Margaret Chappell v̶ ̶ ̶ ̶ ̶ ined at Homerton college̶ ̶ ̶ ̶ ̶ ̶folk for thirty years, twe̶ ̶ ̶ ̶ ̶ ̶arby village school where̶ ̶ ̶ ̶ ̶ ̶ead. She took ten years out of teaching to bring up her three daughters and now has five grandchildren. She was recently widowed after fifty-one happy years and now lives in a converted forge in Bergh Apton, not far from the school where she taught. She has only now found time to write and this is her début novel at the age of seventy eight.

Praise for *Cookley Green*:

'I enjoyed it very much. It seems to me an excellent and unusual piece of work, largely because it rings true throughout. It is unsentimental, sometimes very funny, sometimes moving. The world of the village and its inhabitants from the Edwardian era until the present day is most faithfully represented. It is not only an interesting historical record, but also a very good read'
Elizabeth Jane Howard

www.booksattransworld.co.uk

COOKLEY GREEN

Margaret Chappell

CORGI BOOKS

COOKLEY GREEN
A CORGI BOOK : 0 552 14974 8

First publication in Great Britain

PRINTING HISTORY
Corgi edition published 2003

1 3 5 7 9 10 8 6 4 2

Set in 11/12¼pt Sabon by
Kestrel Data, Exeter, Devon.

Corgi Books are published by Transworld Publishers,
61–63 Uxbridge Road, London W5 5SA,
a division of The Random House Group Ltd,
in Australia by Random House Australia (Pty) Ltd,
20 Alfred Street, Milsons Point, Sydney, NSW 2061, Australia,
in New Zealand by Random House New Zealand Ltd,
18 Poland Road, Glenfield, Auckland 10, New Zealand
and in South Africa by Random House (Pty) Ltd,
Endulini, 5a Jubilee Road, Parktown 2193, South Africa.

Printed and bound in Great Britain by
Clays Ltd, St Ives plc.

To my parents

COOKLEY GREEN

CHAPTER ONE

Mid-April 1999

You think I can't manage without you – but I can and I will! Isn't that just what I've been learning to do over the past eleven months? Don't miss you in the sack much either; it's a case of the less you have of that the less you want, I find. Especially with so much else to worry about – like how to keep a roof over your head and make ends meet with a child to support and no man to help. But good news – you'll be glad to hear, I think I've managed it!

Should you deign one day to call at 39A Hindhurst Street to visit your erstwhile 'partner' (what a blessing we never tied the knot), and your less than perfect son (we shouldn't have left having him so late), you will find a letter and a poste restante address. This is in case you are suddenly moved to send me money for the support of our son. Not that it matters now, for I have found myself employment.

You will not recollect, for I clearly remember your glazed expression when I was telling you about it, that I took a holiday last summer in a little place on the Suffolk coast, where I hired a bike and with Sammy on the back, explored the countryside for about ten miles or so inland. Well, we stayed there again just after Christmas and I saw this job advertised in the local rag. It was for an infant teacher for a small school in a village with an odd name. I remembered the name, but nothing about the village, though I'm sure it was one I cycled through. If you dig deep, you may remember I was a teacher of young children of some eight years' experience, when I first met you and was persuaded to move on to greater things by joining you on the precious and marvellous magazine.

I applied for the post, was called for interview and found myself the only applicant. The reason for this eventually emerged: the school, like so many out in the sticks in East Anglia, is threatened with closure through lack of pupils. Only thirty in this one at present, ages ranging from rising five to nine. They are even willing to take in Sammy, with all his deficiencies. He can be in my class with me; he'll just have to share me with thirteen other children.

I dare say the office folk think me being off all these months with repetitive strain from using a mouse is a tall tale I invented so I could be at home with Sammy. Well, truth is sometimes stranger than fiction – I am only just beginning to regain some use of my right arm. I mean to keep a journal/diary while I am in Suffolk, and this is the beginning. I'm typing it, with difficulty, on my laptop using my left hand. I start the job a week on Monday, so that gives me time to find furnished accommodation for Sammy and me. He would send his regards, I'm sure, if he could remember who you are – which he would probably have risen to if you had spent more time with him. But . . . enough for now . . . I am in danger of acquiring a strain in my left arm just as the right one is recovering . . .

Found a super little cottage, must be over a hundred

and fifty years old, but it's all been modernized like most of the others in this street. It's got two bedrooms, lounge, bathroom, kitchen and tiny garden. The rent's reasonable and would you believe it – I'm living right next door to Pearl, a woman who spent almost her entire life in the workhouse! I think that's extraordinary . . . in these times! Shades of Dickens! Of course, she is pretty old – but she's got all her marbles. Her family had nowhere else to go when her father was killed on the farm where he worked and they were turned out of their tied cottage. She was taken to the workhouse, aged seven, by a young guy called George, after one glorious day at the seaside on a Sunday school outing. I think she fell in love with him then and I think she's in love with him still, judging by the number of times his name keeps cropping up in the conversation. As a matter of fact, I've come across his name already – carved into the bark of an oak tree standing in the garden of a cottage which used to be the old blacksmith's shop. It's alongside the name Ellen, inside the shape of a heart, but I didn't tell the old lady. I expect she's seen it anyway.

Apparently her mother and grandparents died in the workhouse. Her two brothers eventually got jobs on nearby farms, got married and brought up families (probably also in tied cottages), but she herself never saw the outside world again for years. By the mid-Seventies, the place was changed into a hospital for the terminally ill. She says she could have come out sooner but had nowhere else to go. I suspect she had made herself so useful running the kitchens and keeping the accounts that they didn't want to lose her, but when I suggested they had stolen her life, only let her go when she was too old to work, she just smiled. She didn't seem to harbour any resentment. Her only complaint was that they cut off her hair. The children's heads were always shaved against the spread of lice and for easy management, I suppose. 'I had such lovely hair,' she murmured and her washed-out pale blue eyes filled with tears. Going to the cupboard by the chimney breast (we were sitting in her best room, what she called her parlour, all dark brown paint and faded yellow distemper), she took out a cone of brown paper, carefully unfolded it – and out came a long coil of silky yellow hair. It looked as alive as if it had just been cut off a living head.

'I crep' back into the kitchens when nobody wus look'n' and rescued it,' she whispered, 'and I've kep' it all this time!' She held it up where her pink scalp showed through what scanty white hair she had left, and it dangled down beside the withered papery-white skin of her face in dreadful incongruity. It all seemed so eerie and sad. I think she has cataracts now, so she can't see anything odd about Sammy; she treats him just like any ordinary child and he responds in his usual uninhibited fashion.

Most of the cottages in this village have been bought and tarted up by a local property developer named Andrew Gillson – tastefully keeping many of the original features like old beams, fireplaces and Dutch ovens, if the one I have rented is anything to go by. But the old lady's, except for the installation of electricity, is pretty much the same as it was a hundred years ago. It smells of damp and mould and dusty furniture and apples that have been stored too long in the cupboard. She owns it, but has never had the money to modernize it. She even has an outside loo! and old pammets for flooring in the kitchen that actually are highly desirable now. How she came to own the cottage in the first place is a tale I have yet to be told. On a preliminary visit to the school, we met the caretaker, a kind lady who has given Sammy a little two-wheeler bike just the right size for him. Now he just has to learn to ride it.

Andrew Gillson can be seen as today's nouveau riche squire of the village, as he seems to own a good deal of it. The old squire, Lord Summerfield, died shortly after the First World War – of a broken heart, so they say. His ancestral home, Summerfield Hall, which I have yet to see, is about a couple of miles from the village. It has changed hands twice since Lord Summerfield died and is at present without an owner. In fact, it's been unoccupied for the past eight years and is under the auspices of the National Trust until a suitable buyer can be found. It was Andrew Gillson I had to go and see to rent my cottage, and I'm afraid my opinion of his building expertise and taste plummeted as I approached the house he has built for himself on the outskirts of the village. Set well back at the end of a cul-de-sac lined with his so-called 'executive' type houses, it outdid all the others in pretentious hideosity. It had two wide brick pillars, each topped with a recumbent lion, at the entrance to the driveway, and a portico with four Palladian columns framing the heavy, studded, dark oak front door. To the right of this portico, however, stood a light and airy cube-shaped glass structure in which was displayed a single item – a small, delicately made black cart, obviously antique and intricately decorated with feathery gilt scrolls.

I had heard about this cart – it was the one Andrew Gillson was travelling in when he conceived the idea which was to make him rich. He and his father were taking a three-legged cow to the bull (yes, a three-legged cow . . . I tell this tale as it was told to me). This involved quite a journey very early in the morning, as the bull was on some marshes near the estuary of the little river that curves round the village before winding its way through

13

ten or twelve miles of gentle Suffolk countryside and out to sea. On the way they kept meeting farmers coming out of their driveways with carts full of milk churns bound for the nearby railway station and the early morning milk train. I think our hero was about nine at the time, but he had the wit to see an opportunity when it presented itself. Twelve years later he had saved up enough money to buy himself an old lorry and took on the job of going round to local farms, early in the morning, collecting the churns of milk and transporting them to the railway station. Before long he had acquired a fleet of lorries, the farmers had been persuaded to place their churns at the top of their driveways for ease of pick-up . . . and his days of prosperity dawned. Later, he moved into hiring out heavy agricultural machinery and later still, with two grown-up sons to help expand the business, into building – just as the housing boom took off . . .

I fear I am destined never to meet this modern-day squire of the village, this paragon of private enterprise. It seems he is on his last legs, or rather, no legs at all now, being bedridden and very old. I learnt this from the cleaning lady who appeared in the doorway as I approached his house, wearing a mob cap and holding in her hand a piece of cloth from which there emanated a strong pleasant smell of lavender furniture polish.

'Saw you com'n' from the landing winder – what d'you want?' she asked without further preliminaries. When I explained I wanted to rent a cottage, she led me to a large study or office straight out of Ibsen's *Master Builder*, with maps of the locality pinned up on the walls and a huge desk on which lay a large and impressive architectural plan. Other plans lay on smaller desks and tables about the room, though as far as I had been able to tell, as I walked down the cul-de-sac, all Gillson's

houses are basically of the same design, with idiosyn-
cratic embellishments to give the illusion that each is
unique. I felt that all the plans that lay about me were
really for show.

The Missus would deal with me about renting the
cottage, I was assured by the cleaning lady, but she
would have to go and check if she was about . . . and
she left, leaving the door open. I had not been invited to
sit, so I stood, mostly so I could restrain Sammy, should
he become too exploratory . . .

Well, I did indeed meet Mrs Squire. What a sight! Poor
Sammy was mesmerized. An ancient lady, she tottered in
with her fat feet bulging over high-heeled shoes she could
scarcely manage, wearing enough dangling jewellery to
start up a market stall. Over-embellished (like the house)
is about the kindest thing I can say about her, and she
was all made up . . . well, just to give you an idea . . .
she could have been Barbara Cartland's sister . . . and
she came across so regal and condescending I could
hardly keep a straight face! I had heard all about
her, you see, from Pearl. Her name was Christine but
she had recently announced that in future she wished
to be addressed as Christabel. She was the illegitimate
daughter of one Molly Marston (known as Molly
Mattress, apparently, as all the men for miles around had
lain on her). Molly had been barmaid years ago at the
Ploughman's Arms, recently renamed the Moon and
Sixpence. (It seems there is an artist/literary coterie in the
village who mooted for something classier and more
romantic when the pub last changed hands.)

Molly, in her day, had been liberal with her favours
to all except the man who truly loved her – Andrew
Gillson's father – he of the dashing black cart. He wooed
her faithfully and honourably for years (well, as honourably as he could while still being married to Andrew's

15

mother), but with no success. He was the only man to attend her funeral when she died after aborting herself with a crochet hook. (I suppose one illegitimate child in those days was bad enough, two would really put her beyond the pale.) But the really interesting thing about all this is that when the son, Andrew, made his first million, he remembered little Chrissie, last seen when she was about four – and he went back for her. She had been taken in at the Ploughman's Arms with a view to her growing up to fill the gap left by Molly . . . and she was still there. As soon as she realized who he was, she began to play hard to get just like her mother. But Andrew wasted no time paying court to her, bringing her flowers and pleading his cause, he'd seen all that fail with his father. No, he simply fetched her a great clout across the kisser, hauled her out from behind the bar, carried her off and married her . . .

So little Chrissie, or rather Christabel, lived happy and rich ever after and brought forth two hefty sons to help augment the family finances. So if she does put on a few airs . . . who can blame her? The la-di-da voice she assumed for my benefit soon cracked, for Sammy could not help putting out a hand to pull the longest of the dangling necklaces, the one that looped down between her knees as she sat, all queenly, in her dazzlingly patterned brocade chair. Of course it broke and multi-coloured beads rattled and scattered all over the floor, to the accompaniment of my own strained apologies. 'That don't matter,' she muttered indifferently. 'Plenty more where that come from.'

You can see that I find all this absolutely fascinating. You can see too – I am quite aware of it – that I am consistently addressing this diary-cum-journal to you. This is not because I expect or want you ever to read it. It's just that you trained me to write my column on single mothers in a highly personal vein, so that each woman would feel it was addressed to her alone. Now I can't get out of the habit; I'm not even going to try. But I do think I could write a much better column now I am one – a single mum, I mean. However, I'm doing all right. I've solved my three main problems: I've got somewhere to live; I've found a job which will enable me to earn money and take care of Sammy at the same time. Clever me!

So I shall soon be sending formal notice of my resignation to the firm.

Now I know how she came to own her house – Pearl, I mean. Years ago many of the village youngsters left school, sometimes aged only twelve, and got jobs at Summerfield Hall; the girls in service indoors, the boys mainly in the gardens or out on the estate. One such girl was Becky. She started off as a scullery maid, but rose in a very short time to become Lady Summerfield's personal maid. She was older than Pearl, so they could only have encountered each other briefly in the village and at school. Becky devoted her whole life to the Summerfield family, never married, went with her Ladyship wherever she travelled. She became very popular within the family and when her employers died, within a few weeks of each other just after the First World War, the estate changed hands; some of the tenant cottages were sold off; Becky found she had been left the cottage in which she had been brought up, as a reward for her dedicated service. It was then that she took in Pearl and gave her a home. I think she also gave her back her life – the life she would have had in the village had she not been incarcerated in the workhouse for all those years.

For Pearl seems to know everything about everybody, knowledge she could only have got from Becky in the ten years or so they lived together before Becky too died and left Pearl the cottage. She also left her a thick scrapbook about village happenings and a faded photo showing all the village stalwarts. Pearl knows intimate details about every one of them. It seems a woman came round the villages one summer between the wars, filming all the old crafts and country pursuits before they faded into the past. Every now and again the film is toted round the villages of Norfolk and Suffolk so that all can see how times have changed . . .

One of the cameramen took a shine to Becky and gave her the one still photo he took of some of the people in the film. (Some of the youngest could still be alive, I suppose . . .) Men were forever taking a shine to Becky – according to Becky. She and the Summerfield heir were in love, so she told Pearl, but of course they knew they could never marry. He died heroically in the First War, which is why she never married, but remained ever faithful to him, even after his death.

Pearl seems to have taken great pleasure in Becky's tales of conquest, for nothing like that ever happened to her. So, in the photo there was Lord Summerfield's butler (the butler from hell, from what I've heard of him!); he drowned himself for love of Becky. Here Pearl smiled a little (she has a craggy profile: when she smiles her nutcracker chin and beaky hooked nose nearly meet) . . . she smiled and added that he actually jumped into the lake from an overhanging tree just as the beaters of a shooting party emerged from the nearby osier bed. They saved him, just as he intended they should, but he caught a chill and died later of pneumonia. Apparently he was always making suicide attempts over Becky, but always made sure he was saved in the nick of time. There was a footman at Lady Summerfield's sister's place in London who remained forever a bachelor for love of her, and the cameraman came back to the village twice to try his luck.

Pearl pored fondly over the photo, through her large round magnifying glass, and began to point out to me some of the more charismatic village worthies: the wheelwright, Joshua Ableman (aptly named, I thought), and his wife Rose; they had ten children and lost three boys in the war; Kenny Ling the Bumby King (the night-soil operator); his great friend Jacko the rat catcher, with his dog and ferrets; Bent-one the cobbler, who lost an arm in the war. There was Bertha, a big woman everybody called Bossy Bertha, but not when she was around to hear you; she was the unofficial village midwife and layer-out of corpses; she saw people into the world and out, as well as being the caretaker at the school for many years. 'Who is that?' I pointed to a tall important-looking fellow standing very upright in the middle of the front row, with his arms folded firmly across his chest.

'Him – he shouldn't hev bin there,' was Pearl's brusque and disparaging reply. 'He weren't even in the film. He's a foreigner from up north – Captain Kirby – and that woman,' she pointed to the dark-haired young woman standing next to him, who was almost as tall, 'thass Stella Benson. Lady Muck, everybody used to call her. She thought she wus go'n' to be the next Lady Summerfield but she never was.'

'Which one is George?' I asked, then wished I hadn't, for immediately her eyes filled with tears.

'George int there. He weren't allowed in the photo, he wus in disgrace.'

'In disgrace? Why was he in dis—' But I was not to discover why George was in disgrace, for at this point Sammy tripped over the brass fender and grazed his knee and I had to take him back home and put a plaster on it.

*   *   *

And so to school: a small, sturdy building reminiscent of a church, with a rather rickety bell tower at one end. For old times' sake the bell is sometimes rung at ten to nine as it was in the past, to summon lingering pupils to their studies. Some village schools in the county have been much improved, some have heated swimming pools, but the threat of closure has meant that this one has largely remained the way it was. It's not at all what I've been used to – a bit claustrophobic really, with its high narrow windows the children can't see out of and not much sun able to get in. But it's homely, I suppose – a contrast to the last school I taught in, all great glass panels and open plan. (Come to think of it, glass panels and open plan were partly what drove me out of teaching – it was like working in a glass cage at the zoo.)

There are three classrooms, one used as a hall for assemblies, gym and eating lunch; two cloakrooms and a room not much bigger than a cupboard for the Head. There are ten tiny oak chairs in my room that are really museum pieces and rather sweet, but the rest of the furniture in both classrooms is modern plastic. There'll be just me and the Head and a visiting Supply teacher one day a week to take his class while he deals with the administration. Schools nowadays are constantly being bombarded with instructions from above, so I'm told. And yes – the Head is a he, a widower, just right for me!

No, actually, he is not for me. A bit of a hippy really, shortish, bearded, baldish and brown-eyed. He lost his wife and daughter in a horrendous accident, when a lorry mounted a bank in a narrow country lane and tipped its load of concrete blocks onto the back of his car where they were sitting. He comes to school on a bike with a knapsack on his back and I quite think, as summer arrives, he'll be seen in corduroy trousers, sandals and no socks . . . maybe even the kind of diamond-patterned sleeveless pullover last seen on Alf Garnett; who knows? No, I can emphatically state, definitely, without reservation, he is not for me.

Sammy has acquired grazes and bruises on both legs trying to master riding his bike. He's finding co-ordination difficult; but he keeps on trying. You would be proud to see him so determined. Well, you should be.

Poor man – the Head, I mean. He can't get on top of the backlog of accounts left by the previous Head. Still, there are no gargantuan problems here, other than the possibility the school might close at the end of next year's school year. The children are responsive and well behaved. (Well, so far!) I think he took on this job to get away from his former life. He's rented accommodation in the village, so I'm told, like me, leaving his own house empty. Pearl says he can't bear to go there.

Our kind caretaker has found the stabilizers that go with the bike and Sammy is having an easier time now.

Decided to help the poor man get on top of his load of bumph by taking all the kids off his hands for the day. Asked everybody to bring a packed lunch, planned to take them all on a picnic near Summerfield Hall. Seems I've got back into teaching at a very challenging time – for into the schools since I last taught have come a number of thick files expounding the National Curriculum requirements; a whole shelf full of them. Yet it seems much of it has already been superseded by subsequent directives, so I have to admit, I don't quite know where we are. Nowhere in my investigations have I found any directives on the subject of going on a picnic and simply having a good time – so I felt I had to make sure our enterprise was educationally gainful for all.

21

We took the metre trundle wheel, and measured out 1,000 metres, each child taking it in turn to push it and count (everybody counted for Sammy). Then we stuck in a marker. I had marked out a mile the night before, using the milometer on my bike, so everybody could see that a kilometre is shorter than a mile. Then, it's spring: we saw trees bursting into leaf, birds hopping about with twigs of grass and moss in their beaks, lambs in a meadow, wheat, oats, barley, sugar beet, oilseed rape and Bird's Eye peas greening in the fields. There ought to have been tadpoles squiggling in a ditch near the school but we couldn't see any. Modern farming methods have put paid to many of the frogs. Few of the children could name the crops growing in the fields, but then they had not grown enough to be easily recognized. Later in the year we must make another trip, collect specimens on a chart and name and display them. But today all Nature lay about us, blooming in the year's first burst of activity. The best kind of Natural Science, surely?

An avenue of trees, with branches that almost meet overhead, leads out of the village towards Summerfield Hall. At the end of it we came upon two elderly ladies with cloned hairstyles, seated before their easels. They were painting the scene where the countryside opens up into meadows on either side, dotted with sheep and their lambs. The two ladies oohed! and aahed! as we passed. 'Little dears!' no doubt they murmured, for there is no more pleasing sight than a crocodile of young children when you are not the one responsible for them. The ones in front always go too fast; the ones at the back get left behind; those told to hurry then tread on the heels of those going too slowly. We had the added complication of the trundle wheel.

Then there was the traffic. We spent a lot of our time leaping up onto the bank at the side of the road (PE?)

as a variety of vehicles thundered by on narrow, ill-maintained roads that were originally farm tracks winding round and between fields. Still, here was an opportunity to discuss the role of each vehicle – was this one intended for farm, commercial or purely private use? And, it was a jolly good day for a picnic.

The east gate is the first one you come to leading to Summerfield Hall, but we walked on past it, along the road which runs in front of the Hall and parallel to the lake nestling like a great grey mirror in its bed of reeds at the foot of the park. Occasionally a fish disturbed its placid surface, or we would see spreading rings as some insect dipped inconsequently into the water. Beyond the sheet of steely grey the parkland sloped gently upward, dotted with grazing sheep and lambs and clumps of mature trees – and at the crest stood Summerfield Hall in all its glory, its symmetry, its Palladian simplicity . . . (Twenty-two tall windows, we counted on the ground floor.) From that great house, I tried to explain to the children, the resident lord, in times not so long gone, ruled everyone in the villages round about. Now it stands empty, awaiting the next buyer. (Pearl says a Tory cabinet minister was once interested, though how she knows, God knows!) Had they lived in those times, I went on to explain, their whole welfare and means of livelihood could well have depended on the goodwill of the family living in that house.

They quickly tired of my history lesson, and we moved on, turned left and passed the entrance of Hall Farm, on our right, invisible behind its barricade of tall poplar trees. A little further on we came to the west gate, the nearest approach to the Hall, giving a clear view all the way up the drive to the western end of the building and, rather set back, the curve of the wall enclosing the stable yard. The children were in no mood now to stand about listening to me pontificating – in teaching you quickly learn to tell when your pearls of wisdom are doomed to fall on deaf ears; they were getting tired, hungry and fretful, so we walked on.

We had our picnic seated on the grass around the ice house, which was imbedded snugly in the ground a few yards into the park, on a piece of rising land. It rather resembled a wartime air-raid shelter; something which none of these children, I thought gratefully, have any experience of. Yesterday's refrigerator, I pointed out. Ice from the lake in winter was crammed into a deep hole underneath, which cooled the compartment above, so that it could be used for cold storage. The ice would last until almost the following winter and the next frosts. (Pearl was the source of this bit of information – how does she know these things?) Another compartment would be cool enough to store preserved meats, and game from the various shooting parties would be hung there until 'ripe'. That's probably enough of that, I thought. Then, their hunger satisfied, some of them started to explore.

There was a thick layer of turf over the sides of the ice house and a neat, domed, thatched roof over all. At the bottom of four or five narrow steps going down into the ground at one end was a tiny, deepset door. It was locked. Surrounding the door was a nicely curved brick facade, and etched into the very last brick down on the right-hand side, the children found a name: 'GEORGE GUDRUN. 1908. AGED 15.' George . . . of course! . . . the mysterious George! Poor Pearl's livelong love had stood here where I was standing. Very little had changed really, except for motorized traffic on the now tarmacked road. The same trees, but bigger, the same sheep . . . well, perhaps descendants of the original sheep . . . George was embedded in the history of this locality; his name etched into a brick and carved into an oak tree. Remembered no doubt for the things he built and left behind him – and of course for his disgrace, whatever that turns out to be. One day, I thought, I shall find out.

I stood with my corned-beef sandwich halfway to my mouth, saddened by an old familiar feeling: a hunger to belong, to have roots, to have a history in some place other than the succession of army camps we lived in when I was a child, and then the British Army camp in Germany, where I spent my most impressionable years. I remember isolating myself, not only from the citizens outside the camp, but also from all the intricacies of the pecking order within. I had certain status, with my father an army surgeon and my mother an English teacher in the nearby gymnasium – but somehow I could never enjoy it. There were advantages, but they all seemed so petty. I never felt I belonged – but then I never felt that in London, either . . .

Some of the children had been racing round with the trundle wheel over the bumpy grass. Now, I saw, it had fallen apart. Judiciously, they sent Sammy as their emissary, carrying a piece in each hand, to inform me of this calamity. A nut had dropped off, but the bolt was still there. We spread out to make a search and just as we were about to give up – there it was. Now we could begin the long trek home. I waited, taking a last look around me as the children gathered up their belongings. George must have stood here, I thought, on that day long ago, observing the busy comings and goings of a Summerfield Hall teeming with life and activity. Now it stood empty, dead, its windows blank and a wavering line of grass growing up the middle of the drive. Perhaps, after his day's work, he took the short cut home, as we were going to do – by the footpath running closely alongside the lake. What would he be going home to, I wondered. What was life like for him, in the village, at that time? With the children trailing along behind, I started down the grassy slope towards the footpath.

CHAPTER TWO

1908

All morning carriages bearing guests had been making their way up the long gravelled driveway to Summerfield Hall. Now came two cars and though they were not the first he had ever seen, they were novelty enough to cause fifteen-year-old George Gudrun to lower his reaphook – he had been clearing nettles and brambles from around the ice house – and follow their progress as they drove steadily up to the front entrance of the Hall. Once there the travellers, clad in the usual motoring gear of the time – long overcoats and scarves, goggles and leather helmets for the men; the women with their inappropriate hats held down by a variety of gauzy scarves – spilled out onto the gravelled terrace and, talking animatedly, began making their way in through the main door. Articles of luggage were fetched out of the cars by various minions and swiftly transported within. Then the two drivers resumed their seats, started up their engines and after a few convulsive jerks, drove slowly in tandem round the west-facing end of the building and into the stable yard . . . to create pandemonium among those horses not yet unharnessed from their carriages. Terrified by two such strange, threatening contraptions, they plunged and neighed, their hooves beating a frantic tattoo on the hard dark blue cobblestones. Coachmen yelled, the two drivers replied in kind. George couldn't see, but he could hear and well imagine what was happening . . .

He smiled, then turned his gaze towards the entrance of the service driveway behind him and away to his right, which led directly into the back of the stable yard and was designed to facilitate the arrival of more mundane visitors, mostly those bringing supplies. He was waiting for his father to return. He had left over an hour ago, ostensibly to fetch a small tool they had forgotten to include in the tool bag that morning, which they now needed to put the finishing touches to the brick facade they had just rebuilt, round the outer doorway of the ice house. But in the service driveway he saw, not his father returning in his little donkey cart, but the slight figure of a girl in blue he thought he recognized. So intent was his gaze that he failed to notice the approach of two horsemen, stepping noiselessly over the soft turf behind him, until, pausing on the other side of the ice house, one of them spoke.

'I say – we're in luck! Look what's coming our way.' The other rider, the smaller of the two young men, stood upright in his saddle, shielding his eyes.

'Looks like one of the village girls – works in one of the local shops, I think.'

'Well then – now's your chance.'

'Chance?'

'To exercise your droit de seigneur, old man. You've come of age, remember? There must be some advantage in it. Go on,' said the larger, darker of the two, in a conspiratorial whisper, 'there's nobody about.'

The other laughed uncomfortably.

'I don't think you've quite got the hang of life in

the country, Gerald,' he said. 'It isn't like that any more – if it ever was. We've got a certain responsibility for the village people, they have to be handled with respect. You'll probably be treated to a dissertation on the subject from my father, before you leave.'

'Balderdash,' said Gerald. 'My old man used to go on like that about the mill girls . . . and I believed him . . . till I found out he was taking his pick. You've got to get started some time, you know,' he said, looking quizzically at his friend. 'How are you going to cope with all those pretty girls they'll have at the slave market where you're going? Time you got some practice in. Got to do your best for the old country, you know.'

'I don't think that's quite what the Foreign Office has in mind sending me out there,' said Neville.

'Well, I wish it was me going, that's all,' said Gerald. 'Oh, here she comes, look . . . and she is pretty! Yes . . . Eee by gum . . . a fetching little baggage, what? Oh, come into my parlour said the spider to the fly,' and he drove his horse forward then turned sharply, trapping the girl between the ice house and Neville, on the other horse.

'Now, what's your name, where are you off to and what have you got in that basket?' he asked.

'Eggs . . . and oranges,' said the girl timidly. 'For the cook up at the Hall . . . and I've got to hurry.'

'Got to hurry, have you? What's your name?'

'Ellen.'

'Ellen. Well, Ellen, you're not in too much of a hurry, surely, to give this nice young man here a kiss . . . on his birthday?'

Ellen gazed down at the contents of her basket, blushing slightly. 'I don't want to,' she said.

'Oh, come on . . .' Driving his horse close alongside her, he lifted up her slight form from the back, by the elbows, basket and all, towards the other horseman.

'One kiss . . . do as you're told,' he ordered, for she was turning out heavier than he had expected. But Ellen had seven brothers and was used to male methods of persuasion. Twisting adroitly in his arms, she picked an egg out of her basket and broke it against his face. Egg yolk went up his nose and shell and egg white slithered glutinously down his chin.

'You little cat!' he cried, dropping her and spitting and spluttering as he tried to control his horse. 'Now you're going to get it. Now you're going to get what you deserve.'

'Oh, leave her alone, for goodness sake,' said Neville. 'Can't you see – she's only a child.'

His reaphook dangling from one hand, George stepped out from behind the ice house.

'Yes, you leave her alone!' he growled, and found a moment to feel profoundly thankful his voice came out the way he wanted and didn't revert to the light falsetto of early boyhood, as it still, unexpectedly, sometimes did.

'Good God!' cried Gerald, 'what have we here? Young Lochinvar, complete with sword! Will you look at that! "Oh young Lochinvar,"' he sang, ' "came out of the west . . ."'

'Clear off!' said George, 'the pair of you!'

The rear ends of both horses chanced at that moment to turn towards him. Dropping his reaphook he raised his arms high, then brought a hand down hard on each rump with a resounding thwack! Both horses promptly squealed, jumped sideways – and bolted.

Away they went, the two riders clinging on desperately as best they could . . . down over the tranquil sloping parkland (created over a century before by Capability Brown and now nearing the full beauty of its maturity); across the main driveway and on down towards the lake, scattering the sheep and raising a cloud of startled wildfowl as they reached the bottom of the slope. Ducks, coots, geese, rooks, jackdaws rose protesting into the air. Two swans, seemingly in slow motion, stitched a glittering track across the surface of the lake for thirty yards before sinking back once more into the water.

At the edge of the reed bed which encircled the lake, one rider, the slighter of the two men, fell from his horse and was dragged, head to the ground, a short distance before he managed to disentangle his boot from the stirrup. He lay still for a moment, then, George saw to his relief, he sat up, holding one hand to his head. The two horses, both now riderless, plunged on side by side, deeper and deeper into the reed bed until they came to the very edge of the lake and there they stood, two brown lozenges, embedded in a sward of green reeds and bulrushes, gazing out foolishly over the water.

George looked round searchingly for the other rider, the larger of the two men; there was no sign of him, for he had fallen into the reed bed, from which he suddenly rose like a swimmer on the crest of a wave.

George turned to the girl, but if he was expecting to be commended for his courageous defence of her, he was to be disappointed.

'Oh, now I'm short of an egg,' she wailed. 'The cook'll kill me! I bet she'll send me all the way back for another one and it's miles! I had to come all the way round by the road, it not being Sunday.' (There was a short cut to the Hall but its use was confined to those going to church on Sundays.)

'I can get you another one,' said George promptly. 'I know where the head gardener keeps some hens – secretly – in that little copse over there. The estate workers are not allowed to keep hens, you know. Lord Summerfield doesn't like them. Shall I see if I can get you one?'

But Ellen's attention had wandered elsewhere.

'I wouldn't really have minded giving that little one a kiss,' she said, gazing down wistfully towards the lake. 'He was nice – but I didn't like that dark one with the whiskers, did you?'

'Do you, or don't you, want me to get you an egg?' said George, melting as he felt the full force of two blue eyes and a sunny smile.

'Oh, yes please.'

'All right, then,' he said. 'You walk on . . . and I'll tell you what . . . I bet I can run and get one afore you reach the stables. Watch.'

He set off up the sloping parkland towards the little copse with long purposeful strides. He was proud of his running – but when he looked back after the first fifty yards to check that she was still watching, he saw that she had turned her gaze again to the scene down by the lake. He slowed to a walk, then changed his mind and started off once more towards the copse in a furious sprint.

It took him longer than he expected to locate the head gardener's chicken hut. It was well concealed – a low wooden building half buried in blackthorn bushes and brambles, with a small wire-netting run attached. As he broke through the last barricade of nettles and thistles and thorns he was confronted by the back of the hut and the flaps of four nest boxes. He lifted the first flap . . . there was nothing in the box but straw. He lifted the second . . . the same . . . he lifted the third . . . and there sat the bulky back end of a White Sussex hen. As he put out a hand stealthily to feel under her for an egg, she suddenly rose on two pale scaly legs; her whole under-carriage gaped alarmingly like a dropped jaw; a kind of soft convulsion passed over her body . . . and into his hand dropped a warm wet white egg.

Unaware that her precious creation had already been pilfered, she stood quite still for a moment, giving herself time to retract her undercarriage and re-establish her internal arrangements; then she sprang out into the run with a triumphant, ear-splitting cackle. At once, the rest of the hens took up the cry in an uprush of primitive hen sympathy, to be joined a moment later by alarm cries from the two cockerels who sensed an intruder. It all sounded very loud indeed to George but hopefully was too far away from the kitchen garden to alert the head gardener, and by design too far away from the Hall to assail the ears of Lord Summerfield, who, had George but known it, was at that moment cordially conducting favoured guests through the long main corridor and out into the stable yard to the gun room, where each item of his extensive collection of firearms was being checked, cleaned and oiled, ready for the onset of the shooting season.

It took longer than he had anticipated for George to leap, push and scramble his way back through the tangled undergrowth of the little copse, which was by far the wildest, least visited part of the estate, and burst out once again onto the verdant rounded parkland. He saw at once that Ellen had not travelled as far along the service driveway as was to be expected. Perhaps she had waited; more likely, he thought glumly, it was because she'd dallied to watch events unfolding down by the lake. He was too breathless to speak when he reached her, so for a moment they stood silent, watching the distant tableau at the bottom of the slope.

The two horsemen had recovered their mounts and were standing by the edge of the reed bed, attempting to clean mud off the legs of their horses with handfuls, presumably, of rushes and dry grass.

Still breathing hard, George refused to be the first to speak as they walked on in silence towards the Hall. Ellen seemed lost in her own thoughts.

'I shall ask to see the table,' she remarked, after a while.

'Table?' said George, mystified.

'The banqueting table. It's the young Lord's coming of age and there's going to be a banquet and a ball . . . and anybody can view the banqueting table between two o'clock and three. Oh!' she cried, 'that must have been him – the young Lord. Of course! Well, I never. D'you think it was him, George? I've never seen him before, have you? D'you think it really was him?' George informed her grimly that he didn't give a damn whether it was him or not. She gazed at him wonderingly, startled by his vehemence.

'You want to keep clear of the likes of them,' he growled, 'they don't mean no good to the likes of us.'

She looked at him again with a puzzled expression, and walked on. George followed morosely – and nearly walked into her as she suddenly stopped and turned.

'Did you get an egg?' she asked.

George handed it to her without a word.

'Ooh, it's a lovely one! Thank you,' she said. Again the smile and the bright glance . . . he tried to harden his heart, but it was no use. He had to walk on with his head bowed to conceal the flush of pleasure suffusing his face. They had reached the stable yard at last, now deserted and quiet. The horses had been accommodated and the row of assorted carts and carriages stretched out empty, supplicating shafts. At the end of the wall nearest the Hall stood two cars. Ellen mounted the steps leading to the kitchens and looked down at George.

'I could be quite a long time, you know.'

'I'll wait,' said George.

She put out a hand to pull the brass bell hanging from the wall, but before she could do so the door opened abruptly to reveal a plump woman, red-faced, with hands and arms liberally festooned with blotches of flour: undeniably the cook. 'What took you so long?' she snapped. She looked past Ellen and saw George. 'Oh, bin shilly-shallying . . . I see . . .' She grabbed the basket but Ellen held on. 'I'd like to view the table,' she said meekly. 'You're too early,' grumbled the cook. 'That int even laid properly yet. Oh all right,' she said, relenting. 'You can come in. Not you,' she said to George, 'you're too dirty!' She pulled Ellen and the basket inside and slammed the door.

George stood at the bottom of the steps and his face turned red, then white with anger. He wanted to shout that he wouldn't go inside to look at that table for a hundred golden guineas, but there was nobody to hear: he could only stand there. He was about to turn away when suddenly the door opened again, just a little way; a floury hand appeared in the opening and in the hand was a cake. It was probably only a sweetened leftover piece of pastry, but he could see raisins in it. The hand wagged up and down impatiently. George drew himself up and stared at it with immense disdain . . . but he was hungry. His mother had had little enough to give him for breakfast that morning and even less for elevenses . . . and if he and his father didn't finish their job on the ice house by midday, they would not get paid and there would be no money for food for the whole of next week. Before he could stop himself his legs carried him up the steps, his hand went out and took the cake; the floury hand withdrew and the door closed again with a decisive click.

Mortified, he stumbled down the steps and took refuge behind the two cars. He kept the hand holding the cake behind him and well away from his body, as if it was something with which he had nothing whatever to do. When he had recovered a little, he thought he would fake an intense interest in the two cars. He could then nonchalantly bring the cake into his mouth. He felt a powerful impulse then to devour the whole thing ravenously, but managed to restrain himself. He walked attentively round the two cars – one an open tourer with what appeared to be an artist's easel in the back, the other a more sedate saloon – whilst mumbling at the cake with little economical bites. All too soon it was gone and he was going cross-eyed picking precious crumbs off the front of his jersey, when he suddenly heard the clatter of hooves on cobblestones and the two horsemen rode into the yard.

Lest they should think he was skulking behind the cars so as not to be seen, George hastily brushed away the last of the crumbs, not without fleeting regret, and stepped out into full view.

Gerald saw him first.

'There he is – the young blackguard! I'll kill him!' He slid down from his horse. 'I'll thrash him to within an inch of his life!'

Neville put out a restraining hand. 'Don't,' he said. 'Leave it, just leave him alone.'

Gerald gazed at his friend in astonishment. 'Leave it? What d'you mean – leave it? He could have killed us! Look at your ear!' Indeed, Neville's ear, where he had been dragged along the ground, was swollen, bruised and caked with dried blood.

'Just leave it. We don't want any trouble, specially not today. You don't know what you could be stirring up. My father wouldn't like it,' he added, as Gerald opened his mouth for further expostulations. He paused. 'We could even be related,' he said – and could have bitten out his tongue.

Gerald forgot his animosity in a great guffaw.

'Related!' he exclaimed. 'Didn't you say it isn't like

that in the country any more? Aha! Methinks I hear skeletons rattling!'

'Do you have to keep on?' said Neville irritably. 'I don't know anything about it and I don't want to know.'

He was fast becoming aware that the friend he had found so fascinating and original at Cambridge – it was the first time he had met someone from the newly rich of the industrial north – seemed to strike a discordant note in the country.

'I only know the young man's grandfather lives in one of our best manor houses for free. I don't know why. I can't be responsible for anything my ancestors got up to . . . Oh look!' he cried, full of nervous agitation and at the same time thankful for an authentic diversion. 'Stella's here! That's her father's car I'm sure – that's her painting box in the back and oh no, look at me! I'm an absolute mess!' He slid hastily to the ground and gave his horse a sharp slap. Gratefully, both horses set off at once for the stables. A groom came out to meet them, his face registering shock at the state they were in.

'Come on,' cried Neville. 'We'll have to go in via the kitchens and up the servants' stairs. I can't let her see me with a bloody ear like this!'

He ran up the steps to the kitchens and Gerald followed. At the top he paused for a moment and looked back at the lone figure of George standing quietly in the middle of the yard, swaying slightly, balancing on the balls of his feet, arms hanging, fists lightly clenched. The sun caught his tousled fair hair and an incipient gingery beard softened the lower half of his face. He was quite a big lad, Gerald noted thoughtfully, and did not appear in the least afraid.

'Oh come on,' cried Neville, 'hurry up, for goodness sake!'

They burst into the kitchen, kicked off muddy riding boots in the direction of the nearest scullery maid, shouted for hot water and thudded up the bare wooden servants' stairs, leaving behind them the mousy smell of wet socks, damp footprints – and consternation in the kitchen, where lacerations to the ear had been duly observed. Soon they came out into the more opulent part of the house and made their way along the ornate corridor to their adjoining rooms. The hot water duly arrived and along with Neville's a basin of boiled water discreetly covered, a bottle of iodine and some pink boracic lint. Neville used the lint to clean up his ear but ignored the iodine, jibbing at the thought of sporting a bilious yellow ear at the evening's celebration; he had no way of knowing how much he was going to regret that decision in the days to come.

Gerald was first to finish his ablutions. He changed his mud-bespattered riding breeches for a clean pair of college bags but put back on his new riding jacket, specially purchased for this, his first visit to one of East Anglia's stately homes. He had in view, though he did not consciously admit it to himself, an eventual introduction to the luscious Stella, and the new jacket decidedly enhanced the width and symmetry of his shoulders, and highlighted in contrast Neville's somewhat slimmer build. Still, he was not quite sure whether such a sartorial mix would be considered acceptable afternoon wear. He knew there were rules here of which he was ignorant. He almost decided to go to Neville's room and seek his opinion, but then changed his mind and walked instead to the long corridor which ran along the whole length of the front of the house, where a row of fine windows overlooked its setting of magnificent parkland.

The landed gentry certainly knew the best places to

build, he thought, and how to create beauty. From the Hall the ground sloped gently down to where the little local river had been dammed to form the glittering lake. Clumps of trees – oak, ash, elm and beech – stretched as far as the eye could see, with sheep like little puffs of smoke grazing peacefully between. It was all man-made of course, but without a sign of man's hand in it . . . except that a long way off, on the other side of the lake, through a gap in the regiment of trees on the far horizon, a small patch of cut cornfield was lit up in a golden glow by the bright midday sun. He could see a half-built corn stack and a brightly coloured orange and blue farm waggon standing alongside. Toylike figures were leading away toylike horses to their well-earned weekend's rest. It all seemed timelessly tranquil.

Gerald sank down on the nearest window seat in what was for him an unusually pensive and peaceful mood. He felt in his pocket for his pipe, another recent acquisition – but before he could light it there came the sound of hurried footsteps, doors slamming, a low protesting murmur . . . and then a stentorian bellow from some-where below. A full-scale row seemed to be developing on the ground floor.

Grasping his unlit pipe, Gerald tiptoed along to the top of the main stairway and looked down. The main stairway at Summerfield lost some of its glory and grandeur by not descending into the main hall, but into a secondary hall more easily accessible from the domestic part of the house. There below him he saw, in the middle of the chequered tiled floor, Lord Summerfield haranguing some underling, standing before him head bowed, twisting his cap unhappily in his hands. Gerald drew back but kept listening. In the next few minutes he was to undergo a complete reversal of his assessment of Neville's father, whom he had previously considered to be a bland, genial, ineffectual old buffer who scarcely knew, most of the time, what he was about.

'What do you mean – finished for the weekend?' he roared. 'Nobody's finished for the weekend till I say so!'

Again the diffident protesting murmur . . .

'Gone home? Go and fetch 'em back. Tell 'em they are to move that stack, d'you hear? And the waggon. Tell 'em I said so. Now – not Monday. Now!'

It seemed that Lord Summerfield, probably from a window directly below the one Gerald had been looking out of, had spied the plebeian intrusion of a corn stack and a farm waggon into his sweet, carefully created sylvan scene, and was ordering their instant removal.

'I don't care if they have all gone home for the weekend. Fetch 'em back . . . go on. Go now . . . get moving, d'you hear?'

Disconsolate footsteps; if footsteps can be disconsolate, these were. Away went the messenger and away went Saturday afternoon for at least four farmworkers, who had probably planned to do some of their own harvesting – dig up early potatoes, clamp carrots and turnips, and string up onions ready for the winter. The winters were hard for people in the villages to get through and, knowing this, Lord Summerfield, more enlightened than many landowners, had instigated a five-and-a-half-day week – but this was entirely arbitrary and depended on there being no disadvantage to himself.

Gerald stood quite still for a moment, not daring to move or make a sound for fear of attracting attention and the old man's wrath. He heard him snort a bit and thump the floor with his stick (he was a martyr to the gout), then shuffling heavy footsteps, and then silence. Gerald crept back to his window seat, too subdued even to light his pipe, and sat turning over in his mind all that he had seen and heard.

But not for long: Neville appeared, resplendent in heather green tweeds and a new yellow waistcoat, his curly fair hair flattened and still slightly damp, his small moustache pertly waxed at the ends. Gerald braced himself and rose to his feet.

'I thought you said you could see the church spires of three villages from here? I can only see two.'

Neville pulled the curtain to one side and pointed from west to east: 'Summerfield, Silverley and Cookley Green . . . but you can only see Cookley Green when the leaves have fallen.'

'And all that's yours. Everything and everybody in those three villages are under your, or rather your father's, jurisdiction.'

'Well, not quite . . . not as much as it used to be, actually. Even the Church has lost some of its powers, we were affected by the Evangelical movement just like everywhere else, and there are not so many people living in the villages now. Many of the younger generation have gone up north to get work. No, things are not at all as they used to be – there are two Nonconformist chapels in Cookley Green alone, and I've heard tell,' said Neville darkly, 'that Joseph Arch once held a meeting there in the wheelwright's shop.'

'Who the hell is Joseph Arch?'

'Fellow who goes round the countryside trying to get farmworkers to form a union.'

'Aha!' cried Gerald, 'trouble on t'farm! Wants nipping in the bud, that. Oh yes, wants nipping in the bud straight away!'

'I wish you wouldn't keep saying aha in that silly fashion,' said Neville irritably, 'and while I'm at it – do you think you can try and refrain from laughing tonight, when my pater makes his after-dinner speech? I don't want you sniggering and upsetting my mother.'

41

Gerald gazed at his friend in astonishment. 'My dear fellow, what are you saying? Would I dream of doing such a—'

'Yes you would,' said Neville. 'That's just what you would do, so I'm going to tell you now the . . . rather peculiar circumstances of my birth . . . and then it won't come as a surprise, will it? The pater always goes on about it on my birthday and this year is likely to be worse than most.'

'Oooh! Peculiar circumstances!' said Gerald with relish. 'Aha!' He remembered too late and clapped his hand over his mouth. 'Don't tell me,' he went on facetiously, 'you were left on the front steps wrapped in a towel and nobody knows from whence you came. No – your mother had a jolly little interlude with a handsome footman and you were the result.' Then, realizing he had gone a bit far: 'You were born under a gooseberry bush,' he finished lamely.

'I was born in a haystack, to be precise. Well – a heap of hay,' said Neville stiffly.

'Never! A haystack!' cried Gerald delightedly.

'There, I knew you'd laugh. My mother was walking down to the west lodge to look at some new puppies, when she was . . . overtaken by the birth pains . . . just by the ice house. But luckily for her, there was a woman from Cookley Green coming up the service driveway with a bag of clean laundry; she happened to be the village midwife as it turned out, and she whipped out a clean sheet, draped it over the heap of hay and brought me into the world in no time at all and right as ninepence.'

'Well, I'm damned!' said Gerald.

'The thing is, my parents had already lost two children at birth, born in London at enormous expense. My mother always had . . . I don't know . . . complications of some kind . . . but this woman sorted everything out, so now my father swears by her and sends her a box of goodies every year on my birthday. He says if my mother had had her instead of that London lot, he would have had three sons now, instead of one.'

Lucky for you she didn't, thought Gerald, in view of the inheritance, but for once he had the sense to keep his thoughts to himself.

'I saw her the other day,' Neville went on, 'in Cookley Green, near the blacksmith's shop. Funny,' he said reflectively, 'to think you owe your existence to an ignorant old woman with black hair and a moustache. Couple of hundred years ago she would probably have been burnt as a witch – Bertha, her name is. Oh my God!' he exclaimed suddenly, and drew back fearfully from the window. 'There's Stella!'

'Stella? Where?'

'Down on the terrace – don't look!'

Gerald did look, and got a view of the top of a big pink floppy hat and the foreshortened figure of a young woman in a gauzy white dress which fluttered round her prettily in the late summer breeze. Neville, meanwhile, seemed to be trying to disappear behind the curtains. Taking out a spotless, folded, monogrammed handkerchief he pressed it tenderly to his injured ear.

'What's she doing now?' he whispered fearfully.

'Sketching,' said Gerald, 'correction – she's pretending she's sketching. What she's really doing,' he went on, staring down, 'is . . . looking for you.'

'For me? D'you think so? Oh my God!'

'You don't need to whisper, she can't hear you,' said Gerald kindly. 'Yes, I should say she's definitely pretending to sketch. It gives her an excuse, you see, to scan the countryside. I should say she's been told you're out riding and she wants to see which direction you're coming from, when you come back – so she can meet you accidentally on the way.'

'Oh my God – d'you really think so? What's she doing now?'

'Walking away to the other end of the terrace.' This gave Gerald a much improved view of her; the new S-curve corset did wonders for her silhouette.

'Come on – let's go down and you can introduce me,' he said happily.

'No, I want to go to the dining hall and check the seating arrangements,' said Neville.

'Check the seating arrangements – what the devil for?'

'I want to make sure that Stella and my mother are sitting on the side of my good ear tonight.' Still holding the handkerchief to his head, Neville bounded along the corridor towards the stairs.

'Oh hell!' said Gerald, disgruntled – but he followed.

End of April 1999

I must admit I do miss London, but then I've missed it for the last four years anyway, haven't I, being baby-bound while you were out on the town. But our social life here is beginning to take off. We've just taken part in a concert at the Congregational chapel – Sammy (in a bow tie) and me and some of the other schoolchildren. There's a lovely old pub on the outskirts of the village called the Marigold Inn. It's run by a retired gentleman, well known in musical circles apparently. He'd arranged a recital by a quartet and asked if the school could provide some little musical entertainment at the end. So we got several children to play recorders, one girl on keyboard, a little band of seven of my infants did per-cussion and guess who was the conductor? Well, you know what an excellent sense of rhythm he has. He stood on a box in the pulpit and his arms were free to beat time; the rest of them sat on their little oak chairs on the floor below and he managed to keep them all under control. He really looked the part with his little black jacket and bow tie and he obviously enjoyed every minute of it. Everybody clapped and cheered which you can do in this chapel as it is much more informal than the Anglican Church. The chapel is a big barn-like structure built in 1641 by people who obviously felt much more deeply about religion than we do nowadays.

Come to think of it, this is the chapel where poor Pearl's George disgraced himself, but that's as much, so far, as she seems willing to tell me. What on earth did he do, I wonder? A striptease? . . . something blasphemous?

An event even more momentous than our concert is being planned. Summerfield Hall, sold to the Department of the Environment after the death of its last owner, has been under the care of the National Trust for the past eight years. Out of concern for its welfare, an Action Committee was formed in Summerfield village, the village nearest to the Hall, and various events have been organized in the past few years to help raise funds towards its upkeep. The latest idea is for a ball, in August, entrance fee to be a modest £8, to include a buffet, and a bar where people can buy their own drinks. Impossible to describe the excitement this idea has aroused in all the surrounding villages. It means that the hoi polloi will be able to enter those sacred portals that were absolutely inaccessible to their ancestors. Rather like being invited to a shindig at Buckingham Palace.

I'm mad keen to go, but somehow none of the evening clothes I brought back from the flat seem suitable – too flashy somehow. OK for a night at Ronnie Scott's but for an evening in a gracious ancestral pile in deepest

Suffolk . . . no, I don't think so. I've got a length of rough silk in muted green I think I shall use to make a three-quarter length split skirt. I'll be restrained, after all, I am the village infant teacher. Pearl has promised I can use Becky's old sewing machine, an ancient treadle which looks as though it came out of the ark, but still works, at least for straight stitching. I think I'll have to ask the Head to accompany me as I don't know any men (yet). It's to be lounge suits, not formal evening wear for the men, and definitely no jeans! I wonder what he'll look like in a suit? I wonder if he's got one?

Pearl has offered to babysit on the night, which constitutes something of a problem: how can I tell her I'd feel happier leaving Sammy with someone younger and quicker?

I heard some of the children discussing Sammy in the playground the other day. They decided he was Chinese, because of his eyes. I have to admit to feeling hurt, though I know they didn't mean any harm. I decided straightaway to save money for an operation – cosmetic surgery – but after I'd simmered down a bit I thought: he's just right as he is, without guile, without malice, and how many human beings can you say that about? He's a loving merry soul destined to do very little harm in the world.

There's a great bout of lawnmowing going on in the village now it's nearly May, and a lovely summer smell of cut grass . . . Yesterday the Head asked me to accompany him to a parish council meeting next Thursday, as the future of the school is one of the things to be discussed. As I plan to ask him to escort me to the Summerfield Ball, I thought I'd better show willing, so I said yes.

Chapter Three

George sat at the bottom of the kitchen steps and waited for Ellen till he got tired of waiting; then he stood up and went to have another look at the two cars. It was the more dashing of the two, the open tourer, that had first claim on his attention. He leaned in as far as he was able without actually entering it, and for the rest of his life he was to remember the smell of it . . . the smell of oil, warmed leather, metal cleaner and carbide . . . and another elusive smell he could not identify because it was outside his experience – that of a woman's expensive scent. He longed to climb in, seat himself behind the steering wheel, pull the hood up over his head and dream a little . . . there was nobody about . . . but at any moment there could be . . . He hesitated: perhaps he had attracted enough attention already today . . .

He was relieved of his indecision a moment later by Ellen's appearance at the kitchen door. Her eyes bright with excitement, she ran lightly down the steps towards him and began describing the wonders she had seen before she was even within hearing distance.

Oh, the food! The meats! The sweets! The poor little

suckling pig going round and round on the spit in the hearth, and that was what the oranges were for – one was to be put in the pig's mouth, maybe two! when he was cooked. Oh, the great tall rooms, the funny dark old paintings on the walls, the chandeliers! And then the huge dining room, the table, the gleaming white cloth, everything snowy white and sparkly! And not just one wine glass at each setting but several and a regiment of knives and forks. And oh the lovely flower arrangements, the candelabra and Lord Summerfield himself had come into the dining room and asked her name and which village she was from and said to walk round the edge of the room and not breathe on the silver . . . but oh the food . . . most of all the food . . . !

George, his stomach positively contracting with hunger, found he had nothing whatever to say. He walked glumly along beside her and no sooner were they out of the stable yard and proceeding again down the service driveway, than they met up with a gaggle of women and girls on their way to view the table, and he had to suffer the whole recital all over again! In an effort to close his ears to their prattle, he drew to one side and stood for a moment gazing down over the peaceful, sunlit parkland. A thin autumnal mist seemed to be forming over the lake, but through it he could still see the tracks in the reed bed where the two horses had made their mad dash to the water's edge . . . An outburst of raucous laughter from the assembled females brought him back to the present. Stupid lot of mawthers, he thought to himself morosely.

'Stupid lot of mawthers!' he said aloud to Ellen, as, with much giggling and waving, she extracted herself from the group and they walked on together. She looked at him uncertainly from under her brows, her high spirits and confidence beginning to wilt, for if they were silly and stupid to want to look at the table, so, by inference, was she.

'But it's a tradition,' she protested. 'Folks have always gone to view the table before a great occasion. It's a privilege . . . like being allowed to skate on the lake when it freezes over and walk the footpath on Sunday.'

'Some privilege!' said George bitterly.

She felt she could not please him and they walked on in silence.

'The cook showed me something secret,' she ventured after a while, 'she showed me the cake.'

'Cake?' George glared at her blackly.

Poor Ellen actually recoiled. 'The b-birthday cake,' she murmured, 'for the young Lord.'

'Oh, the birthday cake.' George made an attempt at normality. 'What was it like – was it a big one?'

'Huge . . . four tiers! . . . and you'll never guess what was on the top – a model of the ice house!'

'Model of the ice house?'

'In pink and green marzipan. The young Lord was born, you know, down by the ice house – on a heap of hay.'

'That's old news – everybody knows that.'

'Well, the cook has done the whole scene in icing and marzipan and strips of yellow angelica for the hay and a little pink baby on top on a layer of frosted icing.'

'Good God!' said George.

'And the sheep all standing round and Bossy Bertha in the shape of an angel . . . she's got wings . . . like the Nativity scene in church at Christmas.'

'Some angel,' said George, with feeling: along with most of the village children he had, at various times in his young life, been closely acquainted with the flat of Bossy Bertha's right hand.

'It was a lovely cake!' said Ellen, 'and it's a secret until the very end of the banquet. Nobody has seen it but me. Except I thought the baby looked a bit too red,' she said thoughtfully. 'I think the cook used a bit too much cochineal.'

'Very likely,' said George, 'yes, no doubt,' he added, assuming a knowledge of the properties of cochineal which had no basis in reality. They walked on.

'I'm going fishing tonight,' he said. Got to get something to eat from somewhere, he thought, if we don't get paid. 'Want to come?'

'Where?'

He nodded towards the lake.

'Oh no!' she cried. 'Don't – that's not allowed! You'll be seen. You can see anybody down there, from up here.'

'Not by the boathouse,' said George. This was true: willows, poplars, reeds and bulrushes kept the boathouse well concealed.

'I can't. I promised Mum I'd go gleaning with her.'

'Oh well, that's that,' said George. He yawned. 'I'm going to have to wait here for my father,' he said, as they approached the ice house. 'He should be back pretty soon – he went home to fetch a tool.'

'Oh, I don't think he'll be coming back,' exclaimed Ellen, and wished at once she hadn't spoken. 'I saw his little donkey cart outside the Marigold Inn. I thought perhaps he was doing a job there,' she finished lamely. George's face flamed; drinking himself stupid, more like, he thought, though God knows how he's got the money! He walked well ahead to conceal the look of rage and humiliation on his face. Ellen followed, dismally aware that he was now mortally offended; she had no notion of how to begin to put things right. They parted at the ice house without another word being spoken. George refused even to look at her as she set off, a solitary little figure, down towards the entrance gates of the service driveway.

He began picking up the few tools lying around (most had gone with his father in the donkey cart), lining them up ready to be packed away in the tool bag or frail. He wished now that he had taken it upon himself to finish the pointing to the brickwork facade using his thumb or the handle of the putty knife, instead of giving in to his father's spurious show of perfectionism and superior expertise. Increasingly, he was finding his father difficult to work with; he seemed more and more prone to these attacks of excessive punctiliousness, as if he saw George as a threat and needed constantly to demonstrate his superior skills and experience, in order to assert himself.

After all, thought George, it was hardly a showpiece patch of brickwork, not exactly part of a cathedral – yet his father had insisted on going all the way home for the 'right' tool – which was nothing but a homemade artefact of no great consequence. He sighed, knelt, and began picking up all the implements and stowing them away in the frail . . . and there, nestling at the bottom of the bag, was the 'right' tool – which was nothing but a homemade artefact of no great consequence. He sighed, knelt, and began picking up all the implements and stowing them away in the frail . . . and there, nestling at the bottom of the bag, was the 'right' tool – a short section of metal pail handle just the right width to seal the strip of mortar between the bricks, its edges creating a neat line at the top and bottom.

He stared at it with mounting anger and resentment. Had his father genuinely not known that it was there? Had he really gone home to look for it? Or had he pretended it was missing in order to pay a clandestine visit to the Marigold Inn? He was not allowed much time for conjecture; he had barely time to register the muted

51

thud from the hooves of an approaching horse before a shadow fell over him, and he looked up to see the figure of the estate steward looming above him. Normally the steward would have got down from his horse to inspect the work, but he was only a smallish man – on the ground he would have had to look up to George – so he stayed on his horse and simply asked if the job was done.

George had to admit that it was not, quite.

'Then I can't pay you,' he said, with noticeable satisfaction. 'I can't pay for work that isn't finished, can I? Where's your father?' he added.

George muttered something unintelligible.

'Well, I'm sorry, but you'll have to wait for your money till next Saturday. I can't flout the rules.' He began turning his horse's head away, then, noting the boy's stricken expression, he relented.

'Can you get it done first thing Monday – say nine o'clock?'

George nodded.

'Well, do that. Be here Monday with the job done and I'll try to git round to you – sometime afore ten.' He tugged his horse's head round and rode away.

George picked up the frail, slung it over his shoulder and set off down the driveway in a rage. Once out on the winding country lane, thickly edged with hedgerow bushes and trees, he stopped, took a small chopper out of the tool bag and cut himself a stout stick from a clump of hazel saplings. Then he hung the frail on the stick, put the stick over his shoulder, and set out, Dick Whittington fashion, for the Marigold Inn.

The inn was situated by the river before it reached the dam at the lake. It was named after the profusion of marsh marigolds which bloomed in early spring along the riverbanks and the ditches criss-crossing the marsh. Some way along the road there was a short cut across the marsh and over a makeshift bridge to the inn – you could just see the building from the road, nestling among the willows on the other side of the river.

George climbed energetically up onto the stile at the start of the short cut . . . and then stopped. The footpath, little used in the past few months, was overgrown. The whole marsh was a moving sea of luxuriant vegetation: not many flowers in bloom, it being rather late now in the season, but a multitude of seed heads, grass plumes with a few late-blooming poppies, Michaelmas daisies in the drier patches and taller meadowsweet where it was damp. A gentle breeze rippled musically through a nearby bank of reeds, and George felt his anger beginning to evaporate. He gazed about him in a more softened mood. Perhaps there was a reasonable explanation for his father's non-appearance; he could not think what it could be, but perhaps there was one.

He jumped down from the stile and stood at the edge of the sea of waving vegetation. He lightly flicked the grass tips with one foot and out flew a cloud of tiny creatures who had been living their lives there: dazzling white fluffy moths, brilliant orange ladybirds, pale green grasshoppers, honey bees . . . an almost transparent damselfly which alighted for one magic moment on his arm. He could hear a coot piping down by the river and overhead a skylark rose joyously into the air. There was a low continuous hum from all the insects and the murmur of the wind in the reed bed; it was as if the earth itself was breathing . . .

He had a sudden recollection of something that had happened earlier in the year, when he had gone running across the footpath, then bare of vegetation, and stepped heavily on the tail of a grass snake sunning itself on a patch of stones. A vivid picture rose in his mind of the snake as it writhed and twisted in shock, exuding an evil-smelling liquid from its skin, its only defence, before sliding rapidly away into the undergrowth. This whole area was alive with creatures, going about their business, living out their lives; it was impossible to take a single step here, he thought, without crushing countless numbers of them into oblivion. He climbed back over the stile and resigned himself to walking the long way round.

He could see an impressive carriage standing in the yard long before he reached the Marigold Inn. Obviously some more important guests on their way to Summerfield Hall and this evening's celebration, making a brief stop for refreshments and perhaps unaware of how close they already were to their destination. He walked briskly into the inn yard and then stopped, transfixed. He could hear his father singing. Tiptoeing across the yard, he took up a position close to the wall, next to the big bay window of the main room of the inn. For a few moments he stood, pressing his forehead to the moss-veined plaster, his eyes closed, listening. His father was singing 'Abide with Me', thus lending a spurious sanctity to the indefensible fact that he was in the pub when he should have been working. As George listened the tears rose to his eyes and his throat became constricted. His father had the voice of an angel, a tenor voice, not powerful but sweet, plaintive, perfectly pitched. Blinking away the tears, George shifted along to the edge of the window where he had a clear view into the room.

His father was facing away from the window, his cloth cap clasped lightly in both hands behind his back. He was directing his voice towards three men and three women sitting in a semicircle at the far end of the room. They were gazing at him in wonderment, George did not doubt, at having encountered, in such an unlikely venue, such an exquisite quality of sound. For he knew his father had a beautiful and affecting voice. As he came to

54

the end of the lovely old hymn there was a poignant moment of silence, before they all broke into generous and spontaneous applause. George let out a long quivering breath, his mind in a turmoil as anger and resentment battled with pleasure and pride. Then he saw his father begin to move sideways along the semicircle, absent-mindedly, as it were, nudging each traveller with his cap as he passed. He was asking for money.

Dropping his tool bag, George rushed to the inn door, flung it open and burst into the room in a fury. In three long strides he had reached his father. As he moved, he was aware of the blank faces of the onlookers staring at him open-mouthed, some of them with hands raised still in the act of applauding. Lifting his stick high he brought it down with a vicious slash on his father's hands. He yelped with pain, the onlookers started in their seats, the cap fell to the floor and the three gold coins it contained went spinning across the room.

'Get out – go on home!' breathed George through gritted teeth. 'We're not beggars! Go on – before I thrash you!' He pushed him violently towards the door.

'My cap . . . I want my cap,' he whined. Reeling slightly, he bent and put out a hand – but towards the coins, not the cap.

'Leave it,' hissed George.

'But I want them – they're mine!' Lurching forward his father stretched out both hands towards the money. Too late. A tow-headed youth, who had been standing in shadow at the end of the bar, darted forward. In one swooping movement he snatched up the three gold coins and dashed out of the door. Framed by the open doorway he could be seen by all: a violently animated figure, scarf flying out behind . . . fast disappearing down the road to Cookley Green.

May 1999

Went to the parish council meeting with the Head this evening, as promised. Big Mistake! It was held in the so-called main hall at school, as Cookley Green hasn't yet risen to finding a village hall. Only a scattering of parishioners turned up to occupy the chairs facing the table where the council members sat. It was announced that Mrs Knight, who was Clerk to the Council, has resigned because of illness. Before I knew what was happening I was proposed, seconded and voted in in her place. I wasn't even allowed time to protest! In a daze, I found myself seated at the table along with the other members, with a pile of bumph before me, the minutes of the last meeting, the agenda for tonight and a pad and pen. I looked round in some bewilderment at this sudden change in my circumstances and exchanged a smile with the Head. I had intended sneaking off home after about the first forty minutes. I had left Sammy asleep on Pearl's old armchair . . . what if he should wake before I got back? Would she be able to cope?

I must say the Head turned out to be something of a surprise. He's got a sturdy body under those baggy corduroys! All that cycling, no doubt. In a belted red Cossack-type tunic and a dark blue peaked cap, he looked like something out of Dostoevsky and rather romantic. Some say that clothes don't matter – but they do, they do!

The meeting dragged on and on. The discussion about the future of the school was a waste of time. All the talk in the world won't conjure up more children or bring back the days when people could earn a living in the village and bring up their families here. Outsiders have moved in, many · of them retired, or their source of income is elsewhere, or they are too old to have children or their children have grown up and gone. Some of the few who do have them tend to make use of the village school till age eight, then ferry their offspring miles every morning to bigger schools some distance away.

The Head stood chatting to a group of villagers at the gate. He gave me a searching look as I drew near, perhaps wondering if I was upset at having the job of Clerk of the Council foisted on me, or perhaps he was wanting to escort me home. I didn't wait to find out. I ran off as fast as I could with a thick bundle of parish papers under one arm. Lights were shining in some of the cottage windows and some outside security lights flicked on as I hurried down the village street. I found Sammy still asleep, thank heaven, but Pearl was awake, sitting bolt upright in her dilapidated old chair with the scarred wooden arms. She had made herself a mug of hot milk and sat holding it tremblingly to her lips with skeletal white hands; hands, I suddenly found myself thinking with a pang, that were coming to the end of their useful life and would soon be underground.

I apologized to Pearl when I got in. 'I'm sorry to have been so long – I got roped in to be the new Clerk of the Council, would you believe! And I couldn't get away. As it was, two items had to be held over till the next meeting.'

Pearl lowered her mug shakily. 'The missing acre, I shouldn't wonder – and the War Memorial Fund?'

'How did you know?' (How does she know these things – has she got second sight?)

Well, it seems an old biddy called Miss Hastbury (who had a rather heightened complexion) left an acre of land to the village in her will for a playing field. Unfortunately, nobody knows just where it is – it's somewhere near the tennis courts behind the house she used to live in, next door to the Black Bull. The tennis courts are still called the tennis courts though they have long been turned into a bowling green, the better to suit the diminishing energy of today's average villager. It's all very confusing, but it seems that every time the subject of Miss Hastbury's/Raspberry's missing acre comes up there is a tremendous row and nothing gets resolved, so the easiest thing is to postpone the subject till the next meeting and this has been going on for years . . .

'What about the war memorial?' I asked, but at this the shutters came down. Pearl's face assumed the same stony expression it wears when I press her about George; I knew she would tell me nothing more. Maybe she was tired, I certainly was. I left with Sammy still asleep draped over one shoulder, stopping for a moment in the kitchen to slip a £5 note under the bread bin – she's proud and won't accept money unless I force it on her. At last Sammy was safely tucked up in bed, after a lengthy search for Floppy – remember Floppy? Still the first thing he asks for every morning when he wakes. I wasn't long getting to bed either, and soon peace reigned in Fern Cottage.

Neil has very warm observant brown eyes.

CHAPTER FOUR

Cookley Green village square was a triangle, with a pub at two points and a long three-storey building that looked out of place beside the much smaller cottages lining the streets round about. This had been built by a former Lord Summerfield to house certain members of his family for whom he felt responsible, but who in close proximity got on his nerves. How better to dispose of a disagreeable aunt or an irritating cousin than to house her – it was usually someone of the female persuasion – at a safe distance from the Hall, where she could act as a constant reminder to the village inhabitants of his own power and importance in the local scheme of things? In short, a watchdog, or, in crude parlance, a spy. Indeed, a balcony at one of the upper windows of the building did rather resemble an eye, peering out balefully over the village scene below.

The present incumbent was a Miss Hastbury. Not so much disagreeable as odd (she had even been heard to voice support for the Suffragettes), she was known to the village children as Miss Raspberry, because of a tendency to redness at the end of her nose and she shared the house with another eccentric, a Miss Gale, known, of course, as Windy. A grandiose archway at one end of the building, giving access to the gardens and stables at the back (the latter never used as Miss Hastbury could not afford to keep carriages and horses), gave the building a look of importance it did not really merit. The opposite, less regal-looking end incorporated one of the two village shops, the one where Ellen spent her working days.

The third side of the triangle, directly opposite the window with the balcony, echoed the gentle curve of the little river as it wound its way lazily round the environs of the village (the same river, of course, which had been dammed further up to form the lake). Marshland stretched from the riverbank to the very edge of the village square where a willow tree had fallen long ago. Its trunk lay almost completely flat, but its branches had continued to grow upwards, so that it resembled nothing so much as a seat or sofa with a back formed by the perpendicular branches. On this elongated armchair sat two old men smoking their pipes and waiting for something interesting to happen.

The larger of the two was named Kenny Ling, but he had lately taken on the job of night-soil collector, so now inevitably he was known as Stinky: Stinky Ling the Bumby King, to give him his full title. This was a very unfair misnomer, as he had formerly been a gamekeeper and was always immaculately attired in traditional gamekeeper's wear. His buskins shone; a dandelion could well have been seen reflected in them, had there been one growing nearby. He wore brown shiny boots, a well-brushed moleskin jacket, a bright red, white-spotted neckerchief and a soft leather deerstalker hat with a jay's blue feather in it. He had been a skilled and efficient gamekeeper, but was always selling the game or giving it away to family and friends. Two poor shooting seasons had alerted Lord Summerfield to the low quota of birds, so that he personally undertook a mission of enquiry among his seventy-plus estate employees. Kenny got the push and ginger-headed Dick West, universally considered to be the one who had scuppered him, was now the head keeper.

As soil collector, Kenny procured two large barrels from the local brewery and mounted them (in gimbals, to facilitate pouring), on an old cart which was drawn about the locality after dark by his stubby little piebald pony. His round covered several parishes as his customers were far-flung, many people having their own method of sewage disposal. If you had enough ground you used a pail and buried its contents fortnightly (weekly if you had a large family), taking care to mark the spot to guard against digging in the same place next time. The Union Jack flags Ellen sold in the village shop to commemorate Empire Day were found to be ideal for this purpose: you could always tell those who were using this method, as a discreet corner of their garden bloomed patriotically. Another method was to dig a deep pit and construct a privy over it (sometimes with a six-holer seat – holes of assorted sizes to fit every size of bottom in the family). When the pit was full – it would usually last for many years – you filled it in, dug another and moved the whole thing onward. If you left the first for several years and let nature work its wonders, you could grow very good rhubarb.

The people most dependent on Kenny's ministrations were those with little or no garden, particularly those who lived in terraced cottages. Here, the weekly offering had to be carried from the privy in the back yard through the house to Kenny's cart at the front. It was found advisable to add to his modest charge some other small offering – a cake, a bag of pears, some fresh-drawn radishes – to ensure he did not lose concentration and drop a dollop in the front parlour . . .

Seated beside the clean, even dapper Bumby King, Jacko the rat catcher could not help but appear disreputable. His looks were not improved by the ancient wool hat pulled down low over his ears, his refusal to shave more than once a week and trouser legs tied round with string. This last was due to necessity rather than slovenliness, as rats and mice, disturbed in a corn stack for instance when it was being threshed, would not be particular about where they ran for refuge. Jacko's long, dilapidated overcoat hung in a straight line on either side, weighted by two capacious, button-down pockets, so that he looked rather like someone sitting in a sentry box. In one pocket he had two dead rabbits, for he had just finished his yearly cull of the rabbit population and was clandestinely keeping two back for the pot. The other pocket heaved convulsively from time to time and presently the head of an amber-coloured ferret with pink eyes popped out to view the world. Absent-mindedly, Jacko tapped it on the head with his clay pipe, and it obediently withdrew. At his feet his little white dog with one black ear, bred small enough to go at least partway down a rabbit hole, sat gazing fixedly at his master.

Thus the two old men sat, slumped and silent, everything they had to say to each other having already been said . . . but presently something new did happen to rouse them from their torpor. A sooty black pony clip-clopped into view, drawing a delicately balanced, two-wheeled, glossy black cart fantastically decorated along the sides, wheel hubs, spokes and felloes with an intricate arrangement of curly yellow scrolls. In the cart, very upright, sat a man in a black suit and a black homburg hat, and beside him a boy of nine or ten similarly attired. The pony stopped when it came to the

Ploughman's Arms and the man in black got out, carrying flowers, and went into the pub, leaving the boy, still sitting very upright, in the cart. Kenny followed all this with some interest, and presently came up with a question that somehow had the stamp of something that had been asked many times before.

'How dew he dew it?' he said.

'Nobody know,' was the reply.

The thing that nobody knew was, how did Ginty – for that was what the man in black was called (though why he was called that was another thing that nobody knew) – how did Ginty make a living since he had never been known to work: that is, he had never been known to work for an employer? He had a worn-out wife who took in washing, but that surely could not account for his general air of prosperity and the glamorous appearance of his cart.

'Still trailing his wing round that gal Molly, I see,' was Kenny's next pronouncement, which, translated, meant that Ginty was paying court, in the manner of a cock with a hen, to the blowsy barmaid at the Ploughman's Arms. It was common knowledge that he had been paying court to her for the past six years and had got nowhere, which was rather strange as every other male for miles around got everywhere at once with no trouble at all. With Ginty, Molly played the bashful virgin and Ginty appeared not to see the incongruity of this. Before long he emerged from the pub, minus the flowers, looking downcast: the very picture of a lover spurned. Without a glance at the onlookers, or a wave of acknowledgement, he climbed into his cart, flicked the reins and trotted dejectedly away. And that was that. Kenny and Jacko sank back into the willow-tree armchair with the air of those resigned to the fact that the big event of the day was now over . . . but no! . . .

not so! Down the road from Summerfield Hall came the sound of running footsteps and into view came the figure of the tow-headed youth from the Marigold Inn, half running, half walking, gasping for breath, stumbling sometimes in a cloud of late summer dust. He raised an arm in greeting as he caught sight of the two old men, but then swerved into the nearest pub, the Ploughman's Arms.

Kenny and Jacko sat up smartly: obviously something important was about to happen. Sure enough, expectant faces began to appear in the pub window, watching . . . waiting . . . Kenny and Jacko watched and waited too. In fact, so intent was their gaze that the ferret took advantage and got his head and two front feet out of Jacko's pocket and nearly made his getaway. While they were stuffing him back in the tow-headed youth reappeared waving, as if to say – wait and all will be revealed! He then ran across the green and into the other pub, the Black Bull.

Kenny and Jacko waited . . . and waited . . . but nothing happened, because the youth had collapsed at the bar and was in the process of being revived by a pint of ale. He was one of Ellen's brothers, Bernard, commonly known as Bent-one because of an anatomical peculiarity caused by an accident some years before. The youngest of a family of seven boys and three girls, he was the runt of the litter, being puny and none too bright. He had stayed on longer than most at school (you could leave at twelve if you had reached a certain standard), without much being gained; then had worked for a while with his father, Josh, the wheelwright, again with little success. A spell working with a cobbler to learn the trade had ended when the shop caught fire and was burnt down. Finally he managed to get a job on a farm, looking after the stock.

One day he was put in charge of a motherless calf with the task of teaching it to drink milk from a pail. You dipped your fingers in the milk, gave them to the calf to suck and, as it sucked, gradually lowered its head down towards the pail. Bernard was entranced. He loved the calf's liquid brown eyes, velvety nose, warm mouth and sandpapery tongue, but found it largely unco-operative. Its instinct was to look upwards for its sustenance, not down. It mooed pitifully. He was nonplussed – until he hit on the notion of offering, well coated with milk, that part of his anatomy which most closely resembled, in form and situation, the poor creature's natural expectations. Instant success! The calf sucked vigorously and Bernard . . . well, for Bernard, in all likelihood, the earth moved. He may well have experienced dizzy heights of erotic delight. Who can tell . . . suffice to say that with all the love and tender care, plus of course that extra nourishment, the calf grew and prospered.

Unfortunately, it also grew teeth and one day progressed from sucking to chewing. Oh calamity! Bernard was discovered sometime later in a corner of the stockyard blubbing and quite unable to disclose the reason for his distress – until someone noticed riverlets of blood trickling out from under his trouser bottoms, over his mud- and dung-bespattered hobnail boots. All was then revealed, amid general consternation, there being no precedent to suggest how best to deal with such a delicate and alarming situation.

Providentially, a visiting amateur vet, there that very day to geld a splendid Suffolk punch colt, was persuaded to try his hand at restoration. With twenty-three hasty stitches he managed to reattach Bernard's wayward member to somewhere near its original anchorage. Then all were sworn to secrecy and although almost everyone in the three villages knew of the shameful episode by nightfall, Bernard's father, Josh the wheelwright, never knew (he was deaf anyway, and could never be got to hear anything he didn't want to hear). His mother took care never to find out, and everyone by common consent kept it from his sister, sweet Ellen, in deference to her youth and innocence.

Unfortunately, the vet was perhaps rendered nervous by his lack of formal training, for the operation was not a complete success. Bernard's member never again hung quite straight. It was 'on the huh'. It sprang out 'soushun ways'. (Hence his nickname, Bent-one or Bendy.) It became the subject of many a ribald jest, such as: 'How dew he fare this morn'n', Bendy, dew he list to port or starboard?' 'What way dew he favour when he's up-standing – nor' nor' east or nor' nor' west?' and 'Houw are yew ever go'n' to hit the bull's eye, bor, if yew can't aim straight?' In the end Bent-one became so accustomed to being the source of fun and merriment that he quite forgot to feel abashed, and grew to consider his affliction a mark of real distinction.

Ribaldry could not have been further from the minds of Kenny and Jacko (though normally they were two of the foremost and most regular participants) when they saw Bent-one emerge from the Black Bull and come pounding across the green towards them, their sense of anticipation mounting as they saw a knot of people gathering in the doorway behind him, and, once again, faces at the window. They waited, agog, as he flung himself onto the willow tree between them – only to be overcome by a violent paroxysm of coughing. Choking, hawking, dribbling and wiping his nose along the length of his sleeve from elbow to wrist, he struggled to regain his breath.

'Never,' he gasped out at last, 'never did I think to see—' He coughed, they waited, he spluttered. 'A young boy a'trosh'n' of his father!' he finished at last.

Kenny's and Jacko's faces spoke volumes: Who? What? When? Where?

'George Gudrun,' spluttered Bent-one, 'in the Marigold Inn!' and was wracked with another spasm of coughing.

George Gudrun! Kenny and Jacko waited to hear no more; they had to have their say. Well, everybody knew George Gudrun was getting too big for his boots. Now he was beating his father. Bin made tew much of at school . . . finished up running the place, dint he . . . till the parson stepped in . . .

This was true. Poor little Mr Thomas, a Welshman and asthmatic, had grown shorter and shorter of breath and had to allow George, as pupil teacher, to take over more and more of his responsibilities. Indeed, soon after George left, precipitated on his way by the vicar, he ran out of breath altogether; hardly had time to chalk up tomorrow's date and the numbers of the hymns for the next morning, before he crumpled up at the foot of the blackboard and died.

'The Marigold Inn – what d'yew say happened?' asked Jacko, as Bent-one's lungs entered a period of comparative calm. Bent-one opened his mouth to speak, closed it again and pointed.

Down the road from the Marigold Inn came George and his father, or rather, his father first and George following, cringing inwardly as he became aware of all the eyes watching and wishing, no doubt, that he was anywhere else but where he was. He was still carrying the frail in his left hand and the stick in his right, clapped close to his leg where he hoped it would not be noticed. But his father, as they came abreast of the Ploughman's Arms, with its smell of warm ale and recollections of merry, uncritical companionship, veered longingly to the left and had to be redirected by a light tap of the stick, as are cattle when they wander from their homeward route. Sadly, the stick somehow got entangled between his legs and he stumbled, then fell on his knees. Straightway a legend was born which moved instantly and immutably into local folk history: that George Gudrun, aged fifteen, one September afternoon in the reign of King Edward VII, thrashed his father, so that he fell on his knees and begged for mercy, in front of numerous witnesses, in the middle of the village green.

'There's something going on out there,' said Miss Hastbury-known-as-Miss Raspberry, from her seat by the balcony window. 'Come and look.' Miss Gale made no reply. She was trying to work out how long their collection of sweet chestnuts would last if they rationed themselves to four each per day. Lately, the two ladies had decided to try existing on a completely natural diet such as an Ancient Briton, for example, would have enjoyed. The result of this morning's foray into the countryside lay on the table before her: hips, haws, mushrooms, blackberries, chestnuts and hazelnuts. Miss Raspberry stood, in order to get a better view of what was happening in the street outside – but her eyesight was poor and they could never persuade the servant, who was afraid of heights, to go out on the balcony and clean the other side of the glass. 'Windy!' she called peremptorily (she loved using local nicknames and colloquialisms; it made her feel at one with the peasantry). 'Windy – come and look!'

Miss Gale fumed inwardly. This was the third time she had been interrupted and been forced to do a recount. At times like these she always experienced a powerful impulse to call Miss Hastbury, Raspberry . . . but she never did, being largely dependent on her for bed and board. Reluctantly, she joined her friend at the window. 'I can't make anything of it,' she said, as they watched

George in the street below running the gauntlet of what seemed like a thousand eyes.

'There's something going on,' said Miss Raspberry. 'Oh well . . . if we're going to this birthday do at the Hall,' she continued, turning, after a pause, 'we'd better start getting ready. I should leave those where they are.' (The hips, haws and chestnuts.) 'You can sort them out tomorrow.'

'Do you think,' said Windy timidly, 'we could send a message to say we've changed our minds . . . and would they send the pony trap for us after all?'

'Certainly not!' said Miss Raspberry firmly. 'We shall bicycle.'

On the other side of the green sat Bent-one, on the willow-tree armchair, between the two old men. Clenched in his hand, in his right side trouser pocket, were the three sovereigns. He longed to bring them out and show them to Jacko and Kenny . . . flaunt them . . . broadcast to the world his good fortune . . . but a kind of native caution kept him silent. He knew, without any shadow of doubt, that if he did so he would lose them; somebody, on some pretext, would take them away. So he kept mum and for once in his life made a sensible decision: he would use the money to buy leather and a cobbler's last and other necessary accessories, set himself up in his father's shed and mend people's shoes.

CHAPTER FIVE

George walked down the length of the street behind his father with a sick feeling in the pit of his stomach. He had thrown the stick away but he knew his mother would instantly detect a tension between them, and he dreaded the moment when she would realize there was no money for next week's supplies.

Their cottage lay at the end of a little lane which branched off from the main street and ran along the foot of a high bank, almost a hill, except that there are no hills worthy of the name in Suffolk. At one end of the bank was a mill, at the other end the church stood sentinel with a view straight down the main street, past the wheelwright's shop on the right, terraced cottages and the blacksmith's shop on the left, to a grassy triangular village green at the end, with its two pubs and two shops, Miss Raspberry's lookout and the fallen willow tree. The inhabitants of Cookley Green could rest secure in the knowledge that they were being monitored by the church at one end of the village and the squire's emissary at the other.

As they walked in through the little creosoted garden gate, George saw his mother's face at the kitchen window; saw how her soft mouth drooped as his father walked straight past the window to the sheds at the bottom of the garden. Had his father had some money to give her, she knew he would have gone straight in. George stood for a moment before the carefully whitened doorstep of his home, for the first time in his life afraid to go in. When at last he did, however, things turned out easier than he had expected, for he found that his mother had taken in the family from next door.

There they sat, occupying all of the available chairs in the one living room – two elderly grandparents and three children aged about five, seven and nine. George's two sisters were standing at the table playing draughts. There was a savoury smell in the room, for they had all eaten, and above that a delicious smell of stewed black-berries. George murmured something noncommittal and returned to the kitchen where his mother had kept food back for him and his father. He wondered how much she herself had eaten. She had made a thick soup crammed with vegetables – they grew as many root vegetables as possible every year to get them through the winter. At this rate, he could not help thinking, they'd all be gone by Christmas. In the soup floated a few chunks of sausage; the last of the pork from when Bertha had killed a pig. He had his soup seated on a stool in a corner of the kitchen (there was no bread, since his mother had run out of flour). Then he ate the blackberries stewed with apples from their big Bramley tree.

As he ate, his mother asked no questions but kept safely to events that had happened during her day. The mother of the children she had taken in had given birth, next door, as expected, that morning. It had been a difficult birth. She and Bertha had managed to deliver the child safely, but it was frail and perhaps would not live. They had called in the Anglican vicar to perform a

71

christening but he had refused to come, saying he was too busy preparing his sermon. So they had to call on a Methodist lay preacher and he had christened the child Henry James, after his father. The father of this family had been gored to death by a bull three months ago, and the farmer who owned the tied cottage where they lived needed it for his new stockman. He had given the family a stay of eviction until a fortnight after the birth of the baby; after that the destination of the whole family was the workhouse, there being nowhere else for them to go.

As she talked, George could feel his mother becoming more and more perturbed by the non-appearance of his father and presently, on the pretext of filling one of their lamps with oil, he walked down to the sheds at the bottom of the garden, to see what he was doing. The donkey, which he now remembered not seeing outside the Marigold Inn, had obviously made its own way home, as it was wont to do, being adept at freeing itself no matter how well you tied it up. His father had unharnessed it from its cart; now it stood sleepily in its shed, only its hindquarters on view and decidedly 'on the huh' as it rested one limp back leg. There was no paraffin, he discovered, the can was quite empty. He wondered briefly whether he could bring himself to go and ask Ellen at the village shop if he could have some 'on tick', but decided emphatically that he could not.

He went into the second shed and bent to pick up two little chairs which had been used by two little sisters who had died four years ago from diphtheria. At least there would be two more seats available in the house – if his mother could bear to have them brought in. As he raised his head he suddenly found he could see his father, through the gap of the partly open shed door. He was

72

seated on the wooden block on which they chopped sticks to start up the living-room fire, gazing into space. Centuries before, some marauding Norseman must have planted his seed and run, or, more likely, had sailed up the little river and settled, as many of them did, and founded a dynasty. For his father had Viking fair looks, blue eyes and craggy features. Nature had not intended him to be a weak man, but he had married above himself and his pride had been eaten away over the years by the gradual realization that no matter how hard he worked, he was never going to be able to keep his wife in the manner to which she was accustomed.

None of this, of course, was apparent to George, aged fifteen. He observed all his father's faults, his gradual moral disintegration, with the critical scrutiny of the young. He felt he was looking at him over an abyss of misunderstanding that could never be breached, and that what had taken place between them today could never be put right. As he stood watching, there came the sound of cartwheels and the clip-clop of horse's hooves down the lane that ran alongside their garden fence: the local doctor, visiting, rather belatedly, the woman next door who had just given birth. His father stood up hurriedly at the sound and turned to move away, and George saw to his horror that he was weeping. Shocked and fearful, he picked up the two little chairs and went back to the house.

In the cottage next door Bertha brought the baby in its crib into the kitchen for the doctor to examine, carefully closing the door of the room behind her where the mother lay sleeping. The doctor made no apologies for arriving when everything was over – he knew better than to lay himself open to one of Bertha's caustic remarks. She was a formidable-looking woman, standing ramrod straight with a mass of black hair coiled high on her head, beady dark eyes and a grim, rat-trap mouth. She was dressed entirely in black: black stockings, black button boots and a large black apron over a dark dress speckled with a pattern of tiny white flowers.

The doctor's late arrival was, in a way, a compliment. Ignorant and superstitious in some ways though he knew Bertha to be, he also knew that she had practical and manipulative skills in midwifery that far surpassed his own. So he sat down, removed his hat and waited quietly as she took the baby from its crib, seated herself on an upright kitchen chair, and began to remove the infant's coverings.

She had swaddled it tightly in an effort to support its legs, which were dislocated at the hips. Presently it lay before him like a little raw skinned cat, without the strength even to mew. He saw that it had a hare lip. A cleft palate too, most likely, he thought, though he didn't look to see – as if the legs were not enough! He lifted one limp, misshapen limb and let it fall.

'Does she know?' He indicated with a jerk of his head the woman sleeping in the next room.

'No.'

'Don't tell her.' He looked studiously at the floor. 'She may never need to know,' he added and went abruptly into the other room to see the mother.

When he came out, some time later, he was carrying the afterbirth in a pail, which Bertha had kept back for him to check.

'It's all right – it's all there. Bury it,' he said. 'I said bury it,' he repeated, 'd'you hear? None of that stupid nonsense about hanging it on a holly tree. Filthy disgusting custom. She's pretty weak,' he continued. He took a sovereign out of his pocket and plonked it on the table. 'Buy her some nourishing food . . . build up her strength, she's going to need it. God knows what she's done to deserve that,' he said, staring down at the baby, 'I should have thought she had enough on her plate already.'

'Will it ever walk?' asked Bertha.

He hesitated for a second. 'When pigs fly,' he said, and pulled out his watch. 'I shall be down the other end of the village for about half an hour,' he said, 'if anybody should want me.' He put on his hat and left.

Bertha rewrapped the baby and carried it in its wooden crib back into the sitting room. A bed had been brought downstairs for the birth where it was warmer, so the tiny room appeared overcrowded, though normally there was very little furniture in it – a table, a rocking chair with cushions, three hardbacked chairs, a religious text on three of the walls, a rag hearthrug in front of the black range where much of the cooking was done, and a tea caddy and a few ornaments on the mantelshelf above. As she placed the cradle on one of the chairs by the bed the mother woke and struggled to sit up against her pillows.

'Shall I feed it?' she murmured in a weak voice.

'Later,' said Bertha firmly. Going nearer, she whisked away one of the pillows so that her patient fell flat again in the bed.

'The doctor said to rest.' Drawing back the bedclothes she put one hand under the woman's shoulders, the other under her thighs, then, in one deft movement, turned her over to face the wall. Carrying the pillow, she moved the kettle nearer to the fire, took down the tea caddy from the mantelpiece, rearranged two of the hardbacked chairs. Presently, in the course of her perambulations, she stopped and stared down into the crib; then, after a quick glance at the sleeping form in the bed, she lifted up the pillow and dropped it gently inside the crib, running her fingers all the way round it. Placing her hand in the middle of the pillow, she pressed lightly over the spot where the baby's face was. Then she stood, humming tunelessly to herself, allowing her gaze to wander idly round the room – over the bed, the rocking chair, the ornaments on the mantelshelf, the text on each of the three walls. Though they were faded and grey with age, she found that by screwing up her eyes she could just manage to decipher the message on them: 'THERE IS A FRIEND THAT STICKETH CLOSER THAN A BROTHER', 'THE LORD IS VERY PITIFUL AND OF TENDER MERCY', and then the third one, hanging directly in front of where she was standing: 'THE ONE ABOVE SEES ALL'.

A lesser mortal might well have felt daunted . . . but not Bertha. Her face maintained its grim but complacent expression, for she was one of that iron breed born knowing what is best for everybody. She believed she had a special hot-line to God before the term had even been invented. There was even a hint of amused indulgence in her look, for she could plainly see that the One Above had 'botched up' and was now dependent on her, His agent, to put matters right. Still humming, she suddenly thought of something more advantageous she could be doing, and looked round for an object to replace the pressure of her hand. The only thing available was a family bible, standing on a shelf in one corner of the room. She took it down, blew off the dust and laid it gently where her hand had been . . . then went cheerfully into the kitchen and rinsed out the bloodstained birth sheet that she had put to soak earlier in a bowl of cold rainwater and salt.

Fifteen minutes later she returned to the living room, removed the pillow and stared intently into the cradle. Feeling satisfied, she pulled out the rocking chair and placed it facing the woman in the bed. Sinking into it, with her knees wide apart, she flung her black apron over her head and began to keen.

'Oh Lord . . . oh Lord . . . Oh sweet Jesus . . . take this child, Henry James Boggis . . . into your loving arms!' With her feet on the bottom rung of the chair she rocked backwards and forwards, wailing: 'Oh Lord, receive this child! Take this innocent babe into your loving care that he may reside there for ever! Oh Lord, I beseech Thee.'

After a few minutes she stopped, drew back a corner of the apron from one eye and looked searchingly towards the bed, to see if her message had been received and understood. It had. The mother had rolled onto her back and lay staring at the ceiling, too weak to speak or even to sob, tears running in rivulets down the sides of her face.

Bertha got up briskly, picked up the baby and took it into the kitchen, where she stripped from it every article of covering which could possibly be of use to someone in the future. Then she wrapped the little corpse in a piece of old calico, and put it out in the shed. In she came again, threw over her shoulders a fitting black shawl, locked the door of the cottage behind her and set off down the village street to look for the doctor.

He was not hard to find. There stood his pony trap in the middle of the village green, the pony mumbling away at the grass as best it could with the bit in its mouth – and there was he, neat and dapper Dr Weston with his sharp little goatee beard, sitting on the willow-tree armchair alongside Jacko, Bent-one and the Bumby King, in companionable silence. In a dolorous voice, she asked if he would kindly call at the cottage again on his way back, as the baby had taken a turn for the worse. He offered her a lift in his cart and a few minutes

77

later they were clip-clopping down the road together. When she told him that the baby was in fact already dead, and what was needed was a death certificate, he listened without comment and did not appear in the least surprised.

CHAPTER SIX

George Gudrun decided to find some way of easing his mother's problem of having to feed five extra mouths. There was nowhere indoors for him to sit; he and his father could no longer bear to be in the same room. His two younger sisters wanted to go out with him and followed him partway along the lane, but he started to run and soon left them behind. Even the three Boggis children came as far as the garden gate and stood in a row, watching. It was the first time they had ventured out of the house. Though their own home was less than fifty yards away, they were as timid and insecure as if they had been transported to the Antipodes.

There were no other watching eyes this time as he ran down the village street; everyone was settling in for the night. He hastened across the strip of marshland behind the willow-tree armchair which led down to the river path, and then slowed to a walk. A rising mist intensified the familiar river smells. Birds chattered as they sorted out their roosting sites in the blackthorn bushes and the alders. A snipe buzzed overhead and mysterious rustlings in the undergrowth caused him to take care where he put his feet. The westering sun, glowing fiery red behind the tips of the poplar trees, warned him that he had only about an hour of daylight left. He quickened his pace and before long came out upon the footpath that led alongside the lake. High up on his left stood Summerfield Hall, glowing majestically in the sunset. As he gazed up at it, Ellen's artless chatter re-echoed in his mind and visions of a banqueting table groaning with food spurred him on. He felt a familiar hollowness in his midriff, where the comforting effect of the vegetable soup and blackberries had already begun to fade. He thought enviously of the life of ease and plenty going on behind those walls; of the happiness of those who never had to worry where their next meal was coming from.

He had no way of knowing that in reality all was not quite light and sweetness within that edifice. In fact, he was at that moment, had he but known it, passing a Hall full of disgruntled females, faced with the problem of getting dressed for dinner.

Tea had been available in the drawing room from four o'clock and most of the ladies had partaken of it (sparingly, lest they spoil their appetite for this evening's meal). This was the social hour: the getting together of old acquaintances; the making of new ones. Then perhaps a walk in the rose garden before retiring to rest, ready for the evening's entertainment. Now it was time to dress for dinner, and many female spirits were doomed to take a downturn.

The fashion of the day decreed that the female form should blossom forth fore and aft with a wasp waist in between, and a comparatively new garment, known as the health corset, claimed to be specially designed to bring about this desirable shape. Many of the ladies had acquired such a garment, most had a new one stowed away in their luggage, but not one of them admitted to it as they chattered away amicably over tea. Each intended to burst upon the scene that evening and astonish everyone with their singular allure.

But there were difficulties. Those with the desirable amount of bulk fore and aft found that they tended to have undesirable bulk in between; while those who could easily achieve the wasp waist inevitably found themselves short of ballast above and below.

Stella had no such difficulties, possessing a figure that easily accepted the contours of this garment. Her problems were of the mind. Why on earth, she wondered, as she gazed at herself in the tall mirror set in the door of an immense walnut wardrobe, why on earth should I have to gird myself up in that thing . . . so I can neither move nor bend nor breathe . . . and worse still, can't even eat properly! Another evening, she thought, of nibbling away at bits and pieces while the men . . . the men absolutely stuff themselves! It was sickening; she was a robust girl with a good appetite. She took off the offending garment and flung it across the room. It hit the bedpost and hung there, swaying gently, looking for all the world like a medieval instrument of torture.

She crossed the room and stood gazing restlessly out of the window. Her eyes fixed on the figure of George, moving with great loping strides along by the lake. She envied him his freedom, his strength, his wilfulness. I won't wear it, she told herself, why should I? But then she reflected: only a few more days in which to catch Neville . . . bring him to the brink of a declaration, before he set off for two years in the Middle East. Could she really afford to do without this extra weapon? She sighed, picked up the loathsome garment and began to dress.

She was not the only one to spy the lone figure of George running across the bottom of the park. Male

81

guests had gathered in the library for something rather stronger than tea, and Lord Summerfield had joined them, ostensibly to act the jovial welcoming host, in fact to find out, from a convenient window, whether his orders concerning the removal of the corn stack had been carried out. Many of his male guests owned houses and estates similar to his own (though none quite so grand); they would be only too swift, he knew, to notice such a blot on the landscape; only too eager to detect any weakness in the administration of his land, and agree among themselves that he was getting far too old to cope. He had not forgotten certain remarks over the failure of his last two shooting seasons through lack of birds. His prompt dismissal of Kenny Ling had dealt with that.

Whisky in hand he made his way, exchanging greetings and jolly remarks as he went, to a strategic spot. He stood with his back to the room chatting amiably to some fellow whose name, he told himself, he would probably be able to remember once he had rid his mind of anxiety over the corn stack. To the right of his companion he had a clear view of his rolling acres, and saw at once, to his satisfaction, that the stack had been removed. There remained only a solitary farmworker on the site, a dot in the distance, no doubt raking up the residue of straw.

He breathed a sigh of relief. All was well. He raised his glass to his lips . . . and what should he see but a trespasser, running across the landscape at the bottom of the park. Well, there was a footpath down there of course, but, like his five-and-a-half-day week, the use of it was arbitrary. It was for members of his staff, or villagers who lived in far-flung places, to get to church and back on Sundays; not for some young whipper-snapper to go galumphing across as and when he thought fit! His moustache fairly bristled . . . but there was nothing he could do except thump the floor with his stick.

Worse was to follow. His gaze left the lakeside, travelled slowly back up the slope and reached the top of the driveway just as Miss Raspberry and Windy wobbled and wavered into view on their bicycles. He stared, scarcely able to believe his eyes. A foot-wide white banner extended between the back of Miss Raspberry's bike and the front of Miss Gale's. As this amazing contraption slowly drew level with the window there came a puff of wind. The banner bulged towards him – revealing its message in letters of fire:

'VOTES FOR WOMEN!'

In the space of a second Lord Summerfield had dropped his glass, stepped over the broken pieces and snapped shut the curtains.

'The sun, when it reaches a certain angle, has a damaging effect on the paintings,' he remarked loftily. Then he turned abruptly, intending to make with all speed for the main entrance, whither Miss Raspberry and her entourage were undoubtedly heading.

Unfortunately, he collided straightaway with his old friend Brigadier Benson-Brick, Stella's father, who responded by clamping his arm fondly round his host's shoulders (which also enabled him the better to keep his balance, for he had been drinking rather too much). Beaming fatuously into his old friend's face, he launched into an account of his new car's performance and of the superiority of the internal combustion engine over the horse as a means of transport. Lord Summerfield could only stand there fuming (he had heard it all already), and make his getaway as best he could.

There was no-one to be seen in the entrance hall when at last he got there; not even Dolmon, the butler, who should have been in charge. A quick glance through a side window confirmed his worst imaginings – a bicycle was propped up against the columns on either side of his pristine Palladian doorway, and the accursed banner was stretched straight across the entrance so that anyone wishing to enter would have to step over it.

He whirled round twice for want of knowing what best to do, before heading for the drawing room just as Dolmon was coming out.

'Why aren't you where you should be when I want you?' demanded his master.

'I was just looking for you, my Lord.' Dolmon stepped delicately across the vast expanse of hallway and bent to within an inch of his master's ear.

'I fear we have a problem at the main entrance,' he breathed decorously.

'I know we have a problem at the main entrance,' roared his Lordship. 'What I want is somebody to do something about it. I want the whole caboodle carted off as fast as possible, d'you hear?'

'Very well, my Lord.' Dolmon tripped daintily in the direction of the servants' quarters. 'I will relay your message—'

'Relay nothing,' barked his Lordship, 'come back here!' Dolmon came back. 'You are to do it, d'you hear me? Now. Put it all in the barn . . . or the stables, I don't care where you put it – just move it. Roll up that . . . that . . . thing first—'

Dolmon gazed at his employer in disbelief.

'M-me, m'Lord?'

'Yes, you. You! Who else? Go on – get on with it!'

Dolmon stood quite still for a moment, his face going pale. At last he roused himself, and walked slowly to the inner door, brushing down his trousers carefully from the knees. He took from his pocket a pair of pale, limp kid gloves – the ones he wore when he handled the silver – shot his cuffs and, finally, he went.

Lord Summerfield stomped into the drawing room, where he found his wife alone amid a clutter of dirty teacups, dishevelled chairs and dented cushions that the lady visitors, a few moments earlier, had abandoned. Lady Madeleine was draining an exquisite silver teapot of its last drop.

'Where's that cousin of yours?' he demanded.

'What cousin is that, dear?'

'That . . . Letitia . . . or whatever her name is . . . and that mad woman she lives with.'

'Do you mean Lavinia?' It was on the tip of her tongue to remind him that Lavinia Hastbury was his distant relative, not hers, but his flushed complexion warned her that perhaps now was not the time.

'Yes, yes . . . I thought I told you to send a message they would be fetched in the governess cart?'

'I did, dear – but they sent a message back to say they had their own means of transport.'

'Oh, they had, they had – bicycles.'

'Bicycles!' She held her teacup halfway to her lips. 'Oh dear!'

'Exactly. And where do you think they've left them? Propped up either side of the main door.' He couldn't bring himself to tell her about the banner. 'I've just had to tell Dolmon to remove them.'

'Dolmon!' Lady Madeleine let her cup fall into her saucer with a bang, but luckily there was not much tea in it. 'Oh no . . . how did he react?'

'How do you think? Went off in a huff of course. Now we shall have him sulking all evening.'

'Oh dear . . . I do hope this isn't going to spoil things for Nim Nim,' she said, distractedly.

'For heaven's sake, Madeleine, stop calling him that. He's a grown man of twenty-one, remember. He's about to go out and administer – well, help to administer – a most important part of our Empire. Don't you think it's about time—'

'I use it in private,' said Lady Madeleine.

'But you did it the other day, in front of that young jackanapes . . . that friend of his from up north . . . that, what's his name?'

'Gerald.'

'Gerald. You said: go and put your scarf on, Nim Nim . . .'

'Well, it was a very cold day,' she said firmly. 'And you've forgotten – Lavinia is one of your relations, not mine.'

'What's that got to do with it?' said Lord Summerfield. 'I do wish you'd stick to the essentials.'

'What essentials?' asked Lady Summerfield crossly. Then she added in a more conciliatory tone, 'What would you like me to do?'

'I'd like you to find out what those two . . . creatures . . . propose wearing tonight. Because they look an absolute sight, the pair of them. You won't believe this, but that Miss Pale . . . Whale . . . Dale . . . whatever her name is—'

'Gale.'

'Gale – was wearing knickerbockers!'

'Knickerbockers! Oh my goodness!' Lady Summerfield suddenly lost her appetite for tea. 'Oh but I'm sure Lavinia will see they wear something suitable tonight. They will have brought a dress with them. She knows it's a formal occasion, why . . . she said she was even going to root out her mother's tiara.'

'Oh, she's brought the tiara,' said his Lordship, realizing in a flash the source of the weird glinting he had seen around Miss Raspberry's head. 'She was wearing it. On a bicycle! In broad daylight . . .'

'Good gracious me!' said Lady Summerfield. 'How very odd!' But then she added, 'I expect she thought it was the best way of carrying it.'

'She's more than odd, if you ask me. Do you know she's been going round the countryside collecting berries and nuts and cooking things on a fire in the back garden?'

'Oh, I expect it's just another of her experiments.'

'Well, she should do her experiments somewhere else. I wish I'd never let her have that place in the village. She's no help to me at all. In fact, she creates more problems than she solves.'

Lady Summerfield put down her cup and took her husband by the arm. 'Let's go and change, dear. I'll pop along and sort everything out with Lavinia, don't you worry. I'm sure everything will go off splendidly tonight, it always does. Come . . .' Lord Summerfield allowed himself to be led out of the drawing room and they began making their way across the main hall towards the smaller hall and the stairs.

'You always have such a lot to deal with, I know, dear.' She intended broaching a rather sore subject and her voice now took on a soft and coaxing tone. 'You always have had. Now, if you had Nim Ni— I mean Neville, to help, how much easier your life would be. He could take some of the burden off you . . .'

'Oh yes,' said her husband sourly, for he had heard this song before.

'Well, it seems so foolish . . . just when he's finished university . . . just when he could begin to be of some real use to you . . . why, if he were here, he could take no end of little responsibilities off your shoulders and it would be such good training for later, when he . . . when you . . .'

'When I'm past it, you mean, or dead and gone.'

'No, I don't mean any such thing! All I'm saying—'

'Sh!' said Lord Summerfield, as a maidservant emerged from the library carrying a tray full of dirty glasses. 'Eyes and ears! Eyes and ears!'

'Clear the dirty crockery out of the drawing room, Becky, when you've done that,' called Lady Summerfield, 'and straighten the chairs.'

'Very well, my Lady.' Becky passed on to the kitchen quarters.

'I just don't want him to have what I had – the burden of this place before he's had time to spread his wings a little.'

'But he could be of such help to you. You could run things together and all the time he would be learning . . . why, he might even decide to marry Miss Benson.' Stella had made strenuous efforts to jettison the Brick part of her name and to some extent had succeeded. 'Stella . . . she seems such a nice girl . . . and the brigadier is your best friend—'

'Oh for heaven's sake!' cried Lord Summerfield, 'let the boy live a little!'

'You say that . . .' Her voice thickened with emotion. 'But there's the heat . . . and the cholera . . . and yellow fever . . . he might die out there! We might never see him again!'

'Oh nonsense,' said Lord Summerfield. 'Pull yourself together! If it was left to you the boy would be an absolute namby-pamby. Have you checked the dining room?' he added after a pause.

'Yes,' sniffed her Ladyship.

'Good. Let's go and get dressed. Go on . . . up the stairs with you!' They were now in the smaller hall, at the foot of the main stairs. She grasped his arm to help him, but he shook himself free. 'I'm not totally infirm – yet,' he mumbled.

'Oh very well.' She mounted the stairs. A thump and a clatter from behind informed her that her husband had missed his footing and dropped his walking stick. It rattled down to the bottom of the stairs. She paused without turning and after a moment continued upward. Lord Summerfield went down four steps, retrieved his stick and tucked it firmly under one arm. Grasping the banisters with both hands, he began pulling himself up after her.

CHAPTER SEVEN

Unaware of the consternation he had caused in high places, George ran on westward, leaving the lake behind him. He followed the river for a short distance before climbing higher ground leading to the woods at the back of the Hall. He was now trespassing and uneasily aware that he could be plainly seen from any of the west-facing windows staring out at him, over the top of the stable walls. Breathless, he plunged gratefully into the woods at last and made his way swiftly towards the head game-keeper Dick West's cottage.

It stood in a clearing a little way into the wood. The original clay daub and thatch cottage had been built by George's paternal grandfather fifty years before. A year ago George and his father had substituted tiles for thatch, patched up the clay daub, replaced some of the windows and lime-washed the whole a gentle yellow. Now, with a feathery coil of smoke curling up from its chimney, it looked the very picture of a fairy-tale cottage. But George had no time for aesthetics. He hurried across the lush green clearing patterned with the long shadows of approaching evening and filled with the aromatic smell of wood smoke, and knocked at the door.

No-one answered, so he knocked again. This time someone shouted from within. He waited again . . . but still nothing happened so after a moment he lifted the latch and walked in.

The reason for the lack of response was immediately apparent: there sat Dick West, naked in a tin bath in front of a blazing fire, staring at George with a mixture of annoyance and embarrassment.

He was a stringy little fellow, bald, except for a spiky fringe of gingery hair spraying out over his ears. His face, neck and forearms were burnt brick red by the sun, but the rest of him had the pale, translucent look common to many red-haired people. Like a piece of bindweed, George thought, that had been growing under a sheet of tin, deprived of light.

'What the devil do you want?' growled Dick, picking up a piece of old towel he had been using as a face flannel to cover his intimate parts.

'A gun,' said George, and his gaze wandered selectively over the three or four guns lodged on one wall on wooden pegs. 'This one, I think . . .' and stepping carefully around the end of the bath he took down the gun of his choice.

'What the bloody hell d'you think you're doing? Put that back!' Dick exclaimed. He tried to rise but fell down with a splash.

'It's like this,' said George calmly, cracking open the gun and peering down each barrel in turn, and trying out the trigger in the manner of all those in possession of a new firearm. 'My mother's taken in the Boggis family and we need some grub just to tide us over the weekend and I thought his Lordship could well spare us a pheasant or two. But the thing is,' he paused, and turning his attention from the gun, he looked at Dick intently, 'are you going to tell on me like you did on Kenny?'

'Tell? What d'ya mean – I don't know what ya talk'n' about.' He took refuge in bluster. 'I s'pus yew think you're cock of the roost, now you've thrashed ya father.'

George looked at him quickly. 'What – have you heard already? I'm blowed! Don't news travel fast in these parts! Well,' he added, with a grin, 'you know what you'll get if you tell on me now then. All I need,' he continued, 'are a few cartridges.' He stepped over the foot of the bath and gathered up a handful from the rough-hewn mantelpiece, the warmest, driest part of the house.

'Put 'em back, you bugger! Dew I'll give you what for!' cried Dick, without much conviction. He attempted to rise again but sat back almost immediately, his face bright red.

'Cover yourself up, do,' said George reprovingly. 'What a horrible sight!' for the flannel had floated away from its moorings exposing poor Dick's appendage, which was long, thin and pallid and reminded George of an intestinal worm he had once seen, passed by a horse.

'Thanks for the gun anyway,' he said, 'I'll bring it back in about half an hour.'

'I shan't be here,' growled Dick, 'this is my night down the pub.'

'I'll put it in the shed then,' said George. 'Have a good time.'

Once outside he took the well-worn path leading to the enclosure where Dick raised his pheasants yearly for the shoot. The coops and runs were empty now, the birds released and practically mature. The Rhode Island hens he use to brood the eggs had already been whisked away, lest they offend the eye of his Lordship, should he happen to come by. His aversion to poultry in all its forms was known to all.

George expected most of the pheasants to have

scattered since their release, but he felt sure some of them would still be near their place of origin. Not a single bird could he see, however. What he did see, slung from a corner post of the enclosure to the branch of a nearby tree, was Dick's display of the gamekeeper's craft – a long wire from which hung the corpses, in various stages of decay, of other little inhabitants of the wood: a jay, magpie, rook, jackdaw, squirrel, hedgehog, weasel, stoat . . . and right at the end, shot, trapped or poisoned by mistake, a thrush.

Not pausing to look too long lest pity and anger at this row of harmless creatures, now dead, upset him, he walked quickly on. Almost at once a young cock pheasant flew out from under his feet with a startled squawk and sailed away in rather graceless flight. Alarmed cries from a group of chestnut trees ahead told him that was where most of this year's brood had gone to roost. He slowed down in front of the trees, then stopped. The ground was littered with bright green sweet chestnuts, some of the cases split to reveal the gleaming brown nut within. Leaning his gun against a tree, he began gathering up the prickly cases, prying out the nuts and stowing them away in his jacket and trouser pockets. At least there would be something for everyone to eat tonight.

But the shadows were lengthening even more now and the sky was turning a fiery red. It would soon be too dark for him to do what he had come to do. Hurriedly, he took out of his pocket some string and a pocket knife and began tying up the cuffs of his sleeves and his trouser bottoms; then, gathering up handfuls of the prickly chestnuts, he began stuffing them down and finally inside his buttoned-up jacket. At last he could take on board no more. He straightened and turned to retrieve his gun . . . and saw, silhouetted against a blood-red sky, just what he had been looking for – the dark, humped forms of two pheasants, roosting side by side on a branch of one of the chestnut trees.

If he approached carefully, he saw at once, and stood at just the right angle, he had a fair chance of bagging both birds with the one shot. Stealthily he edged out from behind a sheltering branch and raised his gun.

He was too close: the pellets would not have time to scatter sufficiently to hit both birds. Slowly he backed away and then stood for a moment. The two young pheasants sat huddled together, heads drooping. There were others in the vicinity, for from the surrounding shadows came a soft chirruping sound: a sort of 'the day-is-over-please-let-me-sleep' sound that he had heard young chickens make as they settled for the night. He closed his eyes: after all, in a few weeks, he told himself, they might all be dead anyway. He conjured up in his mind the distressing picture of the game cart as it would soon be seen – with dead birds dangling from the edges, like bobbles round the bottom of a lampshade . . .

He opened his eyes, raised his gun and, careful not to drop any chestnuts, took careful aim. The nearest of the two birds lifted her head and bent towards him with a look of mild enquiry, so gentle and so inoffensive that his will failed him. He lowered his gun.

He walked away, passing between tall trees along a wide path worn down by farm carts, until he came out on the agricultural scene concealed from Summerfield Hall by the strip of woodland that had been planted years before. A mosaic of newly harvested cornfields lay before him, some still patterned with curving rows of golden corn stooks like rows of teeth. Spurts of moisture from newly cut corn stalks spattered his boots and his tied-up trouser bottoms. He walked awkwardly, arms held slightly away from his body, legs a little apart. He walked across three fields until he reached the edge of an old sandpit that was home to a rabbit population and known as Kyle's Warren.

It was the Romans who first brought rabbits to Britain for food and fur. It seems they kept them in cages; it was the Normans who gave them free range. They were considered a delicacy and over the centuries most land-owners of substance set themselves up with a warren and employed a warrener to ensure a goodly supply and to guard them from the attentions of the hungry peasants. Like rabbits everywhere, they overreached themselves reproductively and came to be regarded as something of a pest as the popularity of rabbit meat declined and their propensity for damaging agriculture became apparent. One of Jacko's responsibilities was to eradicate them from those parts of the Summerfield estate that bordered farm land, and he had only lately done his work in this particular spot. So when George crawled on his hands and knees, dragging his gun, to the edge of the pit, he expected to see rabbits of all sizes hopping about below.

The sandy sides of the pit were peppered with their burrows and their footprints, but to his surprise he could only see two rabbits. One, the larger, with a dewlap under its chin, he knew to be female, the other was obviously male and was pursuing the female with amorous intent. George could hear his little excited grunts as he came upon the doe from behind and hope-fully applied his chin to her back. She hopped on regardless, nibbling grass as she went; then, as he persisted, she suddenly turned irritably and went for him with her front feet . . . and at that moment George fired.

It was impossible to tell which one of them screamed. The buck was flung backwards, kicking and writhing before finally lying still. The doe sat rigid with shock, then slowly began to turn, like a cat chasing its tail. Round and round she went, faster and faster, while George stared at her nonplussed. Dropping his gun, he leapt down the side of the pit, his feet sinking into the soft sand. As he reached the bottom she gradually stopped gyrating and sat hunched up and perfectly still. As he approached, she suddenly shook her head; her nearer eye bulged, and then, seemingly in slow motion, oozed out of its socket and descended on a bloody string down the side of her face.

Horrified, George hauled her up by her back legs and began striking her repeatedly behind the head with the edge of his hand, an operation he had often witnessed in the harvest field but had never been able to bring himself to do. Holding her across his knee, he stretched her out full length until he heard the bones of her neck crack . . . then he threw her to the ground where, after a few convulsive movements, she lay still.

When he felt the contents of his stomach rising up into his throat he swallowed hard, aware that if he lost his last meal now there would be nothing more till morning. So he stood trying to subdue the spasms and just when he thought he had succeeded, lost control . . .

Disconsolately, he covered with sand what remained of the vegetable soup and blackberries. No longer squeamish now that they were dead, he took out his knife, gutted the two rabbits and buried their entrails. Then he slit between the tendons of one back leg of each little corpse and threaded the other leg through, making a loop for a handle. Holding both in one hand, he scrambled back up the side of the pit to recover his gun, leaving a second line of deep depressions in the sand. (A few days later Jacko, sitting alongside George on the willow-tree armchair and peering suspiciously down at George's boots, was to remark that 'some bugger with big feet hev bumped orf my breeding pair' for, of course, only a foolish rat catcher would be so efficient as to exterminate too effectively, and do himself out of a job.)

George quickly shuffled back with the gun and put it in Dick West's shed, as he had promised. The sun had finally set and the only light now came from an anaemic sliver of moon that appeared and disappeared fitfully between fleeting clouds. Glad of a spell of darkness, and still holding on to his chestnuts, he sped down the sloping parkland, passed the west-facing windows of the Hall, and breathed a sigh of relief as he reached at last the semi-legitimate footpath running alongside the lake. Up on his right the lighted upper windows of the front of the building peered down at him, like a row of eyes. And behind them, of course, the birthday guests, well into their preparations for the evening celebration. Indeed, Lord Summerfield, resplendent in his best evening wear and sporting a new silver-tipped ebony cane, was just descending the stairs and grappling with an old familiar problem: what to do about the staircase? He was dissatisifed with it, as had been his father before him. It lacked grandeur; it should have come down into the main hall . . . but what to do? Altering it would be a major operation. He paused, for one problem had suddenly been superseded by another: what if the accursed bicycles had scratched or in some other way defiled – with oil, for instance – the pristine surface of his door columns? He hastened down the few remaining stairs, stumped across the entrance hall, seized a lighted three-spiked candelabra from a marble hallstand and opened the main door.

To George, standing at that moment with the lake spread out behind him like a bar of silver steel, it was as though the building had opened its mouth; as if the shaft of light which suddenly shone forth had spotlighted him, standing there brimming with chestnuts and holding his poacher's spoil in either hand for all the world to see.

Another minute more and his Lordship might well have found time for his customary check-up, might just have spotted the dark figure silhouetted against the lake. But right at that moment, providentially, Dolmon struck the dinner gong. It boomed out through the open door and across the countryside like the mating call of a prehistoric animal. His Lordship turned and hurried in, thus sparing himself yet another harrowing experience – the sight of a poacher and trespasser, making free on his beloved land. He hastened to join his guests, indulging, for a brief moment, in a delightful fantasy where he would be the one to escort the luscious Stella into the dining room, though he knew in his heart that etiquette (and Lady Madeleine) would ensure he was entrusted, not with Stella, but her mother . . .

Ten minutes later, George was back in his own backyard, thankful to have escaped detection of an offence that could have resulted in a prison sentence. Going straight to the woodshed, he chopped off the head and feet of both rabbits without a qualm. He carried them indoors and flung them on the table before his mother. She seemed about to protest, but said nothing and fetched a bowl of cold salt water to soak the flesh, ridding it of any undue 'rabbity' taste.

In the other room, lit by two flickering candles (his mother was using the only lamp which had any oil), he found his two sisters playing marbles on the floor, watched by the three Boggis children, who still had not raked up enough confidence to join in the game. The Boggis grandparents occupied two of the hardback chairs and his father the big old Windsor chair nearest to the range. Without a word, George pulled the green tasselled chenille cloth off the table and spread it on the floor.

Then, standing in the centre, he undid his jacket, untied the string around his sleeves and trouser bottoms and shook out all the chestnuts onto the cloth. The brown shiny ones already out of their shells he put in a saucepan of water and, stepping over his father's outstretched legs, set them on top of the range to boil. Then he bundled up the rest in the tablecloth and lifted them onto the table, for everyone to enjoy.

'There y'ar – git them down ya!' he said.

'Speak nicely, dear,' said his mother reprovingly at his lusty invitation to eat. She had already skinned the first of the rabbits. It lay on the table pink and shiny. George picked up their largest kitchen knife and began cutting big chunks, while his mother pushed the severed back legs of the other through the skin. She tugged the rest of the skin up and off, and a long strip of bright white curd was revealed, stretching along the whole length of the underbelly.

'What's that?' asked George, puzzled.

'Milk,' said his mother. 'She was a nursing doe. She had young.'

George stood, silently, head bent, his unruly hair flopping down over his forehead. He had his father's Viking locks but the eyes he was so studiously keeping averted were his mother's, warm and brown. She knew her son well, and put out her hand to touch his arm. 'You were not to know,' she said.

He put down the knife he was holding, and stood for a moment looking into the other room. They were all gathered round the table, cracking open and eating the sweet chestnuts. Even the Boggis grandparents had managed to lever themselves out of their chairs. Only his father remained slumped in his Windsor chair, staring darkly into space.

CHAPTER EIGHT

Gathered for the celebration of Neville Summerfield's birthday, guests were now comfortably seated at that other, considerably larger, table in the decidedly grander dining room two miles away. Conversation was just beginning to blossom as they earnestly chewed their way to the end of the fish course.

The liveliest topic, the one causing the greatest degree of animation, featured the dramatic happenings at the Marigold Inn and the singer with the glorious voice. A trifle excessive was the wonderment expressed, as they pondered on the mystery of how an artisan from the depths of rural Suffolk could have risen to such musical artistry.

His Lordship, straining to hear and at the same time trying to conceal how much his ears now failed him, cottoned on at last to the subject under discussion and identified the men as Archie Gudrun, a skilled craftsman, and master of many trades – and his son George, who had caused all that trouble at the school in Cookley Green.

'Trouble – what trouble?' queried Miss Raspberry, her attention diverted at last from her plate. It seemed

George had been kept on at fourteen as a pupil teacher and had instigated a debate on the morality of the British Empire!

'Really?' exclaimed Miss Raspberry, her forkful of pheasant arrested halfway to her mouth. She had abandoned her dietary principles for this occasion and was determined to ignore the glances of Miss Gale, who was still sticking to hers, ostentatiously piling her plate with vegetables.

'How very interesting,' continued Miss Raspberry. 'How is it I've never heard anything about it?'

'Oh, it was nothing serious,' said his Lordship. 'He was simply saying how we wouldn't like it if we were the natives – that sort of thing. Only when the whole school filed out on Empire Day to salute the flag, some of them refused!'

'My word – insurrection in Cookley Green!' she observed. 'But we wouldn't like it, would we,' she added thoughtfully, 'if we were the natives?'

Brigadier Benson-Brick, lately retired after twenty-five years in India, breathed out loudly through his moustaches with a ferocious snort.

'Oh yes, no doubt,' he boomed, 'we should've left 'em to their own devices . . . to their poverty and filth and . . . their favourite pastime – killing each other.'

'Oh, but you're wrong to think the father is just an artisan,' said Lady Madeleine, in an effort to steer the ship away from the rocks, 'he was trained as a boy soprano by an excellent choir master at Silverley church. And when his voice broke, it was even better than it had been before. And he married the girl contralto he used to sing with – against her father's wishes. So very romantic!'

'Romantic – fiddlesticks!' said his Lordship. 'He married above himself and lived to regret it, if you ask me.'

But at the word romantic, all the ladies at the table became tremendously fascinated, and clamoured to hear more. They quite swamped the brigadier, who had more to say on the subject of the Empire, but could only sit smouldering while Lady Madeleine told how the two young singers had been much in demand at the three local churches. They fell in love and waited patiently for six years before they finally got married at one of the Nonconformist chapels in Cookley Green. The vicars of all three Anglican churches refused to marry them without the bride's father's consent. Her father vowed never to speak to her again and for fifteen years had lived the life of a recluse. 'In one of our manor houses – Thickthorn, the best one,' said Lady Madeleine plaintively, 'and it'll soon be falling down round his ears and we don't quite know what to do about it.' She was quelled by a glare from his Lordship and continued lamely, 'The mother died early in the marriage and the girl was brought up by a nanny and housekeepers and governesses . . . all gone now, of course,' she finished feebly.

At this point things fell rather flat; a moment later everybody spoke at once; then each waited for another to speak, and in the silence the brigadier, just working up another head of steam, could be plainly heard demolishing a mouthful of pork crackling in readiness to pontificate further on the subject of the Empire.

At the other end of the table, someone came up with a talking point to save the day, causing the brigadier to sink back once again thwarted. Just suppose . . . just for fancy's sake – one cleaned up the rustic singer and primed him in the ways of the fashionable world . . . what fun it would be to launch him upon the London concert scene as a world-class performer and confound all the experts and critics! Could such an enterprise possibly succeed? . . . that was the question.

Many and varied were the answers, delivered vehemently, phlegmatically, diffidently. Much excitement and interest was generated right through to dessert. The brigadier despaired of getting a word in and Lord Summerfield, only able to grasp that some scheme had been proposed to uplift the peasantry, observed that in his experience the peasantry did not respond well to efforts to improve their lot. He cited, as an example, a former Lord Summerfield's experience with the beans. At this, Gerald looked at Neville with raised eyebrows and grinned, having been treated to the story of the beans twice already. Neville gazed down doggedly at his plate, pawing tentatively at his wounded ear. His father launched again into the tale of how the then Lord Summerfield, genuinely concerned about the plight of the peasants after a series of wet summers and harsh winters in the late 1870s and early 1880s, ordered thirty of a prolific type of bean to be delivered to the most needy and deserving families; the enterprise turned out very successful until the following spring, when it was found that many of the families had devoured all of the beans during the long hard winter instead of keeping some back to sow for the next season. He ended as usual with a reference to Aesop's fable of the industrious ant, and the improvident grasshopper who took no thought for the future . . .

Silence fell at the end, as most of those present could not think of anything significant to add . . . except Stella, who seized the opportunity to tell of her experiences with the natives of India, where she had helped in the local maternity hospital for the final two years of her father's career there, after finishing her schooling in England.

'The natives are just like children,' she declared. 'They need to be told exactly what to do and what to expect.

And no doubt a firm, fair and straightforward method would work just as well with these Suffolk yokels,' she concluded.

Stella could not help glancing at Neville at the end of her little speech.

He had indeed lifted his head from rapt contemplation of his plate and, startled by her implied criticism of his father's administrative methods, was gazing at her in astonishment. Lord Summerfield himself appeared to be nodding his head, having only a vague notion of what was being said.

'The best solution to the problem of the beans,' she continued, 'would have been to appoint one reliable villager to take on the responsibility of collecting an equal number of beans from each family, storing them during the winter and distributing them again, fairly, in the spring: thus incorporating responsibility, co-operation and thought for the future all in the one operation . . .'

'Balderdash!' cried Gerald. 'Typical female poppycock! He'd eat all the beans – or keep the best for himself. Total claptrap!'

'Claptrap!' cried Stella. 'Female poppycock? Why female? Why – Isn't my opinion as valid as yours?'

'No. It never will be!' cried Miss Raspberry in a thrilling tone. 'Not until we rid ourselves of . . . these abominations!' she shouted, dropping her spoon and fork with a clatter. Reaching under the table, then rising to her feet, she waved above her head something that looked like a furled piece of pinkish material. Holding the roll at each end, she turned it so that it began to unfold slowly, like a scroll. It revealed itself to be a woman's corset or stays, rather faded, a bit grey, in fact not particularly clean. Reinforced on either side by an amazing arrangement of whalebone, its laces crisscrossed all the way down the centre with the loose ends dangling into a bowl of blackcurrant trifle, the metal tips tinkling musically against the glass.

'Woman traps! Straitjackets!' cried Miss Raspberry. 'Burn them!' she cried. 'Throw them away!' and demonstrating her advice, she threw the offending garment backwards over her head. It sailed through the air, scattering a few multicoloured blobs of trifle in its wake, and dropped onto the floor about three feet in front of the cardboard figure of Dolmon, standing resentfully at the rear. Only his head moved as he redirected his gaze from somewhere in the middle distance to the object now lying on the floor before him. He stared for a moment in disbelief, then, aghast, turned towards his master . . . only to find that with violent jerks of the eyeballs to left and right, and with constrained but discernible movements of the head, he was being directed to do something.

'GET RID OF IT!' growled his Lordship through clenched teeth. 'GET RID OF IT!'

A look of obstinacy crossed the butler's face. For a fleeting moment, the satisfactory relationship between man and master was threatened, the very fabric of society trembled. Then Dolmon recollected his place. Extending an arm, he took the object between finger and thumb, and holding it well before him with outstretched arm, walked slowly out of the room.

Gerald raised his hands for a round of applause, but when he was greeted with a freezing silence, he let them fall. Some of the guests craned their necks to see what was happening on the other side of the room. Others followed Miss Raspberry and carried on with their meal in silence.

'Perhaps it's time for the birthday cake,' Lady Madeleine suddenly piped up rather nervously.

'Later,' said his Lordship firmly, and rose with an elegant insouciance to make the birthday speech.

Neville breathed out in relief when he realized his father was not going to recount the circumstances of his birth. Of course, most of those present had heard it before. Only the dapper Dr Weston and his wife were newcomers in these circles. Dr Weston was being recognized for his sterling services in shepherding Neville through the vagaries of measles, mumps and whooping cough. He was one of the first to be toasted. Then it was the turn of old Nanny Elton, everybody's favourite. Then the brigadier, who had exercised godfatherly concern as best he could from distant India. Then came a gaggle of governesses, with such nebulous personalities his Lordship could not quite distinguish one from another. Next, the pony on which Neville had learnt to ride, dear old Nobby, who had lived to the incredible age of forty-one! And Thomas the groom, who had saved him one day when the pony pitched him into the lake, and finally, but not least of course, Bertha, the Wise Old Woman of Cookley Green, who had succeeded where all the greedy mandarins of Harley Street had failed and without whose miraculous intervention, down by the ice house, twenty-one years ago, this birthday celebration would not be taking place . . .

And now his Lordship's voice deepened as he arrived at the subject of Neville's imminent departure to foreign parts, to join other stalwart members of the Diplomatic Corps in the service of King and Country.

'The great families of England,' he declared, 'have given generously and freely of their sons, no matter how hard the sacrifice and pain of parting.'

Poor Lady Madeleine's big bruised-looking grey eyes filled with tears. 'And while such families remain, the true strength, the very backbone of Old England, their scions continue travelling to the far corners of the earth in the name of British justice, Britain and her Empire will remain great for ever!'

The guests toasted copiously the Old Country, the Empire, the great families of England, Lady Madeleine and all such mothers who gave freely of their sons. They drank to British rule and British justice and (almost as an afterthought) the birthday boy . . . and finally . . . His Royal Majesty, the King!

At the end of this peroration, his Lordship was seen to be somewhat breathless and swaying slightly, and Lady Madeleine judged it was time now for the birthday cake.

'The cook,' said Lady Madeleine, 'has produced something rather special, and it's all a total secret.' Lady Madeleine had decided to allow the cook to bring the cake round herself, for their inspection.

Enter the cook, in her best bib and tucker, pushing the cake before her on a silver trolley, her fellow members of the kitchen staff clustered in the doorway peeping out at the event.

'Take it all the way round the table,' directed her mistress, 'and come back to me last.' Away went the cook while the guests bent their necks in turn, graciously commending the cook on her creation as it passed. Some who had known the family for many years might well have been thinking that Lady Madeleine was just as hapless and hopeless as she had always been towards the domestic staff – for everyone knew if you gave them an inch they'd end by getting above themselves. But poor Cook! Hardly had she got down one side of the table when it became evident that things were not going at all well – for a kind of contagious fit of the vapours seemed to afflict the ladies she left in her wake. The gentlemen managed to remain stalwart, but the ladies . . . the ladies visibly wilted on viewing the tableau on top of the cake.

Ellen had been quite right – the baby was too red. BLOOD-RED would not have been an inapt description of it, and the one or two spots of cochineal that had splattered on the snowy whiteness of the frosted icing were not reassuring. It was disgusting! In such bad taste! It was altogether too much . . .

Cook came up the other side of the table in a spectral silence. Suddenly she lost all confidence, gave the trolley a tremendous push, as if to shove it off the very face of the earth, burst into tears and ran for the door, where she was half led, half carried by her colleagues back into the kitchen, in hysterics. Nor was this all: as the trolley whizzed to the end of the table, seemingly targeted on the ill-fated Dolmon, Neville lunged out an arm, caught the end rail and stopped it in its tracks. Stepping out from his seat, he nonchalantly swung the trolley round and propelled it back towards his mother and ended up showing clearly his 'bad' ear to all.

'Oh, Nim Nim!' cried his mother. 'Your poor ear! Whatever's happened?' and whether it was from strain, shock or over-tightness of her stays after a substantial meal, she promptly fainted.

CHAPTER NINE

Half an hour later, Lady Madeleine lay recovering on a chaise longue in the drawing room, revived by a whiff or two of sal volatile and kind encouragement from Dr Weston. The rest of the diners had repaired to the ballroom, where an eight-piece orchestra and a buffet had been provided for guests who had been invited to the ball, but not the banquet. Dancing was already in progress, but the somewhat battered and bemused dinner guests seated themselves in small groups around the edges of the room, to give themselves time to recover from what had undoubtedly turned out to be the most eventful dinner party for a long while, perhaps ever. For there was an awful lot to talk about, enough, some of those bound for the metropolis on the morrow might well have thought, to keep the conversation going for many a dinner party to come. One thing they all decided upon: Lady Madeleine was as demonstrably inept and misguided in her handling of the servants as she had always been.

'Who on earth is that appalling woman with the tiara?' someone asked.

'I hear she is a dependent, distant relative of his Lordship,' whispered somebody else.

'But why on earth doesn't he keep her at a distance – as far distant as possible?'

'And what about that sly removal of the corn stack? The lamented former Lord Summerfield would never have allowed such a blot on the landscape . . . without doubt, things are not at all as they used to be.'

In the breakfast room next to the kitchens, Neville lay across three padded chairs, while Becky the housemaid, as directed by Dr Weston, gently poulticed his injured ear. From where he lay he got a delectable view of her milky neck and the soft underpart of her neatly chiselled chin and he longed to bury his face there, or somewhere thereabouts . . .

'Oh, Becky!' he sighed. 'Becky!' He had kissed her once, on his seventeenth birthday, emboldened by a few glasses of wine. Kissed her, and in effect ruined her life, for heart, mind and body she waited ever after for the next bit to happen; waited and would accept no other. Now she was fated to be wedded to the family for all of her active life, rising perhaps in time to the dizzy heights of Lady's maid, with a comparable increase in pay. She received at the moment 2/6d per fortnight, which she handed over straight away to her mother, who lived in Silverley with a sick husband and nine other children. But after all, what did she want with money, with everything here provided?

'Oh, Becky!' sighed Neville again, 'I do wish—'

Becky stroked his cheek with one hand as she cupped his poor ear with the other. 'There, there,' she murmured, 'don't you fret.'

In the ballroom Gerald and Stella were dancing. Surreptitiously, he had asked the band to play a waltz and now he was holding her too tightly and whirling her masterfully about the room. So tightly that she soon became irritated: she was tall, but he was taller and with her head pulled in under his ear she was unable to watch out for Neville's return. As the waltz came to an end at last she saw him, leaning against the wall just inside the door, whey-faced and listless. Resisting a quite savage impulse to pounce on him at once, she moved instead, without a parting word to Gerald, towards the open glass doors leading out onto the paved terrace and the rose garden. Fanning herself languidly with a scented handkerchief as if the room had suddenly become insufferably hot, she passed directly in front of his line of vision with a preoccupied air.

He must see me, she thought, swishing along in her ankle-length midnight blue gown with lace neckline and sleeves, her waist nipped in voluptuously by the accursed corset.

Will he follow me? she wondered. She could feel his eyes boring into her back as she drifted on to the end of the rose garden and down to the path leading to the orangery . . . but some other couple, she suddenly thought, might well be in the orangery . . . She turned right and began climbing the slope to the grassy ridge between the main and service driveways. Under the shadow of a young oak she stopped once and glanced back . . . and yes, there was someone moving behind her, past the rose garden; barely visible as the moon disappeared momentarily behind a cloud, but standing out clearly a second later against one of the lighted windows of the Hall.

Breathlessly she climbed onwards – but not too fast, pausing now and again to remove from her light dancing shoes a non-existent stone. At last she reached the ridge and walked slowly along it, aware that she must be plainly seen silhouetted against the now clear moonlit sky. Behind her she could just distinguish footsteps on the soft grass padding nearer . . . and nearer . . . until, at a neatly judged and appropriate moment she stopped and turned, with a nicely calculated cry of surprise. Then: 'Oh it's you,' she faltered.

'Who did you think it was?' said Gerald. 'You're backing the wrong horse, you know,' he went on kindly, 'with old Nev. You'll never get what you want from him. Take it from me – and I'm his best friend.'

'Oh yes,' said Stella, 'and how are you to know what I want?'

'You want whatt all wwomen wwant,' slurred Gerald a little drunkenly, 'you want a good rrrog-e-ring!'

Stella involuntarily drew back suddenly, for the first time wondering if she could be in real danger. Behind her she felt the rounded roof of the ice house and could go back no further.

'Lemme show you how it's done,' said Gerald, slurring again, and stepping forward he seized her by each wrist and pressed her back against the soft turf which covered the sides of the ice house for insulation, cut short by George only that morning.

'What are you doing . . . stop it! How dare you!' squealed Stella.

Gerald pushed his knee forward, forced her legs apart and, as she arched away, pressed himself firmly on her from knee to neck.

'There . . . s-see how nnicely we ffit; just right!' he said. He made no attempt to kiss her but applied lips and teeth in a series of painful sucking bites all the way down her neck and, as he tore down the soft lace of her sleeve, her shoulder and the upper part of her left breast began to come out of her dress. She pushed him away, but he held her down. She cried out, but found, to her utter humiliation and disgust, that she felt a powerful impulse to give in. Some renegade part of her, she realized, wanted this thing to go on! She managed to wriggle sideways and then, thrusting her knee between his legs, she brought it upwards with all the force she could muster. And found herself gazing down at a strong man brought low, literally low, crouching and clutching his tender parts. Fascinated, she could only stand there and stare. Gerald bent, groaning and drawing in hissing breaths through his teeth. 'You vicious cow!' he growled, hobbling away, leaving Stella there, in the moonlight, with her breast exposed.

· But she was not of a particularly nervous disposition; she gritted her teeth and hurried back to the Hall in the half-darkness, quickly up to her room. Soon she was standing before her mirror. She touched, with curiosity, the little ladder of suck marks running down her neck from ear to breast. She felt surprised at her reaction to the assault, but she was not going to admit this to herself. 'How dare he!' she breathed into her mirror. 'How dare he!'

Half an hour later, she was back in the ballroom, wearing a light blue silk embroidered Chinese jacket over her ballgown, its mandarin collar fastened high at the neck – and there was Gerald, she saw with one swift glance, seated beside and in deep conversation with a petite fair-haired girl of about sixteen, admittedly one of the prettiest girls in the room. At the sight of him her legs went weak – delayed shock, she supposed. She made her way to an unoccupied spot beside the buffet table and looked around for Neville. He was nowhere to be seen.

'What I think I'll do . . .' It was Miss Raspberry speaking, as she emerged from the back of the table with a plateful of sweet pastries. 'What I think I'll do – is I'll start up a tennis club in Cookley Green. Yes, I think that would be a good thing for the village. I'll get that young fellow, George what's his name? . . . Gudrun, to lay out the courts. There's room for two, I think, at the back of my stables.'

With her dessert fork she broke off a large chunk of cream jam puff and popped as much of it as possible into her mouth, ignoring the jammy flakes that overflowed onto her chin. She chewed for a bit, then turned and looked at Stella closely.

'Do something on your own account,' she said sagely. 'Make something of yourself, by yourself, that's my advice. Why wait for a man? I wish I hadn't.' She turned back to her jam puff and appeared as engrossed in this activity as if she had never spoken.

She's right, ruminated Stella. Women are forever waiting for a man to give them a lead. But I can do something on my own. She looked over at Dr Weston and imagined how she might help him in the three villages.

Then Neville can't fail to see who has his best interests at heart, she thought. And I'll paint in my spare time. I'll make Cookley Green famous. Only I don't want to wait years and become famous after I'm dead, that's no good.

As she drifted away she suddenly became aware that Miss Raspberry was looking at her closely again. She sank down deep into her jacket; she was unsure how well the mandarin collar concealed the telltale suck bites on her neck.

'You can be the first to join,' said Miss Raspberry graciously.

'You mean the tennis club? Oh . . . thank you,' was all that she could think to say.

At this juncture Miss Gale joined them carrying a plate on which lay a baked potato wearing a pink paper hat, with two olives for eyes and a slice of red-skinned apple for a mouth. She seated herself close to Stella on her right side, carefully removed the hat and began forking the contents of the potato into her mouth, as Miss

Raspberry settled herself comfortably on Stella's left. It was too much. There on one side was Miss Raspberry with her big bony body, her cottage-loaf hairstyle, flattened by the now abandoned tiara and falling down in wisps round a bland schoolgirl face with rosy cheeks. Some of her redness had strayed to the nose that was set like a small beacon in the centre of her face (she suffered increasingly from rosacea). On her other side Miss Gale was tiny and rodent-like, her greyish, sandyish hair in plaits wound in Eccles cakes over her ears. Her forehead lined up with her nose but there was no chin to speak of.

What a way to spend an evening, thought Stella. Two old maids and another one – me – in between! She sat up very straight and looked searchingly about her, as the band struck up a military two-step and the dancers began surging vigorously to and fro. Miss Raspberry stopped chewing and peered at Stella curiously again. Putting out a tentative finger, she gently pulled down the mandarin collar and examined what she found there with the puzzled interest of a monkey . . . or a very young child. But Stella sat oblivious – for through the serried ranks of dancers she was getting glimpses, almost subliminal glimpses, of Gerald and Neville, sitting at the far end of the room on either side of, and in close proximity to, and obviously vying for the attention of, the pretty, fair-haired young girl. 'Oh no!' Stella declared roundly. 'Oh no – I'm not having that!' and rose majestically to do battle.

Meanwhile, as the birthday celebrations at Summerfield Hall looked set to continue far into the night, the day was drawing to a close in Cookley Green. Many families had already retired to save on lighting. The pubs had closed some time ago and most of their clientele had long since gone home to bed. But Jacko and Bentone, in an effort to prolong the pleasures of the day (opportunities for entertainment in the village being thin on the ground), were sequestered in the laurel bushes outside the barmaid Molly Marston's cottage. They were waiting to find out who she would bring home with her this time from the Ploughman's Arms, when she had finished washing the tankards and cleaning up the bar. Jacko looked his usual disreputable self, but Bent-one was wearing his best cap and a new blue-and-white-spotted neckerchief instead of his customary long yellow scarf. Though it was a fine, cool September evening with a quite adequate moon, the many trees and bushes edging the lane where Molly's cottage stood made it all rather dark and shadowy. The two bickered quietly while they waited, for want of something better to do.

At long last footsteps could be heard approaching and two dark figures walked up the garden path to the cottage door and disappeared within. Bent-one crept forward and applied his eye to the spot in the window where a tear in Molly's curtain afforded a fair view inside the cottage.

'Who is it? Who is it?' hissed Jacko in a strangulated whisper.

'How the hell dew I know?' retorted Bent-one irritably. 'She hint hed time to light the bloody candle yit.'

'Let me look,' said Jacko. 'Thass my turn.'

'No that int,' said Bent-one, pushing him away. 'Thass mine.'

Before there was time for any further fricton there came the clip-clop of a horse's hooves and a familiar soft slurping sound, heralding the approach of Kenny the night soil man and his swinging barrels on his customary Saturday night round. His fat little brown and white pony plodded on past the cottage gate, heading probably for a nice clump of herbage it knew of further down the lane. Kenny came crashing through the laurel bushes to

116

join them. 'I knew yew'd be here,' he cried triumphantly. 'Wass go'n' on?'

'Bugger you orf,' said Bent-one. 'We don't want you here, you stink.'

'No, I don't,' cried Kenny. He prided himself on the care he took over his appearance. 'I washed myself all over afore I come away.'

'Yes, but you dint wash that duzzy horse, did yew? Or them stink'n' barrels. They stink enough to crackle yew, they dew.'

'Hold your din, will yew?' hissed Jacko, with his eye pressed close to the glass. 'They'll hear yew. She's lit the candle. Well, bugger me – thass Dick West! – thass hew that is! I can see his red hair . . . and here come poor little old Chrissie down the stairs in har nightgown and har dodmons. (Chrissie was Molly's little illegitimate daughter, dodmons the rag curlers in her hair.) There – she soon got sent back to bed. Poor little mawther! That don't bear think'n' about what that poor little old mawther must see and hear.'

'See? See what? What are they do'n' then?' said Bent-one, 'let me see.'

'He's a'sett'n' in the armchair . . . and Molly's a'kneel'n' on the floor atwixt his legs,' said Jacko.

'Kneel'n' on the floor – wass she kneel'n' on the floor for?' queried Bent-one, puzzled. 'Whass she do'n' kneel'n' down there for atwixt his legs?'

'Well, if yew don't know that, Bendy bor, nobody dew,' said Kenny succinctly.

'Sssh!' breathed Jacko. 'There's somebody else com'n' – listen!'

They listened, and sure enough another pony trap could be heard approaching. It came rattling down the little lane at a smart pace and drew up sharply at the garden gate. A dark but familiar figure got out, wearing a bowler hat – Ginty, bearing yet another gift, no doubt, for the hard-hearted Molly. Hat and shoulders plainly silhouetted against the sky, above the privet hedge, he walked up the path and knocked at the cottage door.

'Poor old Ginty,' whispered Bent-one, giggling. 'He's in for a big surprise!' But only the narrowest sliver of light showed as, a moment later, Molly opened the door a crack and thrust out a hand. The gift, whatever it was, was swiftly transferred; Ginty probably put forth a hopeful foot . . . but too late. The door closed again, leaving him standing disconsolately on the doorstep, hat in hand, head bowed.

'Poor old Ginty,' murmured Kenny sympathetically, 'he don't hev a lotta luck, dew he?' They watched him stump back down the path to his cart, climb in and clip-clop away.

'Dick is pack'n' it in too,' announced Bent-one deject-edly, with his eye to the window. 'He's now putt'n' on his coat.'

'Well, he's bin put orf, hevn't he,' said Kenny. 'Wunt yew be, with all them 'ruptions?'

'Never even got his money's worth,' said Jacko regret-fully, though his regret was probably more for what he thought he himself had missed.

Subdued, they drew back into the bushes and waited as Dick made his departure, the moon glinting briefly on his bald patch before he put on his hat and walked off down the path. They waited until the sound of his boots had died away, then the three gloomy voyeurs pushed their way back through the laurels, climbed over the wooden palings into the lane and parted.

Bent-one and Jacko set off at once for their homes in the village street, leaving Kenny to make his way further down the lane to recover his cart. It was a pleasant evening, and as he walked Kenny played agreeably in his mind with the thought that, should he ever, at some time in the future, experience a compelling need to call upon Molly, he had no doubt that, unlike poor Ginty, he would carry all before him and she would instantly succumb to his charms. Such a happenstance, of course, would be quite out of the question, unless and until she procured new curtains.

He found the pony where he expected to find her, but there was an unexpected problem. On mounting the bank in pursuit of a particularly alluring clump of green-stuff, a stout pole sticking out from the hedge had poked one of his barrels out of balance and the lid had flown off. Nothing very much was to be seen, because of the deep shadows from the overhanging hedgerow, but a pungent and noxious odour spoke for itself. Picking his way carefully round the periphery of the spill, Kenny managed to climb up the bank, retrieve the pony and guide her down to level ground. Then he stood for a moment assessing the situation. It was too dark and too late, he decided, to take any immediate action – it would have to wait until daylight. He set off for home in a philosophical mood, hoping for heavy rain.

Back at the Hall the band played on, the dancers were indefatigable. But his Lordship was tired and longed to go to bed, where Lady Madeleine and many of the older guests had already taken refuge. He had one more duty to perform, though, before he could truly feel he had done with the responsibilities of this special day. He made his way to the kitchens, closely followed by Edward, the youngest footman, carrying a wicker hamper padded at the bottom with straw and lined with a layer of clean muslin.

'Put in the hog's head . . . the hog's head,' said his Lordship, pointing with his ebony cane. 'Plenty of meat on that yet. And the trotters – they're always useful, so I believe.' Edward following, he went round the deserted kitchen pointing. He opened the meat safe and into the hamper went joints of ham and roast beef, sausages and game pie. In went scones and rolls and twists of bread and a few dessert items deemed not too delicate to stand up to close packing, and some of the fruit still available in the fruit bowls. Finally there remained the birthday cake, still practically whole. Using one of Cook's big carving knives, he scraped the controversial blood-red baby off the top tier into the waste bucket, wrapped the rest in a clean cloth and gave it to Edward with strict instructions: 'Carry that separate. Do as you did last year – take the morning off and use the governess cart. You know where to take it and she'll know who it's from. D'you understand?'

Edward did understand. He would do as he did last year – call in on his parents in Summerfield, his grandparents in Silverley and his married sister in Cookley Green . . . and if the contents of the hamper then appeared to have sunk a little . . . he would take a bit of straw to pack in at the bottom, in case the formidable Bertha should suspect it had been tampered with. There would still be plenty, he reckoned, for her to give to her family and friends. Together they heaved the hamper onto the scrubbed pine table and covered it with a gingham cloth.

'Off you go now,' said Lord Summerfield.

Grateful to have finished at last with the demands of the day, his Lordship started off in the direction of bed, with a feeling of blissful relaxation unfolding somewhere in his central being. But at the door he stopped, retraced his steps, and bent down, carefully retrieving the sugar baby from the waste bucket, which he crumbled into little bits, lest the cook should find it in the morning and suffer a recurrence of the vapours. Only then was he able to continue on his way, satisfied in his mind that he had now done everything that needed to be done. For upon meticulous attention to such myriad details did the successful administration of the kingdom depend.

Mid-May 1999

War Memorial Fund – what war memorial? There isn't one! Neil's supply teacher, who is supposed to relieve him of his class on Fridays so that he can deal with the school correspondence, yesterday failed to turn up, so I volunteered to take all the children on a history walk round the village. His class have been learning about the First World War, so we set out to look for the village war memorial. I'd seen them in other villages round about so I thought there must be one here, though up till now I've not come across it. We found a really heart-rending private one on our walk back from the ice house on the day of the picnic, and the memory of it still haunts me. We took the public footpath alongside the lake, passed an old boathouse buried in reeds and bulrushes and a clump of balsam poplars scenting the air. About halfway along the lake we came to some steps leading down to a landing stage, where obviously there had once been a boat.

In this idyllic spot, with the wind rustling the reeds, the water glinting between the leaves of the water lilies and dragonflies flitting overhead, the Summerfield family have erected their own private memorial to their only son. It's in the shape of a stone figure of a young boy mounted on a plinth; the plinth decorated on three sides by the flints that were commonly used in the construction of East Anglian churches. The boy looks to be about eight, is wearing a sun hat, holding a fishing rod in one

121

hand, a bucket in the other and on the front of the plinth is an inscription:

In loving memory
of our dear son, Neville,
who played fished
and rode his pony here
who died for his country
May 1917.

He, of course, was the Summerfield heir, with whom Becky had been in love and who, according to Becky, had been in love with her. When I got home at the end of the school day, I mentioned what I had seen to Pearl and she told me something so dreadful I can't seem to forget it. I've tried to cast it out of my mind, but it keeps coming back. Apparently Bent-one – he of the mysterious anatomical peculiarity – was always the first to find out what was going on and always knew everything about everybody. (Look who's talking, thought I!) He told her something he heard just before he came out of the army: that Becky's lifelong love did not die heroically during the war. He was shot by two of his own NCOs. He was such a poor officer, made so many wrong decisions and caused so many men to die that they both shot him as he crossed a bridge, thus sharing the culpability. He fell into the river and floated downstream and his body was not recovered until ten days later, when it was assumed he'd been shot by a sniper. I know war is awful, but this seems to me beyond belief and I wish she had never told me.

We spent over an hour searching for the Cookley Green war memorial and at last were driven into asking a smartly dressed, white-haired old gent walking his dog, whether there was one and if so, where was it? He was well spoken, obviously a newcomer, and replied vaguely that he had once heard there should have been one, but for some reason there wasn't.

It was beginning to rain now, soft summer rain, so I decided we should make a dash for the church, which stands sentinel on a ridge at the eastern end of the village. Apparently there was once a mill a bit further along the ridge, but it was blown down in the gales of 1953. At least in the church we would all be dry, I thought, so up the street we scampered, passing several places of historical interest, I noted, on the way: the old blacksmith's shop, snuggled under the stag-headed oak tree which once, so Pearl told me, gave shelter and shade to horses as they waited to be shod; the wheelwright's big black shed across the road opposite – down in a dip, so that you get an almost aerial view of it over the low wall. Pearl says there's a sawpit down there, something the children really ought to see. Then there's the cobbler's shop a little further on, with BENDY ALBEMAN still discernible on a sign above the window and an advert inside offering to mend boots, shoes, buskins and any other articles of leather. Bendy . . . of course . . . this must have been the domain of the inestimable, irrepressible, all-knowing, all-seeing Bent-one!

Further on a building with tall narrow windows, once a Methodist chapel, now converted into a private house. Then a wide yard leading to a number of outbuildings still used by a firm of thatchers to store quantities of Norfolk reeds . . . enough here, I thought as we sped by, to merit several more educational excursions. Halfway up the hill we hastily took the side entrance to the church, scrambled up the wet, slippery, mossy steps and into the churchyard – where the children's attention was instantly captured by three goats tethered at regular intervals along one edge of the main path leading to the church door. They had obviously been assigned the task of keeping the grass short . . . and wobbling around the feet of the nearest nanny was a tiny kid. 'Aaaah!' cried all the children and took off as one towards it, bounding over the graves of those who had gone before without a thought, thought I, of their own mortality.

Deserted, I stood in the rain, ankle-deep in wet grass. There, all around, were the graves of my new friends that I felt were old friends, so vividly had Pearl brought them all to life for me as we pored over the scrapbook and the faded photo: Joshua Ableman, wheelwright, and his wife Rose; Herbert Ableman, their eldest son, cowman (there's a picture of him in the scrapbook receiving a long-service award at the Suffolk Agricultural Show – the princely sum of £20 for working for fifty-five years on the same farm!); Bertha Braddock – Bossy Bertha, no less! – the midwife-cum-layer-out-of-corpses. In the photo she looks a tall impressive lady and she's certainly been given an impressive gravestone. Grave-marker would be a more appropriate word, for most of them in this corner of the graveyard, I now saw, are made of wood, brown oak, many of them with carved symbols denoting the lifetime occupation of the occupant. A wheel for Josh the wheelwright. A scrappy-looking cow for Herbert the cowman. A pair of boots for Bernard Ableman (Bent-one the cobbler). Two rats hanging from a nail for Jack Trett, Jacko the rat catcher. Two barrels – milk churns? – for Frederick Kenneth Ling. An anvil for William Zebediah Cook – Billy the blacksmith – and a plough for Benjamin John Nodd – Old Ben, the plough-man from Hall Farm whose great love was his Suffolk punches . . .

Absorbed and saddened I stood looking about me, but I was not too absorbed to notice suddenly that the children had gone suspiciously quiet. Not a giggle, not a whisper from them – a sure sign usually that something is afoot. Something was: they were all standing in a half-circle gazing at the little kid, and one small child, I saw, was being encouraged towards it. Sammy. I saw his innocent trusting smile as he took a diffident step forward. I saw the nanny stop munching, lower her horns and her body assume a businesslike posture . . . 'Nooo!' I yelled and now it was my turn to go bounding over the graves.

I was too late. Poor Sammy received a powerful blow in the midriff that knocked him backwards and all the breath out of his body, to land with his legs in the air among the wet and grassy graves. Red-faced with fury, I stood him up and held him as he hiccuped and gasped for breath.

'She don't like me,' he sobbed. 'Mummy goat don't like me!'

'She thought you were going to steal her baby – that's how I would behave, if somebody tried to steal you.'

The circle of contrite faces stared at me guiltily. It was a subdued and shamefaced gaggle of children who trailed back through the village, with me stalking along in front holding my son by the hand.

He fell over again later, in the school playground, as if he had lost confidence in controlling his limbs. Neil was already playing football with the older children as we waited for the dinner van to arrive. Our dinners are cooked at another school five miles away and brought to us in metal containers.

Neil came over to Sammy, brushed him down and tried to impart fresh strength to his wobbly legs. Sammy sobbed on, refusing to be comforted. Neil crouched, lifted his chin with one finger and smiled up at him, until Sammy's little screwed-up face cleared and he was able to smile back. Then Neil picked him up, carried him over to a seat by the fence and drew him backwards onto his knees. Hugging him close, with his chin resting on Sammy's tousled fair head, together they sat and quietly watched the football. And I knew Neil was remembering holding, in just such a way, the little five-year-old daughter he would never hold again.

I never once saw you smile into your son's face as this man did, and show that you accepted him the way he is.

Seems it was Josh who made the personalized grave-stones, so Pearl informed me when I went round hers Saturday to stitch my green skirt. As mechanized machinery began arriving on the farms, wooden wheels were no longer needed, so he took to making wheel-barrows, ladders, dog kennels and garden sheds. It was in later years, when he was semi-retired, that he began producing gravestones of wood, which he kindly presented, free of charge, to members of the family or friends who appeared likely to be visited shortly by the Grim Reaper. As his own time grew short, he worked more and more furiously, feeling it incumbent upon him to leave a goodly supply for as many as possible after him. Not surprisingly, not everybody appreciated being thus reminded of the inevitability of their demise, and a certain amount of ill feeling was generated. But, as Pearl sagely remarked, sitting patiently holding the end of my green silk as I stitched, every single one of them came in handy in the end. And it was as well to be prepared, she added, for Bent-one the cobbler died before his father. Apparently he was forever trying to climb the oak tree by the blacksmith's shop. He used to climb it when he was a boy, Pearl said, and perhaps he couldn't believe he couldn't still do it, after he came back from the war. Having only one arm then, he slipped one day and got strangled by his long yellow scarf. Poor Bent-one! What a way to go – I felt quite desolate. Did Josh make you a gravestone? was a question I badly wanted to ask Pearl, but I didn't dare.

All this time Sammy was lying languidly on her scruffy old armchair, reacting, I think, to a positive outpouring of pollen from hedgerows, gardens, trees and vast fields of oilseed rape. Is this to be your main legacy to him, I wonder – a wretched bout of hay fever every year?

CHAPTER TEN

Life went on as usual in the village after the Summerfield celebratory ball. Some good things happened, some not so good. Kenny found himself in bad odour with everybody because of the smell from his spillage wafting in on the prevailing wind. In order to make amends, he got sawdust from Ellen's father, Josh the wheelwright, and coated the spill with a mixture of sawdust and sand. This improved things a little, but not much.

George's father managed to stay in work and out of the pub for once and the two of them continued to work together, though relations between them were strained. They got paid as promised on the Monday for their work on the ice house, so George's mother was better able to cope with the problem of feeding eleven people instead of her usual five. Now she had flour, she could provide George with his favourite thing for packed lunch. Known as a scrap-roll, or turnover, it consisted of rendered-down noodles of pork fat, apple, sultanas and brown sugar wrapped in a layer of thick suet pastry. It was very sustaining and invariably induced in George a feeling that all was well with the world.

During the weekend George had made a coffin for the

dead Boggis baby, but the vicar refused to accept the christening as valid as it had been performed by a novice Methodist preacher not yet on the official circuit list. The Methodist chapel had no graveyard, so a dispensation was usually granted for those of other denominations to be buried in the consecrated ground of the Anglican churchyard, but in this instance permission was refused and the vicar insisted the baby be buried outside the churchyard wall in unconsecrated ground. At this the mother, already depressed, became inconsolable as she pictured her baby clamouring at the gates of heaven for the rest of eternity. In the end George went out one night with a lantern, dug up the baby and reburied it inside the churchyard deep under the spreading branches of an ancient yew, where he hoped it would not be noticed.

In the flickering light of the lantern, he carefully moulded the soil into a tiny grave shape. When he had pressed in a wooden stake at one end and lined the grave with a row of stones all round the base, he stood leaning on his spade for a moment, gazing out at the sleeping village bathed in mist and moonlight below. Midnight, and not a light to be seen, and none, he noted gratefully, from the nearby vicarage, half buried among the trees to his right. No sound, except for an occasional querulous screech from an owl in a clump of tall Scots pine and the faint barking of a dog from a distant outlying farm. He alone in the world, it seemed, was awake.

His mission accomplished, he flung his spade over the wall and, pausing at the top as he began to climb over, he sat for a moment, contemplating, with the aid of the lantern, the consecrated land on one side of the wall and the unconsecrated ground on the other. He seriously doubted that God would have instigated such a differential. It was a man-made device the vicar was using, he rather fancied, as an instrument of power. Because of the difficulties over her marriage sixteen years before, his mother had transferred her allegiance from the Anglican church to the Nonconformist Congregational chapel at the eastern end of the village, which probably explained why the vicar was being so inflexible about the baby. Also, in all likelihood, thought George, looking back, it explained the alacrity with which he had been booted out of the school for refusing to salute the flag on Empire Day. People in country places have long memories: he suspected his mother had not been forgiven.

Still, he thought as he extinguished the lantern, jumped down from the wall, picked up his spade and set off for home, the Boggis mother could now rest assured that her baby had a passport to heaven and could perhaps cease her weeping and put her mind to the future. As this entailed the whole family being relegated to the workhouse a week on Saturday, it was not a prospect from which she was likely to derive much comfort.

The awful truth, he reflected dismally and with shame, was that he was sick of the Boggises and could not wait for them to be gone; not only because of the inroads their extra mouths were making on the supply of winter vegetables, but because of the dreadful pall they cast over the entire household and their apparent inability to lift a finger to help themselves. The three children could at least, he thought resentfully, have gone out into the freshly cut cornfields gleaning, as his sisters had done, or tried to earn a few pennies riddling potatoes or picking up stones from the one or two fields that had, so far, been ploughed. Surely his family had given them as much help as they could be expected to give? Then he recalled his mother's attitude of simple Christian goodness and compassion and felt deeply ashamed.

In need of some kind of uplift for his flagging spirits, he took the long way home, wandering along one of his favourite footpaths, now dark and shadowy but so familiar he could have walked it with his eyes closed. There was a bank which he had come upon one night in June studded with the tiny lights of dozens of glow-worms, as if the stars themselves had fallen from the sky. There were no glow-worms now, and the nightingale which had sung so throbbingly then was silent. Glumly, he made his way back home, put the spade and lantern in the shed, stepped carefully over his mother's newly whitened doorstep and entered the dark cottage. It was pervaded by the delicious smell of new-baked bread. His parents and sisters had long since gone to bed, the Boggis family to their own home to sleep . . . but they would be back again tomorrow, early, with hungry gaping maws . . .

Following his nose, he went into the kitchen, a long narrow room running the entire length of one side of the house. There was a chimney and fireplace at the far end and to the left of this a Dutch oven set in the wall, where his mother had been baking cakes and bread. In the oven she had probably put the porridge for tomorrow's break-fast, in a bowl in a saucepan of water to cook slowly with what remained of the heat. In the corner to the right of the fireplace was a copper and on its round wooden lid four new-baked loaves of bread, and on the scrubbed pine table along one wall two plates of shortcakes. He eyed them hungrily: he could have eaten them all, for he was a big lad and still growing . . . and perhaps just one would be permissible? But he counted six cakes on one plate, intended obviously for the Boggis family, and only four on the other – one for his own and one for his father's packed lunch tomorrow and one each for his two sisters, but not one for his mother, and this checked him.

He knew that if he was to have peace of mind he would have to rise above hunger, so with a mighty effort of will he left them where they were and went to bed.

In the meantime, as the days passed, Bent-one made stealthy preparations towards his future career as village cobbler, made possible by his great good luck in acquiring the three gold sovereigns. He knew that if he was seen to be setting himself up too rapidly there would be speculation in the village as to where the money had come from, so he amazed everybody by taking on all kinds of onerous errands and tasks which normally he would have avoided with his customary ingenuity.

He had hidden the three gold sovereigns in an old sock under the horsehair mattress on his bed. Every night he took them out and counted them. He still longed to tell someone about them; he knew he mustn't so he told the cat, whispering conspiratorially into her twitching ear, 'Not one, not two, but three, Molly!' Molly, looking suitably ecstatic, elevated her back end and swiped a moth-eaten tail across his face.

He had got permission from his father, Josh, to use the small shed at one end of their cottage for a workshop. It already had a bench and a window overlooking the village street. Reluctantly, he took out one gold sovereign and set off to see the widow of his old master, with whom he had spent a number of months learning the trade, before a fire put an end to his apprenticeship and the old man's business. He had managed, with the money he had earned, to buy a few items, but more were needed if he was to be suitably equipped. But when he asked the widow if he could purchase any items left undamaged after the fire, she, thinking he was in his usual impecunious state, wanted no money at all and gave him everything that was left: hammers, files, knives, two lasts, a leather apron, nails, screws, hobnails, buskin moulds, even an ancient treadle stitching machine, a bit rickety but still capable of stitching cloth or soft leather for making gaiters.

Delighted with his new acquisitions, and thoroughly surprised at not having to pay for them, Bent-one packed them all in a new wheelbarrow his father had made and not yet managed to sell. Painted bright blue and orange, it made a delightful splash of colour as he pushed it home, singing inappropriately:

'If I was a blackbird I'd whistle and sing,
And follow the ship that my true love sailed in.
And in the top rigging I'd there build my nest,
And pillow my head on his lily-white breast!'

On his return, he arranged all the small tools on his workbench, ready to fasten them to the wall on hooks when he was able. Then he rubbed the rusty stitching machine all over with an oily rag. Last of all, and still rejoicing, he took the precious sovereign out of his pocket, spit-polished it for the umpteenth time and gleefully put it back with its fellows under his mattress. As he did so a sudden thought struck him: what if he should contrive . . . somehow . . . never to spend, lend, part with, even disclose the very existence of the three gold sovvies? What if they should remain deliciously, secretly and everlastingly – his? Fired up, he set out without delay to earn enough money to buy his next requirement: leather of sufficient thickness and quality to sole boots and shoes.

On the farms round about, the harvest was at last coming to an end, later than usual owing to a cold wet spring and a rather uncertain summer. Harvest festival services had already been held on successive Sundays in the three local churches. Worshippers had already lustily bellowed out that all had been safely gathered in though actually, at that time, it hadn't. George, very in love, helped Ellen decorate the homely little Methodist chapel, for her family were of that denomination, with strings of wild clematis, ivy, autumn berries and the usual offerings of vegetables, fruit and corn dollies. During the coming week she would probably help him adorn the large, barnlike, lath and plaster Congregational chapel that his family attended, ready for their service still to come. But before that, on the previous Saturday, the event would occur that the village children most looked forward to throughout the year: the combined Methodist and Congregational Sunday school outing to the little resort on the coast, where the river that curled lazily around the boundaries of the village finally ran merrily out to sea.

So, on the Wednesday before the awaited outing, the head horseman up at Hall Farm, Old Ben, began preparing the two farm waggons in which the children were to travel on their ten- or twelve-mile journey. In a fury of activity, he swept out into the air a cloud of dust, straw, barley barbs, wheat, oat and barley grains, scrubbed down the sides, wheels and shafts of the waggons so that the blue and orange ('dragon's blood') paint came up as good as new. Both waggons had been made by Josh, Bent-one's father, ten years before and had recently been repainted. Only when the waggons had been thoroughly cleaned and their moving parts re-oiled could Ben turn his attention to the job in which he took real delight – preparing the horses. Dusty, sweat-stained and with overgrown hooves, tails and manes after long hours spent in the harvest fields, they had first to be taken to the blacksmith's to have their feet trimmed and shod. They had gone soft-footed in the fields all summer but would need protection for their twenty-odd-mile journey on the rutted and stony road to and from the coast.

The blacksmith's shop stood just about opposite the wheelwright's in the middle of the village street. There was no spreading chestnut tree but an upright oak and the smith himself was hardly the mighty man of Longfellow's poem. He was small and puny, except for overdeveloped muscles in his arms. He was rather afraid of horses; kinder perhaps to say that he was nervous and distrustful of them. He much preferred the ironwork involved in making farm gates, railings and machinery, and particularly wrought-iron work. He it was who had devised the highly decorative framework from which hung Kenny's barrels, and of these he was inordinately proud.

Normally a visit to the blacksmith would have been for Ben a great occasion, for it meant that the eyes of everyone would be upon his horses as he walked them proudly down the village street; they would have been immaculately turned out for the occasion. But today's visit took second place to the greater occasion still to come on the Saturday. So he waited with unusual impatience as Billy the blacksmith slowly went through his customary procedure of lifting up, cleaning, trimming and reshaping each overgrown hoof, before starting on the fitting of the iron shoes. This lengthy sojourn at the smithy was a pleasurable day out for Ben; almost a holiday. Certainly it was a welcome break from long lonely hours spent out in the fields. The warmth of the glowing forge fire, the unmistakable sign of something going on – the chink of hammer on metal – would usually bring in the old men of the village. Past work themselves, their main entertainment was watching somebody else still at it – with hypercritical eyes.

Today, so far, only a group of children looked in briefly on their way back to school for the afternoon session. Bright-eyed and inquisitive, they stood fidgeting in the doorway, breathing in the delicious acrid smell of burnt horse-hoof, and listening with delight to the wheezy pumping of the bellows and the ringing rhythm of the hammer, as it bounced off red-hot metal and rebounded on the anvil with a bell-like sound. Well aware of Billy's nervousness with horses, one of the children soon reached out and pulled a tail, causing a clatter of hooves, a great upheaval of big brown bodies and roars of outrage from Ben and Billy, as they struggled to restore order among four Suffolk punches crammed into a confined space. Unrepentant, the children ran laughing away.

Reseating himself on a wooden trestle near the forge, where he had a clear view of his precious charges, Ben began at last to relax, unbuttoning his many layers of clothing: jacket, waistcoat, two woollen jumpers, thick flannel shirt and who knows what underneath. Although the weather was not really cold he had already donned his winter gear, and would not divest himself of a single garment, whatever the weather, until well into summer next year. Taking out his pipe, he sat back and prepared to enjoy a long, lazy afternoon, watching someone else work.

Up at the Hall things had not gone particularly smoothly since the birthday celebrations. For one thing, the Benson-Bricks had had to stay on longer than planned owing to the brigadier, on the very day of their proposed departure, falling victim to yet another bout of his recurrent malaria. Stella, hardly able to believe her good luck, gladly agreed to stay on to help look after him. Her mother, on the other hand, decided to return immediately to their home in the Waveney valley (gracious, but not nearly as impressive as Summerfield Hall), lest the servants run amok in the absence of their masters.

His Lordship also took to his bed, on the pretext that his gout was worsening; really, he was suffering from fatigue and a crying need to escape from his responsibilities for a while to recoup. Dolmon promptly followed suit, issuing a bulletin from his bedroom (the biggest and best of the staff bedrooms at the top of the house, the one facing south) to say that he had contracted a fever and did not anticipate returning to his duties for at least a week. Human nature being what it is, the servants at Summerfield, treated on the whole with kindness and consideration, tended to be rather more trouble to handle than if they had lived under a stricter, more oppressive regime.

'Feed a cold, starve a fever,' said the cook, grimly, there being no love lost between her and the recalcitrant butler, and she forbade any transference of food from her kitchen to 'that liar and hypocrite upstairs'. The rest of the domestic staff were as one in believing Dolmon to be suffering from nothing other than bad temper and an iron determination to extract his pound of flesh for what he considered to be his humiliation over Miss Raspberry's bicycle and the flying undergarment on the day of Neville's birthday celebrations.

Quite unaware of subterranean rumblings within her household, Lady Madeleine made an attack on her wardrobe, having suffered, at the birthday party, the experience of seeing another woman in a dress identical to her own, and only learning of the advantages of the newest version of the wonderful 'Health Corset' as the evening wore on. Left feeling ignorant of the intricacies of the fashionable world, and convinced that her waist was at least three-quarters of an inch thicker than it needed to be, she gave way to a fit of petulance unusual for one of her gentle disposition. Flinging open her five wardrobe doors, she began throwing out numerous garments that she was determined never to be seen wearing again. This was to the great advantage of various female members of the domestic staff, particularly Becky, whose star was now definitely in the ascendant within the family. Amazed, they found themselves owning the kind of expensive garments they had never in their wildest moments dreamed of possessing, and that in all probability they would never have occasion to wear. Leaving all the wardrobe doors wide open, after she had finished her operation and the rows of coat hangers hung empty, Lady Madeleine could hardly wait for his Lordship to rise from his sickbed and see for himself that she had absolutely nothing to wear.

As the days passed Gerald, who had stayed on for Stella, received first one, then another telegraphed message from his father to say he was 'wanted at mill' and, even more importantly, when was he bringing back the car? Gerald promptly tore up these requests and threw them into the fire. All three young people eventually became housebound, as Neville's ear obstinately refused to heal and Stella, to Gerald's chagrin, would go nowhere without him. They passed the time playing billiards or cards or backgammon, or quarrelling when interest in such pastimes palled. Dr Weston made daily visits in his pony trap and Becky carried out four-hourly ministrations as he directed. But Neville's ear continued to worsen and by Thursday of the second week, the doctor, perturbed at inflammation so close to brain tissue, decided that more drastic treatment was necessary. He suggested the county hospital, but his Lordship, concerned for the welfare of his beloved son, switched his allegiance, in the space of a moment, back to the formerly despised 'greedy mandarins of Harley Street'. After all, were they not the best, the most skilful, the most highly thought-of medical men in the country? They were certainly the most expensive! Nothing but the best would do for his son.

So it was decided that Neville was to travel to London on Saturday by the early morning milk train; was to be driven to the station by Gerald in the Rolls-Royce 40/50 which his father had lent him to drive down in from Yorkshire to Suffolk, and thus impress his aristocratic hosts. (Gerald was as proud of this car as if he had worked, saved up for and bought it himself.) Lady Madeleine was to accompany Neville and spend any spare time at Harrods, to replenish her wardrobe. They would be staying at her sister's home near Regent's Park and Becky, who had quite won her mistress's heart by her devotion to Neville, would accompany her, as her personal maid.

Stella flung herself on a chair in despair when she heard all these arrangements aired in the drawing room in Dr Weston's presence. Nearly a whole fortnight had gone by and she had got no further with Neville; had not even managed to achieve a significant moment alone with him, because of Gerald's constant, overpowering presence. What could she hope to achieve in the one day that remained?

Tears of rage and frustration blinded her eyes. She turned away from the window and pretended to be following Dr Weston's departure, as he took his leave of Lady Madeleine at the front door and rattled away in his cart down the drive. Behind her, the two young men, who had been playing backgammon until the doctor's arrival, lost the will to continue and began to play the more enjoyable game of ostracizing Stella. They reminisced nostalgically, and more and more mawkishly as they went on, about their time together at Cambridge. They recalled carefree happy days spent on the Cam; picnics on sunny afternoons along the Backs; wild pranks by moonlight involving articles of ladies' underwear and chamber pots; drunken parties and discussions on philosophy lasting well into the night . . .

'Philosophy,' said Stella tartly, for she was a practical young woman. 'I'm sure that'll prove very beneficial to your future careers!'

'Ah, but it's all a good discipline for the mind,' said Gerald, loftily. 'The thing about philosophy is you can question everything – question whether that sheep, for instance,' (there was one, grazing at a distance of about thirty yards from the drawing-room window – how many times had Lord Summerfield resolved upon a ha-ha, to keep the animals at bay, and never got around to it!) 'whether that sheep still actually exists when you are not there to look at it.'

Stella thought the question totally idiotic.

'Ah, but there are learned men,' said Neville, interrupting, 'who can put forth a proposition that things . . . that the whole world, in fact . . . may only exist in our own minds . . . as a stream of sensations impinging on our consciousness,' and he went on to elaborate.

Stella felt herself sinking into boredom. Blinking to clear her eyes, she gazed out at the scene beyond the window. She could see the sheep – a white blob on the green foreground against a wide blue background. Small billowing black shapes flew gracefully from right to left across the expanse of blue rooks, blown by the wind across the sky. She could see the lake as a pale metallic blur in a frame of green and yellow reeds and rushes. But it was not that she had now been dragooned into seeing the objects of her world as a stream of sensations impinging on her consciousness, it was just that her dark eyes were short-sighted. She always saw the world that way.

And now her gaze fixed on a warm patch of colour on the other side of the lake. A moving patch, bumpy-shaped and conker-red, it travelled steadily along the road beside the lake, then turned into the driveway leading to Hall Farm. She rubbed her eyes and stared . . . but she was never to know what it was, for a bank of trees had been planted to hide the farm from view and gradually the shape disappeared behind it. Soon it was gone, as if it had never been. But Ben, for it was Ben – and his horses returning from the blacksmith's – still existed and continued on their majestic way behind the trees to the stables. As they drew nearer, excitement caused the horses to quicken their pace and they almost trotted, so eager were they to get back where they belonged. Soon each was safe in his own stall, munching contentedly at an extra pan of oats, given to them as a reward for their good behaviour.

And now, at last, Ben could begin preparing for the operation he had been working towards for the past three days. Going into the tack room, he began laying out brushes, combs, medals, harness, saddle soap, boot blacking, bells, brasses, beads, ribbons and braids. Tomorrow morning, at four o'clock, he would begin preparing the horses and the waggons for their momentous annual trip to the seaside, on the combined Sunday school outing.

The following morning, the London-bound travellers set off in the Rolls-Royce 40/50 to catch the milk train. Gerald was driving with Stella beside him, Lady Madeleine and Neville in the back and Edward following in the governess cart with Becky and the luggage. Away they went, down the east driveway, through the avenue of trees, across the little bridge and into the village – and there they came upon such a magnificent colourful sight.

Standing on the green were two farm waggons of blue and orange, festooned with streamers and home-made paper chains. At the head of each stood two great Suffolk punches of gleaming conker-red, their harness and brasses sparkling, their hooves boot-blacked, their manes and tails tasselled, braided, beaded and be-ribboned. Around them teemed the village children, some inside the waggons, some out, some in the act of climbing in or out, others tumbling over or chasing each other across the grass. George was there, standing close by Ellen, who, as Methodist Sunday school teacher, was in charge of the children and the food boxes. Kenny, in his smartest gear, was already seated at the head of the Congregational waggon, reins in hand and ready to start. On the willow tree, waiting to be helped aboard, sat the Boggis grandparents and the mother, everything they possessed wrapped up in bundles beside them on the grass. They were to be dropped off at the workhouse on the way to the coast. The Boggis children, granted one happy day at the sea, were to be dropped off on the return journey. A few onlookers were dotted in groups round the edges of the green and, also on the periphery, wistfully watching, was Bent-one, patently regretful that he was no longer a child.

'Stop! Stop! Oh, do stop, Gerald! Look – what a picture that would make! Oh do stop . . . I want to make some sketches.'

'We'll stop on the way back,' said Gerald firmly. 'The train won't wait,' and he drove on steadily, with Stella still remonstrating vociferously, turning in her seat. Further on they came to small knots of people standing at their doors or garden gates, waiting to wave to the waggons as they passed. Then Stella sat up abruptly, facing frontwards . . . and even raised a royal hand . . . for were not these the very villagers who, in the fullness of time, everything going according to plan – her plan – would be under her benevolent jurisdiction? Smiling serenely and slightly inclining her head repeatedly as they travelled along, she left behind her small groups of people gazing perplexedly after the car, unable to account for such unexpected affability and condescension. The great white bandage swathed round Neville's head must have accounted for the rumour that swiftly spread that an Indian maharaja was staying at the Hall.

'Rehearsing your future role, I see,' said Gerald, grinning, while Neville and Lady Madeleine sat quietly in the back.

'Role?' queried Stella, though she knew perfectly well what he meant.

'As the next Lady Bountiful. Ever heard of the saying, don't count your chickens before they're hatched?'

At this point he too felt he should play to the crowd, and revved up the engine in an effort to cut more of a dash. Unfortunately, they had reached the end of the street now and the ridge on which the church and mill were situated, where the road curved round and upwards following the churchyard wall. The engine promptly spluttered and failed, and Edward, rattling in the cart behind, whipped up his pony and would have dashed past the car. Luckily Becky, just in the nick of time and with great presence of mind, managed to restrain him: she knew better than to pass her superiors. So, as the puzzled villagers watched, both car and cart slowly rounded the churchyard corner and disappeared from view.

Back on the village green, they were short of a driver.

Ben's wife, Biddy, had driven one waggon from the farm with the other following driverless, so amiable and well trained were Ben's horses. But she brought the news that Ben himself was ill, with a bad attack of asthma and bronchitis, caused probably by exhaustion after a summer working from dawn till dusk in the harvest fields, plus a heavy inhalation of dust from cleaning out the waggons. The news was received with mixed feelings, for, with a driver other than Ben, they were likely to make much better progress and could probably knock a good half-hour off the journey. Ben, they knew from past years, would contrive to go by every little village or hamlet or even cottage, in order to show off his horses. Well, they were a sight worth seeing, but, it was agreed, that was not the main aim of the journey.

Bent-one eagerly volunteered to be substitute driver but found himself in the unhappy position of being too old to be considered a child and too young to be thought of as adult. Ellen offered, but the consensus was that she had enough on her hands already looking after the children and the food. George had to be kept free to help transport the Boggis elders, the mother, and their belongings up the road to the workhouse, when they came to it. Being a good runner, he could catch up with the waggons again further along the route. So who else was there to drive the Methodist waggon? Ginty? Ginty, it appeared, was off on one of his mysterious expeditions from which he always returned several sovereigns the richer. There was nothing for it but to call upon Jacko, said to be rat-catching down on Marsh Farm. So George set off at top speed to enlist his services. A long wait followed. The children began to quarrel, fall over and fight. Even the horses began to show signs of impatience. At long last he reappeared, with Jacko in tow looking so disreputable that even the children stared at him aghast.

He was holding five dead rats by their tails, which he at once handed over to a reluctant Bent-one, with instructions to guard them with his life, particularly their tails (Jacko got paid so much per dead rodent and had to present their tails to claim his pay). A bucket of water was fetched from the Black Bull with which to wash the dung off his boots. Ellen bravely picked straw and barley bristles out of his wool hat, George brushed him down as best he could with a branch off a nearby tree and Jacko mounted the Methodist waggon, accompanied by his little white dog, and declared himself ready to start. The ferret in one of his pockets, forgotten by all, could well have enjoyed a trip to the seaside, had it not chosen that moment to push out its head for a breath of fresh air. A quiveringly apprehensive Bent-one was once more called upon and the ferret safely tucked away inside his shirt.

Then the children scrambled aboard, George helped up the Boggis elders, the mother and their bags of belongings, and at last they were ready to start. A great cheer rang out, only to die away to nothing as all eyes fastened on the Rolls Royce 40/50, steadily making its way back from the station towards them.

Edward, still following in the governess cart, was waved on peremptorily by Gerald to make his own way back to the Hall – but the car slowed and drew up alongside the Ploughman's Arms. Everyone watched nervously as Stella emerged armed with her sketching pad, took up a favoured position and began to sketch. Gerald followed, carrying the latest in photographic gear mounted on a tripod, which he proceeded to set up carefully at various points. None apparently satisfied him, for he would disappear under the black hood only to reappear a moment later and move on. Subdued, the children, the adults, the horses and the onlookers watched patiently.

'Could you move that horse forward a little?' said Stella to George. 'It's holding its leg at such an awkward angle.' George obligingly took Lady by the bridle to lead her forward. He was anxious to be off. She had been dozing, resting her near back leg, her gleaming haunches decidedly 'on the huh'. Under the impression the journey was about to start, she lunged forward powerfully, causing all her brasses to jangle and the children to fall about shrieking in the waggon at her back.

'A horse's leg is an extremely difficult thing to draw,' said Stella, screwing up her latest effort and throwing it on the grass.

Another five minutes passed; three more sheets of paper hit the grass.

'If we don't get started soon,' said George loudly, 'it won't be worthwhile going.'

'Oh, look at their manes and tails!' cried Stella, abandoning legs as being altogether too problematical. 'What a work of art! I shall never be able to copy all that! What a wonderful embroidery pattern all those braids and beads would make!'

'I'll try and get a close-up photograph so you can see the detail,' said Gerald, moving his tripod nearer, 'then you can work on it later, at home.'

George was losing patience. 'Hold tight!' he shouted to the children. 'We're going!' and with a click of his tongue and a bawled 'Giddy up, Lady!' he seized hold of her bridle. She flung up her head and lunged forward willingly, every magnificent muscle straining. Captain, the leading horse of the Methodist waggon, followed suit and the two outfits set off down the street at a rattling good pace, with George running alongside. The children cheered, the onlookers clapped . . . and Stella was

146

left, pencil poised, staring after them in astonishment, while Gerald, underneath his black hood, found himself focusing on empty space.

'How uncommonly rude!' cried Stella. 'How very inconsiderate! Who is that fellow?'

'No idea,' said Gerald, emerging. He had quite failed to recognize George, clean, close-shaven, in his best clothes, without his cap and with a head of curly fair hair, as the young blackguard who had caused the injury to Neville's ear. 'Damn bad form, if you ask me. Fellow's got no manners at all, whoever he is – but what can you expect of the yokels?'

Conscious of being watched, they attempted nonchalance as Gerald gathered up his gear and they made their way back to the car. Not that the yokels showed any sign of glee or satisfaction on seeing the mighty humiliated. On the contrary: they shuffled their feet and coughed and stared at the ground . . . they knew they could laugh later.

'Tell you what,' said Gerald, as he bundled his photographic equipment into the basket strapped on the back of the car. Stella winced and could not help thinking how his use of such a colloquialism showed his own lack of breeding. 'Let's go back, saddle up a couple of nags and go out for a gallop. Looks as if it's going to be a fine day.'

Stella's mouth assumed a thin look of reluctance. 'Oh I don't think – I want to get started on my picture.'

'Oh rubbish – you can do that later,' said Gerald, robustly. 'There's something I want to look into now that—' He stopped himself, then said, 'For Neville, while he's away.'

For Neville? Well, thought Stella, that does put rather a different . . . yes . . . after all, were not Neville's concerns, her concerns? Or at least would be . . . in the

147

fullness of . . . but . . . out in the country alone with Gerald after what he had done to her at the party? She would be defenceless . . . vulnerable . . . what if he should make a fresh assault on her virtue? She clutched herself with a delicious frisson of excitement and decided at once to go. After all, she would be safe enough, surely, so long as she stayed on the horse.

CHAPTER ELEVEN

If Suffolk punches were capable of observing a code of etiquette, the first edict would surely be that all undue haste is unseemly. By the time they had reached the end of the street and left behind the few remaining villagers waiting at their garden gates to wave to the children as they passed by, they had slowed to their usual dignified walk. George clambered aboard. The children stood lining the sides of the waggons, laughing and waving. In their Sunday best – large white collars were in vogue, frilly broderie anglaise for the girls, plainer Quaker-style for the boys – they looked like a brood of baby magpies about to fly the nest. George settled himself quietly on the floor of the Congregational waggon, hunched up against the side with his chin on his knees. He felt wistful away from Ellen. Resolutely, he averted his eyes from the dismal sight of the Boggis elders huddled opposite, clutching their belongings and half-hidden under the rolled-up tarpaulin fastened at the front of each waggon, to be pulled out for shelter if it should rain. As they reached the churchyard wall where the road began winding upwards, both Jacko and Kenny twirled their whips, shouted, and took the little hill at almost a dash; the children cheered, gave one last wave and the cavalcade slowly disappeared round the bend.

On the outskirts of the village the countryside was a golden patchwork of cut cornfields, some still with a regiment of corn stooks marching across them, only one showing the rich brown of newly ploughed earth. It had been a rather late harvest; rain had kept the trees and bushes along the hedgerows still fresh and green, though laden with the fruits and berries and nuts of autumn. The children, quickly tiring of viewing familiar countryside from a moving vehicle, subsided to the floors of the waggons and began playing such games as were possible in a confined space.

Presently the view over fields was shut out by high hedges, and when they came to an end a stretch of hawthorn and hazel hedge appeared which had just been expertly cut and layered by Ellen's elder brother, Herbert, the only one of her seven brothers to become a farm worker. He was employed by one of Lord Summerfield's tenant farmers and in his dreams aspired to become a farmer himself – a dairy farmer. Aware that the waggons were bound to pass that way, he had walked down to the roadside and was now gently stirring the embers of yesterday's bonfire with his pitchfork. His hedge-layering was a work of art, he had carefully raked up and burnt every scrap of detritus, and now he was waiting to receive his due recognition from the party coming his way.

Kenny, seated at the front of the Congregational waggon, summed up the situation at a glance and knew exactly what was expected of him. With a resounding 'Whoa there!' he brought the horses to a halt, stood up in his seat, turned portentously, surveyed the stretch of hedging carefully from end to end . . . and spoke.

'Thass a wery good bit o' hedge'n', that is!' Then, after

an impressive pause, 'Nearly as good as what I coulda done.'

He sat down, clicked his tongue, flicked the reins . . . and the cavalcade moved on. It was not much – but it was enough. Publicly acknowledged and with pride satisfied, Herbert shouldered his pitchfork and walked back to the farm and his customary Saturday morning job of cleaning out the chicken huts.

The waggons trundled on. Ellen made an attempt among the Methodists to initiate some hymn-singing. She had little success and took to gazing appealingly at George, in the waggon in front. But she got no response; he refused to look at her. She was wearing a large navy blue hat and her hair up, and a high-necked blouse drawn in at the waist by the belt of a long navy skirt. He'd become strangely disconcerted by the absence of her usual plaits and pinafore: she looked older somehow, not the Ellen he knew.

He sat gazing at the floor, brooding on his forthcoming obligations when they reached the workhouse. Sexes were strictly segregated there, so his mother had informed him just before he left the house. Were the Boggis grandparents aware that they would be parted? If not, should he tell them . . . or let events break it to them? How were they going to react to being separated after nearly fifty years together? A nightmare vision formed in his mind of the two old people being forcibly torn from each other's arms, with himself an unwilling participant. He did not feel able to deal with such a situation, yet here he was being drawn step by irrevocable step towards it. The waggons steadily trundled on, making good progress, by-passing many of the little hamlets Ben would have found irresistible.

All too soon, for George, the gloomy red-brick three-storey workhouse appeared, standing well back from the road on the brow of the next hill. It was almost as if they were especially welcome, important visitors, thought George, as he saw men working in the garden drop their tools and hurry to the roadside, where they stood in groups on the banks on either side of the driveway, gazing hungrily down at the waggons on the road below. The high banks had been worn into tiered seats on either side by generations of workhouse inhabitants identical to the scarecrow figures sitting there now – old men too weak and decrepit to work in the gardens, who had somehow managed to drag themselves down to the end of the drive to watch the world go by. There were no women; they were never allowed out, but spent their time working inside the building.

The two waggons came to a halt. The children popped up to see what was to be seen. George jumped out and, conscious of all the eyes watching, began lifting out the Boggises and all their belongings. Arthur Boggis he remembered as a reasonably robust and lively figure of a man; now he seemed only a bundle of brittle bones, his wife as light and fragile as a bird. As George lifted out the daughter the old man, dredging up the tattered remains of his strength, picked up two of the larger bundles and bravely started off up the drive. After only a few yards he stopped, staggered, dropped the bundles and stood swaying and gasping for breath. Silently George went to him, picked up the bundles and waited until Arthur had recovered himself sufficiently to move on. He could think of nothing to say to ease the old man's distress. He helped the daughter down from the waggon and then, carrying all their bundles and with the daughter by his side, he followed the old couple as they set off up the drive on the next, the final stage, of their life's journey.

As they approached the building, a notice marked

MEN directed them to a door at the right-hand end, and George could see a door at the opposite end marked WOMEN. Straight ahead was the main door, but it looked very little used, so they walked towards the right-hand door reached by steep steps that ended in a high wooden railed platform. George mounted the steps to the platform and tugged at the rusty bell. The door opened and an elderly man appeared. He was in his shirtsleeves and had bunches of keys dangling from his belt. Without speaking he gestured to George that he was to bring up the old man's belongings. Then, pointing at the two women, he indicated that they were to go to the door at the other end.

So this was it. It was time for the old couple to part. They stood for a moment staring at the ground; then they turned and looked at each other for a long moment, for the last time. George held his breath. Then the old man turned away and began pulling himself up the steps, holding on to the railings. The mother and daughter set off along the front of the building towards the other door, followed by George carrying the rest of the bundles. When they were halfway along, a big woman in black emerged from the women's entrance and came down the steps towards them. In her hand she carried a metal ring of keys which they could hear jingling as she approached.

Behind them, the old man had reached the top of his steps only to be overcome by a violent fit of coughing. He coughed and coughed and gasped; his wife turned and would have gone back to help the man she had cared for for nearly fifty years, but the big woman with the keys promptly seized the mother and daughter by an arm and marched them swiftly up the steps and into the building. There was nothing left for George to do but follow. He mounted the steps and deposited the last of

153

the luggage just inside the door. When he came out and glanced at the other entrance, he saw that the old man too had gone.

With a lump in his throat as big as an orange, he walked quickly down the drive. The more able of the workhouse inhabitants had already gone back to their work, all hope of further passing parties and entertainment at an end. The human wrecks were still there, seated on the tiered banks, some holding out their arms and calling to him piteously. But George had had as·much as he could stand of Redhill Workhouse and its inmates. As soon as he was out on the road, he began to run.

By the time George was able to catch up with them, the two waggons were approaching the outskirts of the little coastal town and the children were already standing up to get their first glimpse of the sea. A sharp left turn took them to the pier and the promenade and the gravelled park for the waggons. Next door was the meadow where they set the horses free to graze. As it was almost the end of the season there was very little grass left, but Ben had thought to provide nosebags.

There followed the sort of traditional seaside day that children and adults have enjoyed since such expeditions began. The children paddled, made sandcastles, dug holes, floated home-made boats on the pond, ate sand in their sandwiches, played ball, chased each other, laughing and shrieking, along the promenade pursued by an anxious Ellen, fearful that they were making a nuisance of themselves. Best of all, two ladies decided to use one of the brightly painted bathing machines lined up along the wall of the promenade, their rickety metal wheels rusting in the salt air. There was no attendant now in charge, so it fell to the children to push and pull the vehicle down to the sea. They did so with the greatest enthusiasm and then stood back, watching as

154

two strangely clad females emerged to test the water with timorous toes.

Meanwhile, back inland, Stella and Gerald were not having a particularly good day. It took them some time to rise above their humiliating encounter with the yokels on the village green, and they quarrelled rather pettishly on their way back to the Hall. Yes, Stella would like to go for a gallop – but later, when she had sketched in at least the rudiments of what would undoubtedly turn out to be her finest painting to date. So Gerald waited . . . and waited . . . Stella fulminating *ad nauseam* about the problem of drawing horses' legs. The subject in the end so bored him, and he was so anxious to get away, that he racked his brains for a solution. 'Why not surround the waggons with a multitude of children so that not a single horse's leg can be seen?' he suggested.

'Oh, Gerald, that's marvellous!' Stella clapped her hands with a squeal.

The main thing to remember, when drawing small children, she pontificated, was that their heads always seemed disproportionately large in relation to their bodies, whereas with adults . . .

Another twenty minutes passed. Sheets of paper with dwarfs suffering from hydrocephalus were cast away on the ground. Gerald lost all patience.

'I simply can't wait any longer. I'm off on a gallop whether you come or not,' he declared. At last, with something resembling haste, Stella abandoned Art, made her way to her room, changed into her riding gear, checked that the still convalescent brigadier had everything he needed and made her way to the stables.

How very different Gerald was from Neville, she could not help thinking, as they clattered out of the stable yard. No enquiry as to which way she would like to go. But what a fine figure of a man he was! Such broad shoulders . . . and strong thighs! She sighed as she saw the thin figure of Neville in her mind's eye. Gerald was waiting for her now. He was standing upright in his stirrups, pointing down at the thickly wooded scene below them.

'There it is – Thickthorn Grange!'

'Thickthorn Grange?' said Stella, squinting down to where, apparently, there was a house. She thought she could see – could not be absolutely sure – twisted chimneys in amongst the dense mass of trees and vegetation. As they stared, they heard a distant gunshot and above the trees rooks rose in a black cloud, cawing their protest.

'What's so interesting about Thickthorn Grange?'

'Aha!' said Gerald mysteriously. 'Come on – I want to have a closer look.' Tugging at his horse, he plunged down the slope, leaving Stella no choice but to follow.

The best of the day was now over. The sky, which had been clear and bright since morning, was beginning to darken with storm clouds. It was even darker in the woods, which were so dense it took them some time to fight their way through to the house. At last the horses stepped out into a clearing which had obviously once been the front lawn. And there it was – Thickthorn Grange, or as much of it as could be seen through the mass of creepers holding it in thrall. Ivy grew out a foot from the walls and spread its tentacles over the gutters and up the roof almost to ridge height, tendrils of wisteria clutched at the windowpanes, jasmine swamped whatever structure had originally graced the front entrance. Only the twisted brick chimneys, bare of vegetation, seemed to have retained their former glory.

'Good God!' said Gerald, somewhat aghast. He added, after a moment's though, 'It's probably basically sound, under all that. Brickwork looks good, what you can see

156

of it. Windows'll probably need replacing. Just wants some money and time spent on it. Thing is,' he continued, dismounting, 'there's only one old man living here at the moment – Roan, his name is, and when he snuffs it his Lordship says Neville can have it for a weekend cottage. Gave him quite a packet on his birthday, so I understand – old Nev wouldn't say how much – to have the whole place done up. We could all have a jolly good time here, if you ask me,' he continued enthusiastically, 'it's a nice long way away from the Hall and that old ghoul of a butler, Dodman, or whatever his name is, who goes round putting all the lamps out at ten. We could have parties . . . and a ball . . . we could have our own shoot. Get down, Stella, I want to have a closer look,' he said, holding his arms up to her on the horse.

Get down? Just for a moment Stella hesitated, then, with a nervous thrill of anticipation, slid down into his hold. But he turned his back on her and began making his way, with difficulty because of the jumble of bushes and creepers, along the nearest side of the house. Stella followed, tut-tutting as she stumbled along behind him, until at length he turned and signalled for her to stop.

'There he is,' he whispered, as they looked out into what had once been the orchard. 'That must be old Roan. He's got a gun. Must have been his shot we heard. He's been shooting rooks.' As usual, Stella struggled to see what she was expected to see and yes, there did seem to be a figure seated under one of the trees, leaning his back against the trunk.

'We'll go in,' said Gerald excitedly. 'Let's go in the house and have a look round.'

'Go in!' cried Stella in alarm, fearful not so much of old Roan's disapproval, but of Lord Summerfield's reaction, should he hear of their intrusion. 'We can't go in there!'

157

'Of course we can,' replied Gerald. 'While he's out here, we can go in the back door, through the house and out the front – and have a good look round on the way. He won't even know we've been. Looks like he's asleep anyway.' Then: 'You can come or not come – please yourself. I'm going!'

Pleasing yourself was the last thing you could expect to do in Gerald's company, Stella reflected, as, against her better judgement, she followed him in.

It was easy. The back door was ajar. They pushed it open and stepped into a stone-floored kitchen which ran the whole width of the back of the house. A big black range had a coal fire flickering in it and a low, slate-topped wall with arches along one side suggested that the room had once been used as a dairy. This part of the house seemed warm and dry, but from there on every room suffered a miasma of damp and mould. From the kitchen a corridor ran straight through the house to the wide entrance hall at the front, with doors to left and right along its length. Gerald began opening them, inspecting each room briefly along the right-hand side as far as the front hall first, and then back along the left. Stella simply waited in the corridor, determined to take no part in an enterprise she felt they might well live to regret. But when Gerald opened the last door, the one nearest to the kitchen, and gave a gasp of surprise, curiosity got the better of her and she followed him in.

It was unmistakably the dining room, with an impressive marble fireplace, dark oak items of furniture and a large leaded bow window at the far end. What had caused Gerald's cry of surprise and made the room look decidedly dark, was a tree growing up from between the floorboards, just in front of the window. They approached silently and stood in puzzlement, surveying it. Rotted floorboards had been prised up and soil added and nearby stood a jug of water, obviously used for watering. Its topmost branches reached almost to the ceiling while its lateral branches, which filled most of the window space, reached out yearningly towards the light. Imbedded in the lower branches was one end of a heavy dark refectory table. The other end extended out into the room where there stood a carved, high-backed dining chair, in front of it a plate bearing the remains of a simple meal of bread, cheese and pickle. At the other end of the table, in front of the tree and partly buried in its branches, was another place setting – plate, full complement of cutlery, wine glasses and table napkin all carefully set out, as if the tree itself was about to dine.

Gerald and Stella stood surveying this scene for some time, undecided what to make of it.

'He dines with a tree – must be short of company,' said Gerald at length.

'He must be mad,' said Stella. 'Oh do let's go – what on earth are we going to say if he comes back in?' But Gerald did not respond. Seizing the tree by its slender trunk he began rocking it violently, to and fro, so that all its pale leaves shuddered and shook.

'What on earth d'you think you're doing!' cried Stella. 'Stop it, for goodness sake!'

'What d'you think I'm doing?' breathed Gerald, red-faced. 'You can't have a tree growing inside a house – it'll undermine the foundations. What d'you think is going to happen if it keeps on growing?' He resumed his attack and added between gasps, 'Neville asked me to keep an eye on this place,' (Neville had asked him to do no such thing) 'and that's just what we're doing.'

'Don't include me,' said Stella crossly, 'I'm having nothing whatever to do with it. I'm going.' She waited for a moment to see if he would join her, but he stalked into the kitchen instead and returned carrying a sizeable meat cleaver with which he began chopping away at the base of the tree.

Stepping out into the corridor, she took a cautious peep to make sure the old man was not around and then left by the front door. She mounted her horse. She glanced at Gerald's horse and considered taking it too, before setting off down a drive narrowed to a thin, almost impassable ribbon by giant spreading rhododendron bushes on either side. Once out on the road, she hesitated for a moment, then turned left towards Cookley Green. She would take the long route back to the Hall and in all likelihood Gerald would get back first and wonder what had happened to her and worry about her late arrival.

It was getting dark and rain started to fall as she trotted into the village. Everywhere seemed still and quiet and lights in some of the cottage windows indicated that the inhabitants of Cookley Green had already settled in for the night. On the green a blue and orange farm waggon stood desolate, empty of children now, bedraggled streamers dangling from its sides, the two great horses, backs steaming, heads drooping, weary after their long trek to the coast and back. As she trotted nearer, the door of the Ploughman's Arms opened and a towheaded youngster was escorted out – you could say frogmarched – by two old men wearing corn sacks against the rain.

'Why me? Why is it always me?' The youth's plaintive cry rang out across the green. Still protesting, he was bundled up into the driver's seat of the waggon, the reins were placed firmly in his hands, the horses galvanized into action – and away went the waggon down the road to Hall Farm. 'That int fair!' cried the youth as he drew level, bending his head towards Stella with an agonized expression. 'That int fair – is it?' But Stella had had enough of the Cookley Green villagers for one day. Clicking her tongue sharply she galloped off into the gathering darkness.

Back at the Hall at last, she found Gerald in the billiard room, seemingly quite unperturbed by her late arrival. He had ordered a fire to be lit and was sitting by it shaving bark off a piece of old Roan's tree.

'See this slender tip?' he asked her. 'It's just the thing to make into a riding crop.' As he worked, he threw the strips of bark into the fire, where they sizzled for a time before drying out enough to burn. Presently he took a telegram out of his pocket and tossed it without a word into her lap. Addressed to Gerald, it was from Neville to say they had all arrived safely. He had seen the surgeon, his operation would take place on Tuesday, and all being well he hoped to be home early the following week.

Tears of mortification rose to Stella's eyes. No mention of her in the message. No query as to her health or whereabouts, no expressions of anticipation as to when they would be able to see each other again. Nothing. Was she just wasting her time? Perhaps he had assumed her father was now well and she was back at Highlea with her parents? Perhaps there was a letter for her there? Still, it was probably best for her to stay where she was, she decided, if Neville was to be home shortly. Of course, she didn't wish her father any real harm, she hoped and trusted he would continue his recovery . . . but slowly. Suddenly contrite at even entertaining such thoughts, she hurried upstairs and spent the next half-hour being extra solicitous in the sickroom.

Out in the rain and the darkness Bent-one clip-clopped along, still simmering with righteous indignation over his treatment at the hands of Jacko and Kenny. So he was not considered man enough and responsible enough to drive the waggon to the seaside, where he could have had a duzzy good time, but it seemed he was considered capable enough when it came to returning the outfit to Hall Farm, with all that that entailed in the way of hard work! After all, hadn't he already done his whack, and more than was required of him? He'd cut off the rats' tails as requested, even taken them all the way to Marsh Farm to collect Jacko's pay for him.

The fact that he had included two thick old leather bootlaces in with the tails and thus earned himself enough extra to buy two pints of beer was neither here nor there, and no less than he deserved after all his efforts. Beer, he reflected glumly, that he should rightly have been enjoying at this very moment, and that he probably now would not be able to enjoy tonight at all! By the time he had reached Hall Farm, unharnessed, rubbed down and baited the horses and walked back to Cookley Green, the Ploughman's would be closed. He just knew it. He felt overcome by a raging thirst and would have whacked the horses to make them go faster, except that he had a superstitious fear Old Ben would somehow know and he would never hear the last of it. Suddenly, he recollected that George was somewhere out in the darkness, dropping off children who lived in far-flung places . . . and he saw a solution to his dilemma. He would drive his waggon into the stable yard, stick the horses' heads in nosebags and scarper, leaving George to cope with both waggons when he finally arrived!

Tremendously cheered, he sat up smartly and began to sing:

'If I were a blackbird I'd whistle and sing.
And follow the ship that my true love sailed in . . .'

Thus, whistling and singing, he travelled merrily on through the wet countryside.

As did George, some miles away. Dropping off his last two children, he turned his waggon gratefully in the direction of Hall Farm. It had been a good day, he reflected. Over too quickly, as all the best days were. Only blighted, for him, by his two visits to the work-house. All too soon, after the horses had been reharnessed to the waggons, the children helped on board for the homeward journey waving windmills on sticks and balloons on strings, they had reached Redhill Workhouse once again and he had found himself walking up the driveway with the Boggis children – Jack, aged ten, Pearl, seven, and five-year-old Benjy, his dark head a marked contrast to the other two, with their almost albino looks. They obviously took after their pale mother.

Pearl's long silky yellow hair, liberated from its usual plaits, flowed down over her shoulders in a golden cloud. She had spent the journey snuggled close to George's side, brushing and combing her hair so that it streamed out in the wind, George thought, like the tail of a Palomino horse. He couldn't help wondering what life had in store for them in the grim red-brick building ahead. As they walked, the children stumbling a little, tired after their hectic day at the coast, he felt a slim cool hand slip into his.

'I don't want to go there,' whispered Pearl. 'I want to go home with you . . . please let me come home with you.'

'Whatever would your mother do without you?' was all that George, taken by surprise at her gesture, could think to say in reply.

They reached the front of the building and turned left toward the women's quarters. Halfway along they were treated, through a low window, to a view of some of the inmates – children, on wooden benches at long tables,

163

sitting very upright, arms folded, waiting. They all wore a dark uniform and had shaven heads, so that it was impossible to tell boys from girls.

'They're bald!' cried Pearl, horrified. 'They've got no hair! I don't want them to cut my hair! Plait it . . .' She turned to George. 'You plait it . . . please!'

'Plait it?' Poor George. 'I can't. I don't know how,' he said helplessly.

'Yes you do – plait it! I don't want them to cut my hair!' Big tears began rolling down her cheeks.

George put down the bags he was carrying and tried to oblige. Fumblingly, he plaited her hair in one long bumpy pigtail at the back of her head. 'Tighter, tighter,' she implored. Only when it was safely tucked down under her clothing, out of sight, as she thought, did she consent to mount the steps leading to the entrance. The big woman in black opened the door in response to the bell. Silently, George handed the children their various belongings, then stood aside as they filed in wordlessly. Pearl turned her head at the very last and he was the recipient of one final beseeching glance – a glance that was to haunt him for years to come – before the door closed.

There was no-one working in the gardens this time, and it was beginning to rain by the time he caught up with the waggons. Both tarpaulins had been pulled out for shelter and nothing could be seen now of the baby magpies. Only an occasional convulsive heave and a stifled giggle indicated that they were still there under the tarpaulin. Perched up at the front of the vehicles, the stalwart drivers, Kenny and Jacko, peered out from the protection of old corn sacks, traditional rainwear in country areas. As George approached a face peeped out at the back of the Methodist waggon: Ellen, her rather severe hairstyle now in disarray and falling down in long

164

copious ringlets. He was reminded of the days when, aged ten, she had sat in the row behind him at the village school. She looked now as she had looked then, and she was smiling. Lifting the edge of the heavy tarpaulin he climbed in beside her.

The waggons trundled along increasingly wet and muddy roads for about another hour, until they were within striking distance of home. Then, suddenly, both waggons stopped, denominational niceties were promptly forgotten and all those who lived in the village itself, regardless of their religious proclivities, were bundled into the Methodist waggon, while those who lived on the outskirts were left standing with their baggage in the rain. In a twinkling Kenny and Jacko had mounted the Methodist waggon, flicked the reins and set off for home. George, who had climbed out of the back of the Methodist waggon to see what was happening, found he had been neatly outwitted; had been left to gather up the abandoned travellers, take command of the Congregational waggon and make a lengthy detour all the way round the outskirts of the village dropping off those who lived in remote places.

Over an hour later, it was getting dark and still raining when he dropped off his last two children at Lodge Cottage, which guarded the entrance of the southern driveway to Summerfield Hall. It was a driveway very little used except on formal occasions, but you could get the closest view of the Hall from there. He glimpsed lights in most of the windows intermittently, through a curtain of trees and brushwood, as he drove along on this, the final part of his journey. Not so many lights as on the night of the birthday party, but enough to make him wonder what was going on in there.

Without even the protection of an old corn sack, he was now wet, cold and hungry, and his mind readily conjured up visions of great fires blazing and tables groaning with food. He wondered how the young couple in the Rolls-Royce 40/50 had spent their day; whether the aspiring artist had overcome her problem of drawing horses' legs. He frowned, fearing that his cavalier treatment of them this morning had reached his mother's ears. She would think him most unmannerly. He was nearly home now and he was glad . . . glad that his task was almost over. He was unaware – that revelation was yet to come – that he had definitely drawn the short straw – been outwitted, not just by Kenny and Jacko, but by Bent-one as well . . .

He was about a mile from the village now, taking a short cut along a bridle path seldom used. It passed a wall of impenetrable trees and tangled undergrowth behind which lay Thickthorn Grange, where his mother had spent her childhood days. His grandfather Roan still lived there alone, visited only by the intrepid Bertha, who cooked him a meal three times a week and did a little cleaning. She was the only person who dared to venture in to deal with the old man. George had only visited him once, with his mother carrying food, for she had heard that he was ill. But the old man had risen in his bed, ordered them both out and thrown the dinner at the wall. She had never attempted reconciliation again. As he drove by the overgrown entrance, with the mass of rhododendron bushes on either side almost meeting in the middle, so that in the gloom no way in could be seen, he heard a muffled shot. He wondered who could be shooting and at what, at this hour, in the darkness and the rain. He was not to realize until the following day that he had just heard the shot that killed his grandfather.

CHAPTER TWELVE

An excruciatingly discordant sound shattered the peace and tranquillity of Cookley Green about five days later. It came from the wheelwright's shop, where Josh had just finished screwing brass handles onto old Roan's coffin and was waiting for his wife, Rose, and her sister Bertha to come and line it. While he waited he decided to sharpen one of his saws. Setting it up carefully in his wooden vice, he began vigorously filing each tooth at the required angle, and this was the source of the terrible sound. As he filed, he hummed merrily, and being deaf was quite unaware of the added discord.

Soon Bent-one, looking despondent, came down the sloping yard. (The slope enabled Josh to cut down a tree for timber, lop off its branches and pull the denuded trunk home by means of a horse and timber drug, manoeuvring his prize with a stout pole down the yard and onto his sawpit, ready to be sawn into planks.)

Entering the wide doorway, with its black doors folded back in sections on either side to reveal a phantasmagoria of splodges where Josh had swiped excess paint off his brushes for so many years, Bent-one went up to his father and stood on tiptoe to commandeer his best ear.

'Can yew lend me tuppence?'

'He said he would but he didn't,' came the reply.

'Nooo . . . I said CAN YEW LEND ME TUPPENCE?'

'I shouldn't – thass tew late. I should go tomorrow.'

'Da . . . ad!' Bent-one took a frustrated turn about the workshop, then came back and tried the other ear.

'Is there any news?'

'Yes. Somebody's mucked up my saw.'

'I mean about old Roan? The inquest – how he died?' But his voice was lost as Josh made a fresh onslaught on his saw. Despairing, Bent-one seated himself between the shafts of the brightly painted blue and orange wheelbarrow Josh had made in his spare time and for which he had still not found a customer. With his hands clapped over his ears, Bent-one leant back, stretched out his legs and mournfully surveyed his hobnail boots. Then, judging his saw as satisfactory as it would ever be, Josh put it on the bench which ran along one side and the back of the workshop.

'Mended all your boots?'

'Thass no good if I dew – people 'ont pay,' his son replied.

'Thass because they're a bit short, like we all are. Yew hev to wait.'

'I hev waited. I'm sick of waiting. Herbert owe me two bob, but he say he 'ont pay – not till I make him a new harness for that duzzy calf. But I can't, can I – cus I hint got tuppence for a ball of waxed thread. Can yew lend me tuppence?' This to Rose, his mother, and Bertha, as they entered the workshop bearing scissors, sewing box and a roll of coffin lining so white it hurt your eyes. Ignoring Bent-one, they rolled the material out on the back bench. Bertha cut a length for the bottom sheet, closely watched by Rose. Long and close association with her overbearing sister had taught Rose to keep her

168

thoughts mostly to herself, but just for once, she could not help making a comment.

'You've cut that bottom sheet too short.'

'Oh, I hev, hev I? Well, let me tell yew someth'n' . . . nobody's go'n' to see it underneath the piller, are they? Old Roan int go'n' to be in no state to complain – so why waste good coffin lining? Here – ' She quickly cut another, smaller rectangle, folded it and handed it to Rose. 'Yew can sew his piller, then 'haps you 'ont find quite so much to say. Stuff it with sawdust – or shavings, if yew can find enough.'

Rose took the piece of lining, picked up the sewing box, seated herself on a nearby wheeltrestle and proceeded, as usual, to do as she was told.

Edie came in suddenly. She was married to Herbert, Josh's eldest. Edie was a tiny woman crowned by a bunch of hair almost as big as her head. She was heavily pregnant with a fifth child. Seating herself opposite Rose on the wheeltrestle, she took a journal out of her apron pocket and prepared for a few moments' relaxation.

'What are yew do'n' down here?' asked Bent-one, in the wheelbarrow, rousing himself to frown at her severely. 'Done all your work?'

Edie lowered her paper, turned slowly . . . and fired off the only weapon available to her.

'Mended all your boots?'

'Never yew mind my boots. Why dew everybody keep on about my boots? Where's that duzzy calf? I thought you wus s'posed to be lead'n' that duzzy calf out to grass?'

'I have bin . . . thass down the road under the elderberry bush. I'm sick of stick'n' its leg back on. Why hint you made that new harness like you said you wus go'n' to dew?'

'Because I hint got tuppence to buy a ball of waxed thread . . .'

The calf in question came from the farm where Herbert worked. It had been born with only three legs. Considered a non-starter, it was thrown out onto the muck heap to die, but Herbert rescued it and provided it with a wooden leg held on by an ingenious arrangement of leather straps which Bent-one had devised and put together, using his cobbler's stitching machine. The calf was now at an age to eat grass, but as Herbert had no land – the family lived in a tied cottage with only a small garden – it had to be led round the village, by Edie or two of the older daughters, to graze by the roadside. Of this weakly and undersized animal Herbert was inordinately proud; it was a heifer and he saw it as the foundation of his future dairy herd.

At this juncture Herbert entered, unexpectedly. Tall, lean, grey-haired, with a typical farmworker's stoop, he addressed Edie accusingly from behind. She started up violently in her seat.

'What are yew do'n' down here, gal? Why aren't you up the house?'

'Oh, Herbert – yew did give me a turn! I thought you wus up the farm. I thought you wus go'n' to finish that bit of plough—'

'So I wus, only Lady sprung a front shoe, so I've hed to bring her to the blacksmith's. That'll take forty minutes, so he say, so I've come down here to eat my elevenses . . . any objections?'

He took sandwiches and a bottle of cold tea out of a capacious coat pocket and put them on the top of the coffin lid, spread across two trestle tables. He snatched Edie's precious journal.

'You've been wast'n' my money on squitty papers! Look at that – a whole penny that corst! How are we ever go'n' to buy a dairy farm, gal, if you keep wast'n'

170

my money on that squit? Hevn't I told you, we gotta make every penny pay? Where's that duzzy calf?'

'Down the road under the elderberry bush. Thass got plenty of grass . . .'

'Done all your housework?'

'Yes.'

'Grubbed out them carrots?'

'I can't bend, can I?'

'Well, hoe between the rows. I'll grub 'em out tonight, arter I git home. Git them mawthers to take the calf out, when they git home from school – make them a bit useful for a change. What I want this time is a boy, d'you hear, to help out when I git my farm. Four great mawthers aren't go'n' to be noth'n' but a drag. What I want is a boy – are you listen'n' to me?'

'Yes, Herbert.' Chastened, Edie took blue wool and some needles out of her apron pocket and began industriously to knit.

Opening her squitty journal, Herbert spread it out on the coffin lid, placed on it his cheese and beetroot sandwich and bottle of tea, and began his repast.

'Any news about the inquest, Herbert?' Josh asked. He had only just registered the presence of his eldest son.

'Accidental death. ACCIDENTAL DEATH!' roared Herbert. 'SOMEBODY GOT IN HIS HOUSE AND CHOPPED DOWN HIS TREE AND HE FELL OVER IT CARRYING HIS GUN AND SHOT HISSELF TO DEATH ACCIDENTALLY!'

'What – with the barrel in his mouth? Where'd you hear that?'

'GINTY! WHAT GIT EVERYWHERE AND HEAR EVERYTHING, AS YEW WELL KNOW.'

'Oh.'

Apparently feeling he was meant to be satisfied with this, Josh went back to his bench and started collecting

171

up his varnish brushes to be cleaned. Snip! Snap! from Bertha's scissors as she cut out the side linings for the coffin. Josh contentedly started up on the cleaning of his brushes in turpentine. Silent and morose, Bent-one sat in the wheelbarrow, still brooding over the problem of how to get hold of tuppence for a ball of waxed string . . . while Edie dutifully kept knitting. Herbert chewed while Rose stood stuffing old Roan's pillow with wood shavings. There was colour and contrast in this scene. The sun, beaming in through the open doors, set the gold varnish of the coffin all aglow and its brasses sparkling, and, ministering unto it at the back, the dark figures of sisters Bertha and Rose stood out against the dazzling snowy whiteness of the coffin lining piled along the bench behind them. A blackbird trilled in the yard out-side.

The wheelwright's shop stood across the road, opposite the blacksmith's. It was in a dip so that from the village street you looked down into it, as you look down at the stage from the circle of a theatre. It was a large black wooden building; its doors, when open, were folded back in sections on either side exposing the multicoloured area of congealed paint. There was a wide white signboard above the doors proclaiming JOSHUA ABLEMAN, WHEELWRIGHT, CARPENTER, UNDER-TAKER. The board connected the hefty doorposts on either side, forming a natural proscenium arch, and, now, neatly framing the busy preparations for old Roan's funeral going on inside.

Drifting down the village street in Gerald's car, Stella glimpsed the tableau over the roadside wall and cried at once for Gerald to stop.

'Everything's there!' she pointed as Gerald obligingly drew up alongside the low wall. 'Everything,' peering through her recently acquired lorgnette which she felt gave her added seriousness when engaged in her artistic pursuits, as well as helping her to see more clearly. 'There's Life, Death . . . the whole cycle,' she said, for she could plainly see that the tiny woman with the big head of hair was in an interesting condition. 'What a painting that would make! I must go down there and do some sketches!' and she seized the pad and pencils that were her constant companions and jumped out of the car. Unusually compliant, Gerald said she could have an hour, which he intended spending in the Black Bull, following more manly pursuits.

The truth was, Stella was tired of the Sunday school outing painting. It had been relegated to the put-aside-to-come-back-to-later category. She was now determined to arm herself with sufficient sketches to enable her to produce, in the comfort of home, a selection of paintings of local craftsmen and significant Suffolk country scenes. She hoped thereby to persuade her father to set up an exhibition of her work, in London, of course, which Neville, his parents and all their friends and accquaint-ances would rush to view.

'I saw you all from the road and just had to drop in and make a few sketches.' Confronted with blank stares, she became conscious of her gushing entrance and tried to tone down her approach. 'My aim is to make a pictorial record of some of the main crafts and other significant activities being carried on in Suffolk. What is being enacted here today,' she continued gravely, spreading her arms to encompass the workshop, 'will make a most significant painting . . . the whole of life, as it were, depicted in one small remote workshop in the depths of Suffolk . . . and it's a lovely workshop!' she cried, gazing round at the racks of tools, stacks of wood, rows of paint tins – the 'gear, tackle and trim' of country crafts. 'And the smell!' she cried, breathing in the aromatic mixture of wood shavings, linseed oil, turpentine and coffin varnish. 'What a magnificent shape of head!' she exclaimed at Josh, as he turned from his bench clutching a pot full of varnish brushes.

'I really must paint your portrait!'

'Paint what?'

'Your portrait . . . PORTRAIT!'

'My what?'

'Your portrait . . . IN OILS!'

'That is painted.'

'No, you – YOU!'

'Oh.' Josh nodded, not understanding in the least.

'He's a bit deaf,' said Bent-one, helpfully.

'He hear all he want to hear,' Bertha said, from the back of the workshop, ominously.

'He'd make a marvellous subject. I really must paint him – he's so sweet and gentle-looking!' Indeed, Josh, with his halo of fluffy white hair and his perky white moustache, bright blue eyes and pink cheeks, his white carpenter's apron with a row of small tools standing up in slots along the bottom of it and his shiny black boots, was the very picture of a dear old country craftsman.

'Yes, I really must paint him . . . but maybe some other time,' said Stella, abandoning communication with him as being altogether too problematical. 'What an absolutely splendid coffin!' she continued, gazing at it in all its shining glory lying across the two trestles, being tended by Rose and Bertha. 'What a beautiful piece of craftsmanship – oak, surely?'

'Elm,' Bertha let fall grimly from her rat-trap mouth.

'It's beautiful!' cried Stella. 'A work of art. Too good to be put into the ground. What a waste!'

What a waste? A work of art? Struck by the novelty of this approach, Bent-one, Herbert, Rose and Bertha drew near to the coffin and stood gazing at it with fresh eyes.

174

'But please don't let me keep you from your work.' Stella settled herself on a nearby stool, her sketching materials at the ready. 'Do carry on – just as you were doing. Pretend I'm not even here.' Too late: Josh, noting their interest in the coffin, went to look for himself, lifted up the pillow – and found old Roan was being short-changed with a short sheet.

'Yew've cut that bottom sheet too short. Look at that! Cut me another piece.'

'That'll dew – that 'ont show when yew git the piller in. Duzzy old fule!' said Bertha, but not too loud.

'No that 'ont dew,' Josh said, snatching the sheet out and throwing it on the floor. 'I will hev things done properly in the parts yew can't see as well as in the parts yew can. Cut me another bit.'

'I'll cut it.' Edie was fed up with knitting.

'Keep your nose out, Edie,' said Bertha, 'you shouldn't be here at all in your condition – 'less you want to born a monster. Turn yourself the other way!'

'Born a monster?' Stella looked up from her artistic preoccupation. 'Whatever sort of superstitious nonsense is that?'

'Nonsense, is it – thass all you know – ' Bertha took a little black book out of her apron pocket. 'I've got it all down here in print.'

'Ooh!' cried Edie, with a long audible intake of breath. 'She's got her little black book out!'

Bertha opened the book with a portentous air, and read very slowly: ' "A worthy gentlewoman of Suffolk" – Suffolk, did you hear that? Might've bin this very village . . . "a worthy gentlewoman of Suffolk, being with child and passing by a butcher killing his meat, a drop of blood sprung on her face, whereupon she said her child would have a blemish on its face and at the birth it was found marked with a red spot!" '

'What! Absolute rubbish! I never heard such arrant nonsense in all my—' cried Stella, but Bertha struggled on:

' "And I have heard of a woman who, at the time of conception beholding the picture of a blackamoor, conceived and brought forth an Ethiopian." '

'An Ethi – what?' from Bent-one, while poor Edie was heard to murmur faintly, 'Oh my goodness – whatever's that?' Triumphantly, Bertha brought forth her trump card:

' "Another monster represented an hairy child. It was all covered with hair like a beast. That which rendered it more frightful was that its navel was in the place where the nose should stand, and its eyes placed where the mouth should have been, and its mouth was in the chin." '

'Oh my word!' cried Edie, 'whatever next!' while Bent-one's powers of imagination were subjected to heavy strain.

'Mouth was . . . eyes was?' he queried. 'Navel . . . where did you say his belly button was?'

Stella was dazed and shaken. 'This is unbelievable! In these times – I never dreamt . . .'

'Thass all down here,' says Bertha firmly, 'in black and white. Pictures too.'

'Pictures?' Herbert and Bent-one exclaimed simultaneously. 'Let's have a look!'

'Oh no – not so likely! Certainly not,' and Bertha closed the book with a decisive snap and put it back in her pocket.

Abandoning her project, the aspiring artist rose bravely to do battle. 'I've never heard such unmitigated nonsense in all my life—'

'Yes,' agreed Edie fervently. 'I haven't been near the butcher's!'

'That book is an abomination! It should be burnt!'

176

'Come and get it,' said Bertha, picking up the scissors.

'Oh . . . Oh . . . Herbert . . . Bendy . . . dew something!' cried Edie, clutching her bump.

Stella was routed and she knew it. In an unconvincing voice of authority she ventured, 'I must tell you that I am seriously concerned for the welfare of the women in this village if this is the sort of ignorant, superstitious—'

'You leave the women of this village to me!' cried Bertha in a fury. 'I'm the midwife here, as my mother wus afore me and her mother afore her. They learnt me all my know—'

'Well, if that's all you know . . .'

'I know all I want to know.'

'What a thing to say!' persisted Stella. 'Perhaps there are more things in heaven and earth than are dreamt of in your philosophy!'

'In my what?' said Bertha, mystified, and Stella, sensing an advantage, unwisely moved into deeper waters. She found herself dredging up Neville and Gerald's recipe for combating boredom on a grey day.

'Oh yes – some learned men, for instance, as an exercise for the mind, question the actual existence of objects when there is no-one there to see them. Perhaps the whole world only exists, you see, in your own head.'

'Wass that yew say?' said Herbert.

'Think,' continued Stella, rashly. 'Can you prove that wheelbarrow still exists if you go out of this workshop and can no longer see it?'

'I could peep in through the window,' said Bent-one.

'I could run it over your toe,' said Bertha.

'Perhaps you would only be running a wheelbarrow you think you hold, over a foot you only think you see. Perhaps the only wheelbarrow that exists, you see, is the one in your head.' At this, Bertha lost her temper.

'Did I ever say there wus two? I never said no such

177

thing! I never heard such a load of squit in all my life! If thass all the good them learned men—'

'Steady you on, Bertha,' warned Herbert.

'Whass the matter? Whass the matter?' cried Josh anxiously, inevitably drawn into the fracas. 'Someth'n' wrong with my wheelbarrow – whass the matter with it?'

'Noth'n' ' said Herbert, 'thass just . . . she say . . . she was just saying like . . . there's learned men . . .' But the whole thing was too much for him.

Edie, stretching up ponderously to her full height, which was not much, shouted into Josh's best ear, 'She say, you can't prove there's a wheelbarrow . . . if you wus to go out of this workshop, you couldn't prove . . .'

'Prove?' queried Josh, staring round. 'You'd never believe the daft things I think I hear sometimes – I coulda sworn Edie said you can't prove there's a wheelbarrow!'

'Thass right,' cried Edie, nodding.

'Thass right?' Josh gazed round at the assembled company. 'Why, whatever would anybody want to try and prove that for – we know that, don't we?'

Herbert tried, labouring somewhat. 'Ah – thass just where you're wrong.'

'Wrong?'

'You only think you know it,' squeaked Edie.

'Think I know it,' said Josh, 'I know I know it – I made it.'

Bent-one is tremendously relieved and excited. 'Thass right! That is right – he made it! He done it. I saw him chamfer the shafts!'

'I saw him fix the wheel on – thass true. That I can vouch for,' said Herbert gravely, 'and I saw him putt'n' the paint on.'

'I should just think so!' cried Bertha, triumphant. 'What've yew got to say about that, I wonder?'

Stella was getting tired. 'Some people have more faith than others,' was as much as she could come up with.

'Some people have more duzzy cause!' roared Bertha, fully rampant.

'Hold yew hard a minute,' said Herbert, warningly. 'Steady yew on, gal.'

'Well, I never heard such a load of pig's wallop in all my life!' and Bertha stood, arms akimbo, a black column of antagonism backed by the glowing coffin and the dazzling white lining tumbled along the bench behind her.

'Perhaps if you all go back to your original occupations I can get on with my work, and you can get on with yours,' said Stella bitterly. 'I've wasted enough time already – but I'm determined to get the basics of this picture down on paper,' and she seated herself resolutely back on her stool. Crossing one leg over the other, she placed her sketching pad on her knee, picked up her pencil . . . and Bent-one saw his opportunity.

'Hev yew got tuppence worth of shoe-mending yew want done?' he said concernedly. 'Hev you got a nail up?' Neatly he snatched off her shoe and thrust his fingers inside. 'Yeah – I can feel one!' he cried triumphantly. 'I'll soon bang that little devil down for yew. I'll give him what for – see if I don't. I'll put him on my last and bang him down in a twinkling . . . and that'll only corst yew tuppence,' he shouted over his shoulder as he ran towards the door.

'Come back here!' yelled Stella, losing all decorum. 'Give me back my shoe – there's absolutely nothing wrong with it. COME BACK HERE THIS MINUTE!'

But Bent-one had gone. She gathered up her things and hobbled out of the door and up the yard after him. Halfway up, her stentorian cries brought Bent-one to a halt. He stopped and meekly handed over the shoe.

Then, with it under her arm, half hobbling, half hopping, Stella continued on her way, back to the car and, she hoped, to Gerald, leaving Bent-one no further forward with the problem of how to get hold of tuppence for a ball of waxed thread.

Throughout this episode Rose, as was her wont, saw all and said nothing. Josh returned to his bench and his varnish brushes, resigned to the fact that much of what went on in life would forever remain a mystery to him. Herbert gathered up his belongings in readiness to retrieve his horse from the blacksmith's. Edie sat for a moment, dreaming, her hands on her stomach, before being ordered by Bertha to get back to her own kitchen. Then Rose was brusquely told to brush up the spilt wood shavings left over from the pillow. Bertha once had a husband, a groom who died of tetanus, and twin boys, who died of scarlet fever. Turned out of her tied cottage, she moved in with Josh and Rose and proceeded henceforth to boss Rose about in her own home. Josh she had never made much progress with – he took care never to hear a thing she said.

And now the top half of Stella could be plainly seen above the roadside wall, as she hobbled painfully down the street towards the car. 'Good riddance to her!' was Bertha's parting shot. 'Nobody never said I wus sweet and gentle-looking,' she observed sourly, as she rolled up the coffin lining. 'Nobody never wanted to paint my portrait.'

CHAPTER THIRTEEN

How long, Stella wondered, as she limped on towards the car, would she have to wait for Gerald to reappear? An hour, he had allowed her, in his lordly fashion, to get the rudiments of the workshop picture down on paper. He intended meanwhile to refresh himself at the Black Bull, so there was no telling how long it would be before he could tear himself away. Surely no more than twenty-five minutes had elapsed from the start of her encounter with the yokels to her ignominious departure? She found herself reluctant to sit in the car and await his return. It was parked close alongside the low wall directly opposite the workshop. She would be clearly visible to all those within.

She stopped to put on her shoe, and when she straightened, saw to her delight a figure at the end of the street striding rapidly towards her – Gerald, undoubtedly, thank heaven! They approached the car at about the same pace, Stella, as she hurried along, rehearsing in her mind some of the things she would have to say about her recent experience. The insight she had gained into the outlook of the local inhabitants . . . their appalling ignorance . . . the medieval mumbo-jumbo . . . the crying need for someone competent to bring enlightenment and steer them out of the Dark Ages . . .

She and Gerald reached the car at the same moment, and Stella gratefully climbed in. But Gerald, instead of applying himself straightaway to the starting handle, to her surprise climbed in beside her. Throwing himself back in his seat with the kind of gusty sigh which could only be interpreted as an expression of heartfelt relief after much suffering, he exclaimed, 'You'll never believe what I've been through, I can't begin to tell you!' and went on to do just that.

'I was sitting on that old willow tree by the village green waiting for the Black Bull to open, along with a couple of old codgers smoking their clay pipes, when out of the building opposite – the one with the archway – comes this flat-faced old biddy with the red nose we saw at the birthday party. You know – she of the bicycle and the banner, who threw the . . . intimate article of ladies' underwear and upset Dolmon for the rest of the evening . . . Well, she comes straight across the green towards me, dragging a great long chain. "Just what I've been looking for!" she cackles, "a nice strong handsome young man to help me with my enterprise!" and before you could say Jack Robinson, she flings the thing round my waist and over my shoulder and starts dragging me off! Well, what could I do? I couldn't very well start a tug of war, could I – her being just a little old lady? I could hear the two old scarecrows behind me tittering and I remember thinking I'd jolly well like to crack their heads together. But before I knew what was happening, she had dragged me across the green and through the archway. I tell you, now I know exactly how it feels to be shanghaied!'

'But what was it all about?' Stella managed to interpose.

'You may well ask! It made me wonder, I can tell you, what with the chain and all . . .' Gerald decided not to go deeper into that and continued. 'It turned out she's setting out two tennis courts at the back of her house and she wanted me to hold the chain to check the measurements.'

'Of course!' cried Stella, enlightened. 'That was Miss Hastbury. She told me at the birthday party she was planning to start a tennis club in Cookley Green.'

'But that isn't all,' continued Gerald. 'The ground had all been prepared and the measurements turned out to be all right – but then she wanted me to help her tread the soil down. No good rolling it, apparently, you get undulations. You have to tread it . . . so there we were going up and down one behind the other . . . except she kept coming up close and pressing . . .' Here Gerald swallowed and had difficulty in going on. 'As well as that,' he continued lamely, 'there was this other old woman – the chinless one she lives with. She opened one of the top windows and screamed out, "JEZEBEL! CAN'T KEEP YOUR HANDS OFF HIM, CAN YOU?" I've never been so embarrassed in all my life . . .'

Poor Gerald looked away sheepishly and Stella saw to her astonishment that he was blushing. Never before had she known him to be even mildly disconcerted by an event or situation, and this sudden chink in his guise of brash self-confidence seemed strangely appealing. She couldn't find it in her heart to laugh at him or be brusque and offhand in her usual fashion.

'How on earth did you manage to get away?' she asked at last.

'Luckily this young fellow from the village turned up – the one who dug and prepared the courts.' (Once again Gerald had failed to recognize George with his unruly fair hair cropped and an embryonic beard and moustache.) 'She was all for the three of us treading away – with her in the middle, no doubt! – but this chap wasn't having any of that, thank God. He produced an old wooden gate with a rope for a harness and he began dragging it up and down and round and round . . . it flattened everything fine . . . and as soon as the old girl's back was turned, I scarpered.'

He paused. 'Damn, bugger and blast! I've left my riding crop there!' Gerald had successfully bound one end of the piece of old Roan's tree with cord to make a handle, fastened a loop of narrow leather at the other end and created a passable riding crop of which he was extremely fond. It gave him much pleasure and satisfaction to tap it rhythmically against his leg or riding boot, in company, as he talked.

'We can call in for it at Miss Hastbury's on our way back,' suggested Stella.

'No fear,' said Gerald. 'I'm not going back in there – not likely!'

'Then I'll go in and get it for you. You can wait in the car.' So Gerald sat and waited in the car at the edge of the village green, glaring intermittently at Kenny and Jacko as they sat puffing their clay pipes and grinning and gazing stolidly at the ground. Nearly half an hour must have passed by the time Stella reappeared, smiling and animated.

'We are now foundation members of the Cookley Green Tennis Club . . . and so is Neville,' she added. 'I've joined him up as well. Here's your riding crop.'

Gerald took it, reached across and patted her hand, as she seated herself once again in the car. 'Thanks, old girl,' he said, 'you're a real trouper!' This was a rare admittance of obligation on his part.

Gerald leapt out vigorously to crank the starting handle. Stella found her hand stealthily creeping up and unfastening the first three buttons of her high-necked blouse. What am I doing? she thought a moment later. Oh, Neville . . . come back, she cried in her heart . . . come back soon!

Early June 1999

Haven't had time to keep up this journal for a while, what with school sports day and then busy preparations for the village fête. Both events over now, thank heaven! The fête took place yesterday – Saturday. The school's contribution would have been less time-consuming if Neil had not discovered an ancient maypole and a pile of country-dance records in the school garden shed. His face aglow with enthusiasm, he appeared in my class-room one playtime wielding the pole and declaring that all it needed was a new set of ribbons: my infants could give a display of maypole dancing at the fête. I lost no time in putting paid to that bright idea. My infants, I explained, were incapable of following any but the simplest instructions – such as please shut the door. Many of them were unable to tell with any certainty their right foot from their left.

That's the end of that, I thought. But no – next minute Neil had the pole erected on our grassy patch, with a high wind blowing it to a rakish angle and the faded moth-eaten ribbons streaming out, his children screaming manically as they leapt around trying to catch hold of the ends. It was the first time I had seen Neil get really mad. He bellowed and went scarlet in the face . . . but then he saw me grinning and had the grace to laugh. I thought he'd give up, but he persisted – he renewed the ribbons and spent every lunch hour for the next fortnight putting his children through their paces, until they were

185

able to give a good account of themselves on the great day.

Had the location of Miss Raspberry's acre been agreed once and for all, we could probably have held the fête there, in the centre of the village, for it is supposed to be somewhere behind the Black Bull. As things are it had to be held at Chalfont Manor, about a mile away. Once the abode of a venerable family called the Benson-Brick, Chalfont Manor is now a part private, part state-run nursing home for the elderly; one of many that have sprung up in the countryside to meet the needs of an increasingly aged population. Pearl said it was too far for her to attend; even if somebody took her by car she didn't think she would be able to walk round for long. So when my children had sung their songs, played their percussion instruments and danced two of the simpler country dances to tumultuous applause, I gave them all back to their parents, borrowed a wheelchair from the accommodating matron of the home, hurried back to the village and fetched her.

She jibbed at first at the thought of everyone seeing her in a wheelchair, but curiosity won. Yes, she would like to come. Would I please look in her wardrobe and choose something smart for her to put on? I went into the next room, the room she used as a bedroom, opened the rickety wardrobe door – and was astonished to find it crammed with the most beautiful, expensive dresses, blouses and skirts. But years out of fashion . . . the sort of things high-born ladies wore, surely, at the beginning of the twentieth century? Well, they were dresses from a high-born lady of around that time – they were cast-offs, courtesy of Lady Summerfield, bequeathed to Pearl via Becky.

Pearl had shakily followed me into the room and she managed to stand while I dressed her. I chose a glowing gold and green wrap-around voile skirt, lined with cambric, with a deep flounce at the foot. It would be easier to put on, I thought, than a dress. Then she chose a crisp pale lemon blouse, delicately embroidered in white, with big puffy sleeves and a stand-up collar which nicely concealed the contorted sinews of her neck. Footwear was a problem as she now had feet that no shoes were ever designed to accommodate. So she kept her slippers on and once in the wheelchair, they were invisible beneath the deep flounce of her skirt. A large, elaborate pale green hat shadowed her face – there was also a matching parasol, but this she declined.

Away we went and what with the sun and the excitement her cheeks grew pink and you could see that, yes, she had once been young and . . . well, young anyway. In fact she looked quite distinguished, noble, rather grand, not at all like someone who had been brought up in a workhouse. Of course, by the time we reached Chalfont the best of the events were over, the stalls depleted of their wares and some of the stallholders beginning to pack up what was left. Neil had just finished organizing races for the children, something, I realized, I could have helped him with, though he hadn't asked. At the cake stall Pearl allowed me to buy her a ginger cake. On we went to the jumble stall where she bought a yellow blouse with a ruffle at the neck she seemed well pleased with. On we went again to sample some of the other stalls, stopping every now and again to acknowledge greetings from people, all obviously surprised and pleased to see her out and about.

By now it was getting towards the end of the afternoon and the sun, which had done us proud so far, began to cloud over. Everybody started to drift away home and just when I thought I could nicely suggest that we did the same, Pearl asked me to take her to the rose garden. She knew the way, she said, she had been there before – with Becky to visit Stella. It was situated in a sunken part of the grounds on the western side of the building, over-looked by a regiment of grey-looking, net-curtained windows, behind which, I suppose, old people in varying states of infirmity were eking out their days. There was a spread of neatly patterned beds of rose bushes – a few still in bloom – with gravel paths in between. Pearl indicated that she wished me to push her to the end of the broader main path running down the centre, which ended in wide brick steps leading up to a wrought-iron garden seat at the top. From there you would have a view commanding the entire rose garden.

'I come here with Becky, one day,' said Pearl, as we arrived at the end of the path and paused to look up at the empty seat. 'To see Stella. Becky knew her in the old days, you see, at the Hall. Quite the lady, Stella was then – too proud to have anything to do with Becky, who was only a servant – but she was glad enough to have Becky look after her when she was old. I only saw her that once. She was sett'n' on that seat wrapped up in a tartan rug with a black fringe round it and she'd gone gaga. She never even knew who Becky was. She just sat there with her head hanging, fiddling with the fringe. "Is Daddy coming?" she said – just like a child. She'd lorst her memory, you see, or she pretended she had. I'd've lorst my memory,' said Pearl darkly, 'if I'd done what she done!' Then, in answer to my unspoken question, 'Oh no – I can't tell you that . . . not here,' and she looked round as if the world and his wife were watching. There was nobody in sight, so she added, 'That'd take too long,' and she sank back into her chair and closed her eyes. I knew better now than to press her. She had a hard side to her, not surprising considering her upbringing. When she'd had enough of you, she retreated into herself and was unreachable.

It really puzzled me. What on earth could Stella have done? We set off back home, collecting Sammy on the way. Neil came too, carrying the maypole like a battering ram. When we got to Pearl's cottage Neil helped me get her indoors. Then he offered to return the wheelchair for me. Chalfont was not far out of his way, he said – he'd be pleased to do it. It's absurd, but to my horror I felt my eyes fill with tears. You see, nobody but my parents have ever helped me out with things. You never did – it was always me helping you. I was too choked up to speak and of course, he saw; I could tell by his expression that he realized I was on the verge of tears. He pushed the wheelchair out to the garden gate where it could be easily collected . . . and fled. Terrified no doubt at the prospect of female emotion heading his way. Thank heaven we've got a week off school soon. Must remember to stay cool and professional next time we meet.

CHAPTER FOURTEEN

Neville delayed his homecoming from London for another week. Having recovered from the worst effects of his operation he wanted to enjoy the city. He also seized on a delightful opportunity to enjoy Becky's company, free from the restrictions of home and family. An unsuspecting Lady Madeleine was easily persuaded to stay longer. She welcomed a further chance to grace the town in her new clothes. While she gaily socialized in the company of her favourite sister, Neville and Becky made secret assignations; walked together through fallen leaves in Hampstead Heath and Hyde Park in the glory of approaching autumn. Nearby Regent's Park they avoided, lest Becky be recognized by other locally employed ladies' maids and nannies.

For Neville these were golden days. But away in deepest Suffolk, where the leaves still lingered on the trees in shades of red and orange, where autumn does not truly arrive until November, his long absence was having its effect on Gerald, waiting impatiently for his return. In his concern for Thickthorn and its future, for which in Neville's absence he felt himself responsible, Gerald overreached himslf; 'mucked his nest' you could

190

say in the vernacular; wore out his welcome at Summerfield Hall.

Old Roan, in his will, had instructed his solicitor to convey to one Bertha Danby the sum of six guineas for the express purpose of providing a demonstrably impressive send-off for him at his funeral. No more and no less than forty carefully selected mourners were to be allowed to attend and to be provided with refreshments at the long refectory table in the dining room at Thickthorn, after his interment. The only proviso was that they must be willing and able to follow the coffin on foot all the way through the village to the church. There was to be one short diversion past the cottage of old Roan's daughter, George's mother, and back, and as a final demonstration of his implacable disfavour, her name headed the list of those not to be allowed to cross the threshold at Thickthorn for the occasion. George's father came next on the list, then the two girls and then George himself. The next eighteen named were those who had had the misfortune to fall foul of the irascible old man during the tempestuous seventy-nine years of life. The shadow of his disapproval extended even unto the third generation. When George's mother got wind of this, she was overcome with guilt and grief, which brought on one of the virulent attacks of asthma from which she regularly suffered. She had to take to her bed and was quite seriously ill.

When Edward, the youngest footman, brought back to the Hall, after a visit to his sick father in Cookley Green, a garbled version of these extraordinary arrangements, Gerald was thrown into a state of acute anxiety. With Neville and Lady Madeleine in London, and Lord Summerfield and the brigadier on a two-day shoot at the estate of a mutual friend in Norfolk (Stella's father felt himself sufficiently recovered to go shooting but not yet strong enough to face up to his wife and his responsibilities at Highlea), who was there to look out for his Lordship's, or more precisely, Neville's property and guard it from harm? The thought of a crowd of Suffolk yokels holding a funeral wake in Thickthorn, for which he had by now developed a proprietorial concern, was simply not to be borne. He had to get there early, before they arrived, and guard it from harm; contrive at least to count the silver; take cognizance of any small, easily transportable objects. Fired with indignation, he set out to find Stella and inform her of his intentions.

After half an hour he found her in the orangery, sitting quietly painting a watercolour of the vines. The bougainvillea had been particularly brilliant this year, fading now, but she could take steps to counteract that. As she listened to his plans, her smooth dark head industriously bent to her task, she thought she detected in Gerald's emphatic expostulations a cry for help. She said nothing, but waited, and at last it came: of course it was entirely up to her, he was not greatly concerned either way – but she could, if she so wished, accompany him on the morrow in support of his campaign for the defence of Neville's property against the encroaching barbarians. Paintbrush poised, Stella sat for a moment considering the proposition. She could not have said with any certainty whether it was concern on Neville's behalf or her new, softened attitude towards Gerald that motivated her, when she eventually agreed to accompany him.

It had not been easy for Bertha to select as mourners forty suitable (in her opinion), deserving, physically fit, compliant individuals, whom she herself had not quarrelled with over the past ten years. Further back than that she dared not go if she expected to fill her quota of fit people. She felt she was scraping the barrel by including Jacko in all his disreputableness, but he was always in need of a square meal. It was that or start drawing in foreigners from Summerfield and Silverley. Bertha had a strong sense of parochial patriotism; she felt any assets accruing from old Roan's funeral should be enjoyed by the inhabitants of Cookley Green alone.

Organizing the women of the village to cook and prepare bread, meat, pies, sausage rolls, chutneys and pickles, cakes, sandwiches and drinks, and arranging the transport of the food to Thickthorn on the morning of the funeral, was quite an undertaking and brought Bertha to a state of extreme nervous tension. Opening the dining-room door to find Gerald already in possession, with Stella promenading watchfully in the corridor and kitchen area, did nothing to assuage her agitation. In a pregnant silence, and aware of being watched, the women began laying the food out on the table. The men fetched in enamelled tin plates and bone-handled cutlery yellow with age. Rose supplied a giant tea urn normally used for jamborees at the Methodist chapel. So there had been no need for Gerald's anxiety over the crockery and cutlery; they had brought their own. Nevertheless, he stood sentinel in front of the fire he had lit when he first arrived, slapping his leg with his riding crop with a metronomic regularity guaranteed to get on everybody's nerves.

Gerald had thrown old Roan's tree out onto what had once been the front lawn, and he now saw that this was a mistake. Everyone when they arrived tramped out again to look at it, so that the ground around it was now totally flat. Instead of being nicely concealed by the long grass, the tree was now clearly visible. It seemed to have acquired mythical proportions in people's minds, for having gazed on it, as on a holy relic after a lengthy pilgrimage, many were heard to comment that it was nowhere near as big as they had been led to expect.

The conversations that followed concerning the hows, whys and wherefores of old Roan's peculiar end made Gerald feel somewhat uncomfortable. He was glad he had set Stella the task of keeping watch over the kitchen and the butler's pantry so that she was well out of earshot: he had never confided to her fully what he had done to the tree and he hoped he would never have to do so. If he just kept quiet, he thought, nothing more would come of it.

More and more people arrived, all dressed in suitably sombre gear. Soon there were too many helpers for the tasks available and Bertha's voice went up the scale as she sorted out the useful from the useless. At last, with the table laid to her satisfaction, she began arranging her army of hypocrite mourners ready for the funeral procession, in the order she thought appropriate. Standing in pairs, they stretched all the way from the coffin in the entrance hall, back down the long central corridor to the kitchen and curled round as far as the old kitchen range.

With two red spots aflame in her cheeks, her moustache fairly bristling and her back ramrod straight, Bertha marched down the line, making a final inspection of her troops. Then she hurried back to the head of the crocodile as a flurry of activity at the entrance heralded the arrival of Josh and the hearse. It was a rather small, unimpressive hearse, but the one Josh normally used: Ginty's black cart with its gold and green scrolls, pulled by a high-stepping little black mare. And, impressive in their funeral suits, shiny black boots and black hats, the two undertaker's officials, Ginty and Josh.

Gerald, registering the stir of activity at the front door and guessing that the coffin was about to be hauled aboard, began forcing his way down the corridor along the line of mourners. He was determined to be there at the entrance, to ensure sufficient care was taken and no damage done to the main door or its frame as the coffin was lifted out. By standing on his toes and craning his neck he could just see, over the top of an infinite variety of funeral hats, Herbert, Bent-one, Ginty and Kenny slowly lifting the coffin into the air.

With scant regard for anyone else in the queue, Gerald hurriedly pushed his way forward, elbowing everyone out of the way and making good progress until he came to an unsurmountable obstruction, a little fat woman, and was forced to stop abruptly. He became aware of a pattering sensation on his right boot. He looked down, then leapt back as if burnt – the little fat woman had peed on his foot! The little fat woman was Edie, her waters had just broken and her time had come. Staring down aghast at her legs and feet, she let out a blood-curdling wail that drew all eyes. It also drew Bertha, who came clattering down the corridor in her Sunday shoes to stare at her in disbelief for one frozen moment . . . before she fell upon her like an avalanche.

'Don't yew dare! Don't yew duzzy well dare start that now – I'm going to start the funeral!'

Poor Edie shrank back, trembling and apologetic, gazing down at the widening pool of white-streaked wetness at her feet as if she couldn't believe her eyes.

'She can't help it if she hev started.' Herbert pushed his way along from the front of the line and rose in defence of his little wife. 'If the One Above decide her time hev come there int noth'n' nobody can do about it.'

'Clumpskull!' Bertha raised her fist in the un-mistakable direction of the One Above and shook it vigorously.

'Bertha!' cried Rose, scandalized. 'Whatever are you saying!'

'Well can't He see thass mortally impossible for me to

be in two places at once? Why can't people work in with me?' she cried bitterly. 'I've worked my fingers to the bone this week, and now look whass happened. How can I do the funeral and born the baby at the same time? She's done it on purpose, she must have.'

At this point Stella, drawn from the kitchen area by the drama, felt obliged to make her contribution. She observed, in a quiet, firm and authoritative voice, 'The onset of labour pains are normally quite involuntary, though of course there are certain measures that can be taken—'

'Hold your row!' cried Bertha violently. 'Yew don't know noth'n'. I'm the midwife round here – as my mother was afore me and her mother afore her. I've got it all down here in print,' and, fumbling in her copious skirts, she brought forth and held aloft the ill-fated little black book. Ill-fated because Stella promptly snatched it from her and made off down the corridor, holding it before her between two fingers, rather in the manner, she was to think afterwards – when she had time to think – of Dolmon with the article of ladies' underwear.

'Where are yew go'n' with my book?' roared Bertha, setting off in pursuit, as the line of mourners fell back and pressed themselves assiduously to the wall to let them pass. 'Give me that book! Give me back my book this minute!'

'It's going where it deserves to go!' cried Stella, and, marching resolutely into the dining room, she flung the book into the fire. It hit the back of the fireplace and slithered down into the flames, as Bertha, with an agonized cry, stood staring at it.

But all was not lost. Bent-one darted forward, ran his hand along the sooty bricks at the back of the fire and snatched the book out of the flames. Dancing away in triumph, he held it out in a blackened hand, offering it to his aunt for the price of a ball of waxed thread.

'Yew can hev it for tuppence!' Then, suddenly realizing the position of strength he was in, he upped the price: 'Half a crown – yew can hev it for half a crown!'

Weaving light-footedly about the room, he held the book out tantalizingly just beyond her grasp. Unfortunately, travelling backwards at high speed, he tripped over the stump of old Roan's tree left sticking out from between the floorboards after Gerald had chopped it through with the meat cleaver. He landed spreadeagled on his back in the window bay, among all that was left of the tree – shrivelled leaves and twigs.

With a cry of victory, Bertha fell upon him. Snatching the book, she dealt him a resounding wallop, first to one side of his head and then the other. As he scrambled to his feet and fled she followed, delivering a succession of blows to whatever part of his anatomy happened to present itself as he ran out of the dining room and down the corridor, past the column of goggle-eyed spectators.

These were hardly the best circumstances in which to start a funeral; the atmosphere was far from satisfactory; but Bertha was undaunted. Fixing her hat on more securely and straightening her skirts, she retook command. The coffin was already in the cart. Edie was heaved aboard. Josh and Ginty mounted the front seat on either side of her and death and new life set off together through the tunnel of wild and straggling rhododendron bushes almost obliterating the drive. The long line of mourners followed hurriedly. Even Gerald and Stella, carried away by the sudden momentum, joined on the end and had travelled fifty yards before they suddenly realized, simultaneously, that these were not the roles they had come to play. As the funeral procession turned left and took the bridle path leading to Cookley Green, they turned right and began scrambling through the tangled undergrowth of Thickthorn Woods. They were heading for the park, from where it would be an easy walk to Summerfield Hall.

'Here he comes – here comes Ronnie on his final journey.' Miss Raspberry was standing in the doorway leading onto her balcony and had a clear view of the funeral cortège as it emerged from the avenue of trees and began making its way towards the little bridge leading into the village.

'Strange,' she said, 'what a lot of mourners! Who would have thought so many people would want to attend that funeral? Considering he regularly quarrelled with absolutely everybody!' Including me, she thought. Miss Raspberry had once had high hopes of Ronnie Roan. Twice, to be exact – first in his bachelor days, when they had graced the social scene together and were generally considered to make a couple. Again, five years after his marriage, when his wife died – but that was all in the past, had come to nothing and she didn't want to think about it . . .

'What took you so long?' she snapped, as Miss Gale emerged from her bedroom in her funeral outfit.

'I couldn't find my black gloves.' Poor Windy, who had spent her whole life apologizing, apologized yet again and together they descended the stairs, crossed the green and joined the procession. They squeezed in just behind the hearse, as befitted their status.

Meanwhile, Gerald and Stella broke free of the woods at last, and came out into the bright sunlight and soft autumn air of Summerfield Park. They walked, eyes bent to the ground to avoid traces left by grazing sheep, in companionable silence. There seemed no need for words. They were like two travellers who had gone through the eye of the storm together and come out at last into calmer waters. A warm fellow feeling drew them physically closer. Hands touched and then clasped. They reached a great elm at the eastern end of the Hall and moved as one under it – and into each other's arms. No biting, sucking of raw appetite this time: he kissed her with real feeling, with a tenderness she had not thought him capable of.

He had not thought himself capable of it, either, and the sudden discovery put him in a great fright. He shook her angrily, then fell to kissing her again passionately . . . desperately, until Stella, frightened by her own response, pulled away. For a moment they stood staring at each other in astonishment, then she turned and fled, stumbling along the gravelled frontage, past the ten tall windows of the eastern half of the Hall and in through the main door. Only the all-knowing, omnipresent Dolmon marked her passage, as she ran across the entrance hall and up the stairs to her room. It was enough to send him, bearing a silver salver, to the door, where he stationed himself in an appropriately impressive pose – and waited. As he expected, Gerald entered presently, red-faced and looking dishevelled. He was not best pleased to be instantly confronted by the sepulchral figure of Dolmon.

'A letter for you, sir.' Gerald took it without so much as a thank-you and stumped off towards the stairs. Once in his room, he hurled the letter into the empty ewer on his washstand. He could see it was just another missive from his father making the same old demands: what was keeping him in Suffolk and when was he bringing back the car?

Kicking off his boots, he lay down on his bed feeling tense and thoroughly dissatisfied with himself. Alarmed, too, that he had fallen with such facility from his decision to remain aloof towards Stella. Once let a woman get under your skin and it was downhill all the way, he reckoned. He had had nearly twenty-five years of seeing his father trying to please his mother, and never quite succeeding, to substantiate this belief. Feeling round under his mattress, he fetched out a small bottle of whisky, secreted there for just such an occasion as this. He took a great swig and soon, turning his burning face into the pillows, he fell asleep.

A fair distance away, on the other side of the main staircase – Lady Madeleine was quietly efficient in arranging these matters – Stella also lay on her bed, staring wide-eyed at the ceiling. She was undergoing an extraordinary rethinking of all her ideas, trying to envisage a life totally different from the one she had always imagined herself destined to enjoy. Not a continuation of the pleasant country life she knew so well, with its hunt balls, shooting parties, village fêtes and church and charitable work, rising in time, through marriage to Neville, to the role of Lady Bountiful in the three villages . . . but a life with Gerald in the dark, dismal, industrial north (which she only knew of through hearsay and books, never having travelled any further north than Peterborough). A life with, yes – the rich . . . but the newly rich? People in business? People in trade? With vulgar values and strange ways of speaking? Why, even Gerald she sometimes found difficult to understand. A life with a parvenu for a partner? It was a word she had heard her father use, and the disparaging tone and the context in which he used it had conveyed to her the gist of its meaning. It did not bear thinking of, and yet . . . and yet . . . her whole being cried out for more of what she had just been given a taste of . . . in his arms . . . under the elm.

She felt she couldn't face him at dinner while still in such a state of perturbation. She ordered supper in her room and went to bed early. But not to sleep. For hours she lay restless. After all, his room was only at the other end of the building. There was nobody else in the house but servants – suppose he took it upon himself . . . ? She lay quivering from a mixture of fear and anticipation.

He did not come. In the morning she rose early, asked one of the maids to wash her hair and give it the requisite hundred strokes of the brush. She decided not to put it into the usual tight coil at the back of her head, but to let it flow loosely over her shoulders, as she had worn it when she was a young girl. She wanted to surprise him, to appear softer and more womanly. Her stomach tightened with apprehension, she made her way downstairs to the breakfast room.

She saw at once that her father and Lord Summerfield must have returned last night, for there were four places laid at the table. Lord Summerfield had already eaten and was talking to Dolmon in the main hall, but her father's place setting was untouched; obviously he was still sleeping. Where Gerald normally sat, she saw to her great disappointment, a servant was clearing everything away: he had already breakfasted and gone. To Thickthorn, Dolmon informed her in his usual mournful and aggrieved manner. Of course – she remembered Gerald saying he would go there early, to check that everything was in order after the departure of the barbarians. Seating herself glumly at the table she breakfasted briefly on tea and toast, then made her way back to her room to sit patiently by the window – behind a curtain partially drawn – to await his return.

A mile away Gerald stood in the entrance hall of

Thickthorn Grange congratulating himself on a job well done. He had inspected the whole house and found nothing amiss, nothing stolen, nothing damaged. He had achieved what he had set out to achieve: he had saved Thickthorn from the despoilers. Lord Summerfield would be grateful.

Gazing about him, Gerald visualized the possibilities once the house had been made over to Neville and improved to his satisfaction. Well, to Neville's satisfaction too, of course, the better to serve them both in the entertainment of their mutual friends. He stood with his back to the door, dreaming. He saw the room swirling with people dancing; beautiful girls in ballgowns; liveried lackeys serving exquisite drinks; a dais for the orchestra at the far end of the room. Suddenly there came the sound of a door opening and he felt a draught at his back. Some intruder was taking the liberty of entering the house without so much as a pull at the bell! He swung round.

Lord Summerfield stood in the doorway, in brown country tweeds, a green velour waistcoat and a green tweed cap, his boots and the lower part of his gaiters stained with grass from his hasty walk across the dew-wet park. He simply stood there, a solid dark figure silhouetted against the light. Gerald could not see his expression but he could see what he was holding, stretched across the not inconsiderable acreage of his green velour waistcoat. It was the huge key to the door. He stepped to one side, only too obviously leaving room in the doorway for Gerald to depart.

Gerald's pride, self-confidence and satisfaction melted away like snow in the sun. Too late he realized just what he had done. He opened his mouth to speak; to explain that he had acted at all times with his Lordship's best interests at heart . . . but no words came. His head bowed, he stumbled out. As he did so, his Lordship stepped in and closed the door behind him.

Twenty minutes later Stella, from her vantage point behind her bedroom curtain, saw Gerald returning across the park. Even from a distance she could see there was something different about him, something not right about the way he walked. He had lost his jaunty – a week ago she would have called it bumptious – air. His head was bowed and he seemed to slouch. He appeared – she could hardly believe her eyes as he drew nearer, it was so unlike him – he actually appeared dejected.

She felt a powerful impulse to rush down to him and . . . what? Offer comfort? But even to go down and simply greet him with pleasure, it seemed to her, would dangerously confirm that intimacy between them had deepened. Previously his very presence had aroused irritation and hostility in her. Now she was afraid to face him; afraid of where their new-found interest in each other might lead. It seemed to her that even by simply being glad to see him, she could precipitate herself into a future of which she was by no means convinced. So she stayed where she was, a prey to indecision, gnawing yet another fingernail down to the quick.

Gerald, as he reached the gravelled frontage of the Hall where he knew he could be seen, drew himself up in a conscious effort to assume his usual bold stride. At the main door he braced himself again and received Dolmon's 'A telegraphed message for you this time, sir,' with studied aplomb. 'I gave the boy a florin for his trouble, sir. I do hope you approve.' Tuppence more likely, thought Gerald, but he handed over a silver coin in compensation.

This time his father, from Northampton, demanded Gerald meet him there this very day, at Haywards

Hotel, in readiness to drive back to Yorkshire with him tomorrow. Failing that, he intended descending on Summerfield Hall in person to commandeer the car without further delay. Anything but that, thought Gerald, picturing his father's ghastly incongruity in these surroundings.

Resigned to his fate, he went upstairs to pack. All right, he had overshot the mark, worn out his welcome here – for the time being. But . . . let a little time pass . . . a little water flow under the bridge . . . let Neville return . . . and things would be as they had been before. Secure in the knowledge of his easy dominance over Neville, he knew he would be back.

Stella, having spent half an hour filing her nails in an effort to equalize their lengths to match the ones she had gnawed down, drew back the curtain and resolved to go downstairs and face up to her problem. She would confront Gerald with cool self-possession. She had thought the whole thing over and decided that there was too much disparity – disparity was a good word here – too much disparity between the two of them in the way of upbringing and general outlook for her to continue with their courtship. She deeply regretted any injury to his feelings and the disappointment of his aspirations . . . but she felt sure that in the long run he would come to see . . .

She was still standing at her window at this point in her cogitations and suddenly a car, with Gerald at the wheel, emerged from the stable yard, drew steadily along the western half of the house and stopped directly in front of the main door. Almost immediately, out of this door came Edward laden with what was obviously Gerald's luggage, which he piled into the back of the car. Without hesitation or a backward glance, Gerald restarted the engine, passed directly under her window and slowly disappeared in the direction of Cookley Green. He needed to buy petrol there at the blacksmith's shop, enough to keep him going for some distance before having to buy more at another blacksmith's on the way.

Stella stared after him, speechless. He had gone! Without a goodbye or even a wave. She could not believe it! She had wrestled a whole sleepless night with the problem of what to do and say, how to convey her decision to him with the minimum of hurt to his feelings . . . Feelings? He had no feelings! It had all been make-believe on her part. She had made an utter fool of herself; she would never forgive him! Still in a daze, she descended the stairs and had the misfortune to meet Dolmon in the main hall. He hastened to inform her, with ill-concealed glee, that Master Gerald had just this moment set off for Yorkshire.

Down at Thickthorn, Lord Summerfield made a thorough inspection of the property and decided, like Gerald, that all was in order after the funeral. Neither of them had thought to check the outhouses and the garden, where the mourners, after the beanfeast was over, had spent a considerable amount of time. Under orders from Bertha, they had all come equipped with sack, basket, box or bag and with these at the ready, they dug up and shared out old Roan's potatoes, carrots, parsnips, turnips and beetroot, stripped the plum tree of its plums, the greenhouse of its tomatoes, the early apple tree of its apples, the chicken hut of its eggs and its occupants and the garden shed of all its tools. In the silverware, glassware, china, chandeliers, pictures, jewellery and antique furniture, about which Gerald and his Lordship had been so concerned, they had no interest whatsoever.

His Lordship was able to make his way back home

again in a comfortable and contented frame of mind. The way was clear now for him to hand the property over to Neville – not that he would need to go into anything legal, for, after all, the boy would inherit everything, in the fullness of time.

CHAPTER FIFTEEN

In the fullness of time Lady Madeleine, Neville and Becky returned from London, and his Lordship's worst fears were realized when he saw the results of her outing in town piled up at the foot of the stairs. By this time Stella had gone back home with her father to Highlea, so she and Neville did not meet again for almost a month.

Becky came back with a glowing look and Dolmon promptly fell passionately . . . well, possessively and obsessively . . . in love with her. This was not so much because of the look, which was indeed seductive, but because her sudden popularity within the family much increased her value in his eyes. He proceeded to make her life a misery by his attentions; took to leaving little nosegays in her room; showered her with special privileges and considerations which would have made her thoroughly unpopular with the rest of the staff, but for her naturally sweet and unassuming nature.

Miss Raspberry, with characteristic ineptitude, decided to hold a garden party cum bring and buy sale, to provide funds for the up-and-coming Cookley Green Tennis Club. As it was now November, the event could not be expected to be a total success and it wasn't. Rain drove the guests and the stallholders under the archway or into the Black Bull and the meagre profit of £2 13s 6d hardly justified the effort everybody had put in. It was here, bedraggled and wet from hastily carrying the consumables indoors, that Stella met Neville once again and found herself racked with doubt. She just did not know whether she did or could ever find him appealing. Her experience of life suggested there was something missing in Neville. Well, there was – there was an ear missing on the right side of his head. The surgeon had amputated the greater part of it, leaving, for some unknown reason, just a piece of the lobe dangling. This, insecurely attached by an attenuated thread of flesh, bobbed and fluttered in a strong breeze like a leaf on an aspen poplar. Stella could not bear to look at it. Neville, of course, instantly realized this, flushed to the roots of his sandy-coloured hair and fell back on tender recollections of Becky's gentle, indiscriminating touch. 'Love is not love which alters when it alteration finds' floated appropriately into his mind.

He was not best pleased to hear that Stella had signed him up as a founder member of the Cookley Green Tennis Club. However, he took heart when he heard that Gerald had also been signed up. He had always had quite a battle maintaining his friendship with Gerald, of whom his father took no pains to conceal his hearty dislike.

Lord Summerfield, invited to the garden party, feeling duty bound to go and show some interest but reluctant to give up time that could be so much better and more enjoyably spent, suddenly saw that here was the perfect opportunity for Neville to begin preparing for his future role. He could deputize for his father at this minor social event, thus releasing him to deal with more important affairs. Neville affably agreed to help, adding that he was well aware of his father's heavy programme of duties and responsibilities and for that reason had decided not to burden him with any of the decisions regarding the improvements at Thickthorn. All his father had to do was come up with the money when it was required. Neville would need Gerald, of course, as a perfect fount of absolutely ripping ideas. Alarm bells ringing in his head, his Lordship tersely observed that that was something he didn't for one moment doubt.

Neville did not know how long his departure for foreign parts would be delayed – he had missed his official sailing date because of the injury to his ear. He felt it imperative to decide on the plans as soon as possible, so that work could start early in the new year. This meant, he told his father, Gerald coming down again at the earliest opportunity, certainly before Christmas. Vaguely feeling that he had somehow been outmanoeuvred, his Lordship found he could do little other than agree.

So, within the week, there was Gerald, on his way back to Suffolk once again. The hours of daylight were short now, so he broke his journey at Northampton and approached his destination mid-afternoon the following day. His journey was without incident until he encountered George and Josh the wheelwright on Church Hill, just as he entered the village. Josh was trying out a primitive bicycle he had made and George was watching from the bottom of the hill. It was a 'boneshaker', with wooden wheels and frame but no pedals. Josh went whizzing down the hill as Gerald came up in his car behind him. Confident that anyone obstructing his passage would instantly move aside, Gerald began banging on his horn in a series of ear-splitting blasts . . . but to no effect. The scarecrow figure merrily continued to the bottom of the hill, then stopped, and, straddling his machine in the middle of the road, bent to examine his front wheel. George shouted, waved his arms and leapt up and down; Gerald held grimly to his course . . . until the very last moment when he had to swerve violently, then mount the bank on his left. He ended up slewed diagonally across the street. 'Stupid oaf! Get off the road!' roared Gerald, red-faced and glaring . . . 'NOT STUPID – DEAF!' shouted George, pointing at his ears. 'HE CAN'T HEAR YOU.'

This time Gerald did recognize George, who was in his working clothes, as the perpetrator of all Neville's troubles with his ear. He would have liked to have jumped out and given the fellow a good thrashing, but the car had somehow righted itself; he was on his way again and reluctant to lose time settling old scores. Postponing that pleasure to some more convenient opportunity, he drove on. Now there was no-one to be seen except two little girls playing hopscotch in the mud at the edge of the village green.

'What wus wrong with that fulla?' asked Josh. He gazed at George with bright blue innocent eyes and his white hair, blown by the wind, stood up on his head like the crest on a cockatoo. 'What wus a matter with him?'

George shook his head and smiled: too taxing to explain to Josh at the top of his voice that he had nearly caused an accident and hadn't even noticed. There was something else more important he wanted to talk about – how to make a chair for his mother.

His mother had been slow to recover from the asthma and bronchitis that had laid her low at the time of old Roan's funeral. She had been too ill to attend anyway, and George had tried, but failed, to prevent her from knowing that she, he, his father, in fact the whole family, were first on the list of those not to be welcomed at Thickthorn on the day of the funeral. His mother said defiantly she quite understood her father's behaviour, for he had always been irascible and unyielding in his relationships with those who defied his wishes, but George could not forgive the old man the years of misery he had caused her.

On the day of the funeral he had been working in the garden, and he had not forgotten the sight of his mother standing at her bedroom window as the funeral cortège passed and then repassed according to old Roan's written instructions. Clad in her long white high-necked night-dress with her brown hair coiling snakelike down her shoulders to her waist, she had wept.

She still seemed tired and dispirited, not her usual warm and sprightly self. So George had decided to make her a chair, twin to the Windsor chair his father habitually sat in, for he had suddenly realized there was nowhere comfortable in the house for his mother to sit. He made up his mind to ask Josh for advice; there was no-one better, for over the years Josh had made a chair for each new member of his own family as they came along, and as Josh and Rose had had twelve children (ten survived), his knowledge and experience in this field was second to none.

It was when George was descending the slope leading to his workshop with this in view, that he met Josh coming up the yard pushing the wooden boneshaker before him. This was the third bike he had made, he informed George, when he had listened to what George had to say – or, rather, bawled out at the top of his voice. It was impossible to tell whether the old man had taken any of it in, as the history of the boneshakers seemed to be fully occupying his mind.

He had never actually had a ride on one of these bikes, he said. Previously the boys had always grabbed them as soon as they were made, and he never got a look-in. But now that all the boys, except Bent-one, were gone, he said somewhat sheepishly, he was going to have his turn. Anyway, he didn't suppose the boys would even entertain the idea of riding a boneshaker nowadays, not now there were bikes with metal frames and rubber tread on the wheels. 'Come yew into the house, when I've had a go, and I'll show yew all my chairs,' he said, thus revealing that he had heard something of what George had had to say.

Josh's cottage stood in the lane just opposite the top of his yard, so he hadn't very far to go to get to work in the mornings. The incident with Gerald now over, they entered the cottage via the lean-to shed, where Bent-one worked mending shoes. And there he was. He had obviously solved the problem of obtaining a ball of waxed thread, for he was sitting at his treadle machine fashioning a new harness to hold on Herbert's calf's wooden leg. The calf was standing close beside him, the little vestigial knob, which was all it had in the way of a left front leg, propped up on a stool of just the right height, carefully padded with Bent-one's yellow scarf. (Bent-one had a warm regard for animals.) The calf's head rested trustingly on his knee and as the knee went up and down rhythmically to propel the treadle, the calf's head went up and down with it, without the animal showing the least concern. George thought the pair of them must have been in that position for some time, judging by the amount of waste material the calf had managed to add to the general rubbish scattered about the floor.

Picking their way carefully across to the inner door, they opened it and stepped down into the living room of the tiny cottage. It was furnished, of course, mostly with chairs. They stood sentinel along three sides of the room, their backs to the wall, the results of many years of chair production, following child production. A long

212

table down the middle of the room wore an orange chenille cloth with a yellow fringe, and a matching pelmet hung from the mantelshelf above the big black range. Windsor chairs on either side of the hearth were obviously for the use of Josh and Rose and on the floor between them lay a rag rug of many colours, made from the family's cast-off clothing. In an alcove under the stairs there was a small piano, its keys yellow with age. On it the three daughters, two now married and living in Silverley, had learned to play and each in turn had gone on to play the organ at the Methodist chapel on Sundays. Here Ellen, the one remaining daughter of Josh and Rose, and George's sweetheart, regularly still performed.

All the way round three walls of the room, in the space above the chairs, were jingoistic pictures of great ferocity and derring-do. Cut-outs hung beside copies of pictures, made by the seven sons, from the *Boys' Own Paper*, depicting heroic events and deeds in the acquisition and defence of the British Empire. One illustration, featuring two Canadian Mounties heroically quelling a tribe of rebellious Indians, might well have been what lured two of the boys to Canada, George thought, as he moved slowly along in the narrow space between the table and the chairs. He examined the pictures one by one, bending close to each to decipher the name of whichever boy had painted it.

'Rose'd have 'em all back tomorrow, if she could,' said Josh, following his gaze. 'But I tell yew what,' he added softly, 'I get a lot more fuss made of me now they've all gone.'

Where were they now, thought George, the seven boys? Well, five, not counting Bent-one and Herbert. Lads he had known all his life . . . had gone to school with . . . Jack and Reggie in Canada, Henry, James and

Charlie who, along with many other young lads of the village, had gone north to work in factories, mills and foundries. What were they doing at this very minute? Would they ever come back to live in the village?

He could sense Josh waiting for him to turn his attention to the chairs, which he eventually did, reluctantly, for there were a lot of them and if he was about to hear a long recital of the design, the production and the amendments to the design Josh had made over the years, they would be here for a very long time.

He had forgotten that Josh was habitually a man of few words. He touched but briefly on the problems he encountered in his early efforts, then encapsulated the basics of chair design in one simple sentence: 'What yew gotta dew, I reckon, is fit the chair to the man, not t'other way round.' Then he added that he could best illustrate what he meant down in his sawpit. Down in his sawpit? Intrigued, George followed him back through the lean-to shed – where Bent-one had given up stitching for the moment to feed the calf a big bunch of grass – along the front of the cottage and down the yard, with Josh walking jauntily ahead, the wind lifting skywards his halo of white hair.

The sawpit was under a roof jutting out from the near end of the black, timber-clad workshop. It was open on three sides, with two posts supporting the outer edges. The sawpit beneath was a brick-lined rectangular hole in the ground, about seven feet long and four feet wide. It was edged at ground level by thick nine-inch-wide boards. Lengthwise across the top lay Josh's latest acquisition – the trunk of a sizeable oak tree, set up ready to be sawn into planks. On the end wall of the workshop several long cross-cut saws lay across wooden pegs, some of the blades, originally five inches wide, worn down to two in the middle from years of use.

Under the roof, leaning against the end of the workshop, upright and unvarnished, stood an oak coffin.

'Who is that for?' George nodded towards it with raised eyebrows. He was not aware of anybody having died in the village since old Roan.

'Me.'

'You! What about the lid? There's no lid.'

'I aren't in no hurry,' said Josh.

They climbed down into the pit via a small metal ladder fastened at one end. There was a delightful smell of pine resin and damp sawdust. Josh's workshop was situated on the edge of marshland that reached out from the little river as far as the village street, and the floor of the sawpit floated on the water table. Planks squelched under George's feet and a bright green frog leapt agilely into the water through a gap in the boards. A heavy, thick board was available to set across the floor, to give steady purchase to the bottom sawyer as he worked. At the far end of the pit the accumulation of many years of sawdust production was piled up high against the wall in a damp, aromatic heap. At its foot sat a fat, statuesque toad, regarding them unblinkingly. George turned and looked about him; nowhere could he see anything relevant to chair design and he had just opened his mouth to say so, loudly – when he found himself travelling backwards. His mouth open this time in surprise, he lost his footing and sat down heavily in the pile of damp sawdust behind him.

Josh had pushed him . . . and was still pushing! He pressed back George's chest, shoulders and his head, then, grasping him by the lapels of his jacket, he yanked him to his feet. The toad, looking, George thought, displeased, slowly jumped away. There in the sawdust was a perfect imprint of George: his thighs, buttocks and the curve of his spine all the way up to his head.

'There y'are – thass the human frame for yew. Thass the shape yew gotta aim for, when you're making a chair. Have a good look,' and Josh climbed out of the sawpit.

'I can let yew hev some decent wood,' he said, when George joined him at the top a few minutes later. 'Yew can come and work in my workshop of an evening. I've got an oil lamp yew can use to see by. I'll keep an eye on yew, to make sure yew dew a proper job.'

'Thanks,' said George. As he bent to brush the sawdust from his clothes, Josh casually ran a piece of chalk along the underside of a thickish string he had fastened length-wise just above the trunk of the oak tree, secured by metal skewers at either end. Seizing the string between thumb and finger, he twanged it sharply so that a distinct white line of chalk appeared along the length of the trunk.

'There y'are – ready for the first cut. Don't know who I can git to be bottom sawyer though . . .' He glanced at George slyly, with twinkling eyes. 'I've had Kenny and Jacko in the past, only they're gett'n' too old.' (Josh was as old, if not older, thought George.) 'Ginty's no good – got no substance. Tew skinny . . . I'm always afraid he'll fly up with the saw! What I could really dew with,' and here George was the recipient of another sly glance, 'is a nice, strong, healthy—'

'All right, all right,' said George, grinning, for he saw he had been neatly caught. 'When d'you want me?'

'Monday? Shouldn't take no more'n four days.' Josh must have known, thought George, that he and his father had no work at the moment. It was amazing how much he could hear when it suited him!

Miss Raspberry was not going to be best pleased, he thought, as he wandered home. She expected him at her disposal in any free time, dedicating himself wholly to

216

the advancement of the Cookley Green Tennis Club. The courts were seeded, ready for the spring, but there was netting to be erected all the way round and she needed George's help with the plans for a pavilion he was to build next summer. It was to have a roofed veranda so that people could sit in comfort and watch the games. Now George had promised to help Josh in the sawpit during the day, and would be spending the evenings in his workshop making a chair for his mother.

When he reached home he found his two sisters playing an elaborate skipping game in the front yard, and his father smelling of alcohol and asleep in his chair by the fire, a pile of shoes on his lap that he had been trying to mend so they would last a little longer. His mother was coping with the washing in the kitchen, putting sheets through the mangle after she'd hauled them out of the copper. He winced at the sound of her tortured breathing as she cranked the handle. He went into the kitchen to help her, but she had just finished, so he carried the washing basket out for her and hung the heavier items on the line.

June 1999

'Can you tell me now?' I was sitting by the one window in the room Pearl called her parlour, hand-sewing the hem of my green skirt for the ball, with Sammy on the floor at my feet trying to cut newspaper into strips with my second-best scissors. Pearl looked at me blankly for a moment, so I added, 'Stella – what did she do that was so awful?' She sat quiet for a moment, as if mustering up the whole story in her mind before she started.

Stella Benson – Benson-Brick, to give her her full name

– harboured from her earliest days an ambition to be the next Lady Summerfield. She thought she had achieved her aim when, after much effort and many tortuous stratagems, she managed to get engaged to Neville, the Summerfield heir, on the last night of his last leave. She became a nurse during the war. His death in France later that year marked the end of all her dreams. According to Becky, she then turned her attention to his best friend, who survived the war, a rather brash, assertive and worldly-wise Yorkshireman, son of a carpet manufacturer in Halifax. Nothing seemed to come of this, though they spent much time together, and there appeared to be some understanding between them. Exactly what happened in the end is not generally known; suffice to say that Stella was later spirited away to an undisclosed destination for several months, which led to certain conjectures spreading in the village, none of which were ever substantiated.

She came back, everybody said, a soured and disappointed woman, and retired a recluse at Highlea, where her parents were still living at the time. She was brought out of her voluntary isolation a year later by the local doctor, Dr Weston. Concerned for her state of mind, he offered her a job as his assistant. With her wartime nursing experience, he said, she could run a weekly clinic for minor ailments in each of the three villages and thus release him to deal with more serious cases. So Stella ventured out again into the world, resolved to devote herself for the rest of her life to the Doing of Good Works. The doctor's scheme was only two-thirds successful. The Summerfield and Silverley clinics ran smoothly, but sadly in Cookley Green there were such ructions between Stella and Bossy Bertha that even those who might have preferred to use the new clinic there were too scared of Bertha to do so. In the end

Dr Weston had to admit defeat and the Cookley Green clinic was closed.

But Stella continued at Summerfield and Silverley and it was when she was on her way to Silverley one morning, on her bike, in her nurse's uniform, that an event occurred which seemed to signify that her dream was not entirely lost. She was crossing the little bridge leading into the village when down the road came a large car and in it – Gerald! Her erstwhile lover! Clothed in leather and wearing a merrily striped scarf of red, green and yellow, he stopped and leaned out to inform her that he had just bought Summerfield Hall and Thickthorn and was the new lord of the manor. Both properties had been up for sale for barely a year, since the deaths of Lord and Lady Summerfield within a few weeks of each other. Here was the proud new owner and whether it was because he liked her in her nurse's uniform or the fresh air had brought an especially attractive bloom to her cheeks . . . I have to admit this is me trying to see the thing in a romantic light . . . Pearl muttered caustically that he probably saw an opportunity to pay her back for the many times, according to Becky, she had flaunted in front of everybody her preference for Neville. Sadly, what came after does seem to bear this theory out. He grandly issued an invitation which instantly brought about a rebirth of all her hopes and dreams. He said he planned to hold a banquet and ball as soon as the sale was successfully completed; everybody who was somebody would be invited – would she be his hostess?

She closed the Silverley clinic early and cycled madly back home to beard her father in his den, managing to extract from him a sum of money he could ill afford (the Benson-Brick finances were already in a shaky state and the brigadier was to be pretty near ruined in the

1929 crash). Stella and her mother sped off to London on a shopping spree. They bought what amounted to a trousseau, plus an evening dress in Wedgwood blue with white embroidery about the bodice and the hem – costing, Pearl cried out in astonishment, nearly thirty guineas! The two women came home well satisfied and in a golden glow of anticipation, but the brigadier was appalled: all the day dresses they had bought ended at the knee and, even worse, Stella had had her long glossy black hair shorn into an Eton crop! Things were not at all as they used to be, he complained. But Stella and her mother were beside themselves with excitement. The invitation could only mean one thing: Gerald had recognized his need for a capable and accomplished partner to assist him in his new role as a member of the landed gentry . . . someone who was au fait with the ways of that world. A little late, he was about to make an honest woman of her.

Poor, poor Stella! I can't help feeling sorry for her. She had her fifteen minutes of glory – more like two hours actually. As in her dreams, but beside Gerald instead of Neville, she stood in the entrance hall at Summerfield graciously welcoming guests as they arrived. She sat opposite him at dinner at one end of the long table shining and sparkling with all the accoutrements of high living she had spent three months helping him to acquire. She discreetly directed the team of servants she had appointed and trained for the occasion (Becky was one), at the same time conducting conversation with diners nearby. It was a tour de force without parallel in the long history of hospitality at Summerfield, where Lady Madeleine's rather lax handling of the servants, and in particular her recalcitrant butler, sometimes resulted in things not going quite as planned. As I see it, Stella's nearest and dearest probably sat gazing at her spellbound with admiration, united in the conviction that all this was no more than she deserved.

I see her in a calf-length, diaphanous, delicately embroidered gown, with a dropped waistline, wearing a dainty necklace of tiny painted blue flowers. Actually, Pearl says, she wore the Wedgwood blue velvet gown, the skirt shorter in front than behind, with the white embroidery on bodice, sleeves and hemline. The fashion of the day, of course, was for narrow dresses hanging straight from the shoulder, belted at the hip. A slim boyish figure was obviously the ideal, but Stella, so I understand, was blessed with a buoyant bosom that probably had to be subdued by a bust-flattening bra. Anyway, down the years has come this vital and I think rather poignant piece of information: despite her very best efforts she couldn't help appearing somewhat matronly. Well, according to Pearl, she must have been by this time in her early thirties.

Of course those who fly highest have furthest to fall. Stella's descent was fast and final when Gerald stood up to make his debut after-dinner speech. He welcomed everyone heartily to this, the start of a new chapter in Summerfield history; thanked all those who had made the arduous journey from Yorkshire; promised that this was just the first of many similar occasions to come; Summerfield was about to resume its rightful role in the scheme of things . . . He carried on in like vein for some time, before turning his attention to Stella. Without her help, he declared, beaming upon her, he would never have been able to cope. She had been an absolute brick! (A rather unfortunate term, Pearl said, considering how much she had always disliked the Brick part of her name.) Her capable, loyal support had brought about in him the realization of his need for a permanent partner in this demanding new chapter in his life. Stella had made him see that his carefree bachelor days must be at an end, and he thanked God that he had indeed found just such a helpmate. He had great pleasure in introducing to them the future mistress of Summerfield . . . and striding down one side of the table he drew out from her seat a little, gingery, Eton-cropped slip of a thing with the requisite flat bosom and boyish figure – a Miss Felicity Schofield of Harrogate.

'Oh poor Stella!' I couldn't help crying out. 'How could he be so cruel?'

'She had her revenge,' said Pearl simply, 'about eight years later. They only had one son – he didn't intend messing up the inheritance, somebody heard him say. One day the boy was following the hunt when he shouldn't hev bin and his pony tossed him over the hedge. He slashed his wrist on a bit of barbed wire as he went over and knocked hisself out. At the inquest the coroner said if only somebody had bin there to stop the bleeding, he could've bin saved. A very unfortunate accidental death, wus the verdict. The thing is,' she continued after a pause, 'somebody wus there – Stella. With all her nursing experience during the war, she just sat there and let him bleed to death.'

'Oh no!' I cried, horrified. 'How—'

'Bent-one told the story afterwards. He wus pinch'n' apples in the orchard across the road. He climbed up a ladder onto the roof of a shed so he could reach the best ones and he saw everything what happened. He saw the boy fly over the hedge and he wus just go'n' to climb down and see if he wus all right, when down the road come Stella on her bike. She could tell someth'n' was wrong because there stood the pony nibbling the grass without a rider. He saw her look all round, throw down her bike, climb the gate and bend over the boy. Then she sat down beside him . . . and just sat there . . . waiting.

222

And Bent-one, he lay flat on the top of the shed and waited for . . . well, he hadn't got no watch and anyway, I don't s'pose he could tell the time . . . but he waited, he said, a very long time. Then he saw her pick up the boy's arm and let it drop. He said he saw her dew that twice. Then she climbed back over the gate, got on her bike and pedalled away. Then, just as he wus go'n' to climb down and go and investigate, two grooms from the Hall come along looking for the boy. They saw the pony, climbed over the gate and found him – dead. I think the whole thing must've got on Bent-one's mind,' she said thoughtfully, 'and he felt he just had to tell someone. So I said right – now yew hev, yew've told me, and don't yew never tell another soul! And so far as I know, he never did.'

'All those tales of Bent-one's – I bet he made them up, just to get attention.' I thought, but what about the other overwhelmingly tragic story I'd heard? 'What about the young officer Neville shot by his NCOs – I can hardly believe that either! Couldn't it have been anybody? Was it really Neville Summerfield? I'm sure it was just a tale going the rounds in the army,' I said to Pearl.

'Oh no, I don't think so.'

'Well, I do.'

'No – it wus him,' said Pearl firmly. 'Definit'y Neville, it wus. Couldn't hev bin nobody else. He only had one ear, you see – the other wus scraped off in a riding accident. That wus reckoned to be George's fault,' she said. 'Everything what went wrong in this village wus always George's fault.'

It was a long time since George's name had entered the conversation so I sat silent, hoping to hear more.

'Sloppy Joe, his men used to call him,' she murmured after a while, 'because his cap kept sliding down the side of his head.'

I suddenly had a lot to think about. The tragic death of a young man so temperamentally unsuited to the savagery of war. The blessed ignorance of his parents of the way he died; the death of Gerald's son. What about Stella? How on earth did she manage to carry on for the rest of her life with this on her mind?

Apparently she managed quite well. When the brigadier died their old home, Highlea, was sold to meet his debts, but luckily at about the same time Stella's mother inherited her family home, Chalfont Manor, on the outskirts of Cookley Green. Stella and her mother turned it into an old people's home, which Stella ruled for many years with a rod of iron. Her mother eventually became the oldest inmate there and when she died Stella, who was getting pretty old herself, sold it, with the stipulation that she be allowed to remain there, free of charge, in one of the best rooms, looked after by her personal maid who was to be paid by the establishment. For some years Becky occupied this post, but as time went by Stella gradually became more and more feeble-minded and when the couple running the home judged the time propitious, Becky got the push and Stella never even noticed she'd gone. She died, Pearl said, sitting on that seat in the rose garden in the rain, waiting for her father to come.

What a way to go! I thought. What a life, after all her dreams and expectations. Gerald lived on, it seems, to a ripe old age, spent most of his time in Yorkshire where, people said, he had another woman. Young Felicity Schofield of Harrogate remained at Summerfield alone, except for the servants. She was in a wheelchair from age forty, paralysed by an attack of polio. She had only the one child and died aged sixty-three.

I suddenly felt thoroughly tired of all this sewing. I'd gone off my green skirt and I'm afraid I swore as I pricked my finger and blood trickled onto the hem I had just finished stitching – luckily on the inside.

'Is absolutely everybody you ever knew dead?' I asked. Pearl sat quietly, gazing into space, and then said simply, 'Yes . . . nearly everybody. Thass what happen when you get to my age.'

And another one almost died yesterday, she informed me – had I heard? Andrew Gillson had been rushed off to hospital. Andrew Gillson? Of course – our squire of the village. Owner of an executive-type house of the utmost hideosity. It was Andrew who had conceived the idea which was to make him rich while taking a three-legged cow to the bull in his father's famous black cart. I remembered seeing the cart in the display case outside his house when I went to rent the cottage. But . . . a three-legged cow? Still, I've heard mention of this story so many times I think there must be something in it.

I've long wanted to hear more, so I waited . . . but no, today was not going to be the day. Pearl was wearing the yellow blouse with the ruffle at the neck she bought at the village fête, and now her head sank down into it like a tortoise sinking into the leathery dewlaps of its neck. Her eyes closed and in a moment she had drifted away. Her face looked utterly collapsed, like a once strongly defined structure that had crumbled into dereliction.

I gathered up Sammy's strips of newspaper, pushed them into the pockets of my jeans to dispose of later, collected all my sewing kit and bundled up the green skirt. I was getting heartily sick of it but at least now it was nearly done. Then, having shushed Sammy with a finger to my lips, we tiptoed away.

CHAPTER SIXTEEN

1914

'Why is it always me?' Bent-one's plaintive cry rang out across a stretch of estuary marshland capped by a pearly blanket of early morning mist. All he got in reply was a ferocious hiss to be silent from his three companions. He was standing in, or sinking into, a waterlogged muck heap, with Herbert's calf Daphne, now fully grown, clutched under his left armpit and a fearsome great Friesian bull rearing up over his right shoulder. The bull, frothing at the mouth and snorting explosively, glared down at him, showing the white of one wrathful-looking eye. Bent-one felt that he would be much better off in some other place.

Edie's inconsiderate conduct in starting the baby at the same time as the funeral had thrown Bertha into the agonizing predicament of having to preside over the funeral or the birth. She chose the funeral and consigned Edie to the rather more tender care of a midwife from Summerfield. Edie's day of shame ended in a blaze of glory when she finally managed to give birth to a son. Herbert, thrown into a state of euphoria, went round shouting that now at last he would have some help when he realized his dream of establishing his own dairy herd, of which, of course, Daphne was to be the matriarch. But six years had passed; the son was now at school and not even a founder member of the herd had made its appearance.

This was the fourth year poor Daphne had clandestinely been taken to the bull. Clandestinely, because Herbert could not afford the service fee for Felix the Blyth Valley Wonder, Champion Friesian of all East Anglia. Felix had to be taken advantage of by stealth. This meant persuading Ginty to allow Daphne to travel in his graceful black cart, in the dead of night, six miles east along the river valley to the estuary marshes where Felix was to be found. It was timed for them to arrive just as dawn was breaking, and the mist, and, hopefully, his sap, rising. This time Ginty took some persuading. He had just repainted his beloved cart, added creatively to the plethora of golden scrolls and re-covered the seat cushions. He objected to it being desecrated by Daphne's nervous ejaculations as they travelled along. He consented in the end with the proviso that she wore a watertight bag under her tail, a device which turned out to be only partially efficacious.

Ginty and Herbert sat side by side in the front seat, with Bent-one crouched on the floor behind clutching as much of Daphne as he could get his arms round, her head draped tremblingly over his shoulder. Ginty's son, Andrew, who had come along partly for the ride and partly from prurient curiosity, sat perched on the tailboard with his feet dangling. He had instructions to get out and walk when they came to a hill, for Ginty's high-stepping little black mare, Black Cherry, was high-stepping no longer. Not as young as she used to be, her bones were beginning to show through and her hide looked bedraggled despite all Ginty's loving care.

There was a three-quarter moon but the sky was

cloudy, so they rode along through patches of light and darkness. None of the travellers much enjoyed the ride. Ginty sat in gloomy silence, brooding perhaps over his latest rebuttal from the cruel Molly Marston, or the ignoble use to which his cart was being put. Herbert was quickly reduced to a state of irritation by questions he didn't want to hear from the pragmatic Andrew: how long did he reckon it was going to take him to establish a dairy herd when Daphne, who was now nearly six years old, had not yet managed to produce a single calf? How many acres of grazing did you need to support one cow – was it two, was it four? How did he reckon to be able to support even a small herd when the only land at his disposal was the half-acre of common land left over from when they'd marked out the village cricket pitch . . . and anyway, how could he be sure that calves born of Daphne would have the correct complement of legs? Thus, without any real malice aforethought, Andrew would have picked away at Herbert's dream until it was threadbare, had Black Cherry not started showing signs of stress, whereupon he was ordered to get out and walk. Meanwhile Bent-one, struggling to keep Daphne upright, hold her leg on at the front and the bag under her tail at the back, had scarcely a moment's repose.

At long last they reached their destination: there, about half a mile from the farm, was the gate leading onto the marshes where, according to reliable sources, Felix was to be found. The sky was just beginning to lighten, cockerels were starting to salute the dawn and the farm dogs were giving a few desultory barks. Mist encompassed the marsh where Felix (named after a saint with local associations) was allowed out for a short stretch of time in August with the home herd, after a busy season indoors at stud. A sort of holiday, you might say, for he had already inseminated most of the home herd. Quickly and quietly, Daphne was bundled out of the cart and the unfortunate Bent-one assigned the task of leading her into the mist to locate Felix and waft her enticingly before him for the delectation of his barely awakened senses. She was judged to be in an alluring and receptive condition. The plan was to entice the bull towards the gate and the muck heap adjacent to it. The muck heap was a necessary requirement; though well fed and well covered, Daphne was somewhat undersized, and disparity in height was thought to be the reason for last year's abortive effort – and the effort the year before that.

All went according to plan. Felix obediently followed Daphne out of the thickest of the mist towards the gate and higher ground and several members of the home herd, out of feminine curiosity, followed him. They gathered in a circle at a safe distance to watch – to weird effect, for only about four inches of their legs could be seen at ground level and higher up their big foolish faces loomed out of the mist like clowns in a surrealist painting.

With gentle encouragement from Bent-one, Daphne was persuaded to mount the muck heap and Felix showed every sign of being willing, indeed eager, to join her. Everybody's spirits rose. It seemed likely that they would soon see their mission accomplished and be able to make a quick getaway before anyone stirred at the farm.

Unhappily, the muck heap, being waterlogged, did not provide a sufficiently stable base to support Daphne plus the weight of the bull. Despite Felix's best efforts, Daphne began to subside and to the consternation of all, the target began irrevocably to sink below the firing line. Shaken, Felix began to exhibit signs of weakening confidence and diminishing purpose. Everyone stared in consternation. What was to be done?

All seemed lost . . . but Herbert, desperate at seeing his dairy dream ebb away before his very eyes, plunged into the nearest dyke, seized a bulrush and, with an exquisite delicacy of touch – born no doubt of fellow feeling – he used the soft velvety tip to redirect the vacillating firearm. Miraculously, Felix rallied and rose again manfully, or rather, bullfully, to the task. A few purposeful thrusts, a startled long-drawn-out moooo from Daphne – and it was all over. Except that Bent-one promptly burst into tears.

'She don't like it,' he blubbed. 'That int fair! I'm go'n' to take her hoam.' And as Felix subsided backwards onto firm ground, he bent and went scrabbling round in the muck heap trying to release each of Daphne's legs in turn – not an easy task, for they all seemed immovably fixed into the muck by suction. Still complaining bitterly about the injustice of it all, the affront to the susceptibilities of one so sensitive as Daphne, he managed at last to get her back onto solid ground . . . only to find that he was on his own – except for Daphne and the bull. Herbert, Andrew and Ginty were peering at him from the safety of the other side of the gate. With ill-concealed excitement they watched as he gingerly edged his way towards them, carefully keeping Daphne between himself and the Blyth Valley Wonder. There was no real need for alarm. Felix appeared considerably deflated (it had been a long, hard season). Lowering his head, he pawed the ground a few times, but made no other protest, as Bent-one gingerly manoeuvred himself and Daphne past him and out of the gate. In no time at all they were loaded up in the cart again and on their way home down the farm drive, hardly able to believe their good luck.

Sadly, the good luck ran out halfway along the drive. They hit a pothole, the left-hand spring broke and the finely curved, fantastically decorated left mudguard jammed down on the wheel, bringing the cart to a juddering halt. All immediately shuffled over to the right to take the weight off the left wheel, and Bent-one tied Daphne to the right-hand rail with his long yellow scarf. When this did not bring much relief, Bent-one was ordered to get out and push. This unhinged poor Daphne. Deprived of his familiar close presence and support, she began uttering a series of loud, heart-rending moos which threatened to reveal their presence and their nefarious activities to the people at the farm, who were now beginning to stir.

At last, with a wedge normally used to prevent a coffin from sliding about shoved in under the spring to lift weight off the left wheel, and with Andrew and Bent-one pushing mightily from behind, they were able to make their way down the drive and out onto the public high-way. Now they could appear, to any onlooker or fellow traveller, to be on some quite innocuous and legitimate business. So they relaxed. Several carts passed them from farms round about, full of churns bound for the early morning milk train. There were a few jeering remarks such as, 'Why don't ya all git out and walk?' or 'Why not put the hoss in the cart and harness the cow?' for Black Cherry seemed to be finding the going harder and harder, and to be travelling more and more slowly. At last, at the top of only a slight incline, she stopped, shuddered – then dropped to the ground between the shafts.

Pandemonium! Ginty leapt out, ran to the front and stood staring down in anguished disbelief at his poor little mare. Bent-one scrambled in at one side of the cart to rescue Daphne, who was in danger of being strangled by the yellow scarf. Herbert tumbled out, struck his head as he went over and lay stretched out in the road, momentarily concussed. Andrew, who had been pushing at the back with his head well down, was taken completely by surprise and could hardly believe his eyes.

After a few minutes Herbert managed to get to his feet, shaking his sore head. Bent-one managed to haul Daphne down from the cart and set her free to graze by the roadside. Then all three joined Ginty and stood in a silent row as he struggled to revive his stricken mare. He tried to raise her, lifted her head, shook it, breathed into her nostrils, rolled back her eyelids and gazed into her eyes. But Black Cherry was absolutely and irrevocably dead.

For almost twenty minutes Ginty sat silently assimilating his loss. He had dragged himself up onto an old tree stump high on the nearby bank, and sat staring down numbly at the scene on the road below. Occasionally he raised his head, his long thin nose silhouetted like a blade against the sky while the Adam's apple in his skinny neck jerked up and down convulsively, though no tears came. No-one dared speak. At last Herbert, Bent-one and Andrew stirred themselves and began to take action. Carefully they disentangled the harness until they were able to draw the cart away from the stiffening corpse. Still Ginty did not move or speak, until at last Herbert, concerned that he would be late for work, took from the toolbox under the front seat two spades that were normally used for the digging of graves. Then he mounted the bank, confronted the hunched figure, coughed apologetically and asked, 'Where d'yew want her buried?'

'Buried! We can make money out of her – if we take her to the knacker's yard!' This anxious cry came from young Andrew, who had also climbed the bank and who possessed a flair for making money which was to serve him well in the years to come. It didn't serve him very well on this occasion though; Ginty was roused from his state of torpor, but only to give his son a look of withering contempt.

They found a spot by a pond where the verge widened, and took turns to dig. It took them nearly two hours for the ground was hard and stony, they hit a clay layer and Ginty insisted on digging to the depth required for a Christian burial, and twice as wide, to accommodate Black Cherry's outstretched legs. Soon carts began returning from the station, bearing yesterday's empty milk churns.

The bottom of the grave they lined with bracken, moss and dry grass. The body they covered with the plaid rug Ginty and Josh used to cover their knees when officiating at a funeral on a cold day. Finally they shovelled the soil back into the grave, then shaped it to Ginty's satisfaction and added a simple cross to mark the spot where Black Cherry had come to the end of her life's journey. Then Daphne was hauled aboard, the cart's shafts were propped up level on the nearest bank, Herbert and Ginty mounted to the front seat as of old and young Bent-one, with only time for one plaintive cry of 'Why me?' found himself between the shafts. He pulled with all his might at the front and Andrew pushed from behind, and so they made their way back towards home.

It took them another hour to reach the farm where Herbert worked. It was still quite early – about a quarter to eight – but Herbert's working day normally started at seven, so he was late. Gasping for breath and sagging with fatigue, Bent-one pleaded for a reprieve. For a few moments they all waited and watched as Herbert hurried up the drive to his customary Saturday morning job of cleaning out the chicken huts. If he was lucky, his employer would be having a little lie-in and not notice that he was nearly an hour late. If not, he would just have to work till one o'clock instead of twelve.

After a while Bent-one wearily picked up the shafts again with his raw and blistered hands, and on they went towards the village.

CHAPTER SEVENTEEN

'I don't believe it!' Miss Raspberry was standing at her balcony window, which overlooked the village green, fixing extra combs in her hair in anticipation of a strenuous day playing tennis. 'Windy – come and look! Come and see this extraordinary sight. A man instead of a horse pulling a cart. No, don't bother,' she cried impatiently, as Miss Gale began laboriously to climb out of her chair, 'you'll be too late. Don't sit down again!' she shouted. 'We've got to get down to the tennis courts now. Got to make an early start or we'll never get through all the matches.'

'Must I?' said poor Windy. 'I'd rather stay here really.'

'Nonsense. What on earth's the matter with you? Pull yourself together and stop being so feeble!'

Miss Raspberry had changed little in the past six years. She still looked like a gawky, overgrown schoolgirl. Strenuous tennis always brought out the worst of her rosacea, but her general health was as good as ever. Miss Gale, on the other hand, had definitely dwindled; her skin was so etiolated it was hard to see where her face ended and her scanty white hair began. Having no chin, she looked more and more like a mouse – a white mouse.

She was extremely frail, and was within a few weeks of being diagnosed with tuberculosis. It was obviously difficult for her to make the slightest physical effort, and she stood swaying. She longed to sink back again into her chair – but she dared not do other than follow her robust friend down the stairs.

Over the past six years the Cookley Green Tennis Club had gone from strength to strength. Today was a Tournament Day and already well attended by home and visiting players and other interested parties. Lady Madeleine was there, as were Stella and Stella's mother. Gerald had brought a party from Yorkshire who were all staying at Thickthorn: a preponderance of young and attractive girls, as usual, Stella sourly noted, without a single chaperone, so it was rumoured in the village. George was there adjusting the nets; he acted as coach, umpire and player. Ellen spent most of her time in the pavilion dispensing food and drink; she played sometimes, when someone was in need of a partner. All the while she had George in the corner of her eye.

Two semi-interested parties, brought there by a sense of duty rather than true enthusiasm, were Lord Summerfield and Brigadier Benson-Brick. They did the rounds greeting everybody they felt should be greeted, then swiftly repaired to the Black Bull for sustenance and to discuss the trouble in the Balkans and what to do about Belgium? 'Good God – look at that!' The brigadier, standing by the window holding a sustainer, could not believe he was seeing what he was seeing. Involuntarily he looked down at the drink in his hand and tried to remember how many he had had since breakfast – only three surely . . . or was it four?

'What is it?' Lord Summerfield hopped over to the window, swinging his gouty leg.

'Aaah . . . hem – nothing.' How to explain that you

thought you'd just seen a man and a cow in a cart, pulled along by a youth wearing a yellow scarf, with a boy pushing from behind?

'Something's got to be done about that willow tree,' boomed the brigadier. 'Wants clearing right away, in my opinion – encourages idleness.'

Indeed, Kenny and Jacko were fast asleep on it, propped up against each other, their heads drooping onto their chests. Jacko's little white dog with one black ear sat sentinel at their feet. Jacko's ferret had escaped and was snaking its way around under the tree trunk searching for prey. Kenny woke up as the sound of Bent-one's tortured breathing reached his ears. Staring open-mouthed, for he too could not believe he was seeing what he was seeing, he jabbed Jacko repeatedly in the ribs; they the two of them rocked and cackled and rolled about with langhter.

'Giddy up, old hoss! Cubby-whish! Steady you on, bor . . . whoa there!' they spluttered between gasps, along with other commands they had heard Old Ben use when out ploughing with his Suffolk punches.

'Woss happened to poor old Black Cherry then? Hev she dropped dead atwixt the shafts?'

Something in Ginty's frozen expression told them that this was indeed the case; they stopped laughing abruptly and simply watched as Bent-one, almost weeping with exhaustion and humiliation, painfully dragged his loath-some burden across the green. He felt the world was watching him, but attention in the village that day was focused almost entirely on the tennis courts. The cars and carts lined up alongside the walls and windows of the Black Bull were empty of their owners, who were already in the pavilion. Even the village urchins missed the treat of their lives as they huddled under the archway, looking inwards, watching and waiting for play to begin.

Convinced he would never be able to hold up his head in the village again, Bent-one struggled on, bundled Daphne out of the cart when they got to the piece of common land, and left her there. Then, gathering his strength in a Herculean final effort, he took the last fifty yards to Ginty's cottage at speed, rushed into the yard and dropped the shafts with such force and finality that Ginty was almost precipitated out of it. He shot forward and lay draped over the front rail like a rag doll, shouting and kicking his spindly legs in protest. But Bent-one had had enough. Shaking his blistered hands, then tucking them under his armpits for comfort, he turned and without a backward glance limped away.

Out on the road again, he began making his way back towards the village, but he was too worn out to go on. His bruised and blistered feet ached, his shoulders felt as though they had been nailed to an iron bar and soon he had to fling himself down on the nearest grassy bank to rest. Nursing his burning hands, he lay gazing at the sky and reflecting that now he would be the laughing stock of everyone in the three villages. News of his exploits as a horse would spread like wildfire; he would never live it down. He would have to emigrate! Yes – he would go home now, by a circuitous route, take the three gold sovvies out from under his bed and make his way to Yarmouth. There he would stow away on a big ship and sail to . . . to Canada. Of course! Join his elder brothers Jack and Reggie and work in the lumber camp. Then everybody would be sorry.

He could probably have gone back the way he came without attracting much attention, for everyone had gathered round the tennis courts at the back of Miss Raspberry's place of residence. Democratically, at her request, ordinary villagers were allowed, indeed encouraged, to come in as spectators. Few adults took advantage of this dispensation, but the village children spent a lot of time under the archway leading to the courts, playing, quarrelling, bouncing balls and doing handstands against the red brick wall.

They would hang about waiting for Miss Raspberry to play and to shout, 'Balls to you!' which she was in the habit of doing when she came to the end of her service and began patting the balls over the net to the next person due to serve. They would wait patiently for hours to hear her utter her innocent cry. George was never absolutely sure that it was innocent – but it gave the children carte blanche to rush out onto the village green and caper ecstatically about shouting, 'Balls to you!' The phrase was fast becoming a catchword in the village, almost respectable due to its venerable associations.

Today Miss Raspberry was one of those drawn for play in the first game, so there should not be too long a wait for satisfaction – except that Dr Weston, also drawn for the first game, was delayed, owing to the usual medical emergency. So George was asked to fill in the time coaching some of the older, less proficient, female members, namely Lady Madeleine and Stella's mother. He was to coach them particularly in return of serve. 'Gently! Gently!' Miss Raspberry whispered into his ear, for George had developed a quite stinging, often unreturnable, service. 'You'll frighten them to death – serve underarm . . . underarm!' George obligingly patted the ball over underarm.

'Good God – look at that!' exclaimed Gerald disgustedly. 'Calls himself a tennis player . . . the fellow's absolutely feeble!'

There were subterranean tensions other than those born of competitive sportsmanship stirring in the club that day. Gerald was irritated by the proximity of George and the remembrance of the unfinished business between the two of them over the subject of Neville's ear – he would have welcomed some pretext for smashing the fellow's face in, but he couldn't think of one, and the fact that the cad was so obviously a great favourite of old Raspberry didn't help.

Stella was irritated by the proximity of Gerald and the unfinished business between the two of them; by his blatant penchant for the company of younger girls and also by the fact that he looked quite stunningly attractive in his tennis clothes. It was intolerable that she had never been allowed the opportunity to explain, calmly and graciously, why all must be over between them; that she was destined for Neville . . . had been since childhood. Gerald appeared to have no inkling that his behaviour, his erratic attentions, might have compromised her. Suppose someone had seen them under the elm? She often returned, in her mind, to the frightening episode there. True, it happened nearly six years ago . . . but in the country people's memories were long. He simply never referred to the various times when they had . . . had . . . almost . . . overstepped the mark. He was definitely no gentleman.

Resolutely, she gazed up at the sky and decided that it showed every promise of delivering a fine and sunny day. As her gaze wandered it came at last upon the sad figure of Miss Gale, wrapped in a red rug, seated in an armchair on the veranda of the long, low, rather magnificent pavilion George had spent two years building in his spare time. Stella waved, mostly to show Gerald, should he be looking, that there were things other than him that interested her. Miss Gale made no response, for she was already asleep. A pleasant mood of tranquillity and relaxation settled over the courts as everyone waited for Dr Weston to arrive – a mood broken only by the gentle pok pok of George serving balls underarm.

Meanwhile, Bent-one, making his way home over the fields with frequent stops for rest, was almost at the end of his tether. Worn out from pulling the cart, his feet were so tender he could scarcely bear to put one in front of the other. He had missed a night's sleep, and had had nothing to eat since suppertime yesterday. When at last home appeared, he had no difficulty in postponing emigration to Canada until he had at least ascertained what his mother, Rose, was going to produce for breakfast.

On the workbench in his little shed, where he usually sat mending shoes, was the Saturday morning bundle of newspapers he regularly distributed throughout the village. Seven were already ordered, but the rest he would normally hawk round to likely customers. Today would be the day, he reflected, when the inhabitants of Cookley Green would begin to feel the want of him and would have to learn to do without him . . . without someone to mend their boots, run their errands, deliver their newspapers, do their odd jobs. And how would his mother cope with the loss of her youngest son, when she had never got over the pain of the three boys leaving for the Midlands and the north to find work, and Jack and Reggie emigrating? Tears rose to his eyes as he felt the full force of everyone's loss if he, too, went.

The tears, however, did not prevent him from registering, as he passed his workbench, something odd about the front page of the newspaper uppermost in the pile. One short sharp sentence in thick black print . . . what could it mean? Reading effectively was a skill Bent-one had never quite mastered; snatching up the top copy, he stepped down into the living room in search of his mother. There she was, kneeling on the rag rug in front of the fireplace, deftly poking out ash from between the bars. First thing every morning, when the fire was low,

241

she blackleaded the big iron range, where she did most of her cooking, until it shone. He had time to notice, before he thrust the newspaper under her nose, that a place had been laid for him at the table with bread and a piece of ham, and a double saucepan of porridge was bubbling softly on top of the range.

'What dew it say, Mother?'

His mother put down the poker, sat back on her heels and gave the paper her full attention. Was it shock, anxiety . . . fear, he saw in her face?

She took a moment before answering and when she did, what she told him had an electrifying effect on the exhausted Bent-one. Forgetting emigration, fatigue, his empty stomach, his sore feet, he leapt into the air and went capering round the room, yelping with excitement. Then he ran out of the door, snatched up the rest of the newspapers from his bench and ran out into the street. Yelling incoherently, he rushed down the road, stopping to shout over the wall at his father in his workshop. Josh was making a new wheel for an old waggon, carefully squaring the end of an ash felloe with an adze; engrossed, and of course deaf, he didn't even look up. So Bent-one ran on, round the corner past the shop where Ellen worked, along the front of the Black Bull and under the archway to the tennis courts, scattering all the children as he went.

Pok! Pok! came the sound of tennis balls from either side as he ran down the path between the courts. Up the steps he scrambled to where a number of onlookers and waiting players sat along the veranda of the pavilion, drinking glasses of Ellen's home-made lemonade or cups of tea. Starting at the left-hand end he began moving quickly along the line, talking excitedly, and selling newspapers like the proverbial hot cakes as he went.

Suddenly, he realized that the players on the courts

were ignorant of the proceedings. Turning, he pressed the front page of his last remaining newspaper close up against the netting surrounding the court. 'WAR IS DECLARED!' it declared dramatically. But there was no response; the players continued their game.

'What the devil is that stupid clod-head up to?' growled Gerald. 'What the hell is he shouting about?'

'Heaven knows,' said Stella, who had managed to manoeuvre herself onto the bench right next to Gerald, as he waited to play.

A moment later and the stupid clod-head was confronting them. Holding up his last copy, he pointed to each word of the big black headline with a grubby, blistered finger. 'War hev bin declared,' he read slowly, emphatically – and slightly inaccurately.

'War!' Gerald snatched the paper from him and swiftly read what there was to read on the front page. Then, lowering it, he stood for a moment in thought. From the corner of his eye he saw Lord Summerfield and the brigadier emerge from the back entrance of the Black Bull at the bottom of the courts, their faces rosy and smiling, the brigadier with his arm round his old friend's shoulders. It was obvious they were quite unaware of the morning's news. Gerald would be the first to tell them!

Here was his opportunity to renew contact with Neville's father, with whom relations had been somewhat strained of late. The cause lay with Thickthorn, of course, and Gerald's insistence that certain improvements he mooted were just what Neville himself would have wanted, had he been on the spot to give each project his consideration. Neville was due home on his third leave in a few weeks' time and there were certain enterprises dear to Gerald's heart that it was expedient to have well under way (ideally, finished) by then. But everything depended on the co-operation of his Lordship, and getting money – Neville's money! – out of the old sod was like trying to suck blood out of a stone.

Ignoring Bent-one's timidly outstretched palm, he stuffed the newspaper into the pocket of his striped blazer and turned to go, bracing himself for another taxing encounter with the miserable old skinflint.

'You haven't paid for the newspaper,' said George quietly from behind. He had done his duty with Lady Madeleine and Stella's mother and was happily on his way to Ellen's domain for a drop of refreshment.

Not paid? How dared he! The scoundrel! This was it – nemesis! This time that fellow was going to get what was coming to him! Gerald's chest puffed out like a pouter pigeon's and his face grew crimson with fury . . . but he hesitated. Wasn't that someone down below approaching his Lordship brandishing a newspaper? The scoundrel's comeuppance would have to be postponed for yet another occasion. Digging hastily into his blazer pocket, he took out a number of coins, thrust them into Bent-one's hand and went . . . swiftly . . . along the length of the nearest court and then down the steps in between.

He was out of luck. Miss Raspberry had just come to the end of her service. All heard the cry, 'Balls to you!' in ringing tones, as she started patting the balls over to the next person to serve. At this the children, in an ecstasy of delight, rushed out from under the archway and tore up and down at the foot of the courts screaming, shoving, shouting; and by this milling, squirming mass, Gerald, to his absolute fury, was engulfed. There must have been about thirty of them, but it felt like a hundred. He stood there, knee-deep in children, red-faced and striking out with his feet in all directions – until suddenly, as if in response to some covert signal, they all rushed back through the archway and out onto the village green. Too late for Gerald, though: at the far end of the walkway he could see Lord Summerfield and the brigadier in the act of seating themselves on a convenient spectator's bench, where they proceeded co-operatively to peruse a newspaper. He had missed his chance.

As for Bent-one, his great rush of adrenaline was petering down to its final dregs. He limped after the children into the archway, then had to stop to rest, propping himself against the red brick wall. Overcome by weakness after all his exertions, he slowly slid down, scraping off, as he did so, a flurry of leaflets pinned to the club noticeboard. On this noticeboard, in the months to come, would gradually appear the names of the dead – all the young men of the village and the surrounding area who, in a few weeks' time, would be marching off to the trenches in France, and would not return.

So the country was at war – but where, why and who with? Nobody knew. Many thought the Frenchies or the Ruskies or (dim memories of hearing of something called the Armada) Spain. There was no way of knowing. Newspapers were a luxury for the affluent few and, anyway, many older people couldn't read. And where on earth was Belgium?

Recollecting that there was a large world map stuck up on the wall at school (with the pink bits denoting the parts comprising the British Empire), Kenny, Jacko and Bent-one – once the latter had had a rest and a good intake of food – went forth to do some geographical research. The school, built by the Anglican Church in the 1880s with assistance from the Government, was of red brick, built to resemble a church, with a bell tower at one end. The bell was pulled each morning at ten to nine to summon pupils to their lessons. Narrow windows were set high up in the walls so that the pupils would not

be distracted from their studies by outside blandish-
ments. Even as adults and standing on tiptoe, Kenny,
Jacko and Bent-one could barely see into the gloomy
interior. However, they did see Bossy Bertha, who acted
as caretaker and cleaner, filling up inkwells for the
children in the higher standards, ready for work on
Monday. Simultaneously discouraged (Bossy Bertha was
not the kind of person you would easily presume to ask a
favour of), they shrank back and prepared to steal softly
away. But Bertha had spied the three heads above the
window ledge and promptly appeared in the nearby
cloakroom doorway, a daunting figure in her big black
apron and black button boots, a glass jug of newly
mixed black ink in her hand.

'What d'yew lot want?'

When they explained she said nothing, but simply
pointed at their feet and then withdrew. A few minutes
later three pairs of hobnail boots were lined up demurely
at the cloakroom door and, timidly, they ventured in.

The map was as they remembered, rather more faded
and dusty, but you could plainly see the many pink
bits denoting the extent and importance of the British
Empire. A small Union Jack drooped forlornly from the
two upper corners, and secured to the wall on one side
was a fly-spotted portrait of King Edward VII, yet to
be replaced by one of George V. Shuffling their feet,
blinking and scratching various parts, the three stood
studying the map. But Bent-one and Jacko couldn't read
very well and Kenny couldn't see, being long-sighted,
and by this time they had forgotten the name of the
country they had come to locate . . .

Not a very successful enterprise, it was agreed, as they
began making their way back to the village; hardly worth
the trouble of taking your boots off and having to put
them back on again. They should've consulted George,

he would've bin the one. George knew a thing or two, George did . . . read every book in the school, so 'twas said. On the way to becom'n' a teacher hisself, wasn't he? till he got chucked out. And he'd read all them books his mother brought from Thickthorn, when she married: three whole shelves full, so they'd heard tell.

George had indeed read and reread all his mother's books. He'd also benefited from his association with Miss Raspberry, who put her extensive, catholic collection of books at his disposal. She had at first tried to organize his reading, directing him towards writers with East Anglian associations. *The Rights of Man*, for a start, by Thomas Paine, born in Thetford. '*The Rights of Man*?' cried Miss Gale, aghast, in one of her rare moments of dissension. 'What are you trying to do – stir up trouble in this village?'

'Any harm in encouraging a young man to think for himself?' asked Miss Raspberry, innocently. Miss Gale was lost for words and knew no peace of mind until George had moved on to Crabbe and George Borrow. She was the more genuinely Quaker of the two and was not above putting her own favourite reading matter in George's way from time to time.

Yes, George would've helped, they all agreed, but where was he? They met Ginty on the little bridge leading into the village and thought to ask him, but he, white-faced and trembling, was in desperate search of Bossy Bertha. Molly – his beloved Molly – had at last managed to dislodge a child inside that she didn't want and was bleeding badly. No, she didn't want Bent-one to run for Dr Weston. He would be bound to abide by his Hippocratic oath and try to save the baby. Molly wanted Bossy Bertha to come and do what needed to be done.

As they tramped on, leaving Ginty scurrying off to the school for Bertha, Bent-one reflected that the onset of war and Molly's predicament might well turn out lucky for him. It might all occupy people's minds so they would forget his antics as a carthorse – then he needn't emigrate to Canada and the three gold sovvies could remain safely hidden under his bed.

June 1999

Now look what's happened – would you believe it! After all that stitching and eyestrain it's all off – the Summerfield Ball, I mean. The venue doesn't comply with the fire regulations. There was a fire there some years ago, apparently, so they don't want to take any more chances. There's also a rumour – don't know how much truth there is in it – that negotiations are taking place with a prospective buyer, so probably they don't want extra complications at this time.

Trouble is, I'd already asked the Head to accompany me; now I wish I hadn't, as he feels duty bound to take me out to dinner somewhere, because, he says, I'm so disappointed. Well, we all are. Everybody was looking forward to enjoying a spot of gracious living just for once. He's suggested dinner for two at the Marigold Inn.

It was dinner for three anyway, and a complete fiasco, as I knew it would be. The Marigold Inn, all old beams, horseshoes and rusty old agricultural tools hanging about, as I said, is run by an ex-music man from the BBC. At one end of the room, standing on a small stage, was a piano and some drums which Sammy, of course, found completely irresistible. There was to be music later, but the music Sammy produced was not to anybody's liking, and fellow diners were treated to the spectacle of their village infant teacher being unable to

248

control her own child. Neil had obviously decided not to intervene, but when it got to me chasing Sammy round and round the piano he rose, picked up my screaming son and plonked him down at the table, where he proceeded to gobble his food like the little animal he sometimes is. In the end he choked and brought up half his dinner all over the tablecloth. To make matters even worse, we were accosted, after the mess had been cleared up and as we waited for our second course, by a drunken yokel who wandered into the restaurant area from the bar.

'I seen yew,' he cried, leering into my face. 'I seen yew look'n' at them breed'n' bulls, t'other day. I know what yew wus a'wonder'n' – yew wus a'wonder'n' houw they dew it, wusn't yew?' I knew instantly what he meant but tried to pretend I didn't, which only made things worse, for he went on to be more explicit.

Between Cookley Green and the Marigold is a large meadow full of an assortment of different breeds and sizes of bull. They are staked out at regular intervals to prevent disputes, I suppose. They range from the small and stubby to the absolutely monumental and are used for the purposes of artificial insemination; the semen obtained from them is transported all over the world. Not a very fitting subject of conversation at dinner in a public place with people well within earshot, all, of course, listening intently.

'I know what yew wus a'wonder'n' – I know what yew're all a'wonder'n',' he began again, addressing everybody in the room now. 'Houw thaass done,' and he went on to describe in detail the whole procedure which, in case you're interested (well, of course you are – like he said, we all are!) is as follows. A metal frame, cow-sized and cow-shaped, with a cow's hide thrown over the back end, is presented to the bull. (Bulls must be pretty stupid, surely, not to notice the difference – perhaps they employ some potent and alluring pheromone?) The poor creature rises gamely to the challenge with his libido at full throttle and his pizzle at the ready – only to have, at the very last moment, a marauding human pop a hutkin over it and thus neatly steal his joy-juice . . .

All this was explained in a very loud voice and uncouth descriptive language and I must admit to being, for once in my life, extremely embarrassed. To make matters worse, I could see from the corner of my eye Neil's face slowly turning poppy red. He took out a handkerchief and proceeded vigorously to blow his nose. His eyes and his flaming cheeks bulged and I desperately searched for some way of easing his discomfiture . . . until I suddenly realized that he was not discomfited by embarrassment, he was killing himself laughing, or rather, killing himself trying not to laugh and the person he was killing himself trying not to laugh at – was me.

When Neil rose to pay at the bar I followed, determined to contribute my share, only to be seized by the shoulders and swiftly propelled in the direction of the outside door with a sharp resounding blow to my backside. 'Bugger off – I'm paying,' said Neil. I emerged from the inn to find that a rough westerly wind had got up and rain was bucketing down. I'd left Sammy inside. I just had to stand there in the rain and wait for them both to join me.

We set off back to the village in silence. Sammy, what with the rain and the tension in the air, began to grizzle and whine. Neil slung him up onto his shoulders and, heads down, we tramped on. When we came to the cattle-breeding station, there were the poor old bulls, tails turned to the wind, heads drooping, dripping wet and looking the picture of misery. I took care not to show any interest, but as we plodded on a low part of the hedge revealed a black bull of mammoth dimensions just on the other side. Unfortunately he also saw us and poking his great head over the top of all the nettles, brambles and barbed wire, he gave vent to a long, mournful, ear-splitting roar, as if to express his extreme dissatisfaction with the way things were in his world. Poor Sammy screamed and leapt up into the air in fright. Neil spun round just in time to catch him as he fell. We set off again, Sammy walking between us, to a chorus of roars and bellows, as all the other bulls in the meadow seized the opportunity to voice their protest. The noise was deafening; Sammy was terrified and clung in this instance, I noticed, to Neil's hand, not mine.

I was much occupied with the problem of what to say when we finally parted. 'Thank you so much for a thoroughly unenjoyable evening'? 'We must take care never to do this again'? The rain kept lashing down, warm summer rain – but wet wet wet! The wind blew itself into a fury. I had clapped my cream-coloured summer handbag on top of my head, holding it on by twisting the straps under my chin. I didn't care about the rest of me, I just hate getting my hair wet, as you well know. Well, we reached Fern Cottage at last, turned and stood looking at each other, dripping wet. He studied me gravely with the ghost of a smile hovering about his lips. Water dripped off the peak of his cap and the end of his beard. Then he stepped nearer and with a finger gently lifted the dripping brim of the handbag clapped on my head. Then, to my utter astonishment, he drew me close . . .

How can you describe a kiss without killing it? I just have to say I was so startled. He was so totally and unequivocally there – in a way you never were. Even in our most intimate moments I always felt part of you had slipped away and was standing on the other side of the

251

room watching. But then, behind Neil I sense a loving and devoted mum, whereas behind you are all those years at boarding school from the age of seven. What was it you learned there? Never wholly to emerge from your shell, carefully to keep yourself to yourself, for safety's sake.

Eventually I became aware of Sammy squashed between the two of us, his little moon face gazing up at us in astonishment. Neil bent and kissed him too, smartly on both cheeks. Then he walked jauntily away.

Andrew Gillson, our squire of the village, died last week. He went on his final journey on Wednesday in his lovely shiny black cart. It was taken out of its glass case specially for the occasion; it was what he wanted. It was always used for funerals, apparently. They couldn't find a suitable black pony and had to use a brown one, so things were not quite as he planned, but in the picture in yesterday's local rag you couldn't tell the difference.

Mrs Andrew, Christabel – remember Christabel? – is fixing up to go on a world cruise. Seems she's always wanted to travel but Andrew never would. Actually, everybody seems obsessed these days with going, or planning to go, on holiday. Nobody seems to want to work. Pearl says years ago people rarely went as far as the next village and of course they had to walk. How things have changed!

Now Christabel will have Andrew's money to spend. From rags to riches! I wonder if she ever thinks of her poor childhood and her evenings, when she was older, spent pleasing the customers at the Ploughman's Arms in some way or other. I hear she plans to go with another rich woman known as the Black Widow. She owns the house that Neil rents part of. They'll be like all the other merry widows, particularly American merry widows, travelling the world on ships, spending the money their husbands killed themselves earning. Strange to think of two old ladies from Cookley Green cavorting about together in far-flung places.

We've had several cases of headlice at school. A real throwback to older times, I thought, but apparently today's version is robust and thriving and becoming immune to modern treatment in the way rats are becoming immune to warfarin. Oh dear – bodes ill for the future! Hope Sammy doesn't catch them.

Next day (Sunday) Sammy and I got shot at and went in fear of our lives. I took my bike out with him on the back, and we went to collect specimens from the various crops growing in the fields. We missed the first crop while we were busy preparing for the village fête. The pea-binders came like great booming prehistoric monsters and droned all night harvesting the peas. They carted them off to the factory in the morning ('Picked to frozen in 2½ hours'). But now the corn in the fields was in ear and ripening fast; now would be the time to collect specimens so that the children could learn to identify and name them.

The first obstacle to our expedition was that yesterday's storm roared on through the night and brought down into the village street a large bough from the stag-headed oak tree standing next to where the smithy used to be. A group of village worthies were clustered round it trying to decide whose tractor to borrow to clear the thing away. Seems it fell just after midnight, narrowly missing a coachload of members of the WI on their way back from a visit to Windsor. I could see it was going to be some time before the tractor problem was resolved, the talking done and the bough cleared away, so I heaved my bike with Sammy on it over the lowest, most accessible part of the obstruction and pedalled away. The wind had dropped and there was no sign now of yesterday's storm except some big puddles, and leaves and twigs scattered over the road. It was a sunny summer day.

We quickly collected specimens of wheat, oats and barley and then some baby sugar beet that had some way to go before being ready for harvesting in the autumn. Then came a glorious stretch of linseed in bloom, so blue it looked as though the sky had fallen. Sunflowers were being tried out; global warming is thought to be creating here the kind of Mediterranean climate they need. Maize, just coming into ear, took up the last bit of space in Sammy's rucksack and, festooned with plumes of herbage, we turned for home. And it was then that I saw the board pointing to Thickthorn.

I must have passed it several times before and not noticed it. It had been pretty well grown over with ivy, but yesterday's storm had blown the leaves aside. Thick-thorn: once an important part of the Summerfield estate, sold off separately some time back, so I'd been told by Pearl, to an entrepreneur from London. I was curious to see it and the driveway looked enticing, long, narrow, winding, made shadowy and mysterious by tall mixed woodland on either side. The high canopy above us was almost overwhelming; we stopped and gazed up at it in wonder, so seldom nowadays do we find ourselves in the company of mature trees; so many, along with miles of hedges, have been cut down in the interests of efficient farming.

I walked on, pushing the bike with Sammy still in his little seat, clasping the bag of specimens and peering out at the world through a wispy assortment of corn stalks. Presently the lane became even narrower, lined on either side by giant, ungainly rhododendron bushes. They were past full bloom, a bit blowsy now, but still somehow magical. There was hardly a sound to be heard, only the soft rustle of wind in the trees. All the birds were silent, for the time for singing was over, they were probably busy feeding their young. As I was thinking how peaceful it all was, how far from the world's ignoble strife and all that, a shot rang out, just to the right of us . . . and then another . . . and something smacked into the bushes on the other side of the road, too close for comfort.

'Don't you dare shoot us!' I shouted, as a figure in camouflage gear, holding a gun, stepped out into the road in front of us. He was aiming his gun, not at us, I was thankful to see, but at the spot where his previous shot had landed. From here another man, in similar gear, suddenly rose from the bushes and set off hotfoot for cover, deeper into the woods with the other in pursuit. As the sound of their boots crashing through the undergrowth died away, there came more shots from further along the lane and I could see other figures dodging about among the trees. What on earth was happening? I didn't wait to find out, for there came another shot from our left and another missile struck the bushes close to where we were standing. Swiftly I swung the bike round, remounted and pedalled furiously away, back to civilization and safety. Recently local police raided an isolated farmhouse and discovered it to be a hideout for drug traffickers – could two rival gangs be shooting it out in Thickthorn Woods? Could it be an army exercise of some kind? One thing was certain, this was not the shooting season and anyway, these hunters seemed bent on shooting each other, not game birds.

Before we got very far our way was blocked by what looked to be a brand new hedge-cutting machine, shiny and brightly painted. It was turning itself round in the middle of the road to continue its attack on what had been one of the few remaining mature hedges to be seen in the locality. Both sides of the mainly hawthorn and holly hedge had been cut or rather mangled, and the machine now began tearing off the top. The result was obscene, with the bare, chewed-off ends of branches sticking out in all directions like the bones of broken fingers, and detritus from the operation lying inches thick all over the road. Efficient, fast and labour-saving – but not an achievement to be proud of, I thought, as the man in charge of the machine saw me and nodded. Should I try and tell him, over the roar of his engine, that men were trying to shoot each other in Thickthorn Woods? Could he do anything about it? I decided not, and pedalled on. I would call in at the Moon and Sixpence (once more prosaically known as the Ploughman's Arms), the first pub you come to as you enter the village from the west, over the little bridge. I would ask Fat Harry, the proprietor, what was the best thing to do.

I propped my bike up against the railings outside, left the rucksack on the saddle, took Sammy by the hand and walked boldly in. The lounge was crowded and a smell of the usual pub Sunday cooking filled the air. There were women here, but at the bar further in I was met by a barrage of male stares. Did I imagine concerted resentment in those eyes that I, a single female, should venture into this sacred male preserve? I had suffered this experience before, many times, since being on my own, but it didn't help. I was daunted as usual and cravenly sought a moment's respite by making for the loo.

They were outside across a paved yard, standing side by side like two sentry boxes trying to prop each other up. LADIES it said on the first door and underneath, feelingly: OH WHO AMONG YOU WILL EASE MY PAIN? and under GENTS next door, rather more succinctly: THIS IS WHERE THE BIG NOBS HANG OUT! Well, yes . . . there is a touch of poetry here, I thought, for as music is to the Marigold, so poetry and fine writing are to the Moon and Sixpence. Here the local literati meet to read and discuss their poems and short stories and other literary outpourings. Even Fat Harry, a rough-looking, red-faced fellow with a crew cut, a beer belly hanging out over his jeans and gypsy earrings, is an unlikely dab hand at versifying, so I've been told.

When I came back in he leaned considerately towards me over the bar and indicated that I looked as though I had something to say and that if I did, I should whisper it into his ear. This ruse instantly caused everybody round the bar to stop talking. So I said, very loudly, for the benefit of all, that I had just seen men shooting at each other in Thickthorn Woods, in fact they had nearly shot Sammy and me – ought not the police to be informed?

I very quickly became aware of grinning faces all round the bar; then came a loud guffaw and a ripple of contagious laughter began its travels, but was promptly quelled by a glowering look from Harry.

'Don't yew worry your poor little owd hid about that, my mawther, dew yew'll dew yourself a injury,' he said kindly. Now, although his family has long had connections with this locality, I know for certain he was born and brought up in Watford, but he prides himself on having gone native and acquired the East Anglian dialect. (Songs he has written, I've been told, rather resemble those by Norfolk's Singing Postman.) 'Thass only them owd London lot. They pay good money to cum down hair and go chas'n' round in them woods shoot'n' each other with paintballs.'

I crept out feeling a perfect fool to find that the wind had blown the rucksack down off the bicycle seat, our precious specimens were scattered all over the road and my bike had a puncture; no doubt a result of the hedge-cutting operation. We would have to walk the rest of the way home. It wasn't very far, but Sammy was getting tired and hungry. I gathered up the specimens, hung the rucksack on the handlebars and off we went. Halfway down the street we saw a group of people standing in a ring, staring up at the oak tree. Not the same people I had seen there this morning, surely? No, the fallen bough had been removed. This group, I now realized to my dismay, largely consisted of members of the parish council. Oh help! It was too late for me to turn and try and get home by a different route.

I gingerly tried to squeeze through at the back, without drawing attention to myself, as they all continued staring upward. I nearly succeeded but was pounced on at the very last moment by a grey-haired lady. Did I know that a bough had fallen in the storm last night and nearly hit a coach full of members of the Women's Institute? Obviously the tree was dangerous; didn't I agree that it ought to be cut down? I mumbled something about needing more time to think about it and wriggled past her, hoping I didn't sound too discourteous. Mrs Greyhair is quite a bigwig in the village. She's on the parish council, she's a governor at the school, is involved with the church and the Mothers' Union and runs the local branch of the Conservative Party – so I don't want to get on the wrong side of her! But I knew Sammy was fast coming to the end of his tether and would shortly be liable to disgrace both himself and me. So we hurried on.

At last we were back home and I quickly prepared a late lunch. Afterwards we went round to see Pearl, and just for once I was able to tell her something she didn't know. She knew Thickthorn had been sold but she had not heard about plans for a sports complex there with, eventually, a golf course, tennis courts, swimming pool, saunas and jacuzzis – according to Fat Harry. She also didn't know that paintballing was already in full flow.

'Well I never,' she said. 'There's always bin funny goings-on at Thickthorn, mostly nasty things,' she added, but she didn't elaborate on what those nasty things were. Just when you think you're going to hear something interesting she closes her eyes and won't say another word. Is she really as old as the century, I wonder? She certainly looks it, but I never dare ask.

So that's that. Now we're back home again. I've prepared all my lessons for next week as a supply will be taking my class. I'm going on a refresher course to bring me up to date with the latest demands of the National Curriculum, as I've been out of teaching for some time.

Here we are at the start of the last half of the summer term. I wonder how we two colleagues are going to conduct ourselves after that kiss, when I drop Sammy off at school tomorrow morning. We'll both be calm and completely professional, no doubt. Do hope I can rise to it and not come over all blushing and embarrassed like a silly teenager.

CHAPTER EIGHTEEN

Bertha got the baby out in bits and pieces, but Molly had died. They were both to have been buried in a pauper's coffin but Josh, after one look at Ginty's grey face, made an oak one free of charge. The baby's father was thought to be Dick West, as it had gingery hair.

Ginty was in a terrible dilemma; he wanted to give Molly a decent funeral but since Black Cherry had died, he had no horse. He began obsessively cleaning and polishing his black cart, and Bent-one, fearful that he was about to be persuaded into a repeat performance, promptly disappeared. He went and stayed with his uncle who kept the mill, resolving only to return when he judged the whole thing to be over. In the end Ginty had to borrow Kenny's little Welsh mare, the one who pulled the bumby cart. She was brown and white, fat, stumpy-legged and hairy and poor Ginty could hardly bear to look at her when he got her between the shafts.

His son Andrew was to drive the cart as Ginty wanted to walk behind as chief mourner, indeed sole mourner – for it appeared that all the men of the district who had keenly partaken of Molly's favours when she was alive, now found themselves heavily committed elsewhere.

Well, she was not respectable, but the meagreness of her send-off, the tendency among the rest of the villagers to consider her beyond the pale, caused Rose and George's mother to don their funeral gear, take poor little Chrissie by the hand and join in the sad journey to the Congregational chapel about a mile away at the eastern end of the village.

Although the month was August the weather had hit a bad patch. It was cold, the wind blew at almost gale force and as the coffin, to the sound of Chrissie's sobs, was lowered into the ground, it began to rain torrentially. They all got drenched and George's mother, proverbially, caught her death of cold – caught the cold which was eventually to lead to her death. She was concerned for Chrissie, now left alone in the world, but was soon too ill to act on her behalf. But Chrissie would be all right: she was to be taken in at the Ploughman's Arms and would be all set, in a few years, to provide the same valuable services as her mother.

Molly's cottage could now be relet. Hovel would have been a better description of it. Nevertheless, as the first few shovels of earth fell on the coffin, some of the poorest women in the village fell upon Molly's home and ransacked it. They grabbed old mats, hairless blankets, chipped plates, rusty knives (after all, Molly would have no more use for them), even the holey curtains which had provided so much free entertainment for dedicated voyeurs. Apart from Ginty and little Chrissie, no-one really mourned her passing, and life in the village went on as before.

The flush of fervent patriotism that swept the country when war was declared was slow to manifest itself in Cookley Green. People there were habitually wrapped up in their own affairs. The big events earlier in the century – the election of a Liberal government, the death of a king, the crowning of a new king – had little bearing on life as they knew it. The introduction of an old-age pension of five shillings a week probably made the biggest impact. So the arrival of an army recruiting unit on the village green one day aroused little response except among the children. People just hadn't the time to pay attention to it. Some of the harvest still had to be got in, potatoes lifted, fruit and vegetables picked, stored, jammed, pickled or chutneyed, carrots and beet clamped, firewood stored for the winter. The recruiting sergeant shouted himself hoarse to little effect, and the soldiers marched away somewhat subdued after forty minutes' energetic effort.

Lord Summerfield was incensed when he heard of this lack of response. He had just come back from more sophisticated parts where the recruiting drive was going apace and he was truly aggrieved to find the young men so remiss in Cookley Green. Well, both sexes, young and old, had often to be chivvied into regular church attendance; he would have to do something, somehow, to point any available young men of the district (and there were some, not all had left for distant parts to find work) towards their proper duty. Neville, due home just after Christmas, could undertake such a mission! Young himself, he would be able to make the right appeal, uphold the honour of the family.

Having solved the problem neatly in his own mind, his Lordship felt much more comfortable and set off the following day, with old and valued friends, on the season's first shoot. He wore himself out plodding about the fields, woods and marshland, stubbed his toe badly stumbling into a rabbit hole and was incapacitated by the subsequent attack of gout on and off until Christmas.

In the meantime more letters than normal began arriving for various families in the area; many versions of the same letter – from Coventry, Birmingham, Leeds, Halifax, Sheffield.

'Dear Mum (Dad, Grandma, Grandad, Uncle Cecil, Aunt Mary . . .)
Just a few lines to say I shall not be coming home for Christmas this year as I have joined the army. A lot of my pals kept enlisting so I thought I'd better do my bit. My new uniform is all right but a bit scratchy round the neck. They have cut my hair short, Mum, and I've got blisters from all that marching. Don't know when I'll be able to get home again. Will write again soon. Hope you are all well as it leaves me, your loving son Frank (Bob, Henry, John, Alfred . . .).'

Josh and Rose received a similar letter, rather later, all the way from Canada.

'Just to say we are on our way back to England, as we have joined the army. A recruiting officer kept coming to the timber yard trying to get people to join up and fight for the Old Country. He wouldn't take no for an answer. Don't know if we can get home for a visit, when we land. We'll just have to wait and see. Hope you are all well. Jack and Reggie.'

So while Lord Summerfield lay in bed waiting for Christmas and Neville to come, mulling over events and problems past and present, a military monster, rendered even hungrier by depletion of its forces in early battles, began another massive intake of fit young men, not just in Britain but all over Europe. Below stairs at Summerfield Hall, Christmas preparations, extended to encompass the young master's homecoming celebrations soon afterwards, continued unabated. Two miles away in Cookley Green, George's mother struggled to live, the sound of her tortured breathing rattling and rasping throughout the house. A combined effort from Bossy Bertha and Dr Weston pulled her through bronchitis and pneumonia, but she developed pleurisy and they could not save her. In the end her heart gave out and she died on Christmas Day. In the sudden silence it was as if the whole house had died with her.

Up at the Hall, relaxed after his enjoyable Christmas and munching his morning toast with his gammy leg propped up on a stool, his Lordship's thoughts turned to the exciting prospect of his son's imminent return from foreign parts. How long, he wondered aloud, should he wait before he could nicely introduce the notion of Neville organizing a local recruitment drive? A week? Ten days? Time enough for him to recover from his travels and settle once more into the comfort and familiar routine of home? A week! Ten days! Lady Madeleine rose in indignant defence of her precious single offspring: a month would not be long enough for her boy to recover from his suffering – from the heat, the flies, the filth, the fevers – not to mention the villainous Arabs, she added swiftly, neatly forestalling his Lordship's cry of scornful incredulity. 'We'd better stage a homecoming ball,' he said instead, cunningly, and noted with satisfaction how her face brightened.

This time the recruitment drive was a notable success. Everything went swimmingly, particularly in Cookley Green. Now there was a band, and behind the band a neat block of soldiers of the Suffolk Regiment marching as one to 'Speed the Plough' (played slowly), and behind the soldiers members of the Queen Alexandra Imperial Military Nursing Service with Stella, conspicuously not yet in uniform, bringing up the rear. Overnight there had been three or four inches of snow, but Kenny had hitched his little fat mare to the village snow plough and cleared all the local approach roads. So the marching feet made crisp contact with the stony road surface and the sound echoed back and forth with stirring effect between the blacksmith's shop and the low wall opposite.

Though he was deaf, even Josh became aware that something unusual was happening. He felt some vibration, thought it might be thunder and emerged from his workshop looking skywards for storm clouds – but thunder, with snow? He shook his head in perplexity, went back in, and quite missed the procession as it made its way down to the end of the street and swung smartly round the corner. Here the band changed thrillingly to 'Rule Britannia' as the soldiers and the ladies joined Neville and Gerald and local youths and onlookers waiting on and around the village green.

Perhaps Neville's voice sounded a little lightweight after the recruiting sergeant's stentorian tones, but this had the effect of causing people to move in closer the better to hear what he had to say, stamping their feet and banging their arms across their chests at times in an effort to keep warm. What he had to say was more or less what had already been said, but he was able to add an account of what he had seen as he sailed into port on his arrival home – troopships crammed with brave lads setting out for the battlefields of France, with bands playing, flags waving, people cheering, as they answered their country's call to arms – as every young Englishman must surely do who had blood in his veins . . .

Then it was Gerald's turn to speak of the effort and sacrifices being made in the north; of the factories, mills and foundries releasing their young men where possible to fight for the greater good; of the young women who

265

were taking their place in factory, mill and foundry – particularly in the munition factories. As for the Mothers of Britain . . . well, on behalf of the Mothers of Britain – but whatever Gerald had in mind to say of the sacrifices of the Mothers of Britain went unheard, for the band, probably deciding that enough had already been said, burst in gloriously at this point with Blake's 'Jerusalem'. When that came to an end, on a somewhat lighter note, Stella and the rest of the ladies, who had been occupying themselves putting up posters of Kitchener and his pointing finger declaring 'YOUR COUNTRY NEEDS YOU' and pictures of the women of Britain with the statement 'THE WOMEN OF BRITAIN SAY GO', gathered into a little group and sang, rather self-consciously at first but then with increasing vigour: 'We don't want to lose you but we think you ought to go . . .'

If only I could go, thought George, lounging with his hands in his pockets against the wall of the Black Bull, hunched deep into his jacket against the cold. How could he, now that his mother had gone, leave his two sisters with a father who, when he was not drinking himself into oblivion at the Ploughman's Arms, sat in his chair by the fireplace staring into space? Perhaps in April, when he had planted up the garden with all their requirements for the coming season and the next winter . . . but what about the season after if the war was not over by then? Everybody had forecast that it would be over by this Christmas – but that hadn't happened. He desperately wanted to go, anywhere, just to get away from here. Involuntarily he straightened up as the band swung gloriously into 'God Save our Gracious King . . .'

It was enough. Ginty was the first to sign. He had lost Molly and his little mare, he didn't like his wife or his son much either, for that matter. There was nothing left here to stay for. Though the general requirement was for young men in their late teens or early twenties and Ginty was well over thirty, his extreme skinniness made him look younger and no probing questions were asked. Two of Kenny's grandsons, fishermen home from Lowestoft for the weekend, signed next. Then a grandson of Jacko's, who normally worked at the mill. Then twin sons of Old Ben who were not yet even eighteen. (Old Ben was not really old – he had just always seemed so.) Next, smiling bashfully and writing his name slowly and with difficulty – Bent-one. Well, it was a long difficult name – Bernard Bartholomew Ableman.

Lord Summerfield was extremely pleased with the recruitment campaign when the results filtered through to him from the three villages. Fifteen from Cookley Green alone! A fine result, with at least half of the young men working away elsewhere. He felt the same kind of satisfaction and inner content that he experienced after bagging a goodly number of birds during a particularly successful shoot. He was not quite so sanguine when he found that two of the volunteers were under-gardeners at the Hall – but they could probably be replaced fairly easily by younger boys. He was seriously displeased, however, when he found that he was also faced with the loss of Edward, his youngest footman, for this presented him with a problem of considerable gravity and cast him into the depths of gloom. What was he to do with the intransigent Dolmon if Edward was not going to be there to look after him now that he was incapacitated?

Edward, driving Dolmon for a check-up with Dr Weston in the governess cart, had come upon the recruitment drive in Cookley Green just as proceedings were drawing to a close. Dolmon was in splints and a head bandage, having broken an arm and a leg and knocked himself out during one of several carefully contrived suicide attempts, due to a heart broken by the elusive Becky. This time he had swung out from the fifth step of the main stairs on a rope hooked round his neck, carefully knotted to be non-slip, just as the family came out from dinner. The rope, tied to a wrought-iron candelabra fixed into the ceiling at the foot of the stairs, was set at just the right length for his feet to touch the floor, should help not be immediately forthcoming. Unfortunately the candelabra was not as securely fastened as it looked and the whole thing fell on top of Dolmon, knocking him unconscious so that this time he was not even able to enjoy his moment of high drama. However, he was soon recovered enough to make the utmost of his injuries.

Edward pulled the pony to an abrupt halt at the edge of the snow-covered green just as the band and the soldiers and the ladies were beginning to reassemble, ready to move on to the next village. He saw in a flash that here, if he was quick, was his way of escape from the onerous task of looking after the impossible butler. The job had been assigned to him, he knew, because of his amiable nature, his low status in the footman hierarchy and because nobody else would even consider taking the old devil on. He had only a few moments, it was clear, to make his bid . . .

He leapt out of the cart and raced across the grass. A few brief words, a quick flourish of the pen – and it was accomplished. He had signed away servitude: the prize was his! His face aglow, he ran back to the cart, climbed in, ignoring Dolmon's ferocious stare, flicked the reins and trotted merrily on to Dr Weston's. In a few days, with a joyous smile on his face, he would be joining the ranks of all the other fit and eager young men marching away to death on a shilling a day.

The show was over. The soldiers, the band, the ladies

were ready to move on – to Summerfield and then Silverley. Spectators began to drift away. Soon only George remained, reluctant to go home and be reminded that his mother was no longer there but six feet underground in the Congregational chapel graveyard. He leant against the pub, his hands lightly clasped in front of him, one knee bent with the sole of his foot resting on the brick wall behind him, idly watching as the recruiting unit moved off. This time the members of the band were carrying, not playing, their instruments; the only sound was that of marching feet. He saw one of the women followers break rank and come walking in his direction. He saw that it was Stella, and lowered his knee to let her pass. As she did so she murmured something unintelligible and thrust something into his hands. He gazed after her in surprise and then looked down to see what she had given him: it was a white feather.

On the other side of the green Neville and Gerald sat waiting in Gerald's latest car, allowing enough time for the marchers to reach the next village before joining them for another recruiting effort. This time the car was a two-seater Cadillac, not as impressive as the Rolls Royce 40/50, but at least it was Gerald's own. The two of them sat for some time animatedly congratulating themselves on the success of the campaign so far. Eventually they fell silent and sat watching fat snowflakes drift down past the windscreen.

'Did you hear what that fellow said?' ventured Neville at last.

'What fellow?'

'Oh – some fellow in the crowd . . . just as you ended your bit. He said, why don't you two go?'

They fell silent again for quite a long spell. If the Government brought in conscription (it was to do just that a year later almost to the day), Gerald's father had assured him that he could get him exempted on the grounds of his indispensability as manager of their latest venture – a fair-sized munitions factory. But was that what he, Gerald, wanted? He thought not – but it was something to ponder. He discussed it with Neville. Freedom, excitement and adventure beckoned. Next morning they got up early and drove forty miles along snow-packed roads to the nearest army HQ to sign on for officer training. There was some uncertainty due to Neville's want of an ear, but when it was proved that hearing was unaffected, the way was cleared and everything went ahead without further delay.

When Lady Madeleine found out what they had done she was, as the saying goes, beside herself with anxiety. The heat, the flies, the filth, the fevers, to say nothing of the villainous Arabs, were now as naught in the face of this new threat to her beloved son. The Embassy, seen up till now as a harsh, impersonal establishment where her boy's needs and idiosyncrasies could never be properly catered for, she now saw as a veritable haven of security far from the violence and danger of war. But for his Lordship's instigation of a local recruitment drive, he might well have gone on contentedly and completed his stint there, assured that he was doing as valuable a job as anyone for King and Country. By the time he finished the war could well have been over; he could have come back home, married dear Miss Benson and begun gradually relieving his father of the most burdensome of his problems, while also learning to manage the whole estate. This idyllic picture of the future so gripped her that she wept openly, and vehemently blamed his Lordship for the loss of it.

Lord Summerfield had to admit (but only to himself) that Neville's decision to enlist was something he had not anticipated and did not want. It was not necessary, he thought angrily. 'What the devil did the boy want to go and do that for?' he muttered to himself.

Yet somewhere in the back of his mind a still small voice asserted that if it was right for other men's sons to risk all for King and Country, then it was equally right and dutiful for his. But he did not, could not, admit that through his own action his son's – his only son's – life could be endangered. He blamed Gerald, who, right from their Cambridge days, had exerted too much influence over Neville. Had he not predicted, from the very first, that no good would come of their association? This was simply an extension of Gerald's presumptuous inter-ference at Thickthorn that he had had continually to battle with during the six years of Neville's absence. The fellow was an absolute thorn in his side! Yet somewhere, deep down, the question of his own culpability rankled, the more potent for being repressed, so that he was angrier than he might have been when he summoned Edward to interview.

Edward had been expecting to be called. He paused for a moment outside his master's study door to arrange his features in a suitable expression of melancholy regret, before responding to the bellowed order to enter. He saw at once, from the bright red cheeks, quivering moustache and hard blue stare, that he was in for a bad time. So he approached diffidently, gazing contritely at the floor, his whole demeanour suggestive of a cringing spaniel, aware that it was guilty of something though it knew not what. Yet in his heart he felt triumphant and dared not raise his head lest his eyes betray his joy and exultation: he was free! He had burst the chains that bound him – escaped the abominable Dolmon and his Lordship's constant and demeaning demands.

Wringing his hands a little in the way he sometimes did when under stress, he stood and waited for the storm to break. When it did, it was on so many fronts at once that he was soon quite unable to discern the crux of his Lordship's grievance. Loyalty was mentioned, or rather his lack of it, in contrast to his father's long years of faithful service; dereliction of duty; the perfidious effect of a unilateral decision taken without regard for the burdensome consequences that others would have to shoulder . . . It all went on for so long and with so many permutations that Edward got quite lost – until it suddenly burst upon him, like a thunderclap, what his Lordship's real problem was: what the devil was he to do with Dolmon with Edward gone?

The interview, in the end, resolved itself into this simple question. Having padded the proceedings out to preserve his dignity and authority, his Lordship in desperation simply asked if Edward had any suggestions as to who would be the most suitable person among the household staff to take on the task.

'Becky?' suggested Edward innocently – and had the satisfaction of seeing his master about to burst a blood vessel. Well, of course, everybody both above and below stairs was aware of the ongoing saga of Dolmon's suicidal obsession with Becky; of Lady Madeleine's demand that Becky be allowed a bolt on her bedroom door and that Dolmon be moved to the other end of the house; that his Lordship had stamped his feet in a rage and retorted that if servants were to be allowed to have a bolt on the inside of their doors, where would it all end? They could smuggle in a supply of food, lock the door and declare themselves on holiday! And NO he was NOT going to move Dolmon, because if he did there would be no end to his bad temper, sulks and tantrums. He would sack him, yes, he was ready to do that; but in Lady Madeleine's family, as she had reminded him more than once, when you took on a servant you took him on for good or ill, in sickness or in . . . She had never let him hear the last of getting rid of Kenny Ling! So no, he would not be sending Dolmon packing: it was stalemate.

In fact, sacking Dolmon was the last thing his Lordship wanted to do. To begin with, there would be the question of a reference, and Lady Madeleine would insist on a glowing one. Furthermore, not just in his Lordship's social circle but also in more elevated circles in London, Dolmon was the focus of perennial interest and speculation. He could well imagine a reference proffered by him getting into the wrong hands and going the rounds to gales of derisive laughter. Better to keep one's problems to oneself. Other people, he thought bitterly, had butlers who glided unobtrusively about as if on castors, whereas he was stuck with Dolmon, from whom there was no escape. He felt much afflicted, like Job. He sank even lower in spirit when he realized he had dismissed Edward without even wishing the lad good luck and God speed, as he went forth to risk all in the service of King and Country. Thoroughly disgruntled, he stumped along to the drawing room, hoping for a cup of something light. He could have done with a stiff drink, but it was too early and Dr Weston had said to ease up on the alcohol and rich food, unless he wanted another fat foot.

He opened the door of the drawing room and to his dismay saw there his wife and Stella, deep in conversation, obviously agitated. He tried to back out swiftly – but it was too late. They both descended on him.

Did he realize what he had done? Had he thought of the possible consequences when he began the recruitment drive? Why couldn't it all have been left until Neville had gone back at the end of his leave? And, as he gazed at them, driven back against the doorpost like a stag at bay, 'The ball! The ball! Neville's homecoming ball!' they

273

cried, almost in unison. Hadn't he thought . . . didn't he realize . . . the ball would have to be cancelled! Stella's face was white with shock and strain.

As well it might be. She had ridden all the way from Highlea that morning on the splendid grey gelding her parents had given her for her twenty-fifth birthday. She had spent the hour the journey had taken her coming to a firm decision about Neville and her future. She would allow him just this one last leave to declare himself. If there were no developments beyond the occasional cuddle and intermittent hand-holding, she was going to cut her losses and switch her interest to Gerald. Never mind his lack of breeding and vulgarity. He was rich, or at least his father was . . . and he was a man! Her heart quickened at the thought of how, when they danced together, she could feel the vibrancy of active desire coiled within him like a spring, quelled only, she felt sure, by a mammoth effort of will. She delighted in taunting him to the edge of a breakdown of his defences and savoured the feeling of power it gave her. But Gerald sensed in her a will as steely and implacable as his own, which put him in a great fright. He was not the first man, and would in all probability not be the last, to determine to confine his interest to malleable young girls who would gaze at him starry-eyed.

And where were they now, her two stalwart lovers? thought Stella, viciously gnawing her last good finger-nail to the quick. Down at Thickthorn arranging for the place to be looked after during their absence, packing up for the drive to London tomorrow, for Neville to explain his change of plans and put things in order at the Foreign Office. And then – to war! She had lost them. Not one – both. There was nothing else for her to do but enlist in the Nursing Corps and join them in the war effort, a decision she had deliberately delayed in the hope that

Neville would make a declaration. But he never would – she saw that now. What she had been clinging to all these years was nothing more than a dream. She rode back to Highlea in a state of black depression. She did not know it, and it was as well she did not, but she had just joined the ranks of thousands of other young women, in Britain and all over Europe, who, as a result of the ensuing slaughter of young men on the battlefields, would go manless and childless into the future.

An atmosphere of tension and expectancy hung over the three villages in the next few days, as parents faced the prospect of their sons leaving home (some had never previously gone beyond the perimeters of their village). Mothers wondered how on earth their dear boys would manage the small everyday tasks of life that they had always done for them. Sons lay in bed at night contemplating the future with a mixture of elation and dread. Most found there were last-minute jobs to be done. Ginty polished his cart yet again and for the last time and then stowed it away in his best shed. Naomi, his fat, flat-faced stoic of a wife, busied herself as usual with the washing she did for people who could afford to pay. She had never been the recipient of much of his affection or attention – Molly had had that – so she didn't expect to miss him when he left. Rose went about her housework silent and withdrawn. Except for Herbert, who was doing essential farmwork, she was losing all her sons, even Bent-one, the youngest.

Bent-one had two worrying problems.

'Tell me again, Mum – which is my left leg?' When she told him, he clasped it tightly in both hands and ran all the way down to his father's workshop where he painted his left thumbnail and his left big toenail with orange (dragon's blood) paint. No, he wouldn't be able to see this toenail when it was inside his army boot, but he could see his left thumbnail and know without a doubt that his left foot was straight down under it.

He was very much taxed by his other problem – what to do about the three gold sovereigns under the mattress on his bed? There were two double beds in his bedroom from the days when seven brothers had slept there head to tail. What would happen to the room when he was gone? Mightn't his mother fly into a frenzy of spring-cleaning, throw out the extra bed, flounce, clean and turn the horsehair mattress, under which nestled the precious gold coins in their long grey knitted sock? Where could he hide them, safe and sound, until his return?

That night, his last night, he still had not solved this problem. Leaning out of his bedroom window in his nightshirt, he gazed down at the moonlit street below. Traces of snow still lingered. The whole village lay in a chill winter's sleep. A thin straggle of smoke rose from the forge chimney and drifted up among the branches of the nearby oak. From the marshes behind his father's workshop a snipe flew across the night sky, buzzing melodiously, and an owl in the oak tree, where it yearly raised a brood of owlets, answered with an ear-splitting shriek. It was too cold to linger at the window; he climbed quickly into bed, pulled the chilly bedclothes up to his chin and lay frowning into the darkness. What to do about the precious gold sovvies? Presently he found the answer, turned and with a smile on his face he fell asleep.

Late June 1999

Well, I did blush and felt an absolute fool, as soon as I met Neil at the school door. He pretended not to notice and carried it off rather well, I thought, by handing me an old log book he had found in one of the cupboards. Perhaps I'd like to look at it, he suggested, grinning, if I got bored on the computer course.

I was a bit worried as to how Sammy would react at having a stranger for a teacher instead of me. I'd carefully explained to him what was going to happen, but as you know, you can never be sure how much he's really taken in. However, Neil made parting easy by taking him off quickly to feed the school rabbit, so I was the one left feeling a bit disorientated. Sammy and I have rarely been parted, and, as well as that, Neil has shaved off his beard and moustache and looks ten years younger. Rather handsome, in fact: nice teeth, healthy-looking, clean-cut, *kissable* mouth was what, despite my best efforts, sprang irresistibly to mind, causing a fresh flood of colour to go creeping up, I felt, to my very ears! I kept my head bent and pretended to be studying the log book as I walked away.

It seems the school was a dame school in the beginning, providing lessons for those who could afford to pay. Then came lessons at the vicarage under the auspices of the Anglican Church. Finally, some years (eighteen to be exact) after the Education Act of 1870 stipulated that elementary schools were to be built in all districts not already satisfactorily provided for by religious bodies, the present little red-brick school was built.

The log book dates from 1888 till just before the Second World War and provides a vivid picture of the life of ordinary villagers during those years. One of the first things that struck me was the odd names of some of the pupils: Christmas Bell, Shed Royal, Forrest Pine, Heffer Dawnbrake, Needy Sizer along with other more common and biblical names. Most were children of farmers and labourers, craftsmen, tradesmen or shop-keepers, whose forebears all had connections in and around the village.

Today's children are a much more mixed assortment, with connections all over the place. They possess every conceivable toy, have never known a time without television, take to computers like ducks to water and often holiday abroad in exotic places.

However, things are not quite so simple as I first thought. The children are sweet, but some of them have troubles – a new man in the home who is not their father, or a succession of such men. In two instances it was the wife who absconded, leaving the children to be brought up by the fathers. (Pearl was scathing about this: what sort of a woman goes off and leaves her children? She's not a woman at all!) Twin boys in Neil's class have accumulated eight sets of grandparents, a fact they constantly remark on, as if they can't make up their minds whether it's something to be disparaged or a mark of real distinction.

School attendance in the old days was haphazard, with children being called on to help in the harvest, pick up potatoes, scare birds, pick fruit, or collect stones to clear fields for ploughing. Some families had one pair of shoes for two children, who took it in turns to come to school. All went home to dinner at midday, sometimes quite a distance, the reason for the long two-hour dinner break. If it rained, few came back for the afternoon session for want of suitable rainwear. Children would be absent because their boots needed mending; girls would be kept at home to look after younger siblings on Mondays while Mother did the washing and on Fridays when she baked for the weekend.

Yesterday's pupils were poor, ill clothed, perhaps not that ill fed in summer when much food could be home grown, but winters were hard to get through. Every year deaths were recorded from TB, scarlet fever, diphtheria, whooping cough and complications arising from measles. Others were affected by rickets or permanently crippled by polio – childhood diseases that have been more or less eradicated now. Let's hope they never come back.

There was something in the log book about George, who was at one time pupil-teacher at the school. He was thought to be a bad influence for some reason not recorded and he got the push. Must show this bit to Pearl and see if she can shed any light on the matter. She's gone all cagey on the subject of George: I've a feeling there's something she doesn't want me to know.

The saga of the dangerous oak tree is gathering momentum. News of its proposed removal and the ructions this has caused in the village has filtered into the local press. Yesterday (Saturday – I am writing this as usual on Sunday night) a contingent of Greens appeared in the village at ten o'clock in the morning. They joined hands and danced, as far as they were able, around the tree. Then they tried to stage a protest meeting in the middle of the village green, with placards and a loud speaker calling for clemency for the noble oak. They arrived on the green just as Sammy and I came out of the one remaining shop on the corner (there used to be three shops). At the same time, a group of morris dancers, clad in their traditional gear and carrying two-foot wooden poles, emerged from the Moon and Sixpence opposite.

It looked as if there was going to be a battle for possession of the green, but no – the morris dancers quickly took centre stage and the Greens, along with other interested spectators and children, formed a respectful circle and waited for the dancing to begin.

To the accompaniment of lumpen music from a giant ghetto blaster, the morris men began: stamping their feet, slapping their knees, the bells on their cross-gartered legs tinkling, clashing their wooden poles together. Our dancers were all ordinary Englishmen, keeping alive an ancient English tradition which, did I not agree, was wholly commendable? Well, I would have agreed but for the fact that something had momentarily stunned me: I had just recognized one of the dancers – Neil, smiling merrily as he clashed his stick, slapped his knees and spun round like a whirling dervish. I suddenly realized – this all ties in with the maypole dancing: here he is making another effort to preserve yet another ancient English custom!

A moment later the ancient English custom was interrupted by the thunderous arrival of a great black Range Rover, followed by a Willys jeep, from down the road that leads to Thickthorn. They roared up to the very edge of the green, causing the nearest spectators to remove themselves with all speed. Then, rather more slowly, both vehicles turned right and began making their way more carefully along the back of the ring of spectators, to draw up finally under the windows of the Black Bull. Five young men in army camouflage uniforms wearing face masks with visors like knights of old, carrying guns and with ammunition dangling from their belts, jumped out of the Range Rover, and four young men similarly attired stood up in the jeep and gazed over the heads of the crowd at the strange spectacle on the village green. Unperturbed, the dancers danced on. The four young men jumped out of the jeep and, followed by the five from the Range Rover, threaded their way through the ring of spectators to get a closer view. They were this week's consignment of paintballers from Thickthorn – I could tell because various parts of

280

their clothing bore splodges of variously coloured fluorescent paint, where they had been successfully 'potted' by their opponents. As the Marigold is to music and the Moon and Sixpence is to literature, so is the Black Bull to the huntin', shootin' and fishin' fraternity and also, since very recently, the intrepid paintballers from the big city. The local hunt meets regularly outside the Black Bull in winter, so I was told by my informant; often objectors stage a protest and the police have to be called.

Today, disorder had not been a problem – so far – but now the paintballers could not forbear from taking the mickey, jeering, cheering and guffawing . . . until one of them could not resist thrusting out a foot and tripping up the nearest dancer as he flew by. It happened to be Neil, quiet, kindly, gentle Neil – who instantly turned, and, grasping his pole, advanced on his tormentor with an expression of aggression and fiendish delight that I would never have expected to see on his face. Abandoning the dance, the rest of the morris men at once took up the challenge and advanced on the paintballers brandishing their poles and spoiling for a fight. The paintballers saw they were outnumbered and retired hastily to the safety of the Black Bull, where they were shortly to be seen standing on benches, drinking their beer and following events through the window.

The morris men had come to the end of their repertoire. All fired up, they were ready now for another old English custom, one particularly associated with East Anglia – the noble sport of dwile flonking. (A dwile is any bit of rag used for mopping up the floor or clearing drains or even something worse, with which you wallop your opponent with all your might.) Fat Harry brought forth a bundle of odorous old rags and a pail of what looked to be slops from washing up the beer mugs, for there was a layer of yeasty-smelling scum floating on the top. The morris dancers whipped off their shirts, untangled their cross garters, dipped their dwiles and set to.

They had formed into two teams but, try as I might, I was unable to discern the rules of the game, if there were any, or the method of scoring. There are rules and structure to this game, I now know, but this time it seemed just a free-for-all, for soon onlookers began to join in and then there was a definite suggestion of old scores being settled. Some of the children followed their elders and pulled off their T-shirts to use as weapons, Fat Harry's supply of dwiles having run out, I even saw Sammy wielding a sock he had found in a pile of discarded clothing.

The fun was infectious; too much for the watchers inside the Black Bull to resist. Next moment they were to be seen cutting up, with a great knife the like of which they all wore in their belts, one of the tablecloths much prized by the proprietor of the Black Bull for its erratic (and erotic) pattern of rampant black bulls. He remonstrated, but to no avail – they ripped the cloth into sizeable pieces, then streamed out, dipped their weapons, plunged into the melee and started laying about them thick and fast as Fat Harry kindly came out with another bucket of slops. The first was used up, much of its contents now forming a big muddy patch in the middle of the battleground.

I'm getting fonder and fonder of this place, I thought. What a way to get rid of all stress, resentment and tension! How much more tranquil afternoons in the office would be if you could spend ten minutes every lunch hour walloping the boss with a wet rag! No need to go to a counsellor with your emotional problems, except perhaps to give him a good walloping . . . and think how your average MP would fly about doing his job if he knew he could be subjected to regular dwile flonking by his constituents . . .

The general air of happy abandonment was contagious. I have to admit that when a small boy from Neil's class, whom I had occasion to reprimand last week for coming to lunch with filthy hands, took his opportunity for revenge by swiping me across the face with his revolting dwile, my one thought was to acquire a similar weapon and get after him . . . Just at that moment there came a tremendous clatter and crash. Neil, locked in combat with the biggest of the paintballers and wielding his dwile with the utmost ferocity, had overreached himself; he lost his footing in the soft mud and fell backwards, striking his head on the rim of Fat Harry's latest bucket of slops. It tipped and he landed with his head inside it, the contents flooding out all over his face. Then he lay still, concussed – or drowned.

Providentially, as if on cue, a cacophony of sirens sounded as a police car followed by an ambulance came caterwauling down the street. Somebody, obviously a newcomer unfamiliar with Cookley Green's little ways, had alerted the police to the fact that violence had erupted during a demonstration by the Greens in defence of the threatened oak tree and was fast getting out of control. Two policemen climbed out of the car and after overseeing Neil being stretchered into the ambulance, noticed what appeared to be a number of walking wounded oozing blood. However, on further examination the blood turned out to be red paint, liberally spread about by flying dwiles from the paintballers.

Things had gone flat now and people began gathering up their belongings and making for home. The Greens had had such a festive time they had forgotten about the oak tree and they marched away singing, back to the bicycles and motorbikes they'd left at the other end of the village. The police departed, finding no actual legal transgression to have taken place. Neil emerged from the ambulance with his head bandaged and declared himself fit to walk home. Sammy and I took the bucket and the dwiles back to Fat Harry and then made our way home. So ended an eventful Saturday in tranquil, sleepy Suffolk.

Later that evening, after I had regaled Pearl with a lively account of our doings, I felt I had a duty to check on how Neil was feeling after his mishap. Concussion can sometimes result in problems later. I had never been to his place, but it was not hard to find – a pleasant walk on a summer evening. It was just past Chalfont Manor, a granny annexe attached to one of Andrew Gillson's executive-type monstrosities.

Neil's part had a separate entrance and his name on the wall at one side, but to my surprise his door was opened by a black-haired (dyed, I thought), vividly made-up woman. The Black Widow? Christabel's supposedly octogenarian travelling companion? Why, she wasn't old at all, not much older than me, but, I have to admit, far better turned out. Pneumatic, too . . . and she was quite brusque and proprietorial. Was I a friend? A member of the family? Was Sammy my son or was I one of the village childminders? No, I said lamely, Neil was just a colleague and I was concerned lest there should be repercussions from his injury. No, she said firmly, he was fine. He was going to be perfectly all right for she lived next door. He was not well enough to receive visitors of course, but I had no need to worry. He was in safe hands – hers.

Routed, I departed. I know I'm not very big, it's one of the reasons why I chose to teach small children, with older ones I think it helps if you're on the tall side – but by now I felt so slight a puff of wind could have blown me clean away.

Sammy didn't catch them, I did – the headlice, I mean. Had to have a day off dousing my head in some evil-smelling stuff from the chemist's: the last defence, so I've heard.

CHAPTER NINETEEN

1915

Spring came; the sun shone, the birds sang, and soon the recruiting unit made another round of the villages and this time garnered in George. He had just had a blistering row with his father over his sisters being bundled off to live with Josh's brother and his wife, and easily succumbed to fervent patriotic rhetoric and the stirring strains of a military band. Desperate to get away from a home which now only contained his father, he joined the residue of other young men of the district who, thrilled to be noticed at last, marched off eagerly to fight for a country not one square foot of which, George could not help thinking, did they or were they ever likely to own. So they went off to fight for those who did own it and found themselves in the grip of a system which depended on unquestioning obedience to those above. It was a system which was anathema to him, with worse to follow: with his rooted aversion to killing anything un- necessarily, he was being trained and equipped to kill his fellow man. It was a situation entirely of his own making and he bitterly regretted his lapse of judgement. He resolved to go no further down that road. He spoke to his commanding officer, and made his position clear.

They also had it in writing. He had chosen to volunteer, and he claimed the right to resign. Now in his quarters, he piled up all his equipment and most of his uniform on his bed. Then, wearing just his boots, socks, trousers and shirt, and with his army jersey tied by the sleeves round his waist, he climbed up onto the roof of the hut nearest to the boundary fence. Taking a deep breath, he jumped onto the fence as near to the top as possible, then scrambled up and over it. He landed on his back on the other side in a clump of thistles, and stood up prickled and festooned with fluffy seed heads. Brushing himself down briskly, he set off for Cookley Green with a song in his heart.

It took George only two days to walk there, with one night of discomfort spent sleeping in a damp straw stack wishing he had not discarded his army jacket and great-coat, for the night turned out quite chilly for late August. He arrived home in the middle of the afternoon, hoping not to encounter his father, whom he had not forgiven for sending off his sisters. The village was deserted. The gate to the cottage was open and there in the yard stood the donkey, still hitched to its cart, eating great mouth-fuls of his mother's oxalis. It had probably unhooked itself from its tethering post as usual and made its own way home – which meant that his father was probably in the Ploughman's Arms and likely to remain there for some time.

The house seemed cold and unwelcoming. Dead, with-out the glowing presence of his mother. Quickly, he went into his bedroom and changed into his working clothes. Then he bundled up all his army gear in a large piece of sacking – his boots proved to be the biggest problem – and tied the parcel with a piece of binder twine from a bunch that hung from a nail in the garden shed. He attached to it a home-made label addressed directly to a

Major Bendrick: he was anxious not to be accused of stealing army property. He would leave the parcel with Ellen at the village shop and the carrier could take it to the station first thing in the morning.

He was ready to go now, but as he made his way towards the gate the donkey stopped eating, turned and looked fixedly at him, a string of herbage dangling from each side of its mouth. Was it surprised to see him after three months? George thought it more likely it was thirsty and was mutely asking for a drink. Setting down his parcel, he went over to the well in the corner of the yard and, seizing the handle, let down the bucket at a rattling good pace. It hit the water forty feet below with a resounding smack and immediately submerged instead of floating gently on the surface, as often happened if you didn't let it down with sufficient force. Steadily he cranked the brimming bucket back up, as he had done countless times before, ever since he'd been tall enough to reach the handle. Then he unclipped the bucket, extracted the usual couple of struggling earwigs, and set it down before the donkey.

Leaving her to drink, he wandered round to the back of the cottage to see how his father was coping with the vegetable garden. Most of it, he saw at once, was a mass of weeds, with just a few patches of new-turned earth where his father had dug up early potatoes. But the carrots, turnips, parsnips and swedes George had planted so carefully before he left in the spring had not been hoed or singled out, and were smothered in weeds. Cramped for space, many had already bolted – gone early to seed. But did it matter, he wondered, now there was only his father to feed? The two girls were no doubt being well looked after by Josh's brother and his wife at the mill. Having no children they had been very happy to take in the two girls.

There was the new problem of where he was to stay now he was home – not with his father, that was out of the question, and the last thing he wanted was for Miss Raspberry to know he was back and offer him accommodation. Nor did he want to make any demands on Ellen and her family. He was determined to be a burden to nobody and to involve no-one in any repercussions resulting from the unorthodox way in which he had left the army. And there probably would be repercussions . . . At least the donkey was being well looked after, he saw, when he looked in the little shed where she was stabled. The floor had been swept clean and a row of sacks stuffed with straw for bedding stood against the end wall.

Putting the bucket back on its hook above the well, he said goodbye to the donkey, picked up his parcel and set off down the street. The village still seemed dead. There was nobody about and he was glad. He didn't want to be questioned about why he had returned; at the moment he felt he hardly knew himself.

When he came to the shop at the corner, he found Ellen busy with a customer. He could see between the shelves of articles in the window that she had her hair up again in the way he didn't like, and was wearing something dark. She was busy weighing something on the scales, chatting to her customer; this was not the time to contact her. He walked swiftly on, past the windows of the Black Bull and the front of Miss Raspberry's residence, and then in under the archway leading to the tennis courts. He stood for a moment leaning against the wall, then placing the parcel beneath him he slid down onto it and sat with his back to the bricks, hugging his knees, waiting, brooding and uneasy, for Ellen's customer to depart. He was in trepidation lest he encounter Miss Raspberry, who would demand why he was home again. She had not approved of him going in the first place – for how was she to manage the tennis courts without him? And anyway, he didn't even know, nobody did, she said, what the war was about. To which he had replied that joining the army was the best way of finding out.

But he was no nearer knowing. It seemed you were not expected to ask, or to want to know. He had encountered men crippled at Gallipoli and listened with incredulity to their tales. It was beyond him to understand how Britain was being defended by landing troops on a beach in a far-flung country, with the enemy shelling them from the cliffs above. He was reminded of long ago when he lay at the top of the sandpit firing at the helpless rabbits down below. All those lives wasted . . . and for what? The rabbit's eye, which he hadn't thought of for many years, oozed out of its socket and slowly descended on its bloody string . . .

He straightened up restlessly and looked about him – and saw something he had not noticed hitherto: a sheet of paper pinned to the club noticeboard on the wall opposite. He could see it was a list of names with a black border round the edge. With a dreadful feeling of foreboding he scrambled to his feet.

It took him some moments to realize that Gilbert Henry Nathaniel Ginton was Ginty – nobody had ever used his real name. Ginty was dead, never to be seen in the village in his smart black cart again. Death had come to Old Ben's twin sons on the same day. Edward the young footman's bold flutter out into the wide world had ended almost before it began. Rose and Josh had lost two of their sons and the blacksmith had lost his apprentice. All this in the three months he had been away. Now he understood the stillness as he walked down the street; the silence from the smithy; Josh's workshop's half-closed doors. The whole village was in mourning – yet here he was. He sank back with his head in his hands. Later he was to learn that a cousin of his in the Sandringham contingent that fought with the Norfolks at Gallipoli had just disappeared along with many others. Everyone in the village, he thought, must be suffering from grief and shock. Worse was to follow, of course, in the next three years.

Later that week, Lord Summerfield was taking tea informally with Lady Madeleine in the drawing room. He was standing at the window, making one of his swift surveys of his estate, when he saw something stirring in the reed bed on the far side of the lake. A small group of soldiers, surely? They were apparently combing the undergrowth and slowly making their way towards the boat shed at the western end of the lake. He gave a startled exclamation, which he immediately turned into a cough, for any mention of soldiers or the war was enough to send Lady Madeleine into a paroxysm of anxiety over Neville, from whom they had not heard for nearly four weeks. He took a sip of tea, then peered out for a better view, while trying to convey the impression that there was nothing of special interest out there.

What could be the meaning of the activity? He had given no permission for army exercises on his land. He would send Edward, who was young and fleet of foot, to find out what was happening. Then he remembered that Edward was no longer at his, or anyone else's, beck and call. He sighed heavily. Cracks were beginning to appear in the smooth running of his world. Two of his under-gardeners had just joined up . . . and his long-time estate steward who lived in Silverley was at home ill, following the news of the death of his son. He would have to fall back on the one infallible source of information, the servants, in particular the kitchen staff. It was always a matter of puzzlement to him that the kitchen staff, who rarely seemed to venture far from their working environs, even on their few but legitimate days off, always seemed au fait with everything that was going on in the three villages.

Placing his half-empty cup back on the tray, he mumbled something unintelligible and set off for the kitchens. Lady Madeleine was so distraught she scarcely noticed his departure.

The kitchen staff, taking tea themselves in a rare moment of relaxation at the long pine scrubbed table, looked up startled at his Lordship's sudden appearance. An unusual occurrence, it made them nervous and probably more voluble than they would normally have been. Oh yes, they knew what was going on. Military police had been in Cookley Green for several days, the men staying at the Ploughman's Arms, the officers at the Black Bull. They were after a deserter who, as everyone knew, was hiding out at the end of the lake in the boat shed. He was from Cookley Green. Nobody had actually told them where he was, but someone had suggested they follow the girl who worked at the village shop on the corner, who was visiting him once a day and taking him food.

Lord Summerfield was incensed. To think that a deserter was hiding out on his land! He was ashamed to hear that it was a local man who had so little concern for the defence of his country and so much for his own welfare. The quicker the wretch was apprehended the better . . . he deserved to be horse-whipped! No doubt the army would soon catch him. If he knew what was good for him, he would never dare show his face in the district again! He fulminated on in this vein until he ran out of breath. His audience continued to gaze at him attentively. They said nothing, for they had deduced that, as usual, their opinions were not called for.

Red-faced and still breathing hard, his Lordship stumped back towards the drawing room – only to be confronted in the middle of the marble-floored entrance hall by the ominous figure of Dolmon.

'A letter for you, m'Lord.' He held out the usual salver with one letter on it. A letter, not from Neville, his Lordship saw in a flash, but from . . . oh, horror of horrors . . . from the War Office!

Lord Summerfield glanced at it – and quickly looked away. When he looked again he found it was still there. Reeling slightly, he went to the nearest window and began examining the sill closely for signs of woodworm. Dolmon followed and with a look of beady intensity again proffered the letter. Lord Summerfield recoiled and moved away, this time towards the main door, where he sank down heavily on a hard ladder-back chair standing close up to the oak-panelled wall. Dolmon followed and, tipping the salver slightly, watched as the letter slid gently into his Lordship's hands. The old man stared round the room for a moment, then, drawing a deep breath, he confronted his ghoulish oppressor.

'GO!' he snarled and gave the butler a look of such ferocity that Dolmon at last was quelled. He went . . . straight to the kitchens, still limping from his fake suicide attempt with the candelabra.

His obsession with Becky had subsided somewhat since Lady Madeleine, working on the old adage that out of sight is out of mind, had sent Becky to work for her sister in London for six months. However, three months of near normal behaviour from the problematical butler had not been enough to lull the rest of the staff into true tranquillity. The row of faces on either side of the table looked up as Dolmon entered the room. A tense and uncomfortable silence fell as they gazed at him, fingering their teacups and shifting in their chairs.

With an air of solemnity, he approached the nearest end of the table and stood gazing sternly down at his captive audience. A lengthy silence was interrupted when Heather, Becky's stand-in, a thin, highly strung girl of about fourteen, burst into a fit of giggles before she found the sense to thrust her fist into her mouth. Dolmon gazed loftily at the kitchen clock and waited for quiet before announcing, with fitting gravity, that there had come what every household in the country, rich or poor, great or small, daily dreaded – a letter from the War Office! His Lordship was sitting in the entrance hall, afraid to open it. Lady Madeleine was in the drawing room, unaware as yet that it had come. It was undoubtedly to inform them that the sole heir to the Summerfield estate was dead . . . killed in action.

Gasps of dismay greeted this, as yet unsubstantiated, announcement. Highly strung Heather burst into noisy sobs and was sharply shushed by the cook. Dolmon waited once more for calm. Then, drawing out the empty chair at the end of the table, with doleful exactitude he seated himself, clasped his hands together, eyes closed, and bowed his head. After a moment of hesitation, everybody followed suit.

In the entrance hall Lord Summerfield sat gazing at the letter and did not, could not, believe a word of it. There must be some mistake. His only son could not have gone through that dark door to nothingness and he not know it . . . feel it . . . in his innermost being. Neville was lying somewhere, injured. He had lost his memory . . . forgotten his identity. Like a flash of light in the darkness an answer came to him – Neville had left the army and made his own way home! He was down in the boat shed hiding . . . afraid to face the wrath of his father. But he felt no wrath. Patriotism, duty, courage, cowardice . . . what did they matter? At that moment he would have gladly given everything he possessed for his son to be still alive . . . back on home ground . . . down in the boat shed. Safe.

He sat on, the letter in one limp hand. Sat on for another twenty minutes and knew, at the end of that time, had to admit to himself . . . that this was not so. His legs buckling under him so that he had to stop at intervals to gather his strength, he made his way across the hall towards the drawing room and Lady Madeleine, holding in his hand the letter that he thought in all likelihood would kill her.

Thus Summerfield Hall joined the ever-growing number of grieving households that already existed throughout the land. But this was only the beginning. Soon conscription rerestored the depleted forces in the battlegrounds and the war went on for three more terrible years. At last it was over, and those lucky enough still to be alive began to come home.

July 1999

Haven't got round to this journal for a while. Been off school suffering a bout of summer flu. Missed the annual school outing – the supply had to take my place. Sammy missed it too as I couldn't let her take on the extra responsibility of him, he can be a bit difficult with someone he isn't used to, as you well know. I went back too soon and was knocked out again for another week – haven't been getting enough sleep. I keep settling him down in his own bed but he wakes up and creeps back in with me. I put him back but after a few minutes, in he comes again. I've hardened my heart – one of us has got to give in and it isn't going to be me!

A strange thing happened on Friday. The tree surgeons came to trim our ancient oak and make it safe so no more boughs threaten to fall on members of the Women's Institute. Sammy and I walked down the street to see how they were getting on. That old tree must have stood there for over a hundred years. Shading the horses as they waited to be shod. Sheltering George and Ellen as they finally plighted their troth and George carved their names into its bark – still clearly visible. The tree must have listened to the sound of marching feet during the two wars, and stood swaying loftily as poor Bent-one perished among its branches . . .

There was a hole at the top of the tree, at the base of one of the biggest boughs, where, ever since anyone can remember, tawny owls have nested. Knowing that the bough would have to come down, Neil has made a nest box for the men to fasten near the original site and everyone's hoping the owls will accept that as next year's des res. The bough with the big hole in it had just been sawn off and was being gently lowered to the ground on ropes as Sammy and I arrived on the scene. 'This is where Mother Owl reared her babies,' I said, once they had settled it at the side of the road, and we bent and peered into the hole. Sammy thrust in a hand and brought out some dried sticks, old feathers and a cluster of tiny bones. Then, to my surprise, he pulled out a small leather pouch covered in muck and mould, carefully oversown along one edge. One of the workmen lent me a knife, I slit the stitches . . . and out rolled three gold sovereigns, looking as fresh and shiny as if they had just been minted!

What an extraordinary thing to find in an owl's nest! Nobody can think who they could belong to, or who put them there. Until further enquiries have been made they've been left in my keeping, as I, or rather Sammy, found them. I've put a notice up under the archway to say money has been found in a leather pouch, but not how much or where, or that it is in the archaic form of gold sovereigns. Sammy has a verruca.

Another week has gone by and there will soon be little left of this term. No-one has come forth yet to claim the gold coins, so on Friday at the parish council meeting I brought the subject up. If they were never claimed, I said, why not put them towards some worthy village cause? Like the War Memorial Fund, I suggested, straight off the top of my head. Must have floated up from my subconscious, I think, looking back – I've long been curious about this mysterious fund, over which there seems to be a collective conspiracy of silence. I was hastily commended for my suggestion and the meeting ended abruptly with the whole thing being held in abeyance, in time-honoured fashion, till the next meeting. Seems to me I've heard this song before, I thought. Well, by then it should be clear whether anyone has genuine entitlement to the money. That's as far as we've got at present. In other words, not very far.

I walked home with Fat Harry and inadvertently learnt more about the chequered history of the fund – at least from around the end of the Second World War – than I had ever managed to before. What happened after the First World War seems lost in the mists of time, or rather, I suspect, has been blanked out in local folk memory. But Harry was quite clued-up and emphatic about what happened after the Second World War, for it concerned his uncle. He was one of the returning heroes when, in 1946, the subject of the War Memorial Fund came up again for consideration.

The terrible losses of the First World War were, thankfully, not repeated in the Second. Nine local lads went to war in 1939; seven returned. The two who were lost had gone to live in Lowestoft some years previously, to work on the fishing boats. When war came they joined the Merchant Navy, where there was heavy loss of life from the activities of German U-boats. When the subject of a war memorial came up for reassessment, it became apparent that Cookley Green suffered from a deficiency of dead heroes. Were the two who had gone to Lowestoft to be counted?

Taking a firm grasp on the situation, the seven surviving heroes got on their bikes and went to Lowestoft and, by means of the latest in box cameras, procured irrefutable evidence that the two poor lads who went down with their ships were already commemorated on a memorial there. So what to do with the money? Why wait for yet another war? Why not reward the living heroes – surely now the way was clear? Nobody could remember what the original fund was worth but it must have been accruing since 1919, when the money was first collected. Who knew to what heights it had risen?

I certainly didn't, though I have to say curiosity had driven me to scour through what parish papers were in my possession in an effort to find out. All I found was that a separate committee of ancient ex-parish council members meet every February to check on its progress. But nowhere did I discover any report of their findings. Maybe it's another of those items held in abeyance in perpetuity?

Rumours, Harry said, flew round the village at the time. The money could be divided between the returning heroes to the tune of £50, £70 . . . even £100 apiece! At a time when farmworkers were battling for £4 10s a week, this must have seemed riches indeed. Too much, said Fat Harry bitterly, for other people to bear. Jealous, people were, he said. Why, with that money his uncle, an ex-paratrooper who miraculously survived the landings at Arnhem, could have abandoned his horse and cart, bought himself a small lorry and greatly extended his household goods and ironware round . . . but it was not to be. Those who were in a position to decide fell back on the premise that legally the money must be used for the specific purpose for which it had been originally collected.

There then followed a series of meetings in the village school which were better attended than any parish council meeting before or since. Everybody was concerned as to what was to become of the money. It has to be said – I got this later from Pearl, not Harry – the returning heroes thoroughly disgraced themselves in the end. They rose in a body, shook their fists, stamped their feet and shouted: 'WE WANT OUR MONEY!' The dust rose in such clouds from between the ancient floorboards that people began to choke and had to take refuge outside. The meeting broke up with nothing being resolved and the whole problem being held in abeyance ever since.

Strangely enough, it's the dust rising in clouds from between the ancient floorboards that convinced me of the truth of this version of events (there are other versions), for I remember Neil telling me that when he first took over the school and tried out country dancing with his class, the dust was such that they were all nearly asphyxiated and several children were away ill the next day. So that weekend, he hired a machine and sanded and sealed the floor. So there you are. The most likely version, I think, of what happened to the War Memorial Fund. I must say I find all this absolutely fascinating!

*   *   *

Another week has gone by. This has been a sunny summer, but that's pretty usual apparently in East Anglia, which is flat, I'll grant, but has these great big beautiful blue skies.

Something weird is going on at Summerfield Hall. I took my class for a nature walk on Thursday because the tiles in the infant cloakroom were being replaced. I decided we should go out into the countryside in search of tranquillity.

We marched smartly up the avenue of trees leading to Summerfield, the children looking like miniature members of the French Foreign Legion, their sun hat back-flaps flapping. I planned to do our favourite walk – past the Hall by road as far as the ice house and then back by the footpath alongside the lake. But before we'd got far Sammy began to limp and several of the other children began to look flaked out – it was a pretty hot July day. So we went down the drive to the east gate, the first entrance to the Hall you come to, intending to get straight onto the footpath along the southern side of the lake. It's the route I usually like to take coming back, but the ground would be softer there for Sammy's tender foot. Right at the other end of the lake is a clump of balsam poplars where we could rest in the shade and take turns to dip into the water to see what we could find.

The east gates stood wide open and we had just walked through them when down the drive behind us, looking like a funeral procession, came a fleet of shiny black cars – limousines, the front one with a flag on the bonnet whose insignia I was unable to recognize. Foreigners? Pop stars? Royalty? Jumping nimbly onto the bank at the side of the drive, we stood in a row, for all the world, I thought, like an assembly of estate workers

300

welcoming home their feudal lord. (Had I a forelock now would have been the time to pull it.)

As the cars swept by I briefly glimpsed hooded, black-clad, female figures in the first two. In the third car were young girls also wearing some sort of headgear. The last car drew to a stop about fifty yards into the park and out tumbled a number of black-haired, dark-skinned boys of no more than ten or twelve. They were dressed in colourful shorts and gaily striped T-shirts. They charged round shouting excitedly, as children will who have suffered a long journey in a confined space. The car slowly drove on again and after a moment the boys sorted themselves out and hared off after it. What on earth was happening? Nobody in the village can tell me anything about it. Anyway, that was the end of the excitement for that day.

Later I said to Neil that I thought the new tiles could be a sign that the school was due for another reprieve – surely no such expense would have been incurred if it is scheduled to close next year? But he says at the governors' meeting last week, Mrs Greyhair (who now has a blue rinse!) tripped over a broken tile in the infant cloakroom when inspecting the loos, and sprained her wrist clutching at the coat pegs for support. She insisted, 'Something is to be done. At once!'

Neil says the school is due to carry on for at least another year, so I suppose our jobs are secure till then. We only need three or four couples with young children to move into Cookley Green and we could keep going indefinitely. It would be such a shame to close yet another village school; it really takes the heart out of a community, and then there's the problem of ferrying what children there are to schools elsewhere.

Another really warm week. It's getting near the end of term and the children are tired and fractious. The heat is keeping down over East Anglia a pall of industrial pollution drifting in from the Continent, according to Anglia television, making everyone feel ill. Well, I suppose that makes a change from our own industrial pollution that sometimes drifts down from the north or, nearer to home, the stench from battery chicken farming going on about a mile away.

The two children whose mothers absconded have fallen to bits. The little girl, who is only five, would like to spend all day sitting on my lap. She follows me everywhere. When I go to the loo, she puts her hand in through the gap at the bottom of the door and holds on to my shoe. The boy is less demanding but actually in a worse state; he takes nothing in, just sits twiddling his hair, waiting for his mother to come back. She was once a pop singer, and achieved a measure of success until marriage and two children put paid to her career. I'm told she's gone off to try her luck at the holiday camps along the coast – maybe she'll return when the season is over. The flip side of women being encouraged to do their own thing, become someone in their own right rather than just a wife and mother, is that it obviously can result in wrecked lives for children.

Pearl says such things never happened in her day. Real village women, she said, would never have dreamt of leaving their children. It was all these strangers moving in, changing partners, getting divorced, that were ruining everything. Does she mean me? Am I still a stranger in this village? What does it take to be accepted, I wonder?

I've found out what they've done with the war memorial money – nothing. It must still be around somewhere, quietly accumulating. Somebody really ought to bring the matter up again for discussion at a parish council meeting. It's a real hot potato, so one thing's for sure – I won't be the one to broach it!

I'm busy every evening now writing school reports for the few pupils I have. Sammy, like the rest of the children, is tired and fretful – lack of sleep because of the light evenings. Haven't made much progress getting him to sleep in his own room, but I'm still trying.

I suppose if I really wanted to make waves I could start trying to find out what happened to the missing acre! I could ask Fat Harry whether he knows anything about it. Come to that, I could ask him to tell me all about George. Actually I think I'll leave it to Pearl to tell me in her own good time.

CHAPTER TWENTY

1918

Of the seventeen young men who went to war from Summerfield, four returned; of the eighteen who went from Silverley, five; from Cookley Green, the smallest of the three villages, only three of the twelve who went came home at the end of the war. Josh and Rose lost another of their sons – Jack came home for a brief visit, grey-faced and uncommunicative, then left for Canada alone, Reggie having been buried in pieces somewhere near Vimy Ridge. Bent-one arrived home weeping and continued to weep. He was missing part of his left arm, which had been amputated at the elbow. The arm had been crushed against a wall when he valiantly tried to restrain a horse that had bolted with a cart full of medical supplies.

He was regarded as something of an oddity when he went to enlist. His anatomical peculiarity aroused considerable interest and his bashful inability to explain the reason for it drew the attention of one of the chief medical officers, who took a fancy to him and wanted him on his team as a kind of mascot. So Bent-one spent the war years behind the lines working in a field hospital, fairly safe from danger of death but not from the sight and sound of injured men.

Towards the latter part of the war, he was sometimes sent out onto the battlefield to collect the injured and the dead. Numbed, by now, by the horrors of human suffering, he found the dreadful spectacle of dead and injured horses more than he could bear. And when he came home, he could not forget them. However, before long Miss Raspberry offered him work on the tennis courts. Unused during the war years, they were sadly in need of an uplift. There were simple jobs he could still do with his one arm, so he stopped weeping and began to cheer up. She took him on as a kind of stopgap, while she waited for her favourite, George, to return. But George was a long time coming; he was sitting out his latest prison sentence for refusing military service in Gabarie Prison, Egypt, where his regiment was stationed during the latter stages of the war.

The soldiers Lord Summerfield had spied making their way towards the boat shed arrived to find their quarry missing. George had left the previous day and Ellen had gone with him. They had decided to get married. Wanting no truck with any of the local chapels and churches – anyway they probably didn't have time – they went by train to Gretna Green, got married over the anvil in the blacksmith's shop and then began a slow journey back home, with George doing odd building jobs on the way. He had had time now to consolidate his position in his own mind: the war was a madness with which he wanted nothing whatever to do. He was a builder, not a destroyer. Yes, he had volunteered, but he'd had second thoughts and claimed the right to change his mind . . .

The profligate expenditure of young lives in the early stages of the war meant that the supply of eighteen- to twenty-year-olds began to run out. Older men were called for, and soon the Conscription Act made it evident where a young man of George's age should rightly be. He went into a small market town one day to buy drain rods, was seized by military police and returned in hand-cuffs to his regiment. Ellen was left to make her own way home, back to her old job in the village shop.

The army has time-honoured methods of breaking the will of any recalcitrant member jibbing at military discipline, and it used them all. But George possessed the kind of will which hardens irrevocably in the face of opposition. It would have been so much easier to have acquiesced, but he was constitutionally unable to do other than hold on to his convictions. He felt at all times alone in his opposition to the war, but in fact he wasn't. Members of the Bloomsbury Group and a fair number of dissident intellectuals had a voluble spokesman in Bertrand Russell. Quaker pacifists had Fenner Brockway, who fought for the right to have conscientious scruples concerning war service taken into consideration. Possibly as a result of such efforts, George was brought at last before a military tribunal to state his case.

Perhaps if he had claimed solely religious scruples, or even that he heard voices from above proclaiming Thou shalt not kill! he would have received a more sympathetic hearing. He was ready to work as hard as any man for the good of his country, he said, but he was not prepared to kill for it. To the much-used question: then what would you do if a vile Boche assaulted your sister? he replied that that was for him to decide if and when it happened. Was he a pacifist? Was it this war or all wars that he repudiated? Yes, he was against war as a method of settling differences between nations. It was uncivilized. There had to be a better way. (But some poor fellow centuries ago, he found himself thinking, tried to teach a better way, and look what happened to Him.) So far as he could see, he said, this war was madness and the

306

frightful loss of young lives an absolute crime and totally unacceptable. Was he then presuming to question the strategies of top military decision-makers? Yes, he was; from what he now knew of military decision-makers he wouldn't trust a single one of them to lead him to the privy.

To speak the truth at all times as George had been brought up by his mother to do may sound commendable, but is seldom wise. Inevitably, he soon found himself back in his prison cell lying naked on the stone floor beside the uniform he refused to put on, his legs kicked black and blue by fellow conscripts under orders to persuade him to march. A few relished the task of forcibly dressing him, manhandling him out onto the parade ground, then thumping and kicking him back and forth in an effort to get him to co-operate, while the NCOs stood by, grinning. But a number of the new conscripts, he noticed, were ashamed, unable to meet his eye. They had not yet been indoctrinated and brutalized enough to carry out such orders with an easy mind.

*   *   *

Nearly three years passed after the Armistice before he was finally released, the army probably delighted to be rid of him. He returned to Cookley Green in midsummer, unsteady on his feet, with a staring look and weighing nine and a half stones instead of his usual thirteen. He sensed a simmering resentment in some of the villagers, and before long was to receive two more white feathers to add to the one given to him by Stella, the day when Ginty, Bent-one and the others signed on. Well, he didn't expect to be welcomed with open arms by those who had lost sons, brothers, fathers, husbands at the front, but he was most apprehensive as to how he would be received by Josh and Rose, who were his in-laws now he and

Ellen were married. Appalled to hear they had lost another of their sons, he decided to face up to them first and quickly made his way to Josh's workshop.

Both doors stood wide open, the riot of congealed paint on their exposed inner sides brighter and more fantastical than ever. The smell of linseed oil, paint and coffin varnish was as it had always been, but Josh was not there. Somewhat daunted, George made his way slowly back up the sloping yard and along the front of the little cottage, which had once been alive with children. The door of the lean-to shed at the further end was open and after a moment's hesitation, he walked in. Here, Bent-one normally sat at his bench mending shoes. His rickety stitching machine was still there, his lasts, tools, spools of thread, strips of leather and a pile of boots and shoes waiting to be mended – but no Bent-one. He saw that the door into the cottage was ajar, pushed it open and stepped down into the living room.

There stood the long narrow table in the middle of the room, covered with the familiar orange chenille tasselled cloth. Round the room, backed like sentinels against every available stretch of wall, were the ten chairs hand-made by Josh, each a mute reminder of the child who had once sat there. On either side of the big black range were the Windsor chairs used by Josh and Rose. On the floor between them lay the rag rug made by Rose from the family's cast-off clothing . . . and there, just above the backs of the chairs, around the whole length of three walls, was the line of drawings of heroic happenings, executed by the seven boys in their youth. A few pictures on the end wall, on either side of the window, of animals and birds and over-crinolined ladies, were obviously the work of Ellen and her sisters.

George moved slowly along between the table and the chairs, studying each of the drawings in turn, trying to decipher the name of the artist beneath, as he had done so short a time, it seemed, before. Nothing here appeared to have altered. Four years of war had left this world untouched. But then Josh entered the room silently from the doorway leading to the stairs. 'We've lost Albert, Wilf and Reggie – I expect you've heard?' he said. He was wearing his customary white carpenter's apron and his rolled-up shirt sleeves displayed forearms spattered with bright orange dragon's blood paint.

'So you're back. I expect Ellen was glad to see you.'

George nodded. He had just felt the gulf between a man who had lost three sons in war and a man safely home who had refused to fight.

'Madness, all this fighting and killing,' said Josh bitterly, pressing back with one palm Reggie's picture of the heroic Mounties quelling a tribe of Indians, where it had come adrift from the wall. 'Oh God, scatter those that delight in war! Rose is ill, you know – but what can you expect? I'd better git back to her,' and he began moving towards the door. 'I don't know what to say to her,' he cried bleakly. 'I jest don't know what to say!' Josh had always been a stout member of the Methodist Church, but his religion, George noted, seemed to have failed him. However, he stopped in the doorway and turned, his face brightening. 'I could dew with a bit of help in the old sawpit, come Wednesday,' he said hopefully, 'got a nice bit of elm I want cut into coffin planks . . . shouldn't take no more than four days . . .' George nodded and smiled, too choked to speak. Perhaps, after all, everything could be as it had always been.

Strangely enough, it never occurred to him until years afterwards to wonder whether Josh, who wasn't averse to using his deafness to avoid hearing what he didn't want to hear, actually knew how and where George had spent the war years – but by then time and fresh enterprises had swallowed up the past and rendered the subject irrelevant.

George and Ellen were now much occupied with the problem of where they were to live to start their proper married life – with Josh and Rose or with George's surly and unpredictable father? Luckily the problem was solved for them by Miss Raspberry, who, in the fullness of her heart and with a view to accomplishing her own plans for the future, offered them free accommodation in her tall, rambling house. Its ground floor was un-inhabitable as it was used to house fuel supplies, store vegetables, accommodate garden tools, tennis gear, apparatus for wine-making and mushroom production and Miss Raspberry's and Windy's bicycles.

George and Ellen could have two bedrooms up above, a kitchen George had converted from a bedroom years ago, and the long west-facing sitting room with the balcony overlooking the village green. Some furniture was already there and the happy couple quickly moved in. Miss Raspberry took herself off to the pavilion where poor Windy lay, in bed, on the roofed-in veranda so that she could benefit day and night (except in the very bitterest weather) from the freshest East Anglian air, blowing straight in from the North Sea. This was in keeping with the prevailing treatment for people suffering from pulmonary tuberculosis.

Miss Raspberry, on the other hand, was to be domiciled inside the pavilion, and George, before the onset of winter, was to add a boarded inner lining to the whole building for insulation and install a chimney and two fireplaces – one in the living room and one in Miss Raspberry's bedroom. In the spring, he was to build a swiss-type chalet in a meadow at the furthest extremity of Miss Raspberry's property, so that the two friends eventually could live there, in peace. But before he started all that, said Miss Raspberry, could George please resurrect the tennis courts, so that at least one tournament could be held to mark the rebirth of the Cookley Green Tennis Club before winter set in.

With the somewhat wayward assistance of Bent-one, George set to, with a scythe in the first instance, to try and rediscover the lush green turf he had created so lovingly nearly seven years before.

It took him almost a month to get the turf back to somewhere near its former glory. Ellen, meantime, made a home for them: cleaned their new living quarters throughout, painted walls, put up curtains, made cushion covers, set bowls of bulbs out on the balcony for everyone to enjoy in the spring, as they passed by or stood gossiping on the green. After the turf was restored, George replaced some of the tall netting surrounding the courts that had succumbed to winter gales – and finally Miss Raspberry declared herself satisfied. Now there could be a tournament, just one, before winter set in. The third Saturday in October was to be the great day – Reclamation Day! – when the past was to be recaptured; when everything was to be as it had always been . . .

Well, almost. The day dawned fine and bright but with a bank of dark clouds looming threateningly in the west. Kenny and Jacko settled themselves early on the willow tree, confident that today at least there would be something for them to watch. They should also be able to earn themselves a copper or two unharnessing people's horses from their carts and carriages and taking them off to graze on the small area of common land at one end of the village. At Jacko's feet sat his latest little dog, with a patch over one eye this time, instead of one ear. It sat gazing fixedly up at its master, as had its predecessor, and didn't even turn its head when the

311

sounds of strange voices, car engines, cart and carriage wheels signalled that people were arriving on the other side of the green.

Village children began to wind their way between the parked vehicles to stand gazing bashfully into the archway, before they mustered up enough courage to creep in. Miss Raspberry appeared early too, and seated herself, pad and pencil in hand, on a bench at the inner end of the archway, ready to welcome old club members as they arrived.

It was seven years since the last tournament and today's took a long time getting started. Dr and Mrs Weston, as usual, were going to be late, he having been called to the bedside of a long-sick patient now at last resolved to die. Gerald and his entourage of boisterous Yorkshire blades and flappers turned up looking the worse for wear after a late-night party at Thickthorn. They arrived just in time to ruin the dignified entrance of Stella and her mother.

Designedly late, Stella stepped daintily into the archway, inclining her head graciously to left and right – until she realized she was wasting her favours on a gaggle of giggling children. She walked swiftly on . . . only to have her entrance into the courts proper effectively eclipsed by the arrival of Gerald and his raucous band of followers just behind her. She deliberately ignored his greeting and also, inadvertently, Miss Raspberry's, which did nothing to endear her to one with whom she was already not particularly popular. Head in air, her mother following and stumbling in an effort to keep up with her, she swept on along the path between the two courts.

Bent-one, sitting cross-legged like a garden gnome inside the wire barrier of the first court waiting to discharge his duties as a ballboy, smiled shyly; George, bounding down the pavilion steps with a measure to

312

adjust the height of the nets, raised an arm in greeting. They both got short shrift; Stella swept on, straight up the steps to the refreshment room where Ellen was dispensing coffee and tea. Spectators were already seated along the length of the veranda and among them, of course, poor Windy, in bed, half sitting, half lying, propped up high with pillows so that she would have a fair view of the games.

Coffee in hand, Stella walked out onto the veranda and stood glumly surveying the scene. There were people now standing along the sides and the foot of the courts. She saw that Gerald and his acolytes had got no further than the back door of the Black Bull. They were waiting for the pub to open and the chance, she thought sourly, to get more of the dog that had bitten them the night before. The children, growing bolder, had managed to slip past Miss Raspberry, busily engaged in writing down the particulars of four aspiring members, into the cobbled area between the foot of the courts and the pub. In an outburst of high spirits they began chasing each other round and round the pump, which stood by the back door of the Black Bull. It served as a water supply not just for the pub but for several cottages round about. Soon one boy seized and vigorously cranked the pump handle and the rest, screaming with delight, began splashing each other and people nearby.

A thunderous bellow from Gerald put an end to that activity. Subdued, the children backed up against the pub wall and stood in a huddle, looking contrite. The bellow had drawn all eyes, but Gerald was unfazed and went on chatting amiably to his companions.

Various rumours concerning Gerald and Thickthorn regularly went the rounds in Cookley Green: that he had bought it; leased it; that Lord Summerfield, who, as everyone knew, was becoming increasingly incapacitated and depended on Dolmon to push him about in a wheelchair, never went near the place and had no idea what was going on there. In fact, Gerald was using it as he had always used it – for his own convenience, as if Neville were still alive. He employed Kenny as a gardener and Bertha as caretaker in his absence. A cook from Silverley obliged when he and his friends came to stay.

The truth was, his Lordship no longer cared about Thickthorn, the Hall, the estate or the people working for him. He had lost interest in life altogether and despite Dr Weston's best efforts could not be roused from a state of extreme lethargy and depression. At this very moment his concerned long-time friend, Brigadier Benson-Brick, having dropped off his wife and Stella at the archway, was on his way to the Hall in his latest car, to fetch his Lordship to the tournament. He hoped that the resurgence of the Cookley Green Tennis Club and a taste of things as they used to be would boost the spirits of his old friend.

Meanwhile, Gerald waited with mounting impatience for the pub's back door to open, stamping his feet at intervals and slapping his leg with his riding crop – *the* riding crop, which he carried with him at all times and which so often played an enlivening role at social gatherings, when he would regale all present with the story of its origins and of old Roan who lived with a tree. The tree grew mightier with the telling and his Herculean struggles with it, before he took to the meat cleaver, would frequently hold everybody spellbound.

From her vantage point on the veranda, Stella looked down on him bitterly – that he should still be alive and Neville . . . Neville . . . it did not bear thinking of . . . With a mammoth effort of artifice and cajolery she had managed to get herself engaged to Neville on the last night of his last leave. She was still wearing his ring; all it

314

signified now was the death of her hopes and dreams. She was racked by the injustice of everything: that she had backed the wrong horse; lost her chance of changing her choice; had never even been allowed the satisfaction of turning Gerald down; that he had risen to the rank of captain and had three pips to Neville's two . . . that the wrong man had survived . . . that there he was preening himself, his friends clustered round him. She glared down at him. The girls, she noted, were wearing the shortest skirts she had ever seen. Now she looked down at her ankle-length flared skirt and long-sleeved, high-necked blouse and found herself feeling frumpish, as if somehow, without her noticing it, her youth had slipped away.

Gerald and his cohorts continued to wait, but the back door of the Black Bull obstinately remained closed. Presently, however, the front door facing the green obligingly opened to admit an old and valued customer – Lord Summerfield and his gouty leg. The leg came in first, the rest followed, supported on one side by Dolmon and on the other by the brigadier. Slowly they manoeuvred him in through the door and across the room to the window overlooking the village green. The brigadier ordered drinks and Dolmon accepted his position sufficiently to take himself off with his glass to a settle on the far side of the room. But he continued to keep a beady eye on his master, was punctilious in attending to all his wants; got up and walked over to adjust his whisky glass when he missed the coaster; was there in a twinkling to wipe dribbles off his cravat.

The brigadier suddenly felt he couldn't stand another minute of the solicitous butler. Ordering another drink for him, he told him to sit tight and enjoy it, then he grasped his old friend round the middle and the pair of them hobbled across the room, through the kitchen to the back door. The publican rushed to open it, and, with the gouty leg preceding them, they stumbled out onto the cobbled area at the foot of the courts – just as the antagonism which had festered for years between Gerald and George (mostly on Gerald's part) came to a showdown.

Everything had been going swimmingly. All expected former members had arrived. Not the Westons, of course, or indeed Lady Madeleine. She, as only family and close friends were supposed to know (though in fact almost everyone knew), was 'resting' in a home for those with nervous troubles about half a mile from her sister's house near Regent's Park, where Becky visited her every day. She could not be expected to appear, but eight new people had now joined the club, which augured well for the future.

Miss Raspberry closed her notebook with a snap and looked about her. She saw that the sky had darkened. The storm clouds in the west had moved appreciably nearer . . . were almost overhead! Surely it was not going to rain? She rose, ready to make her way to the pavilion to get things started – but down between the courts came Ellen with a cup of tea, so she gratefully sank back again into her chair. Ellen was wearing tennis gear, for she expected to play some time during the day. Round her waist she had tied a tea towel to protect her dress while she coped with the refreshments. She meant only to stay for a moment but as she started back, George came out from the nearest court, thrust a racket into her hand and demanded that she join him for a few minutes of practice knock-up . . .

It was the pok! pok! of their tennis ball that drew Gerald's attention. Going close up to the net he stared through. That scoundrel, that blackguard! He was back . . . had dared to show himself in the village again . . . was flaunting himself in front of everybody!

'What's that bloody lily-livered conchie doing making free with the courts?' he yelled. 'Get him out of there. Get him out!'

'He's got as much right on the courts as you have,' retorted Miss Raspberry, rising swiftly from her chair to defend her democratic principles. 'He's an honorary member!'

Gerald did not, or chose not to, hear her. Striding onto the court he snatched Ellen's racket from her and shouldered her aside – just as George served a gentle ball over the net. In a trice, Gerald had hit the ball back straight into George's face. Nimbly George leapt to one side and returned it. Again Gerald struck the ball back with all his force. But George was a better player than Gerald had anticipated: again the ball came back . . .

An almost tangible tension gripped the onlookers. Everyone pressed forward for a clearer view as they realized that a game of more than ordinary competitiveness was taking place. Even Windy suddenly sat bolt upright amid her pillows and leaned forward, beady-eyed, the better to enjoy this clash of the Titans. The ball flew back and forth almost like a metronome. Everyone waited to see who would be the first to fail.

It was Gerald: while reaching out in vain to return a wide shot, he tripped and fell sprawling, to a chorus of jeers and guffaws. Leaping to his feet, he jumped over the net and punched George in the face. George sprang backwards in surprise, lost his footing and fell flat. He lay still for a moment, then slowly sat up, shaking his head. Ellen, who ran to his assistance, Gerald roughly elbowed aside . . .

There are times when pacifism, like patriotism, is not enough. George's expression changed; his face flamed and he leapt up and launched himself at Gerald with fists flying. For someone who disapproved of violence, he

317

was giving quite a good account of himself. He had no idea why he was being attacked – felt vaguely that perhaps he was being publicly chastised for his unorthodox behaviour during the war years – but to Gerald, everything was crystal clear. Every blow was for Neville and long overdue: for his ear, even for his death, for which in some mysterious way he held George responsible. The sound of their blows and heavy breathing was all that could be heard as onlookers pressed themselves to the outer netting, transfixed.

The pair seemed evenly matched; it was only when they fell to the ground and continued their struggle that Gerald was seen to move into the ascendancy. He was by far the heavier; George had not yet regained his normal weight. The sight of her favourite young man's face being shoved into the turf caused Miss Raspberry to decide it was time to put an end to the fight. Trotting over to the pump, she picked up a bucket that providentially had earlier been filled to the brim with water by the children in their play. Crossing quickly into the court she held the bucket high, then, with a crow of sheer delight, tipped its contents onto the squirming bodies below – to an uproar of cheers and laughter.

Swamped, the two combatants disentangled themselves and stood, dashing water from their faces. Tenderly, Ellen wiped George's bloody nose with the tea towel from around her waist. 'You leave my husband alone!' she hissed at Gerald, her blue eyes flashing fire. 'You didn't ought to be here if you don't know how to behave!' It was the first time she felt truly married. Head held high, she took George's arm and together they made their way to the home Miss Raspberry had provided for them, where he could dry himself and change his clothes.

The rain which had threatened now arrived, with a

sharp gust of wind to show it meant business. Big slow drops began to fall, soon increasing in speed.

Miss Raspberry rattled her pail handle for attention and shouted, 'Play will resume when the rain stops. In the meantime, would you all seek shelter in the pavilion. I wish to discuss future plans for the club.'

People were already hurriedly making their way there, holding jackets, bags, newspapers, books over their heads. In the rush, Gerald found that he was able to make a dash for the back entrance of the men's changing room without exposing himself further, wet and dishevelled, to public gaze.

Only his Lordship and the brigadier made a vain effort to go in the opposite direction – back to the warmth and sustenance of the Black Bull. They found their way blocked, at the bottom of the pavilion steps, which they had painstakingly climbed in order to get a better view of the fight, by the stalwart figure of Miss Raspberry. Her rosacea in full bloom, she stood, legs astride, hands on hips, effectively commandeering the whole pathway.

'You first,' she said graciously, indicating that their way was up the steps, not down. 'I'm so glad to see older members still taking an interest in the club . . . very gratifying! Very gratifying indeed, I must say,' and she stood her ground.

There was nothing else for the two old friends to do but turn and mount up to the pavilion. His Lordship hopped backwards on one leg with the brigadier lifting him from behind, step by step; the gammy leg pointed skywards, increasingly soaked with rain.

Soon all were safely gathered into the pavilion, except of course the disappointed children, who took refuge under the archway. Were they to be denied the pleasure of hearing Miss Raspberry's famous utterance at the end of her service? Some of them had not even been born when the last 'Balls to you!' had echoed across the courts, but the saying had entered local folklore. There wasn't much fun to be had under the archway either, with grumpy Kenny Ling and smelly Jacko also taking refuge there.

Inside the pavilion, to the accompaniment of rain rattling on the roof and cries of 'Speak up!' Miss Raspberry began to expound on her plans for the future of the club. In its early days, she said, she had been able to run the whole thing herself, with twice-yearly meetings. Now was the time, she thought, to put matters on a more orthodox and democratic footing – with president, secretary, treasurer and possibly six committee members. She herself, regretfully, must withdraw from all responsibility. Though she would, of course, continue to take a keen interest and give support as she was able, her time was going to be much taken up with caring for her dear friend Miss Gale. At this point she suddenly remembered that, with a westerly wind blowing, her dear friend out on the veranda might well be getting rained on. As George had now reappeared, dry and in better shape, he and Ellen were quickly dispatched to draw Windy's bed in under cover and dry her if she was wet.

With this problem dealt with, the meeting could proceed. The brigadier, after a feeble protest, was elected president, Stella secretary, her mother treasurer and six others nominated to form the committee. Gerald, coming to the meeting late after much time spent restoring himself to his usual state of sartorial elegance, was seriously displeased to find everything had been settled without him. In his view, there was no-one better suited to be president than he, and he quite failed to appreciate his good luck when he was voted onto the committee, in spite of the fact that he was known locally as 'that damned know-all from up north'.

The main business concerning the club was now over, but it rained on. The brigadier took the opportunity to announce that the War Memorial Fund, which he had taken on the responsibility of organizing, now stood at £5 7s, and a meeting would be held shortly to decide on the design of the memorial and where it could best be sited. The Anglican vicar now scuttled in, very wet from cycling all the way, to announce that a special memorial service for the war bereaved was to be held at the church on Remembrance Sunday at eleven o'clock. It was hoped that all those who had lost loved ones during the war would attend, to give thanks for victory and peace.

The vicar seemed to be directing his words very particularly at the peasants in the assembly – the ordinary villagers who were clustered together at the end of the room. They had come to the tournament as spectators and would never have presumed to attend the meeting but for the rain, which had driven them into the pavilion. They stood shuffling their feet and gazing unresponsively at the floor.

The vicar turned to Lord Summerfield for support. In the past, he would often help by chivvying people in his employ and living in his tied cottages into more regular church attendance. This time, however, there was no support to be had: his Lordship sat with his bandaged leg stretched across two chairs, his back bowed and his chin on his chest. Miss Raspberry, on the other hand, with her customary regard for fair dos for all – in this instance, fair dos for all religious denominations – leapt to her feet. There were to be similar services, she announced, on the same day, at two p.m. at the Methodist chapel and four p.m. at the Congregational. And what a pity there was no Quaker meeting house in the village, for a Quaker service would have been a truly enlightening experience for all. However, she hoped the bereaved would rise above their religious differences and attend all three . . .

The vicar got ready to cycle home, blessed and said goodbye to all; wished Miss Raspberry well with a look that suggested he really wished her further – and departed. There seemed nothing more to do or say. Reclamation Day had been a failure. Golden yesterday could not be recaptured. Stella organized a quick auction of the food Ellen had so carefully prepared, which now would not be needed, and Bent-one gobbled up the leftovers. The children wandered disconsolately away. Kenny and Jacko got soaking wet fetching back from the common the horses they had only just put out to graze, and the cars, carts, carriages and people gradually dispersed. In the refreshment room Ellen, George and Bent-one collected, washed up and put away the crockery, while Stella and her mother bickered as they waited for the brigadier to pick them up after he had taken his Lordship and Dolmon back to the Hall.

It rained on. It was also raining a hundred miles away in the vicinity of Regent's Park, where Lady Madeleine sat in her small cosy room penning yet another letter to her boy. She found little new to say – just hoped he was remembering to eat a substantial breakfast before going out to face the day, and not forgetting a warm scarf now that winter was coming on. She hoped she herself would soon be better, well enough to get home to Summerfield to organize a really memorable party when he came home on his next leave. She sealed the letter, directed it as usual to his unit in France and stuck on a stamp. Then she placed it on the top of the small cabinet beside her bed – she would give it to Becky to post when she made her customary visit this afternoon.

Meanwhile, deep in sleepy Suffolk, in driving rain, the brigadier sadly drove Lord Summerfield, and a Dolmon rather the worse for wear after too many pints of ale up the gravelled driveway to Summerfield Hall. Single-handedly he helped his Lordship out of the car and in through the main door. Dolmon followed unsteadily. The wheelchair stood inside the entrance; the brigadier helped its owner into it, then stood for a moment looking about him. With an aching heart he realized there was nothing more he could do for his old friend but consign him to the mercies of his abominable and rather drunk butler.

Mid-July 1999

We've had an open day for parents and governors. My class exhibited their paintings, handwork models and their workbooks for inspection. Neil's class set up an exhibition of relics of the past and it was amazing what the children came up with: old tools, old books and maps, wartime letters (both wars), clothes – even a shepherd's smock – a shepherd's crook, household items such as butter-pat shapers, iron kettles, flat irons, those you filled with hot coals as well as those heated on top of the stove; oil lamps . . . even an old carbide lamp from somebody's ancient bicycle.

Interestingly, as well as the old photo of the village worthies taken just before the Second World War, there were also two sepia-tinted and much faded photos of even older times, produced by the school caretaker's mother. One was of two old men, a little dog at their feet, sitting on a garden seat in a leafy arbour, peacefully watching the world go by. Pearl says (I took the photos home to show her) that it was not a garden seat but the trunk of a fallen willow tree which used to lie along one side of the village green, just opposite the archway leading to the tennis courts. (Now bowling greens, of course.) The branches of the tree continued to grow upwards forming a back, like the back of an armchair or settee. It was quite a feature in the village at one time, so Becky told Pearl, and so were the two old men – until somebody complained about it, and the whole thing was sawn up and cleared away.

The other, larger photo contained the caption on the back: 'Reopening of the Cookley Green Tennis Club, 1922'. Fat Harry said no, he'd seen the photo before and it showed the *opening* of the club – the very first tournament, before the war, in 1914. The reopening of the club after the war was a washout, his father had told him. It rained and rained, and everybody had to shelter in the clubhouse so they couldn't have taken a photo that day. 'Look at their clothes,' Harry said, and when I studied the photo more closely I saw the women were all wearing the clothes and hairstyles of pre-war days, so I think he's probably right.

Because I am so familiar with the people in Pearl's old photo, I could recognize some of them again in this one: Lord Summerfield and the figure in attendance at his back, Dolmon, Harry informed me, his impossibly difficult butler. Brigadier Benson-Brick, Stella's father, he of the protruding waistline and walrus moustache, standing with his arm across his Lordship's shoulders. And the tall imposing figure, standing in the middle of a row of young people at the back – Captain Kirby, surely, the carpet manufacturer, despised by all his aristocratic associates because he was in trade. And there was Stella gazing at the camera with disdain (lucky for her, I thought, she didn't know what the future had in store for her). Then her mother, and next to her a bohemian-looking person – a hippy of the time, perhaps? Miss Hastbury, Harry informed me, commonly known as

Raspberry, who had started the club. Seated next to her the diminutive figure of Miss Gale, who was to die of tuberculosis. In the foreground, cross-legged on the grass, a row of children and one rather larger than the rest, peeping out from beneath a spiky fringe of hair. Of course – Bent-one, who else!

'Well, there they all are.' I had taken the photo home to show Pearl, and with some satisfaction moved her magnifying glass slowly along the rows of faces. 'Are they as you remember them?'

'I don't know – I never knew them, did I?' she said crossly. Of course she didn't, I thought . . . except by hearsay. She spent her days in the workhouse, while the life she should have lived went on elsewhere.

'Which one is George?' I ventured, moving the glass up to the two rows of young people at the top of the photo, all in tennis clothes, some clasping rackets. 'He's there somewhere.'

I saw her hands begin to tremble and heard a sharp intake of breath. 'How should I know?' she retorted. 'I don't even know what he looked like when he was grown-up. I never saw him after that day he took me to the workhouse. He was only fifteen. When I come back to the village to live with Becky, they told me he'd been dead for forty years. The fascists killed him,' she added.

'*Fasc— Fascists?*' I couldn't believe my ears. To my alarm, her head drooped sideways onto one shoulder as if she no longer had the strength to support it. I could see a pulse fluttering wildly in her neck and began to feel frightened for her. She was very upset. I had never dared ask how old she was – someone had once said as old as the century; someone else, I remember, had hoped she would live to get her telegram from the Queen . . .

I lifted one limp wrist and was trying to find a pulse when she suddenly revived. When she met my anxious gaze she sat up and tried to shrug her shoulders. I took down her heart tablets from the mantelshelf and offered her one, but she refused it. 'I'm all right,' she muttered irritably.

I went into the kitchen and made her a mug of hot milk. I offered to wait until she'd drunk it and then help her to get to bed, but she shook her head and looked so furious I thought it better not to insist. She has a home help who comes in twice daily and frequent visits from social workers and can give them a really rotten time, so I've heard, if she happens to be in a bad mood.

'He wouldn't do something he believed was wrong,' she continued suddenly and clearly, as I gathered my belongings and bent to pick up Sammy, who had fallen asleep on her saggy old armchair. I straightened up quickly.

'Who wouldn't? Who d'you mean? D'you mean . . .' but I dared not mention his name. She went silent again. I slung Sammy up over my shoulder and we returned to our cottage. I gave him some supper and put him to bed in his own room, hoping he would stay there. Then I stood by my kitchen window in darkness and waited for the light to go off in Pearl's living room and on in the other downstairs room she sleeps in, so she doesn't have to mount the stairs. When, after a longish interval, the light went off there too, I knew she was safely settled in bed and began to make my own preparations for sleep.

But for a long time my mind went round in circles. *Fascists? In Cookley Green?* This blessed spot. This oasis of tranquillity. My home, my refuge, deep in the heart of Suffolk . . . far, so I thought, from the madding . . . It just isn't possible!

CHAPTER TWENTY-ONE

1921

'I suppose you won't be wanting to come to the service,' said Miss Raspberry to George early on Remembrance Sunday, a fortnight after the tennis club reopening had been rained off.

'Why not – why shouldn't I?' George spoke violently and his face flamed. Did she think he was ashamed to show himself in his own backyard?

'I meant, I don't suppose you want to come with all us women?'

'Oh, that.' George's ire subsided. He noticed that his hands were trembling and put them in his pockets. 'I may come later,' he said lamely.

'Do,' said Miss Raspberry briskly.

She was organizing a round trip for the bereaved mothers, taking in the three services. She believed the experience would be beneficial for all: a demonstration that grief can transcend religious differences. She had asked Ellen to help. They were all to assemble under the archway at half past ten, attend the Anglican service at eleven, return to the pavilion for a cold lunch, attend the Methodist service at two, the Congregational service at four and return to the pavilion once more for a light tea. All the food was to be prepared previously by Ellen.

From the balcony window George watched them all arrive – the ten black-clad women who had lost their sons, accompanied by some ten or twelve relatives or friends. The bereaved fathers Miss Raspberry had not been able to organize; they preferred to come, if at all, on their own. Soon he watched them walk away, past the Black Bull and round the corner. Tall and ramrod straight, Bertha was leading, superseding even the power and authority of Miss Raspberry, who was almost as tall. He, too, would attend all three services, George decided, would remain staunch in his convictions and be seen to be so. He was not going to be forced into a role of shame. Going into his bedroom he took out his one set of decent clothes and began to dress himself in brown tweed breeches, woollen socks with wide turnovers, knitted for him by Ellen, a belted tweed Norfolk jacket and a dark brown deerstalker hat. Finally, from a jam jar on the mantelshelf he took down his three white feathers and tucked them into his hat band. But then he paused: in church he would not be wearing his hat, he would be holding it in his hand. He took the feathers out again and tucked them into the top left breast pocket of his jacket, where they would be plainly seen by all.

He was late arriving. There was no-one about as he approached the church door, but he entered to find the inside at least three-quarters full and everyone seated, waiting silently for the service to begin. He gazed across the forest of black hats and bowed backs. What was he trying to prove? That he had acted from conviction, not cowardice? How could that count with people who had lost . . . had lost . . . He sank down on the pedestal of the font and tried to muster up the will to go on.

The organ began to play softly and a stray beam of

late autumn sunlight suddenly struck the stained-glass window above the altar at the far end of the church. He stood up, hat in hand, and began to walk steadily towards it, down the middle aisle between the two blocks of seated figures. Nobody moved. He seemed to take an age to get to the pulpit at the front of the aisle. Once there he paused, took a deep breath and turned. The organist stopped playing. There was a hush as all eyes fastened on the dark figure silhouetted against the light of the window at his back. For a moment he hesitated, then, gathering his strength, began a slow, deliberate walk back . . .

He caught a glimpse of Ellen's strained face beneath the only blue hat in a sea of black; heard gasps as he moved steadily along, the three white feathers there for all to see. He felt his legs beginning to fail him, but managed to carry on. At last he had passed them all, run the gauntlet, he felt, of a thousand accusing eyes. He had reached the altar. The pew to the right of it was unoccupied and he sank down, overcome by an uncontrollable fit of trembling.

'Relax the mind and the body will follow,' he had been advised by an unusually sympathetic prison doctor in Egypt, when his shattered nerves could no longer be attributed to his latest bout of malaria. But George had been unable then, and was unable now, to follow that advice. He gripped the top rail of the seat in front and tried to subdue the spasms by an act of will. He failed now, as he had failed then. 'Why not let me try and get you to a hospital back in Blighty on a breakdown ticket – neurasthenia? Anything would be better than this, surely?' and the doctor glanced round George's dismal cell. 'You mean you can get me back home to a loony hospital,' said George, 'so I can be written off as insane. No thanks – it's this war that's insane, not me.'

When the service started he began to feel better. After a while he managed to stand for the hymns and bow his head for the prayers. The service was as he, as everyone, expected: a thanksgiving for peace, for victory, for the bravery and self-sacrifice of the sons of the village, the sons of the nation, the Glorious Dead . . .

He closed his eyes and ears till the end of the service. He sat immobile while the congregation began to file out of the door. All avoided looking back at him. Even the vicar had decided to act as if he was not there. At the very last came the bereaved mothers, Bertha, Ellen and Miss Raspberry. Ellen stood waiting at the end of his pew.

'Come along, Ellen,' said Miss Raspberry sharply.

'I'll be along in a minute,' said Ellen.

'I want you now,' said Miss Raspberry firmly. 'I need your help with luncheon.'

'I said I'll be along in a minute,' repeated Ellen, with a steely look Miss Raspberry had not thought her capable of.

Still, she was determined to have the last word. 'Very well – but don't be long!' A moment later George and Ellen were alone in the church.

The Methodist service was to start at two. The Methodist chapel, opposite the churchyard's lower entrance, had been two cottages that had been made into one, with the ceilings removed to achieve some semblance of grandeur within. There were two Gothic windows on either wall. The building was on a slight rise, with a flight of steepish steps at the entrance. It seemed to have attracted a rather larger congregation than had the church, George thought, as he mounted the steps and entered – but that could have been because the building was smaller and more readily appeared congested.

At the opposite end to the entrance was a platform

or dais on which Josh's father had created a splendid carved oak pulpit, too heavily ornate to blend in with the varnished, wood-panelled simplicity of the rest of the building. To the right of the pulpit stood the organ, where Ellen's two sisters and Ellen in her turn had played for the hymns twice every Sunday, and where Ellen still performed. George seated himself in the exact spot where in his younger days he had enjoyed watching Ellen's silky golden curls drift back and forth across her shoulders as she played. Now she had her hair up again, confined under a blue dowager's hat and not a single curl to be seen.

George could see all of the Ableman family, those that remained, bar Jack in Canada and Henry, the only one left up north. Tiny Rose sat beside Josh; difficult to believe she was sister to brawny, black-haired, over-bearing Bertha. Next to Rose sat her daughter-in-law, Edie, still with the big bunch of hair. Then Herbert and the miracle child, born the day of Roan's funeral, now at school. Next the four daughters of assorted sizes and questionable value in their father's eyes . . . and, at the end, Bent-one, twirling, for want of something better to do, an empty sleeve where his left arm used to be. Four sons now instead of seven.

George made no attempt this time to draw attention to himself. He had not gone to the pavilion with the women to eat, but had made himself a cheese sandwich at home, which he had been unable to force down. Now he was beginning to feel faint from lack of food. He leaned his elbow on the nearby window sill and, chin in hand, dozed fitfully through virtually the same sermon he had just sat through at the church. Thank God for peace, for victory and the glorious sacrifice of the country's sons, fathers, husbands, brothers . . .

Out in the street again an hour later, along with the

rest of the congregation, he found himself once more totally ignored. Nobody looked; nobody spoke. The consensus was that he was now beyond the pale. He had flaunted his cowardice at a commemorative service for those who had sacrificed their all in the service of their country.

A November fog, which had thinned at times during the day to let a few beams of sunlight through, now showed signs of closing in for the night. It was growing colder. There was a general buttoning up of overcoats, turning up of collars and tucking in of scarves. George quite expected to see most of the worshippers make a beeline for the comforts of home and Sunday tea, but, to his surprise, this did not happen. Perhaps, under the beady gaze of Miss Raspberry, they didn't dare. A contingent of between thirty and forty people, Anglicans, Methodists and Congregationalists alike, set off, after a brief consultation, for the Congregational chapel on the outskirts of the village. Miss Raspberry shot George a glance of sheer triumph as they started off and she proudly joined on the end – probably to make sure, he could not help thinking, that nobody absconded from her religious marathon. Only Ellen forsook the party, having been despatched back home to minister unto Windy, who had been left alone too long.

George hesitated, then he too began to walk. Having come this far, he thought he'd better see it through to the end. He found himself alongside Bent-one, who regaled him yet again with gruesome stories of his experiences in a field hospital during the war, and his horrified obsession with the fate of the horses, which always reduced him to tears. George tried to close his ears, but by the time they reached the chapel his nerves were in shreds.

The Congregational chapel was a large barn-like

structure with a high, double-pitched roof which had probably once been thatched. It was timber-framed with walls of lath and clay-daub. Built in 1647, its size indicated that it was intended to serve a wide area. People must have come considerable distances to escape the power and authority of the established church. Lighted now from within by oil lamps and candles, its small-paned windows twinkled out into the dusk with a welcoming Christmassy effect. This was the chapel to which his mother had transferred her allegiance after all the Anglican-imposed difficulties over her marriage. George glanced across at the corner of the graveyard where she now lay, cold, still and alone in the darkness. He moved towards the main door of the building, and joined the end of a trail of worshippers slowly entering.

Inside, he found that the suggestion of warmth and comfort was, as usual, illusory. Paraffin stoves, oil lamps and candles barely took the edge off the chill in the large and draughty interior. George breathed in the familiar smell of paraffin, candles, mould and mice, vividly reminding him of happier times when the whole Gudrun family had regularly attended services here, twice on Sunday.

A tall varnished pole, reputed to have once been a ship's mast, supported the part of the ceiling where a plain wooden pulpit under a suspended canopy looked down on a block of crude wooden benches already almost fully occupied by parents and young children. Along the wall opposite the pulpit there was a row of box pews, like pony traps without wheels, with little doors which people could close and then sit in cosy isolation as they listened to the sermon.

Up above was a gallery reached by stairs, with rows of rickety seats mounting almost to the ceiling. Many of the older children had escaped the clutches of their parents and made their way up there. It was a favourite refuge for them and the sound of their voices and thudding feet, as they scrambled about among the seats, reverberated throughout the building. He stood for a moment, remembering . . .

At Harvest Festival services, George recalled, you could throw down grains of wheat, barley or assorted berries – or you could spit – on the heads of worshippers below, without fear of retribution. George's family pew was the second one in from the door, but it was fully occupied now by Miss Raspberry and her bereaved mothers, their families and friends. Bertha, he saw, had grabbed the first pew for her followers and was sitting stiffly upright.

He squeezed himself onto the end of one of the central blocks of seats directly beneath the pulpit. Thunderous noises from the gallery drove some parents, sitting behind him, to make a feeble attempt at discipline. They waved and shushed, but no-one went up to deal with the miscreants. George sat quietly, checking, as far as he could, without moving from his seat, the various repair jobs he and his father had done over the past years: repairs to benches, window sills, the main door, the pulpit steps . . .

Presently a cacophony of squeaks and wheezes signalled that the organ, old and decrepit, was about to be played, instantly causing a row of giggling faces to appear along the top rail of the gallery above. George gazed fixedly at the floor, trying to fight off his own rising surge of hysteria as the poor organist tried to wring something resembling a hymn tune from the instrument's worn-out interior.

The preacher, a thin, pale-faced, earnest fellow with a somewhat prominent Adam's apple, now mounted the pulpit steps to begin the service. He stared up reprovingly at the row of giggling heads, shook his fist and cried for silence. To no effect – until Bertha took command. Opening the door of her pew, she stepped out into the aisle and simply stood, hands on hips, treating the faces above to a hard imperious stare. Instantly the children wilted, withdrew to the safety of the inner recesses of the gallery and were heard from no more.

The preacher was a lay preacher, determined to do justice to this grave and memorable occasion. That it is impossible for ordinary mortals ever to understand God's mysterious ways was the gist of his address. That the best way was to accept His way, even if His way appeared inexplicable. (Inexplicable was a word he rather liked and he used it generously.) Only in seeing and accepting God's will in everything would we find peace, and keep the memory of the Glorious Dead forever fresh in our hearts . . .

He had taken some time to arrive at this juncture and showed every sign of going on for longer – but George could not bear another moment of it. Leaping from his seat, he ran up the pulpit steps, hauled out the preacher, pushed him down to the floor below and substituted himself.

'Waste!' he cried passionately, grasping the edge of the pulpit with both hands. 'Wicked, wicked waste! Not God's will – man's! Madmen, not God, sent your sons . . . brothers . . . husbands over the top only to be mown down. For a yard or two of ground that was lost again next day. Why were they made to go on doing it when for weeks there was so little gained?' He paused and waited for the strength to go on. 'There was nothing glorious about their deaths . . . blown to bits . . . shot and left hanging on the barbed wire . . . or buried in mud, sometimes by a shell that fell short from our own guns. They had to be brave. They knew if they didn't go over the top when they were ordered they could be shot by their own officers . . .' He paused again and stared down at the sea of blanched faces gazing up at him. As a boy, he had often accompanied his mother as she cleaned the chapel and changed the flowers. Sometimes he would climb into the pulpit and imagine himself delivering a sermon to a spellbound audience below. Now here he was . . .

'This is the third place of Christian worship I've been in today,' he continued more steadily, 'and what have I heard? Thank God for victory over our enemies. Whatever happened to Thou shalt not kill? Love thine enemy.' He paused; he was losing his voice. 'These feathers,' hooking a finger into his pocket, he pushed the feathers forward, 'these feathers are a badge of cowardice, but if you think standing out against a vast military machine because you believe war is evil . . .' He stopped, unable to go on. Nobody spoke, nobody moved. 'Better to be a dead hero than a live one,' he continued bitterly, 'like the poor devils going round the towns and villages now, trying to make a living selling things nobody wants. Crippled or gasping for breath because of the gas. Finding out that nobody . . . nobody . . .'

Gripping the edge of the pulpit with white-knuckled hands, he stared down at the upturned faces staring back at him. 'Look what came for me in the post the other day.' He pulled a brown paper package out of his pocket and waved it aloft. 'Medals!' He took out three medals and swung them by their ribbons. 'For three years' meritorious conduct in the service of my country, it says here – which I spent in military prisons being kicked, bullied, beaten, half starved and hung up in chains in the Egyptian sun. Because I refused to fight my fellow man. No doubt some of you have received similar medals in recognition of the sacrifice of your men. Well, now you see what they are worth – they're dished out to everyone.

Even me.' He leaned far out and dropped the medals one by one. In the silence with a succession of sharp thuds they fell on the brick floor below. 'If all men thought as I do,' he said quietly, 'there would have been no war. Your men would still be alive.' He became aware of women weeping, of Rose's anguished face staring up at him.

He had told them the brutal truth – but what they wanted, what they needed, he now saw, was the comfort of lies. Lies that made senseless death acceptable. Now he had denied them even that. Always . . . always, he thought, it was the innocent who suffered and all he had done was to add to their suffering. After all he had gone through, the people of his own village . . . the victims . . . were more than he could bear. He stood swaying. His legs gave way. He slumped down to the bottom of the pulpit and put his head in his hands.

The silence went on interminably. Everyone was in a state of shock. At last the preacher, deeming it his duty to bring things back to normality, timidly mounted the first few steps of the pulpit. Recollecting that it was already occupied, he stopped halfway up and put his hands together. 'We will pray,' he said. 'We will pray for our brother . . . that God will help him to see . . . to see.'

He got no further, for suddenly Miss Raspberry burst out of her pew. With eyes shining and her rosacea at full throttle, she pushed past him, ran up the pulpit steps and leaned in. 'Bravo, George!' she shouted. 'Bravo!' There followed another deathly silence, broken this time by the sound of Rose's pew door opening. She was leaving. Ashen-faced, she stepped out into the aisle. Without a glance to left or right, she set off towards the door, followed a moment later by the rest of the women in her pew. Bertha came out last. The women in the other pews followed suit, then gradually the rest of the congregation.

In the soft light of the oil lamps and candles, they looked like pilgrims in a medieval painting as they jostled their way towards the door. The children bounded down from the gallery to join them. But Miss Raspberry was not done.

'Bravo,' I say,' she shouted at their retreating backs, drawing herself up tall and apocalyptic in the pulpit. 'Praise be to God – we have heard the truth this day! WARS WILL CEASE WHEN MEN REFUSE TO FIGHT!'

Unheeding, the congregation trailed out into the gloom of a cold November evening, leaving behind just one small boy, lingering to pick up the medals. Carefully, he hung all three from his coat buttons, before running out into the darkness.

In her excitement, Miss Raspberry tripped in the chapel graveyard and twisted her ankle. She couldn't walk and had to be pushed home on her bicycle, supported by George on one side and Bent-one on the other. The bicycle had first to be fetched by Bent-one, while she and George waited, in the darkness and the mist, seated on a cold, damp, fallen gravestone. Next day George developed a high temperature which turned into an attack of tonsillitis lasting nearly a fortnight and leaving him in a state of nervous debilitation. Ellen had to take time off from the shop to look after three invalids; three, because poor Windy was already suffering from a secondary lung infection probably brought on by the wetting she received on Reclamation Day at the tennis club. They were all housebound for over a fortnight, so there was no way of knowing what repercussions there were in the village as a result of George's outburst in the chapel. All seemed tranquil – but, underneath, a grim game of consequences began to be played out.

The brigadier's meeting to decide on the site for the war memorial and what form it should take was held at the end of the second week. It lasted for about twenty-five minutes and ended in disarray. It took place in the school and almost everyone in the village attended. Even Kenny and Jacko put in an appearance, for various rumours had been circulating. First, that the favoured spot for the memorial was the middle of the green, which Miss Raspberry was said to oppose because it would obtrude on the view from her balcony window. Second choice was said to be the edge of the marsh directly across the green, which would mean doing away with the willow-tree armchair. Perhaps there was some truth in these rumours. Perhaps some people would welcome the chance of cocking a snook at Miss Raspberry in her absence; perhaps it was a chance too good to be missed. Then again, although the fallen willow tree was acknowledged by most to be a feature in the village, the brigadier was known to be much fazed by seeing people lolling about on it when they ought to have been gainfully employed. Kenny and Jacko slouched in at the back of the schoolroom accompanied by a strong smell of ferrets, prepared to voice vociferous objections if their place of refuge was to be threatened.

Gerald, who had come down from Yorkshire specially to attend the forthcoming first committee meeting of the tennis club, had spent the past three days helping Stella to do a final collection for the War Memorial Fund. He undertook the job of arranging the seating for the meeting – school chairs at the front for the bereaved and their families, then benches for other interested parties and heavy lidded wooden desks for the hoi polloi to perch on at the back. Bertha, as school caretaker and cleaner, did not approve of his arrangements. Her view was that people should have been made to stand,

339

thus ensuring that the meeting would not last long. But Gerald arrived early from Thickthorn and swept all before him. With military precision he set out the seats, straightened up the world map on the wall, whipped away the redundant portrait of Edward VII and replaced it with a shiny new rendering of George V. Thus, in the space of a little under half an hour, he brought Cookley Green safely into the 1920s.

A large rectangular table with attendant straight-backed chairs, loaned from the Black Bull for the occasion, faced the assembled villagers and accommodated the VIPs – the brigadier, Gerald, Stella, her mother, and, in the fullness of time, Lord Summerfield. He was trundled in by Dolmon, in a wickerwork invalid chair. A shocked silence fell as everyone took note of his trembling, disorientated condition. He would have been best left in his chair, but Dolmon laboriously got him up out of it and took an unconscionable amount of time coping with the gouty leg. He had to sit sideways at one end with the leg thrust out into space. Finally, Dolmon took up a position just behind his master, where he continued to adjust his chair, flicking imaginary specks of dust off his shoulders, or wiping dribbles off his chin. Sickened, the brigadier decided to start the meeting, despite the non-arrival, as yet, of Dr Weston, to fill the remaining chair at the table.

He began by welcoming everybody and commending them on their interest in the project in hand. He had special praise for his daughter – here he beamed upon Stella fondly – and of course for Captain Kirby, for they had taken it upon themselves to do a final collection round. The sum now stood at £7 11s 6d, an advance of £2 4s 6d on the original amount. He was personally prepared to bring this sum up to a round total of 10 guineas, which, so far as he had been able to ascertain, should be sufficient for what they had in mind. Now they could decide, not just on the site of the memorial, but what form it should take. He had obtained illustrated leaflets showing the designs that were available, which he now proposed to pass round for their perusal. He then judged that he had said enough, and in an expectant silence went to hand out the first leaflet to the person sitting at the end of the front row. But into the silence came a still, small voice. Rose's voice.

'I don't want my boys' names put on a war memorial.'

The brigadier paused, startled. Surely he had not heard aright? 'Of course, the exact details . . . how the names are to be arranged . . . is a problem for later,' and he began handing out the leaflets.

'Hold yew hard a minute.' It was Bertha speaking this time. The bereaved and their families were seated at the front on low school chairs. Knees, of necessity, were almost up to chins; bottoms overflowed the small hard seats. Bertha, taller than most, had difficulty in rising, but rise she did: a long, dark, forbidding column.

'Dint yew hear what my sister said? She don't want her boys' names put on no war memorial.'

'What? What?' spluttered the brigadier.

'None of us want our boys' names put on,' ventured another of the mothers. Indeed, the rest of the bereaved mothers were now seen to be shaking their heads in unison.

'I don't quite . . .' began the brigadier. 'I don't understand – what is the problem?'

'I'll tell yew what is the problem,' said Bertha calmly. 'They don't want to be reminded, every time they go down the street, that all the morn'n' sickness, backache, varicose veins and piles, all the nappies they boiled, dinners they cooked, shirts they ironed, socks they mended, taters they peeled and great piles of bread and butter they cut . . . wus all for noth'n'. That their sons hev just bin blown to bits. From their point of view there int noth'n' to commemorate. I don't know why women let men dew it,' and she glared down balefully at the mothers, crouching like a covey of submissive hen partridges on their low chairs. She turned to the ring of startled faces round the table. 'They want to believe their boys are still up north, sav'n' up their money and com'n' home for Christmas,' she said simply. She turned again to the women as if for confirmation. They gazed back tremulously, some of them weeping. Then they all got up and walked out.

A stultified silence followed as those remaining tried to accept an entirely new view of the situation. Bertha sat down quietly. The brigadier, now thoroughly confused, was at a loss to know what to say. He cast round for help, turning to his old friend. His Lordship's head drooped onto his chest, his eyes were closed. He had obviously drifted to some place far away. Gerald, stymied by the presence of a superior officer (even though one retired), waited for action from the brigadier. Waited . . . but no lead came, and when Gerald finally got to his feet, cleared his throat loudly and prepared to take command, it was too late. Bertha was already orchestrating a general exodus. Everyone filed out – except Kenny, Jacko and Bent-one, who were neatly ambushed at the door and made to help move back the furniture. Everyone else, in what seemed no time at all, found themselves out in the school yard, quite bemused.

Gerald's first impulse was to gather everybody together and get to the bottom of this bizarre affair here and now . . . but he hesitated. He realized that he must have been unaware of subterranean goings-on.

People began to drift away home, down the road and then left towards the little bridge that led into the village.

Only Dolmon, pushing his master stalwartly before him, turned right and started up the long avenue leading to Summerfield Hall. His Lordship sat hunched in his wicker chair, head bowed, a scarf wrapped around the lower half of his face, his cap pulled down over his eyes. This was to be his Lordship's last appeareance in the village, for he deteriorated rapidly in the weeks to come and died early in the spring.

His Lordship was making his exit, but no-one marked his passing. Everyone walked quietly away in the opposite direction, wrapped in their own thoughts, pondering, no doubt with some bewilderment, this latest turn of events. The brigadier, who had come on horseback, soon trotted ahead of everyone else. Gerald and Stella walked with the stragglers at the end of the procession, Gerald interrogating Stella vigorously as to the reason for the women's strange behaviour. Stella, who had been away during the extraordinary debacle in the chapel, had heard garbled versions of what happened from various sources, all transmogrified in the telling.

As he listened to her own vague account, Gerald became incensed. Of course – the lily-livered conchie was at the bottom of all this! He was a subversive, a traitor to his country! He deserved to be horse-whipped . . . drummed out of the district! He personally would see to it; this time George would really get his comeuppance!

Stella stole a glance at Gerald's reddened cheeks and glaring eyes as he continued his savage diatribe. He seemed not even to realize she was there, to have forgotten everything that had passed between them – the episode under the elm, the times they had danced together, when she had felt . . . knew that he had felt . . . the latent fire between them. Those stolen moments when Neville was not around . . . when she had almost yielded in his embrace . . . now it was as if she walked with a stranger.

They reached the village green to be assaulted by the sound of wild screams from some children performing acrobatics on the fallen willow. Gerald, in his inflamed state, strode onto the green and roared at them to clear off. They rapidly disappeared round the nearest corner. 'That tree has got to go!' he declared, still breathing heavily. 'The brigadier's right – it's nothing but a source of trouble in this village. I'll get old what's-his-name . . . the wheelwright . . . to saw the whole thing up and cart it away.' He strode off purposefully in the direction of Josh's workshop.

'You may have trouble making yourself understood,' called Stella, as she struggled to keep up with him. 'He's a bit deaf, you know.'

She knew better than to accompany him down the yard to speak to Josh. She had bitter memories of her own difficulties in communicating with him and his family, on the day they were busy lining old Roan's coffin. She stayed by the gate at the top of the yard, leaning her back against the wall where there was a slight curve which hopefully would conceal her from the gaze of passing villagers. She waited.

She heard 'mumble mumble' from down in the workshop, then 'mumble mumble' a bit louder. Then she heard Gerald beginning to shout and an uncomprehending reply from Josh. Presently she heard 'SAW' roared out very loudly; and then 'MORE WHAT?' from Josh. Then 'SAW' bellowed louder still, with, no doubt, Gerald illustrating his requirement by appropriate movements of the arm. A long silence . . . Finally Gerald reappeared at the bottom of the yard and began making his way up, carrying a long cross-cut saw, which he had some difficulty controlling as the wind caught it.

'Stupid oaf! The man's an absolute clod. Couldn't understand a thing I wanted. So I said lend me a saw

344

then – I'll saw the bloody thing up myself! But he couldn't even understand that, till I wrote SAW in the dust on his bench. Then he had to do something, so he took me to his sawpit. He's got a coffin in there, his coffin, would you believe! The sooner he gets in it, the better, if you ask me. There was a collection of saws pegged up on the wall, some of them with six-inch-wide blades worn down to two. Anyway, he let me have this one. Looks as if it's never been used. Here – hold the other end.' Reluctantly, Stella did so, and they set off down the street, the long saw wavering in the wind between them.

'Oh no,' she said firmly, when they reached the willow tree and it seemed he expected her to operate at the other end. 'Oh no – I'm not going to make an exhibition of myself, even if you are.' Luckily, or rather unluckily, for him, Bent-one arrived on the scene just at that moment, worn out by his exertions with the school furniture after the meeting.

'Whass go'n' on?' he asked, incautiously drawing near. 'What are yew tew up tew?' and then, as Gerald indicated that he was to take the other end of the saw, he flapped his empty coat sleeve pathetically and shook his head. 'Lorst me arm in the war,' he said, but it didn't do him a bit of good – Gerald simply thrust the saw at the arm remaining and poor Bent-one was trapped.

Gerald was still wearing his army greatcoat, of which he was very fond. He now flung it off to set to with the saw. He started in the middle of the main trunk, the thickest part. Rage sustained him for the first fifteen minutes. Bent-one danced about on the other end, doing his best to contribute as they sawed back and forth. Presently Kenny and Jacko appeared at the edge of the green and stood by the railings of the Ploughman's Arms, looking aghast to see their favourite place of refuge being attacked. When Gerald stopped at last, his face bright red and running with sweat, it was evident that all the effort had had little effect. With a curse, he yanked out the saw blade and started again, on a bough of less daunting dimensions.

Stella draped his overcoat over the cut in the trunk and sat down forlornly to wait – in the spot usually occupied by the two old ghouls now leaning against the railings on the far side of the green. It had not been a bad day for late November, but it was beginning to turn cold and damp. Why don't I just walk away now, she wondered, take up medicine and make something of myself? Why can't I abandon all thoughts of life with this man? she thought – I don't even like him! She eyed him stealthily as he threw himself conscientiously into the job in hand.

The saw flew back and forth with Bent-one almost airborne on the other end. Then suddenly it began to go slower . . . and slower . . . and slower . . . and then it stopped altogether. 'Pull, you oaf!' shouted Gerald and Bent-one pulled, lost his grip and shot backwards, heels over head, to land in a bunch of nettles on the edge of the marsh behind them. The blade had jammed.

There was nothing to be done. The saw was irrevocably stuck in its groove. Gerald heaved to no avail, then lost all patience. Grabbing his coat, he yanked it out from under Stella, almost causing her to topple backwards and join Bent-one in the bed of nettles. Abandoning the saw, Stella, and the whole vexatious problem, he stalked off through the archway to the parking area at the back of the Black Bull, where he had left his car.

Stella followed, aware as she crossed the green that the two old ghouls, chortling with delight, were already on their way to reclaim their throne. There they sat, along-side a Bent-one worn out with the demands of the day, for nearly an hour. The daylight began to fade, the sky to darken, a pearly blanket of mist rose above the marshland behind them . . . and Josh appeared out of the gloom, humming and carrying a stout pole under one arm. With a casual nod of greeting, he bent, inserted the pole directly beneath the saw-cut – and gently elevated the bough. The cut gaped and he drew out the saw. Then he went off, still humming, using the pole this time as a walking stick, with the long saw drooping over his shoulder. It was his least favourite saw, the one he never used. Its teeth were too small, the metal of the blade too thick and the whole tool somehow unsympathetic to the hand – but it did fill up an empty space on his wall. Behind him, the three gnomes on the willow tree went into paroxysms of delight at the simplicity of the solution to Captain Kirby's problem. Their only regret was that he had not been there to witness it.

Their glee was short-lived: at the first committee meeting of the Cookley Green Tennis Club, Gerald railroaded through two resolutions. That the willow tree be cut up and removed, under his auspices, by workmen from the Summerfield estate chosen by him. That George and Ellen, due to treacherous, unpatriotic behaviour and the calamitous effect this was having in the village, be permanently barred from membership of the club. Whether they were still to be employed by Miss Raspberry in its upkeep was a matter for her to decide, but they were not to be allowed to play on the courts or take part in any of the club's social activities. Both resolutions were swiftly passed to the satisfaction of all those members thought to matter most. Then came a few innovations, some minor adjustments to the rules . . . and the first committee meeting was acclaimed a success.

Gerald was one of the last to leave. He hung about judiciously, allowing time, so he thought, for Stella's father to take her home. He felt they had been seeing too much of each other. Elated by his triumph over the willow tree and George, he bounded merrily down the pavilion steps, along the cobbled walkway at the foot of the courts and through the archway to the parking area . . . only to find Stella admiring (equally judiciously) his latest car, a 4-cylinder, 20 h.p. Morris Cowley, a more comfortable ride than the Cadillac on long journeys. Forgetting all caution, Gerald found himself loftily offering to drive her home in it. She readily jumped in. Her split skirt slid back revealing a long slim pale leg, and her perfume mingled with the smell of the leather interior. And somehow it was not at Highlea, the brigadier's Victorian mansion, that they finished up, but at Thickthorn. This was ostensibly so that Gerald could show Stella his plans to lay out tennis courts there, if his Lordship was sufficiently *compos mentis* one day to be persuaded to agree to the idea and come up with a suitable sum. On the way the spirited sound of the engine, revved up in keeping with Gerald's ebullient mood as they swept round narrow lanes and splashed through the puddles of recent rains, the bickering when Stella wanted to try her hand at driving, her questioning his directions – all these built up an emotional tension between them they had first sensed all those years before.

So, when they finally reached their destination, bursting through the heavy portals of Thickthorn, Gerald took hold of Stella . . . and Stella yielded . . .

Oh, how she yielded! How Gerald's long lean limbs stroked her, to her infinite delight! Well, limited delight to start with, but heightened satisfaction as the night wore on (yes, she stayed the night in his bed). She unwillingly did harbour, at about the midnight hour, amid the transports, the thought that he was – as she had always suspected he would be – far better at this sort of thing than Neville could ever have been. Now Gerald would have to marry her. Now he was committed and she was compromised. Such were her thoughts as she nestled for the night, her head on his chest.

Gerald woke when the rooks started circling noisily above the house as they decided what route to take for this morning's forage. Frail and spent, with panic lurking in the pit of his stomach, he looked fearfully at the sleeping Stella and felt weak and defenceless at the thought of her clinging limbs.

She was awake now, her head deep in the pillows, a little smile playing about her lips. She was awake and dreaming of a married life at Thickthorn. She knew Gerald had been waiting for a favourable opportunity to broach with his Lordship the subject of buying it. It was not the Hall, which she'd always aspired to, but near enough. His father, the Carpet King, might well buy them something better later, as children came along. She turned and smiled at him winningly, causing him to scramble out of bed and lurch over to the window.

'Oh my God – who the hell is that?' He leaned forward and stared: someone was trotting on horseback down the long, meandering avenue of rhododendron bushes, leading another, pale grey horse – Stella's horse! It was the brigadier come in search of his daughter!

'Christ – it's your father!' Panic-stricken, Gerald tore off his nightshirt, grabbed various garments and began to dress. 'Get up – get out of that bed! Get yourself dressed,' he hissed. 'I'm not waiting for you!' Even when he had gone, she did not seem inclined to move. She lay back, stretching luxuriously. She felt she hadn't a care in the world. She didn't even care if she got pregnant. She calculated that it would only mean bringing the wedding forward by a few weeks. She lay smiling contentedly . . . did not even move when she heard her father jangling the brass bell at the front entrance. Only when he began to thump the door and call her name did she rouse herself.

Climbing out of bed, she slipped on Gerald's discarded nightshirt over her nakedness, then, barefoot, stepped out onto the landing. Yawning and fluffing out her hair above her temples, she walked languidly down the stairs to greet her father. Halfway down, she was startled to hear a car motor being started up and then revved violently. Dashing down the last few stairs, she flung the door wide . . . and was just in time to see, beyond her father standing on the step and the two horses on the gravel below, Gerald, driving off with all speed across the terrace and down the narrow ribbon winding between the rhododendron bushes.

She was not to see him again for nearly three years, when he was to greet her cockily as the new owner of Summerfield Hall and Thickthorn, as lord of the manor in all but title. It was then that he invited her to be his hostess at his forthcoming ball, only to deal her the final blow of his wedding announcement at the ball, a blow from which she would never really recover.

In the meantime, the news that George and Ellen had been thrown out of the tennis club hit Miss Raspberry hard. She now saw that her favourite young man had been safer under her dictatorship than under the fledgling democratic system she had, with good intentions, instigated at the club. She hastened across from the pavilion to her former place of residence to commiserate with George, leaving poor Windy, despite the fact that the courts were sparkling with the first frosts of winter, still lying in a bed out on the veranda, clinging to life by a thread. George himself was not too well and was feeling very down. 'Never mind,' Miss Raspberry predicted, 'in fifty years' time it'll be acknowledged that the war and the way it was conducted, with the wiping out of almost a generation of Europe's young men, was an absolute madness. And the settlement even madder and likely to cause another war sometime in the future. Perhaps we're the only sane people in a mad mad world!' she added. Then after assuring the young couple that her house was still at their disposal and that her wish was for George to continue to be employed by her as before, in the upkeep of the tennis courts and other enterprises, she trotted away, back to her failing friend.

George sat gazing morosely at the floor. He saw himself as an outcast. Yet this was his home . . . where he was born, where he belonged . . . and where he was going to stay. But the village had no reason to turn against Ellen, he thought angrily, and expel her from the club after all her efforts. In a burst of energy that surprised her, he gathered together their tennis clothes and began suspending them from coat hangers and bits of string all the way round the top rail of the balcony, where they flapped merrily in the wind. Then, as Ellen watched anxiously, he wrote out a notice:

FOR SALE
2 tennis rackets
1 pair tennis trousers
1 tennis dress
1 pair tennis shoes size 10
1 pair lady's ditto size 4

He pinned the notice on a board and hung it down the centre of the balcony for all the world to see. Then, as Ellen watched, mystified, he hauled the board back up again.

BALLS TO YOU! he added.

Mid-summer 1999

Sounds extremely unlikely, but I've been told by Fat Harry that members of Mosley's National Union of Fascists did go round the countryside in the mid-Thirties in support of farmers who were fighting against paying tithes to the Church, obviously hoping to enlist their support in return. Apparently, some of the farmers did get carried away and joined the party, only to let their membership lapse a few years later when the country went to war with Nazi Germany. Even Captain Kirby, by then the new owner of the Summerfield estate and lord of the manor in all but title, had a brief flirtation with the movement. He let members use Thickthorn as their headquarters and organize meetings and events in the villages round about. It seems it was after a particularly rousing event one summer evening in Silverley that a couple of young militants decided to carry out one of their favourite stratagems – beating somebody up. By some terrible trick of fate, they decided on George.

Fat Harry had an uncle who lived in the locality at the time, so if this isn't straight from the horse's mouth, it's as near as makes no difference. George, despite the post-war depression and his general unpopularity due to some nefarious action on his part Pearl has never made clear to me, seems to have done quite well for himself. Miss Raspberry gave him a leg-up in the early days and, being a good builder and master of multifarious skills that often go with a country upbringing, it seems he was never short of a job. Even those who were most against him overcame their animosity when it was a question of them getting a job done well.

So George prospered and with Ellen's help built himself a house on a piece of rising ground on the outskirts of the village. It had a seven-foot fence round it, which suggests he suffered from a siege mentality, at least in the early days. But he must have relaxed somewhat by 1936, for the gate was wide open when the two young black-shirts entered it that peaceful summer evening. George had also had to dig himself a well and it was to this he turned when the two asked for water, as their car radiator had run dry. As he bent to let the bucket down the well, he was felled by a blow from a wooden truncheon on the back of his neck. After a moment he managed to sit up and gasp, 'What the devil did you want to go and do that for?' 'This is what we do to communists,' was the reply, before they went on to elaborate on their intent.

George a *communist*? George part of a communist cell plotting revolution . . . in *Cookley Green*? Apparently he was kicked and beaten black and blue and had to spend a week in bed. When he got up he seemed to be making a good recovery, but he had been bleeding internally and presently suffered a massive pulmonary embolism. A few days later he was dead, and Ellen was left to bring up their three children alone.

No-one was ever apprehended for the crime. The local police expediently suppressed the political implications. Bearing in mind the excesses that had been going on at political rallies in London at the time, it was perhaps understandable that they didn't want that sort of thing spreading to their neck of the woods. So when poor Pearl finally left the workhouse-turned-hospital in the early Seventies – and in her early seventies too if she really is as old as the century – expecting and longing to see again the one whose memory she had kept in her heart all her life, she found him long dead, buried beside his mother in the Congregational chapel graveyard.

Sammy and I did pop round to see her that evening and I did try to bring up the subject of George. His story is so bewildering – but I couldn't get through to her. She was sitting looking through the old scrapbook Becky had given her, using her magnifying glass on a newspaper cutting yellow with age. She got me to read it to her. '"Cookley Green three-legged cow gives birth to calf,"' I read.

'But it was no good,' Pearl muttered, 'it turned out to be a bull calf.' Now what on earth can you make of that? It was on the same page as a picture of Josh's eldest son Herbert, and showed him receiving a Long Service award at the Suffolk Agricultural Show. Twenty pounds for working fifty-five years on the same farm. What a stint! And what a measly award! I wanted to go on looking through the scrapbook and perhaps find a way of getting her round to the subject of George, but after a while she nodded off – so we crept away.

Last week was the last week of term and not a happy one. Everything seems to be going wrong. To begin with, there was an ambulance outside Pearl's cottage when I got home from school Monday. She had had a stroke and was carted off to the county hospital and is now in intensive care. I can't help wondering if my obsession with the history of this place is going to be the catalyst that shortens her life, deprives her of her telegram from the Queen? I find this too awful to contemplate.

The children finished school on Wednesday and Neil organized an end-of-term party lasting from half past three till five. Sammy and I stayed on afterwards to help clear up, and in the general atmosphere of relaxation Neil suddenly said he would like to cook a meal for me, at his place, Sunday. Great! I thought. Something to look forward to and a nice way to start the long summer break. We used Thursday for clearing the classrooms ready for cleaning, and Friday for getting on top of the latest convolutions of the National Curriculum. This has proved, in the past, to be rather like trying to grasp hold of a bubble of mercury which changes shape even as you grapple with it.

Just as we were about to leave on Friday with the prospect of five weeks' holiday, who should appear at the school door but the Black Widow, in search of Neil. His parents had had an accident in their car and were both in a Chester hospital. His mother was in a state of shock, under sedation. His father's injuries were still under investigation; it was feared he might have a skull fracture as well as crushed ribs and a broken collarbone. Of course Neil dashed off at once to get his car and drive to the hospital.

That was Friday. Saturday I learnt that Pearl has been transferred to our little local hospital, where her needs are to be assessed before it can be decided what next to do with her. I went to see her this morning (Sunday) on my bike with Sammy on the back, and came away utterly dejected. She was half sitting, half lying, in a bed at the end of the ward looking absolutely bleak, glaring at anyone who came near her. I don't blame her – she can't speak and is more or less paralysed all down one side. I knew I couldn't speak either without starting to cry, so I just took her poor dead hand and held it. The only move she made was when Sammy went to her other side, stroked her arm and gazed into her face. Using her good arm she drew him close. One eye focused but the lid of the other just drooped. She tried to smile but it only happened on one side of her face; it was grotesque. I couldn't stand any more, so we left soon after and that travesty of a smile has haunted me ever since.

So now we're home and it's evening. No school tomorrow or for the next five weeks . . . a great block of time for me to fill up somehow with worthwhile pursuits. What on earth am I going to do? Neil's gone and Pearl is gone and I now realize I know hardly anyone else here – just Fat Harry and the school caretaker and the caretaker's mum . . . and some of the parents, vaguely. How long does it take to feel you really belong in a place? A lifetime, I rather fancy; I never felt I belonged in London either.

I should have been enjoying a meal with my teaching colleague at this moment, to celebrate the end of the summer term. I'd managed to get the caretaker's mum to babysit, so we could have an evening to ourselves, but I've had to cancel that. All my plans have fallen through. Instead, here I sit over the ruins of a pizza (out of the freezer) which neither Sammy nor I have been able to eat. He seems a bit feverish and out of sorts. Probably going down with the summer flu I had a few weeks ago; or perhaps chickenpox, which has been going the rounds at school. Some of the childhood diseases we thought we were on top of are getting immune to treatment, apparently. Perhaps it's just as well I'm not going out. I've put him to bed early – in his own room of course (I'm still trying!) and now I'm left with a long evening ahead of me. There's nothing I want to see on television. I'm feeling really low. I've opened the red wine I got from Fat Harry to take to Neil's, and I'm already half-way down the bottle. Can't think of anything better to do.

I've written you a letter which I may or may not send. It is to tell you your son is dead and will therefore embarrass you no longer.

That's right, Sammy died three weeks ago today of meningococcal meningitis. He is buried in a corner of the Anglican graveyard along with the Methodists and Josh's personalized gravestones. I wish Josh was alive now so he could do one for Sammy. I'd like him to carve Floppy on it, and under Sammy's name: HE DID VERY LITTLE HARM. Few people came to the funeral, for few people really know us. Anyway, there's a big scare about the disease possibly spreading. People are staying, and keeping their children, indoors. I wish Neil would come back.

As I stepped back from the grave I saw, deep in the shadows beneath an old yew, another tiny grave edged round with stones and with a broken wooden cross at one end covered with lichen, moss and mould. Someone, I think, must have buried a cat or a little dog there, long ago. At night, perhaps, secretly, because they wanted their beloved pet to lie in consecrated ground and they didn't want anyone else to know. So Sammy has company; he would have liked that. I keep trying to make sense of it all, but I can't. Where has he gone?

I've had a letter from Neil to say his parents are now out of hospital, but he is staying with them to make sure they can cope. He seems to get on very well with his parents – with his whole family.

In the letter Neil also said new school sports gear should be arriving sometime late August and please could I see that the caretaker puts it in the green shed, locked by the new padlock I'd find in the top right-hand drawer of his desk. Today, this brought me outside for the first time for a while, and the first person I met in the street was one of the mums. What she wanted to know, I realized after a few minutes' conversation – oh yes, everybody was so sorry to hear about poor Sammy – was whether my employment at the school was to continue next term. If so, had proper medical advice been taken to ensure there was no danger of me spreading the infection to the rest of the pupils? Well, I could understand her concern – but it made me feel just great . . . like a leper, so welcome, so wanted, just the thing to bolster up my faltering confidence and restore my will to live, as I endlessly and uselessly mull over the past and think how different it could all have been.

Because Sammy died from the promise in a kiss. It's true. Something for me, I thought, something at long last for me! and I really moved him out of my bed to let someone else in. Yes I did. If I'd kept him with me I'd have seen how ill he was. If I hadn't been too fuddled with wine to check on him properly last thing that night, I would have seen how much he had deteriorated. He lay arched in his bed, breathing quickly, and I simply pulled the duvet up, afraid of waking him. And in the morning if I'd gone to him at once, instead of spending time looking for something for my hangover in the medicine cupboard, I could have got the doctor sooner. If . . . if . . . if I hadn't just for once relaxed the close guard I've kept on him, day and night since birth, all my attention and vitality utterly consumed, as with every other lone parent. If only I hadn't wanted, just for once, something for me . . .

I've done nothing all day, hardly moved out of my chair. There's no reason for me to move, so I just sit here. All day. But at nightfall I still sometimes get this compulsion to write, as if words on paper can change reality somehow. I know writing can be therapeutic. Years ago I wrote myself out of an entrenched compulsion to think ill of myself when I learned, during a psychology course, that it is usual for a child to feel he or she is to blame when a parent cuts off and leaves the family. My guilt was compounded by my mother, when she told me a few years later she was dying of cancer. Her only comment was, 'What's left to live for? I've been dying ever since he

358

left me,' which I interpreted as meaning that I was of no value to her, had no significance in her life. I don't want to sink back again into that black trough – but how can I not?

Neil's come back. The Black Widow told him about Sammy and he arrived here upset and appalled and so sorry he had not returned sooner. I said I knew he was looking after his parents and anyway, there was nothing he could do; there was nothing anybody could do.

He looked at me very closely for a long moment and then said, 'Where are they?'

'Where are what?'

'The pills. You forget – I've been there. I know all about the if onlys . . . if only I'd started earlier, gone a different route, gone a different day . . . Oh yes, I've been through all that. It alters nothing.'

He peeled back the newspaper I had hurriedly spread across the breakfast table when I heard his voice at the door, and there they were – a bottle of paracetamol and one of aspirin and a small packet of sleeping pills the doctor had prescribed and I'd taken care not to use. He swept them all up and put them in his pocket. Then he took them out again and stood them in a neat row on the mantelshelf. 'Get yourself togged up,' he said. 'Put some decent shoes on – we're going for a walk.' He paused in the doorway. 'Life goes on,' he said simply, 'whether you like it or not. I'll be back in about an hour.'

He was back in rather less than that, with a rucksack stuffed with food and a flask and carrying a tartan rug under one arm. When he found me still in the same state as when he left, he said nothing but went into the bedroom and rooted round in the bottom of my wardrobe until he found some suitable walking shoes.

Kneeling, he patiently put them on my feet; then found the top which went with the tracksuit bottoms I was wearing. Then he hauled me to my feet and there was nothing for it – we were ready to go. 'I'm sure you know all the best walks,' he said, as we stepped out into the sunshine, 'you lead the way.'

We went down the street, past Josh the wheelwright's workshop on the right, now derelict, Forge Cottage on the left and the saintly oak and the one remaining shop on the corner. There were several Jeeps and Land Rovers parked on the village green, suggesting that a meeting of the farming fraternity was taking place in the Black Bull. On we went past the Moon and Sixpence and over the little bridge towards the school. But then I turned left and we started up the long avenue of trees leading to Summerfield Hall, the walk I had last taken with all the children . . . with Sammy . . . seemingly a lifetime ago. It was cool and shadowy under the trees, with a gentle breeze stirring the topmost branches. A hen pheasant clucked in the brushwood at the side of the road and then stepped out cautiously to cross, with her brood of youngsters scuttling along behind her.

At the end of the avenue the countryside opened out into meadows on either side; there were no clone-haired aspiring artists painting the scene this time, but the sheep were still there with their lambs now half-grown. If Neil was aware I was repeating previous walks, he made no comment. Neither of us seemed to find it necessary to talk until we were walking down towards the east gate and I remembered the long black limousines and their hooded occupants about whom nobody in the village seemed able to offer an explanation. Neil knew nothing about them either – but he had heard that delicate negotiations were taking place with a prospective buyer, and now at last there was the possibility of a sale.

Everyone said they'd heard all that before, however, and it never amounted to anything positive.

As we turned right onto the footpath running along-side the lake, I fancied I could still see our footprints in the grass from that day when I had walked along there with all the children and Sammy . . . that day when I had no inkling of what was to come. We stopped for a few minutes where we stopped before – at the sad little memorial to the Summerfield heir, who was so cruelly killed in the First World War. Further on, it seemed natural to settle under the balsam poplars, by the boat shed, to eat our lunch as we had done before. Neil spread out the circular tartan rug, and opened up the sandwich tin and coffee flask.

Behind us, high on the soft green crest of the park, stood Summerfield Hall . . . gracious . . . imposing – but empty, as it had been for so many years. Here in this tranquil spot the children had fished, taking it in turns with the nets. Here Sammy had brought up a bright green frog which sat in his net motionless for a moment, before springing up into the air and back into the water again. I started to tell Neil about the frog but the words stuck in my throat and I began to weep. He put down his sandwich and his coffee mug and drew me close.

We walked past the ice house for about a mile, then turned right and began making our way back along the road which runs past the Marigold Inn. There were several cars in the forecourt and we could hear someone playing the piano rather well, but we didn't go in. Soon we came to the cattle breeding station, and, sure enough, there was the same old black bull peering at us over the same dip in the hedge. This time he was silent; he stood there with a mournful, haunted look.

We were far from the parkland of Summerfield Hall now and into a corn-growing area, where hedges, ditches and trees had all been removed to enlarge the fields to accommodate today's farm machines. Eventually Neil stopped at a footpath sign pointing straight across a vast field of gently swaying wheat. Of course, the farmer should have delineated the exact route of the footpath when he planted the wheat, but he hadn't, so we began to walk it . . . from the sign at the side of the road, straight across the sea of ripe golden ears.

Other fields round about had already been harvested, and the combine harvester, ready and waiting to cut this one, stood at the boundary. Neil walked into the middle of the field and I followed, placing my feet carefully between the rows of corn stalks. When he finally stopped he turned, hung the rucksack from my shoulder, clamped my arms down by my sides and walked closely round me once, then again further out . . . then as I watched perplexed, again further out . . . round and round . . . until he had trampled down a sizeable corn circle, with me in its centre. As I stood there bemused, he took the rucksack from my shoulder, dropped it at the edge of the circle, moved me to one side and carefully laid the tartan rug on the trampled corn stalks.

'We need to activate the life force,' he said, gazing at me gravely. Then, in answer to my puzzled look, 'You once told me you always wanted to be made love to in a corn field.'

'I said that? I don't remember—'

'Oh I do. Oh yes – we lads take careful note of things like that . . . in case we're in there with a chance, one day. Like now,' and he slowly pulled me down.

He meant to be careful and considerate and take his time, I could tell – but my response was so immediate and ferocious that he lost his cool.

So much for the Black Widow, was the thought that flitted across my mind. Warmly entwined, we lay gazing

362

up at a huge East Anglian sky reduced to a clear blue circle fringed round with corn stalks.

'Let's get married,' he said after a while, fanning his face with a sprig of wheat.

'Married? Oh, Neil, nobody bothers with that nowadays.'

'But I want you with me, always,' he said. 'In the same house. In the same bed. Of course the vicar wouldn't like it,' he said after a pause, tickling my chin with the sprig of wheat, 'if we weren't married, would he?'

'Nor Mrs Greyhair!' We collapsed into giggles.

'Better do things properly – perhaps next half-term. If we could have a baby every year for the next few years,' he continued solemnly, 'we could keep the school going and ourselves in a job.'

'But would it be wise . . . after Sammy?'

'Don't.' He turned and faced me. 'Don't go to that dark place.' He took me by the chin and lifted my face to meet his gaze. 'I want you with me – really with me. All of you. I want your company, I want your thoughts. I want your attention . . . well, most of the time! And I want . . .' He began deftly removing what remained of our disabling clothing before demonstrating, this time with rather more control, what else he wanted . . .

There should have been a skylark soaring and singing above us in the blue, I thought later, as we lay in our secret place, far from the world and all its troubles. But intensive arable farming methods tend to wipe out the conditions birds need to breed. So no skylarks. Just a threatening rumble from the combine harvester at the edge of the field, which quickly mounted to a roaring crescendo, causing us to scramble madly into our clothes . . . on our hands and knees, because standing we could be seen by the driver high up in his glass cabin. There had been a light rain during the night and he had probably been waiting for the corn to dry out. Now, its roar reduced to a steady throb, the huge machine began to move. At last, fully dressed, we were able to stand, lace up our shoes, gather our belongings together and begin making our way to the end of the footpath and out onto the road – nonchalantly, as if we were just two dedicated walkers.

Now it's Friday and except for the weekend, the last day of our summer holiday. It'll be back to school for us on Monday. The children don't start till Wednesday, but we have a lot to do before then, getting everything in the classrooms set out and work ready for the new term.

I showed Neil my long letter and I think he was somewhat appalled. Anyway, he suggests I write another one – 'a bit kinder' was the way he put it. He says you can't have been too bad, since I had once loved you.

Today, in the late afternoon, I took Neil to meet Pearl. She has been moved to Chalfont Nursing Home, where Stella and her mother ended their days. It was hoped a place could be found for Pearl in one of the local state-run homes, but neither had a vacancy. The Social Services are paying her fees at the moment, but when her house is sold the proceeds from that will be used, so Pearl's spell as a house-owner did not last long.

They had dressed her and she was sitting in a wheel-chair at the end of the ward, by the window overlooking the sunken rose garden and the bench where Stella sat and breathed her last, waiting for her father to come. Pearl looked much the same, with her mouth still twisted and one eyelid drooping. I introduced Neil and tried to explain that our relationship was now something other than professional. To my dismay I found myself shouting, as if she was deaf as well as dumb, and I stopped in confusion. Neil simply smiled, drew me close and kissed me, and I think she got the message. Her active eye had been darting to the left and right of us and I realized, after a moment, she was looking for Sammy. I started to explain, but couldn't go on, so Neil took over. Kneeling, he held her good hand and gently told her what had happened. When he had finished, she cried out something incomprehensible, snatched her hand away and twice pointed vehemently at herself. I think what she was saying was: it should have been me! It should have been me!

It was raining now. In the window the rose garden and the bench disappeared behind a haze of raindrops on the glass. We promised we would come again and push her out into the gardens, one day when the weather was fine. Then we left. Outside in the courtyard, we went to the corner of the building where steps lead down to the rose garden and looked up at her window. We could just see her figure, silhouetted against the blurred wet glass. I knew now she would tell me nothing more about Cookley Green and its inhabitants. She was still alive . . . just . . . but her tongue was stilled for ever.

Will I ever know what George did? Somehow I find the need to know is gone. From now on we will be making our own history. Let the village keep its secrets. I have roots now – my place is here with Neil, near Sammy. Nobody has claimed the three gold sovereigns so they have been left in my keeping and since Sammy was the one who found them, last night I went out in the moonlight and buried them at the foot of his grave. Some day, no doubt, somebody will dig them up and wonder how on earth they came to be there . . .

I think I'll start a new journal, for here we are at the beginning of a new school year. I shall concern myself with the present and the future, not the past. How's this for starters:

We called in at the Moon and Sixpence after visiting Pearl. I had an orange juice. At the back of my mind is the thought I may be pregnant; if so, this time I mean to do everything right – eat all the right foods, take all the tests. We carried our drinks out onto the patio at the back. There were no other customers, so Fat Harry soon joined us and regaled us with the latest startling news. The explanation at last for the long black limousines, with the insignia I failed to recognize, the boys allowed out to chase the car and the girls in the car in front who were not. I had witnessed the arrival of a large family coming to view their new abode for the first time. The start of a new chapter in the ongoing saga of Cookley Green and its inhabitants – Summerfield Hall has been bought by a rich Arab.

THE END

NOT ALL TARTS ARE APPLE
by Pip Granger

At least, that's what seven-year-old Rosie finds out at school one morning. 'You haven't got no proper mem and dad. *Your* mum's a tart', she is told by her friend Kathy Moon. And with this, Rosie's safe world – her home above the cafe in Old Compton Street, watched over by her devoted Uncle Bert and Auntie Maggie – is turned upside down.

A cafe in post-war Soho is a strange place to bring up a child. Rosie is used to being with a motley group of grown-ups – Mamma Campanini at the deli, Madame Zelda (Clairvoyant to the Stars), Sharkey Finn (a clever lawyer, but bent as a two-bob watch), Paulette (French Lessons) – and the mysterious Perfumed Lady, who makes an appearance from time to time. Usually the worse for drink, she laughs a lot and wears clothes like a princess. She brings Rosie presents – silver shoes and glittery jewellery and satin ribbons. Rosie thinks she is her fairy godmother. But she is, of course, Rosie's real mum . . . and one day, might want to reclaim her.

'A warm-hearted début novel guaranteed to please'
Woman's Own

'A poignant story with a strong authentic backdrop'
Woman and Home

0 552 14895 4

A SELECTED LIST OF FINE NOVELS
AVAILABLE FROM CORGI BOOKS

14060	0	MERSEY BLUES	Lyn Andrews £5.99
14685	4	THE SILENT LADY	Catherine Cookson £5.99
14579	3	SCORE!	Jilly Cooper £6.99
14450	9	DAUGHTERS OF REBECCA	Iris Gower £5.99
14451	7	KINGDOM'S DREAM	Iris Gower £5.99
14895	4	NOT ALL TARTS ARE APPLE	Pip Granger £5.99
14896	2	THE WIDOW GINGER	Pip Granger £5.99
14537	8	APPLE BLOSSOM TIME	Kathryn Haig £5.99
14538	6	A TIME TO DANCE	Kathryn Haig £5.99
14770	2	MULLIGAN'S YARD	Ruth Hamilton £5.99
14771	0	SATURDAY'S CHILD	Ruth Hamilton £5.99
14820	2	THE TAVERNERS' PLACE	Caroline Harvey £5.99
14692	7	THE PARADISE GARDEN	Joan Hessayon £5.99
14603	X	THE SHADOW CHILD	Judith Lennox £5.99
14773	7	TOUCHING THE SKY	Susan Madison £5.99
14772	9	THE COLOUR OF HOPE	Susan Madison £5.99
14822	9	OUR YANKS	Margaret Mayhew £5.99
14823	7	THE PATHFINDER	Margaret Mayhew £5.99
14872	5	THE SHADOW CATCHER	Michelle Paver £5.99
14753	2	A PLACE IN THE HILLS	Michelle Paver £5.99
14947	0	THREE IN A BED	Carmen Reid £5.99
14792	3	THE BIRTHDAY PARTY	Elvi Rhodes £5.99
14905	5	MULBERRY LANE	Elvi Rhodes £5.99
14867	9	SEA OF DREAMS	Susan Sallis £5.99
14903	9	TIME OF ARRIVAL	Susan Sallis £5.99
14908	X	APPOINTMENT AT THE PALACE	Mary Jane Staples £5.99
15046	0	CHANGING TIMES	Mary Jane Staples £5.99
14853	9	THE COTTAGE	Danielle Steel £6.99
14846	6	ROSA'S ISLAND	Valerie Wood £5.99
15031	2	THE DOORSTOP GIRLS	Valerie Wood £5.99